I0689944

COSMOSIS

ALSO BY RAINER REY

Replicator Run

Day of the Dove

COSMOSIS

A Novel

Rainer Rey

TURNER

Turner Publishing Company
424 Church Street • Suite 2240 • Nashville, Tennessee 37219
445 Park Avenue • 9th Floor • New York, New York 10022

www.turnerpublishing.com

Cosmosis, A Novel

Cover design: Nellys Liang
Book design: Kym Whitley

Library of Congress Cataloging-in-Publication Data

Rey, Rainer.
 Cosmosis : a novel / by Rainer Rey.
  pages ; cm
 ISBN 978-1-62045-992-8 (alk. paper)
 I. Title.
 PS3568.E86C67 2014
 813'.54--dc23
        2014036434

ISBN: 978-1-62045-992-8

Printed in the United States of America
14 15 16 17 18 19 0 9 8 7 6 5 4 3 2 1

For My Wife, Jan—and Her Love of Books

Acknowledgments

My sincere thanks to Diane Gedymin,
my agent, who shared my vision and who persevered
in launching and sustaining my writing career.
And to Ed Stackler, whose early editing and
encouragement gave shape to this novel.
Finally, appreciation to Christina Roth
for her diligent polish to its final rendition.

COSMOSIS

PROLOGUE

Near Huntsville, Alabama
August 24, 1993, 5:13 A.M.

A SEA OF FROGS SANG Arthur Kelton back to consciousness. He heard them as water trickled down his cheek.

Sensing the chill on his abdomen, he imagined himself sprawled on ice, but the notion was swept away as he opened his eyes and found himself face down in the mud. Sheets of rain passed overhead, spattering the back of his trench coat.

Arthur shivered. He shifted his weight, causing a rib to unhinge in his upper chest. Searing heat shot through his right shoulder. Something had shredded at the base of his neck. His collarbone had snapped and his right arm lay crumpled beneath his body.

Then he remembered the tree falling—the skid—the sound of breaking glass.

Biting through the pain, Arthur strained to lift his chin. He peered back at the wreck.

In the dim morning light, the overturned Jeep loomed some twenty feet behind. Its one unbroken headlight shot an anemic beam into the woods. Steam rose from the engine compartment, and the upside-down passenger door hung open.

Where was Carville?

Perhaps he'd been thrown clear.

Arthur took a deep breath to prepare to shout Carville's name, but a sharp ache knifed through his side, and he could only mutter, "Carville, are you there?"

No response.

Arthur braced his left forearm in the mud but found he couldn't rise. He had no feeling in his lower back or hips. As he flexed his thighs, his abdomen gave way. No core strength at all. Everything below his sternum felt like mush. A strange stickiness wadded his eyelashes at the corner of his right eye. He brought his left hand to his forehead. His fingers came away red. Blood gushed from a deep cut in his scalp below the hairline.

All right, he told himself, you won't bleed to death. You can still crawl. Then he realized it might be a good idea . . . he smelled gasoline.

The Jeep's tank had ruptured. It could blow.

"Carville," he croaked, wishing he had his driver's help. The Army National Guard corporal had been assigned to transport Arthur through this stormy night.

More fumes. He had to move. Bracing himself, he flexed one knee and instantly regretted the severe cramp that wracked his left hamstring. He straightened the leg again and used his left elbow for leverage instead. Half dragging himself, he belly crawled through the muck.

Exhausted after three body lengths, he slumped to the crabgrass and lay still, listening to his own breathing.

The bog was eerily quiet—just frogs, rain, and trickling water. Finally a cool breeze teased his hair, swishing through the long grasses, rustling cattails near the ditch.

Arthur arched his neck to look across the road. The hulking trunk of a great willow lay across the drenched asphalt, its twisted branches snaking into the gloom. The jeep had rounded the bend as that tangled mass of green crashed down into their headlight beams.

Carville had no time to stop. He had shouted an obscenity, put the vehicle into a wild skid and careened onto the shoulder, where the left front tire dug into soft gravel, launching Arthur through the vehicle's canvas roof.

Had wind taken the tree down? It must have.

Arthur's gaze followed the trunk, coming to rest where the roots should have been. In the murky morning, he shuddered at what he *didn't* see: no mound of fresh earth, no splintered break—instead, a glistening smoothness at the trunk's base, as if it had been cut by a chain saw.

Arthur pushed up on his elbow. Beyond the long grasses near the road, hulking shadows of forest—willows, some elm and bleached birch trees—etched the darkness.

Chain saw. Somebody was out there. Someone had ambushed them. Why?

The evening's events had been surreal. Arthur had been forced to leave the NASA Flight Control offices in Pasadena after Davenport's manic request; after rushing onto that archaic B-52 to Birmingham, then the wild ride with Carville through Alabama's backcountry had ensued. "Hide the negatives," Davenport had said. "Get them to Huntsville."

The negatives.

Curling his left hand into the flap of his trench coat, he managed to reach under his right arm. The sealed manila envelope was still there—thoroughly wrapped and dry, though his sweat-drenched shirt certainly wasn't.

He lowered his head, heaving for air, trying to gather strength. He caught his breath. The frogs had stopped chirping. Something had disturbed them. Above the trickle of water in the ditch, Arthur heard a sloshing in the bog—nearer now, with the sound of tall grass being crushed. Someone was trudging through the swamp near the jeep.

Was it Carville coming this way?

Arthur strained to look back. "Over here."

No reply. Arthur saw the light, carried by a silhouette that appeared from behind the vehicle. The dark figure plodded toward Arthur.

"Keep your head down." It wasn't Carville.

"Hey. I need help."

"Shut up. Do what I tell you." The hint of an accent.

Arthur dropped his head. He looked sideways to his right as the man stepped forward onto the gravel shoulder in a pair of striped pant legs and brown Italian shoes.

"Where's my driver?" Arthur asked.

"When did you last see him?"

"I don't know. I was out cold."

A gloved hand holding a gun pointed at Arthur's head. "Show me your hands."

"I can't move my right arm."

"Then roll over. Slowly."

Arthur put his left hand under his chest for leverage and pushed off, gasping in agony as he rolled onto his back.

The gun's silencer pointed at the bridge of his nose. A broad-shouldered, shaggy-haired blond man in a black raincoat glared down at him as water dripped from the man's wide-brimmed hat.

"Who the hell are you?" Arthur asked.

"Where are the negatives?" The voice rang cold, like the clank of steel. He reached out with his other hand.

Arthur was stunned. "What?"

"You know goddamned well. The Mars mission."

"How could you possibly—?"

"Give them to me." The handgun twitched. "If you please."

Awed by the exchange, Arthur reached inside his trench coat.

The envelope was dry against his body warmth. He pulled it out and handed it over, looking up into the rain.

The gloved left hand accepted it. The gun hand gestured. "Back on your stomach."

Arthur winced as he rolled over. Blood mixed with rain dripped off his nose into his mouth.

Paper crinkled, and Arthur saw the glow of a flashlight illuminate the mud nearby. In Arthur's lilliputian field of vision, tiny blades of grass sprouted vibrantly green against the darkness.

The man grunted in frustration.

Arthur sneaked a glance as one of the gloves was removed and the man reached into his vest, pulling out a combat knife. He severed the heavy cellophane tape at one end of the envelope. Arthur heard the prints being pulled from the folder. "I suppose you thought these shots would support your theories about Mars."

"What do you mean? I wasn't allowed to examine them."

"Then you're a fool. Risking your life without knowing why. Don't look at me."

The light doused. Arthur strained to see as the envelope rustled, being tucked away. The knife was deposited in the man's front vest pocket. Its steel handle was visible. Could Arthur reach it?

"Why have you done this? Who hired you?" Arthur asked.

No reply. One at a time, the man's expensive-looking shoes stepped a few inches closer. The handgun dropped down next to Arthur's face. He suddenly realized he might never go home—never see his wife again. The knife in the vest was at arm's length. "Please don't kill me," Arthur said as the muzzle came to rest against his temple. It was colder than anything he'd felt in his life. "Dear God, no." His six-year-old son could lose a father tonight. "Oh Jace," Arthur whispered.

PRESENT DAY
St. Mark's Cathedral
Ann Arbor, Michigan

BLANCHED BY THE SEPTEMBER MOON, wispy ground fog crept through the wrought-iron fence, tucking like a blanket around the gravestones. Cold mist drifted across the cemetery grass near the rectory wall, while crickets chanted their anthem to an ebbing Indian summer.

In the second-floor bedroom of the rectory, Father Navarro had eased into deep slumber, relaxed by the Napa Valley port his sister Inez sent from Sacramento.

Father didn't hear the crickets humming outside his window nor the grating rasp of the graveyard gate as three hooded men entered the church grounds.

Accustomed to the hazards of their work, the commandos moved quickly and easily, armed with combat knives and nine-millimeter handguns. They spaced themselves, one by the fence, a second on the rectory path, and a third—their leader, known as Shag—crouched in the shadows of the mausoleum portico.

Shag unsuccessfully tried the handle of the carved mausoleum door. He lit a small acetylene torch and began to cut through the latch—a quiet, convenient method of breaking the lock. The small blue flame danced in the crack of the doorjamb as the brass bolt smoldered and gave way.

He extinguished his torch and set it steaming on the stone threshold. He pushed on the door and stepped inside the darkened columbarium.

Using his flashlight, he searched the musty chamber with its granite floor and wooden walls, lined in black mahogany partitions. Each smoked-glass-covered niche was marked with a metal plate denoting the name of the departed.

Shag moved from column to column, his flashlight beam darting across the gray panes. He briefly touched each name placard with his black leather glove as if communing with the identities of the dead.

His hand came to rest at the name he'd been seeking. The sunken letters on the plain, slightly tarnished brass plaque read MARRO.

Shag wasted no time. He pulled his nine-millimeter gun from its holster, and using the butt as a hammer, he shattered the glass. Brushing the pieces away, he trained his light within.

As expected, he found two urns. Reaching past the vessel inscribed

TENILLE, he grasped the urn marked MASON. Laying his flashlight into the Marro niche, he placed Mason's urn in the crook of his left arm and used his combat knife to pry the lid.

He grunted and strained, but the seal held.

Shag considered getting his blowtorch, but lacking time and patience, he grabbed the urn with both hands and lifted it high over his head. He paused, captivated by his own silhouette reflected in the glass of the opposing wall. With his hood and broad shoulders, he resembled an enraged ghoul in some subterranean cave.

For a moment, the apparition amused him, since he frequently envisioned himself as a harbinger of hell. But he cast off the fantasy and hurled Mason Marro's remains to the floor. The marble vessel shattered.

Shag dropped to his knees and found what he was after—the small tan scroll tied with a black band protruded from a pile of Mason's ashes.

Feeling blood pound in his head, Shag tucked his flashlight under his arm and brushed the dust away. He untied the ribbon, unrolled the paper, and examined the parchment. The odd geometric writing and detailed pictoglyphs were exactly as Cho had described in his e-mail from Beijing.

Shag was now convinced he'd located Mason's mysterious treasure—what had been called the Peruvian Prize. He smiled as he tucked the scroll into the kangaroo pouch of his black sweatshirt. To celebrate his find, he removed a small flask from his back pocket and sipped his schnapps, enjoying the sting at the back of his throat. Dousing his flashlight, he stepped outside, collected the acetylene torch by the door, and joined the others.

The ground fog had layered nearly waist-high. Moving off under a harvest moon, the three men seemed to float through the cemetery gate, leaving swirls of mist in their wake as they disappeared into the night.

The fog in the cemetery again settled into a frigid calm.

Even the crickets had been driven to their shelters by the midnight chill.

The only remaining sound in the churchyard, barely audible through the open stained-glass rectory window, was an occasional grunt from Father Navarro, who continued to dream.

PART ONE

1

A Day Later
Aboard the Trawler Tripe
Off the Sabine Coast, Gulf of Mexico

WARM FIFTY-MILE-AN-HOUR gusts tossed sheets of spray across Jace Kelton's tan, unshaven face as he gripped the resin-covered rail of the *Tripe's* rocking stern.

Jace watched a flock of seagulls trail the boat, flying north as if fleeing impending disaster. Judging from the heaviness of the air and the dark band of southerly clouds, the seagulls were right—the worst weather was yet to come.

The boat's churning wake dwindled on the horizon where, forty miles to the south, Jace had left the relative security of the spar oil rig, *Neptune.*

Ahead lay the uncertainty of Texaco's damaged floating oil rig, *Aurora.*

Jace hoisted the collar of his black slicker and turned from the gale, squinting forward, where the charred frame of the floater hovered eight hundred yards off the bow.

The hulking giant had taken the lives of twelve men. Through a twist of fate, Jace was driven into not only assessing the damage but also insuring that the *Aurora* wouldn't entomb fifty more.

According to the accident report, a gas explosion had blown a hole in the *Aurora's* main deck and a portion of the pipe deck. The blast had also torn a hole in the southeastern tension leg, one of the huge vertical hollow tubes that floated the rig. Rough seas had filled the lower part of the tube with water and the football-field-sized platform labored with a ten-degree list that could no longer be adjusted by cable tension off the ocean floor.

In the face of a coming storm, the repairs wouldn't happen soon enough. The rig was 482 miles offshore and the wind was picking up.

Jace felt the shiver of anticipation as he stuck his head inside the wheelhouse. "Any boats in range?"

Cameron Logan's angular face was bathed in the green glow of the Furuno radar scope on the console. "Nothing I can see, Jace. They're all running for port."

"What's the latest weather?"

"They're calling this depression as a Category 4 hurricane. It just crossed the twenty-fifth parallel with winds upward of one-forty, bearing northwest, toward the Mexican coast. If she comes farther north she'll be right up our pipes."

Logan's tone conveyed the obvious concern—neither the damaged floating oil rig *Aurora* nor the *Tripe* might survive the onslaught.

Jace stepped outside. Wiping salt spray from his blue eyes, he gazed at the exposed bridge on top of the wheelhouse. Barton Kluge, the boat's master, stood at the helm in a yellow slicker. "The storm's gaining. We've got very little time," Jace shouted.

The pilot of the thirty-eight-foot boat turned from the on-deck tiller, his freckled face taut with tension under the brim of his nor'easter. "What do you want me to do?"

"Hold your course and come in from the north side. Better than being slammed into the rig by the wind."

Kluge wasn't just nervous, he was pissed off about being assigned to ferry Jace to the *Aurora;* his small tool craft had been the only supply boat in the vicinity.

"But what's the plan?" Kluge asked.

Jace responded with a reassuring smile. "The *plan* is to stay dry."

Jace stepped back into the companionway and fought the sideways tumble of the hull as he hung on to the handrails, joining Logan at the control panel. The wiry Irishman was a good mate, steady and capable. Jace found himself wishing that Logan were at the wheel instead of Kluge.

Logan made room as Jace picked up the handset and dialed channel nine on the VHF radio that hung on the console. Remember, he thought. Don't get too wired. You're "Hamilton" now, not "Kelton" . . . Jace Hamilton. "Calling *Aurora.* This is Jason Hamilton aboard the *Tripe.*"

A voice broke through the crackling staccato. "This is Stewart. I read you."

The hairs on Jace's neck bristled at the name. He was about to confront someone who'd been hiding for over twenty years. Ironically, one aliased man was hunting another. "We're making ready a few hundred yards off your southerly deck."

"I'm switching to channel fifty-eight," Stewart countered. With the approaching storm, the hailing channel would be burning with emergency calls. It was procedure to change to another frequency quickly.

Jace dialed 5 8.

Stewart was back. "I see you now. You're pitching badly. Didn't they have a bigger boat? Over."

"This was the *only* one. It's me and a crew of two. Need help to board. Over."

"All right, keep heading for the lee side. Don't try to tie up in these rough seas. We'll lower a net. Let it settle on your aft deck before you climb in. When you're secure, give us a sign and we'll pull you up. Over."

Jace visualized himself being slung on the deck like a haul of tuna. "That's the best way? Over."

"It is now. The catwalks are down due to the blast."

As Jace climbed the ladder to join Kluge on the bridge, the adrenaline rushed through his brain. Years of searching and humiliation were about to end. He was about to confront the man who, according to Jace's intelligence connections, wasn't George Stewart at all, but rather Roger Carville, the Army National Guard corporal who had disappeared the night Jace's father was murdered . . . maybe even committed the crime.

Jace hoisted himself onto the bridge as the trawler shuddered from a crashing wave that flooded her bow, sending salt spray across the rails.

"So what can you tell me?" Kluge shouted through the wind.

"Tell you?"

"Once you're up on the platform. What the hell do I do?"

Kluge had set the additional responsibility for the boat's safety on Jace's shoulders. Jace's title as safety consultant for the Southland Insurance Company gave him no authority over oil company supply boats. Yet he fully understood Kluge's apprehension—as far as the eye could see, waves had begun to tower. "The rig is my call, Kluge. What you do with your boat is up to you and Texaco."

Kluge's eyes were wide with concern. "Fuck that," he drawled. "I'm here because of you."

"You're here on your supervisor's orders."

"I'm asking you to help me decide." Kluge spun the chrome wheel a quarter turn. "After I drop you off, I can't tie her up. She'll come apart. If I put her on a tether and let her ride, the ropes might not hold." He took a deep breath and gazed at Jace. "I better head back to the *Neptune*." Kluge would have to answer for the loss of the company's boat. "I'm like a guy with his leg stuck in the outhouse shitter with a bear at the door."

Jace brushed a hand through his drenched black hair. "Look at it this way—you come up there with me and you might lose the boat . . ." He nodded out to the churning sea. "You head south forty miles and you could lose your ass."

Kluge's eyes were anxious, searching. "But what if the *Aurora* herself doesn't make it? Can she take a hurricane banged up like she is?"

"That's what I'm here to find out." Jace stared at Kluge, musing the drastic career change that had brought him to this unanticipated emergency. After three years of education he had acquired his Occupational Safety and Health certificate. Then two years on the job before he was granted the inspection of the *Aurora*. Five years of sacrifice to reach this moment.

Left without answers, Kluge changed the subject. "Tell Logan to find the goddamned grappling hook. We're going to need it."

As Kluge guided the trawler toward the floater's north side, the *Tripe* passed by the southeastern corner of the oil rig, and Jace got a good view of the damage.

The *Aurora*, one of the tension leg rigs launched in 1996, had been operating over the Saturn oil field at a depth of 650 feet. Like other rigs of its design, the *Aurora* depended on four pontoonlike tension legs that were attached to the ocean bottom for stability. But two days ago, for reasons still unknown, liquid petroleum gas from one of the ten pipe shafts had ignited and started a fire. Moments later, flames ignited nearby gas and diesel fuel tanks. The explosion knocked a large hole in the main deck and took out portions of the pipe deck below plus all the catwalks in between.

The twelve dead and nineteen injured had been flown off the *Aurora* and a repair schedule was set. Everything would have gone according to plan if a storm front hadn't appeared in the western Caribbean. Jace had expected to find Stewart on the *Aurora*. What he didn't expect was the unanticipated accident and complications of a killer storm.

The *Tripe* changed course, yawing around the platform's northeast corner.

"Hold on," Kluge shouted.

Jace gripped a cleat with both hands as Kluge fought the wheel, bringing the boat to a firmer heading. The trawler's bow came into the wind as Kluge edged into position twenty-five yards off the *Aurora*. Within the rig's frame, waves crashed back and forth, and Kluge pivoted the boat so that the stern faced the platform.

Securing his cell phone and wallet in a waterproof pack at his waist, Jace watched as two hundred feet above, men in bright orange windbreakers appeared on the ledge of the north deck. They waved their arms, signaling the crane operator who was situated some thirty feet back to guide a steel cable over the side.

A flimsy cargo net attached to the wire cleared the platform's edge, swaying in the gusts as it slowly descended. The *Tripe* rose and fell with swells on the ocean surface as the rope basket approached overhead, hissing in the wind and smelling of wet hemp.

Logan was ready with the grappling hook and snagged the webbing as the *Tripe*'s aft deck bucked. "Need a lift?"

Jace smiled, lending a hand with the net. "Isn't that an old vaudeville line ... 'I asked for an elevator, but they gave me the shaft'?"

The crane operator on the platform did what Stewart had forecast and let out enough cable for the net to fully collapse on the deck boards. The slack wire line lashed back and forth in the gale above Jace's head as he and Logan tried to loosen the net's top-knot. Kluge looked on from the tiller as Logan spread the neck of the rope basket, and Jace fought the heaving deck as he climbed inside. He got both legs over the rope folds and went to his knees as the net surrounded him like a cat in a limp cage.

Wondering what kind of hostility he might encounter from Stewart once the cat was out of the bag, Jace lay down on his back.

On the bridge, Kluge shouted from the wheel, "Hurry up. I can't hold her."

Jace responded immediately. "Give them the sign, Logan. I'm ready."

"Let's go." Logan twirled an arm in the air and the men on the platform mimicked Logan's wave. Somewhere beyond, the crane operator shifted gears and slowly the cable began to ascend. As the thick wire tightened, the trawler's stern sank into a trough between swells and the boat fell away under Jace's body. The net clamped around Jace as the deck dropped. The crest of the next wave caused the twenty-thousand-pound *Tripe* to buck violently, lunging the boat deck upward, causing a collision between Jace and the floorboards.

Jace was dashed to the deck and found himself dragged across the hardwood. He tried to regain his balance, but the *Tripe* plunged into the next trough and the aft deck once more dropped away.

Jace hung perilously in the air, unable to do anything but wait for the next wave.

"Go," Logan yelled, waving his arms at the platform. But the men above misinterpreted his panic and the cable stopped spooling.

Helplessly suspended, Jace struggled to roll onto his side. The stern of the boat pushed high on the crest of the next wave, and the rising deck slammed into Jace's torso.

He felt like he'd been hit by a truck.

"Up, goddamn it, up!" Logan shouted.

The cable began to reel again as the trawler dove into the hollow between waves.

"Kluge," Jace shouted as he dangled midair. "Get out. Pull away from me."

Kluge hit his engines, swinging his stern to starboard to maneuver the *Tripe* from under Jace. But he timed the move badly, and the stern didn't pivot enough. The next wave lofted the rising stern rail upward, and it smacked Jace on the side of the head. He saw a flash of white light and fought to keep his senses.

As the *Tripe* hit a trough, Jace's limp body cleared the stern entirely, and he swung out over the ocean, colliding with the crest of a following wave. Foaming brine crashed through the netting, and Jace was suddenly submerged in white water.

Dazed by the blow to his head and unable to breathe, Jace replayed a memory. At nine years of age, he had fallen through an ice pond behind his Amarillo foster home. As Jace thrashed about in panic, a strong hand had reached into the freezing water and gripped him by the collar.

Cory Jackson's rescuing hand wasn't here now, and Jace pondered why he was snarled in white froth. He instinctively clutched the wet ropes above his head and tried to climb hand over hand toward the ocean's surface. His strength began to fail as his upper body suddenly felt weightless.

With his hands tangled in the webbing, Jace inhaled a mouthful of seawater, and everything went black.

2

Stag Lake
Cascade Mountains, Washington State

LIKE A MIRROR, THE WATER'S surface reflected gray cliffs that rose to the west against an azure sky. The naked granite spires provided a stark contrast to the lush browns and greens of the forest that rimmed the lake.

On the southeastern shore, where sunlight dappled the pine-needle carpets at the water's edge, Madison Marro crouched in the shallows. Wearing hip boots over her jeans, Maddy waited for a small orange tadpole to make its approach through the reeds. She remained motionless with her flannel shirt rolled up to the elbows, holding a small mesh hoop in one hand and a plastic jar in the other—still enough that a dragonfly landed on her shoulder. While Maddy watched the turquoise-colored insect settle, she stood like a statue knee-deep in water to avoid frightening the approaching pollywog.

Her reflection on the surface made her smile. Here she was, one of nature's secret guests, camouflaged among the rushes. She gazed down at her likeness, amused by her earth muffin appearance—her frumpy forest garb hid her shapeliness.

Her mother had fantasized about Maddy becoming a model, commenting how her even-featured face and big eyes were ideal for the pages of fashion magazines. Maddy wouldn't hear of it, having rebelled against things cosmopolitan. She preferred to view herself as a country girl and was pleased that, sans makeup, her skin still revealed the faded reminiscence of teenage freckles.

She felt more at home here, roughing it with her auburn hair pinned back, wearing flannels rather than silks.

The meandering pollywog continued to gently fishtail toward her through sprouts of bottom foliage, nearly close enough for capture.

As Maddy watched and waited, her nose began to itch. Her nostrils stung with an irrepressible tickle that would lead to a sneeze. She couldn't risk moving her hands, so she closed her amber-colored eyes and scrunched her face.

The facial contortion caused her head to move slightly and the dragonfly took flight. Ignoring its departure, she focused on conquering the sneeze, fighting not to laugh at the absurdity of her predicament.

Finally, the tickling passed and she was able to open her eyes. The pollywog, unaware of her battle of mind over matter, had been about its business only two feet away. She could see it quite clearly now, its small tail undulating back and forth through the reeds.

The amphibian was not unlike a human fetus in the moisture of the womb, innocent and evolving, kindled by the miraculous energy that ignited all life.

Maddy could name all the tadpole's anatomical parts and identify each plant through which it swam. Her scientific background included a master's in biology and a bachelor's degree in geology and to her, each lichen, every pebble had a story to tell.

Yet living creatures were far more than just specimens. She believed that animals possessed their own spirituality, bonded by the laws of a fragile ecology.

Maddy gently placed the mesh hoop behind the tadpole's waving tail. In one smooth underwater maneuver, she captured the creature in the webbing and then deposited it in a jar.

She held the pollywog at eye level. The tiny creature remained motionless in the clear glacier water and Maddy turned the jar 360 degrees to get a full view. To her dismay, one of its posterior limbs was missing.

Of the eight pollywogs she had collected today, she had released seven normal specimens. Yet one, which she'd kept, had been disfigured, having grown an extra set of gills on its right side.

The frequency of these deformities was disturbing.

A field researcher for the Environmental Protection Agency, Maddy had spent two weeks checking frog larva in mountain pools on the eastern slopes of the Cascades. She had been charged to prove that ozone depletion above the upper lakes of the Cascade Range did, in fact, cause abnormal life forms.

The tiny tadpole in her hands had become a victim.

"I'm sorry," she whispered as she tucked the jar in her backpack. She had never gotten over the fact that she'd come from an ecologically abusive family.

Whenever she encountered a creature crippled by environmental damage, she couldn't help thinking of her youth growing up near Detroit and the millions of gallons of poisonous gas that had been generated on the shores of the Great Lakes.

Poisoned minds advocate poisoned air, she thought, wading toward shore. Her father—Mason Marro, a top automotive GM executive—had lived what he believed, helping to poison the environment while he was poisoning himself with his lifestyle and dying from it.

Maddy had been raised in an alcoholic, chain-smoking household. This was likely the reason she loved being miles from civilization, an escapee from chaos, away from the tainted air, the drone of traffic, and the banality of empty conversation.

A decade ago, seeking clean air and a fresh outlook on life, she had moved to the University of Michigan, away from Mason's smoke and Tenille's cocktails.

She devoted her postgraduate study to ecology. Shortly thereafter, her aversion to the past was reinforced by her parents' deaths . . . first her father and then her mother, both of lung cancer.

Maddy waded through the dark marshy shallows and climbed the soft shoulder of the lake bank.

She sensed something move to her left and glanced toward the north shore. A few swallows cavorted among the branches of thick firs along the water's edge. Ducks swam lazily between the reeds . . . but there was nothing out of the ordinary.

She turned and walked toward a large stump where she'd left her hiking shoes and her sample kit, a plastic tackle box refitted to hold her jars. One water-filled container already held the first crippled pollywog.

She unslung her backpack, removed the newest tadpole from the canvas bag, and knelt down, placing the second next to the first. She looked around.

Light had broken through the forest. Layers of moss showed bright green on the trunks of the trees in pockets of late-September sunshine.

Maddy retrieved her hiking shoes from a clump of moss and, with her back to the lake, sat down on the stump. She tugged at her stubborn waders. Placing the hip boots at her feet, she leaned over to tie the laces on her hiking shoes. She hesitated.

A sharp snap had echoed across the placid surface of the lake.

Something large had broken a branch on the north side . . . the same area where something earlier caught her eye. She stood and turned, anticipating the presence of a deer or an elk; instead, the silhouettes of two men disappeared into a pine grove.

Maddy watched, disturbed by the way they'd moved—slinking, darting, intent on not being seen. Why? If they were hikers, they were much too evasive. If they were poachers, they would have carried rifles.

Had they been stalking her? Watching the whole time? If so, nothing would prevent them from following her as she took the five-mile hike back to the Klakamas Inn.

Her imagination churned with possibilities. The thought of rape crossed her mind.

Angered by the intrusion and unwilling to become the prey in some back-woods game, she decided to do some stalking of her own. She was a compe-tent woodswoman and knew the surrounding topography, but she'd have to be quick and travel light.

Stashing her wading boots and tadpole samples behind the stump next to her backpack, she casually strolled off in an easterly direction. She walked into the forest until she was sufficiently shielded by foliage. And then she began to run. Hurdling downed timber, dashing through the thick tree trunks, she changed direction every fifty yards in a zigzag route. After five hundred yards, she cut north up the slope toward Cougar Heights.

She was now several hundred feet above the valley floor, looking down at the lake with the sun in her face. Seeing no movement below, she traversed the tree-lined ridge toward the west and hiked down a rock-strewn gully. When she finally reached the shore, she began to work back along the bank.

Minutes later, she arrived at the spot where she'd seen the men. All was quiet. Two mallards paddled between the reeds. In a nearby grove, a wood-pecker tapped a refrain.

The soft ground showed two sets of tracks that led off to the east. Judging from the size of the prints, the men had been of medium build, wearing what appeared to be flat-soled sneakers.

Shielded by rows of spruce and pine, she followed the trail, keeping a watch-ful eye ahead, now realizing that the tracks led to where she'd stashed her gear.

As the moss-covered stump came into sight, her heart sank. Someone had taken her backpack and, along with it, her cell phone. Thank God she'd been carrying her wallet.

Her gratitude changed to dismay. Her sample kit lay shattered on the ground. The first pollywog sample had been smashed, and the small amphibian lay crushed in the plastic debris.

She bent down and picked up the second jar. At least it was still intact. The tiny creature inside hadn't been tampered with.

Suddenly, off in the distance, she heard the sound of a dirt bike. Another motor kicked into gear. The whine of two bikes seemed to head east, or had they turned south? With the echo of the motorcycles reverberating between the cliffs of Stag Lake, it was impossible to tell.

Were her stalkers leaving or simply repositioning themselves, preparing to ambush her during her hike back?

THE SUN WARMED MADDY'S FACE as she emerged from the cool forest shadows, relieved at what she saw. Three hundred yards to the west, perched on a bluff called Eagle Ridge, the Klakamas Inn stood out against the late glow of the day.

Maddy had used the inn as a home away from home—her base of operations in the wilderness. Today in particular, the sight of the inn lifted her spirits. She looked forward to the warmth of a crackling fire and the brassy taste of Wayne Foley's coffee.

The confrontation at Stag Lake had disturbed her. She began to recall other incidents, minor events that may have indicated she'd been stalked before—a scrap of paper on the trail, an occasional echo in the trees. One day she had smelled the odor of gasoline out in the middle of nowhere, something she now correlated with the mystery off-road bikes.

Throughout her three-hour return to the lodge, she had stopped frequently to listen for engines. Her paranoia caused her to wonder if she might be able to work in the forest again without being spooked by the slightest noise. Whoever those bastards were, they had robbed her of more than her backpack and her phone; they had stolen her peace of mind. She vowed to report the theft to the sheriff.

She would drop off the pollywog sample, Foley would get the jar off to the lab in Seattle, and then she would take the one-hour drive home, where a hot bath and a good night's sleep would put things into a more measured perspective.

Scents from the inn already made her feel better. A gray column of smoke rose from the river-rock chimney. The radiance of faux candle chandeliers glowed through the inn's leaded windows.

Maddy stepped over the split rail fence that bordered the property. The familiar ferns and salal rustled underfoot as she walked. The landscaping had been kept in natural, unaffected beauty. Chipmunks cavorted in stately pines that threw long shadows across the two-acre complex.

The Klakamas was known as a bed-and-breakfast in the summer months, but in winter it became more of a private home. The proprietor, Wayne Foley, stayed year-round, and park rangers and cross-country skiers stopped at the lodge when blizzards howled through the Cascades.

For Maddy, the inn was ideal; it was centrally located within her research area, and samples could be picked up by a delivery van that made daily stops.

Maddy's boots crunched across the gravel parking lot, and she found her teal-colored Suzuki 4x4 where she'd left it. Its muddy exterior showed signs of off-road trips she'd taken in the last two weeks. The marginally comfortable truck was her vehicle of choice because of its low carbon emissions.

She fussed with her keys, opened the vehicle, and stashed her gear inside. Then she took the surviving tadpole and headed for the lodge.

The low sun bathed the cedar pillars of the front porch as Maddy climbed the stairs. She stepped beneath the rack of antlers and opened the knotty pine door, feeling the radiant heat of the fire as she entered.

A few late season visitors whittled away the hours in the large common area. A middle-aged couple played checkers at a shellacked corner cedar table. A young man in a logging cap took a swig of beer and lined up a shot across an ancient pool table. He hesitated, smiling at her.

Wayne Foley was seated on the river-rock fireplace wearing his red wool shirt, jeans, and suspenders. His gray Clark Gable eyebrows knitted in recognition as she appeared, and he set aside an issue of *Sports Illustrated*, getting to his feet—his fleshy face reddened by the effort.

Foley's midfifties complexion had been hewn by harsh weather and even harsher whiskey, which sometimes affected his memory. "You're just in time for coffee," he said, shuffling off toward the hot plate on the counter. "I just made a fresh pot."

"Has the delivery truck been here?" Maddy asked, trailing behind.

"Nope. Still comin'." He paused and looked back. "You had a couple of messages."

Very few people knew how to reach Maddy in the field, and she immediately thought of her best friend Christine, who took care of her house and her animals. "And?"

As usual, Foley took his time answering. He turned and held a mug in his square hands. "There you are, nice and hot."

Maddy took the cup and smiled, trying to disguise her impatience. "Who was it, Foley?"

Foley dug in the pocket of his pants and retrieved a crumpled note. "Well, let's see . . . oh yeah." He pronounced the syllables with reverence, "Father Joseph Navarro."

"From Ann Arbor?"

"Yep. Wants you to call when you can."

Navarro had been the family priest at St. Mark's Cathedral in her hometown and had baptized Maddy. She couldn't imagine why he would have resorted to calling long distance. Certainly no family crisis. After all, her only remaining relative, Uncle Robert, lived in Rhode Island, and he would have contacted her himself. She was fond of Robert, though he was somewhat eccentric and prone to mood swings. Perhaps Father Navarro was again soliciting her for church fund-raising, as he had after her father died.

Foley noticed the pollywog in her hand. "Got another sicky?"

Maddy handed him the jar. "Yes. Please see that this gets on the evening run."

Foley squinted at the tadpole. "What's wrong with this one?"

"Rear leg." Maddy took a sip of the coffee.

"Well look at that little nub," Foley said in a childish singsong. He was accustomed to the routine. "Off to the EPA?"

"Yes, please. You still have the address?"

"I sure do . . ." With jar in hand, Foley shuffled toward the registration desk. After placing the jar in a mail pouch, he returned. "Oh, there was one other thing. Some doctor dropped by. This morning after you left." Foley scratched his head and dug for another note. "Name was Bellamy."

"I don't know a Dr. Bellamy."

"He said he was with the Ecology Department."

"Which one?"

"The University of Washington, I think. Asked where you were. I told him you were at Stag Lake."

Maddy flashed back to the two silhouettes in the forest. "Oh Foley, you didn't." The gray-haired couple by the window looked up.

Foley's brows knitted in confusion. "What's wrong?"

Maddy had overreacted. "Sorry." She lowered her voice. "It's just that I was stalked by someone."

"God. You want me to call the sheriff?" he whispered.

"No. I'll do that. Nothing happened. But there were two . . . you say this guy was alone?"

"Far as I could see."

"Describe him."

"Thirty-five maybe. Light hair. Kind of pudgy."

Maddy shook her head. Before Foley mentioned that the stranger was pudgy, she had thought it might be Kit Lassiter, a tenacious old boyfriend who had the annoying habit of suddenly showing up unannounced. But Kit was over six feet and certainly not overweight. Whoever the surprise visitor was, his appearance at the lodge, the coincidence of strangers in the woods, and an odd message from the family priest made Maddy suddenly feel compelled to call Christine to make sure everything was okay at home. She reached for her phone and then remembered. Among the other calls she would make, she'd have to inform the phone company to cut off her cell service.

She glanced at the pay phone by the front door. "Foley, I need some quarters."

3

The Aurora

THE AMYL NITRATE BURST THROUGH Jace's sinuses. He shook his head as the chemical penetrated into his brain. Though he wanted to sneeze, he kept sucking large gulps of ocean air instead. He opened his eyes.

A man in a bright red Texaco cap withdrew a small cotton inhaler from under Jace's nose and shouted over the roar of the gale. "He's coming around."

Another burly looking guy with shaggy gray hair and a blue peacoat bent down. "Can you hear me, Jason?"

Jace felt a chill. Thick black clouds raced overhead and strong wind chopped at his face. He was wet to the skin, lying on a stretcher on the metal deck of the *Aurora*. Several gawking men in bright orange windbreakers lingered nearby.

Some forty yards beyond, bent blackened metal plates blossomed around a gaping hole that had been caused by the explosion.

The man in the peacoat extended a hand. "I'm Stewart. You making sense of things?"

Jace took Stewart's firm grip, trying to focus on the man's eyes. The honesty in them bothered Jace. The man he was prepared to hate didn't look like the cowardly villain he'd imagined. He had a ruddy, outdoorsman-like appeal that reminded Jace of his father. Jace fought the feeling as Stewart pointed to Jace's head.

"You took a nasty bump."

Jace brought his hand up to his temple. A goose egg had grown over his right ear. Then he remembered. "Where's Kluge?"

Stewart pointed to the rear. "They're bringing them up now."

Jace heard the hum of the crane hydraulics off to his right. He rolled up onto one elbow and watched the cable ascend as the dripping net came into view above the lip of the platform.

Dressed in rain gear, Logan and Kluge clung to the net basket rather than riding within.

"I should have done that," Jace said.

Stewart nodded. "They learned from your experience. We never had to bring a man aboard from a small boat in seas this rough."

"Now you tell me."

"You didn't ask," Stewart faltered apologetically. "We had to scuttle the *Tripe*. No way to lash her with the swells we've got now."

Jace sat up. As he checked to make sure his cell phone and wallet were still secure, he heard the roar of waves crashing into the *Aurora's* tension legs below. The deck still listed to the south.

"How long have I been out?"

"Twenty minutes maybe."

"What's the latest on the storm?"

"They're calling it Hannah. She's still tracking for Matamoros on the Mexican coast. Kicking up wind speeds of one seventy now. God help us if she turns north."

Jace desperately wanted to find a way to get Stewart alone, but there were professional obligations . . . like saving the crew. "I better take a look at the damage," he said. He got to one knee, and the listing deck seemed to suddenly list even more.

Stewart's hand caught him by the arm. "Are you all right, Jason?"

"Yeah." Jace took a deep breath, squinting the pain away. "But call me Jace. How do I access the pipe deck?"

"I told you. The catwalks fell away during the blast." With his gray hair wafting in the breeze, Stewart glanced at the crane. "We'll have to drop you through the hole on a cable."

Jace followed Stewart's gaze to the spot where Kluge and Logan touched down. "You mean back on that thing?"

Stewart smiled. "No. We have a winch-driven gondola our painters use. It wouldn't have worked for the *Tripe*, because it's got a shorter range and it's clumsy. But it's made of aluminum, and with the way the wind might bang you around, it's safer for you to stand inside it." Stewart pointed. A small tractor approached, towing a flatbed wagon. A ten-by-three-foot metal container that resembled a large canteen cup sat on the wagon's wooden boards. A gearbox with a set of handles protruded from the rail at the center, which apparently controlled the winch cylinder and its engine that attached overhead to a basket-like metal frame.

Stewart nodded toward the Asian American tractor driver. "The gondola moves up and down on its own. Sammy Chen there will run the winch while you make your survey."

Ten minutes later while Kluge and Logan had hot coffee in the mess, Jace and Sammy Chen were suspended over the forty-foot-wide blast hole.

Forced to delay his plans for Stewart, Jace stood in the ten-foot gondola, dressed in his deck shoes, workman's jeans, a green flannel shirt and one of the *Aurora*'s bright orange windbreakers. Sammy pulled back the gear handles. The winch spool mounted on the metal cage above their heads doled out cable through a buckle to the red crane jib one hundred feet above.

Jace's head still throbbed inside the hood of his jacket, but he felt well enough to take the ride. And he liked Sammy, who displayed an unflagging spirit, shouting dirty one-liner jokes in Jace's ear over the noise of the gondola being rigged.

Jace was intrigued by Sammy's southern drawl, an unexpected accent from a man whose face looked classically Asian. Sammy explained that he'd grown up in Texas and was third generation Chinese American.

Working the gears, Sammy nodded toward the sky. "Man, it's dark. Might as well be night."

Thick black clouds obscured the sun. It could easily have been four in the morning rather than four in the afternoon.

Driven by the force of the rising wind, the gondola swayed back and forth as it descended through the opening in the deck. The air filled with sound . . . the whir of the winch engine, the roar of the wind overhead, and the crashing of the waves far below. A powerful southerly gust forced the container to stray northward, and Sammy seemed concerned by the proximity of the cable to the ragged deck's edge.

"Hey, Dave," he shouted into the two-way radio he had strung on his sleeve. "Pivot south about ten degrees."

Dave Gill, the cable operator in the cab on deck responded, slowly moving the crane's jib. The new position compensated for the force of the gale, and the gondola centered itself into the blast cavity.

Satisfied with the correction, Sammy lowered away.

Jace looked down at the heaving seas. After his near-drowning accident as a child, he had forced himself to restore his confidence with water by joining the U of Texas freshman swim team, one of his many athletic pursuits. But the white water below was far from welcoming. The ocean surface within the cradle of the oil rig's frame thrashed between the four tension legs that supported the floater. Jace conquered any creeping misgivings by concentrating on his singular objective: the sooner he finished the inspection, the sooner he'd corner Stewart. "Take me down as far as you can," Jace said, looking over the gondola's lip.

Sammy pushed a lever forward. "I've only got a hundred fifty feet of cable."

"That's fine."

As soon as they dropped below the main deck, the blast damage beneath became visible. The destruction of the pipe deck had done the most damage to the southeast tension leg. Using a powerful long-stemmed flashlight, Jace was able to determine that as the pipe deck's cross members tore away, they had pulled plating from the tension leg, which had ripped a seam extending to sea level. As large ocean swells had developed, the water had poured into the tear and was flooding the hollow tension leg compartment.

Dave's voice came over the radio. "You copy, Sammy?"

"We're here."

"Stewart wants Mr. Hamilton to know that the Coast Guard has just issued an advisory for the Sabine coast. Hurricane Hannah just turned due north. She'll start to get here in a couple of hours. What have you got down there?"

Jace shook his head and Sammy responded. "Nothing yet. He's still checking."

Jace directed his gaze upward to the tension leg, along each riveted row of metal plating. The structure at sea level seemed relatively sound, and nothing there indicated that the storm would cause further damage provided the supports were solid up above.

"Take me up there." Jace pointed to the upper section of the tension leg.

Sammy cranked a handle and the gondola rose slowly, swaying as it went.

It began to rain harder now, and stinging droplets blew sideways in the wind. Jace shielded his eyes as he directed the flashlight along each riveted section during the ascent. His gaze came to rest at the top where the tension leg met the main platform frame. A shadow under a thick two-foot beam caught his eye . . . something ragged where the frame met the tension leg.

"You see that?" Jace shouted.

Sammy glanced toward the framing. "What?"

Jace pointed to the main joint. "Ask the crane operator to take us closer to the south edge." Sammy's face flooded with anxiety. He checked the hundred-foot length of cable that attached at the tip of the crane jib. Wind whistled past the cable that swung only twelve feet from the deck edge.

Sammy looked at the shredded girders that once held the catwalks, only a few yards to their right. He pointed. "When that cable starts coming into contact with those deck plates, it's going to affect the sway on this bucket."

"There's a split along the main brace up there," Jace said. "I need to see how deep it is."

Sammy shouted into the radio. "Another five degrees south, Dave, but take it slow."

The crane jib swung ten feet southward and the gondola followed. Sammy yanked a gear lever and the gondola began to rise.

As they ascended, Jace saw what he feared. Rivets holding the tension leg and the mainframe brace had been sprung by the explosion.

"Not good," Jace said, peering at the damage. "Tell Dave to get us closer. I have to be sure. If that stress fracture runs along the shadow of that elbow, that tension leg could give way if the deck flexes due to the storm."

Sammy's gaze rested on the shredded girders of the catwalk. He hadn't moved. The gondola swayed in the wind.

Jace turned in surprise. "What's the problem?"

Sammy's eyes danced nervously. He pointed to the shredded remains of a catwalk staircase. "I don't want to get hung up on that trash. We can't move over any farther unless we intentionally swing up under the deck. If we do that, I won't have any control at all. My job is to take you back on deck in one piece."

"I understand, but there are fifty men up there who may have to evacuate this rig in rough weather. I can't guess on that decision—I have to be sure. There's no other way to find out." With Southland the insurer of this Texaco rig, Jace's documented decision would be crucial should something fail.

Sammy reluctantly spoke into the radio, instructing Dave to take them north and then south again so that the gondola would swing under the deck.

Sammy and Jace hung onto the gondola rail as Dave complied. They swung north, then south again. The crane jib halted with a jerk, letting the gondola swing like a plumb bob on a string. The crane's momentum aimed them up under the damaged deck.

As the gondola reached the apex of its arc, Jace's flashlight shone on the brace and he got the view he needed. The weld along the seam between the upper deck and the tension leg had broken. The main beam had partially detached from the tension leg.

Jace shouted to Sammy, "I've seen enough. We're in trouble."

"No shit." Sammy grabbed the rail of the gondola as a sudden gust of wind caught them, pushing them east as well as north. The gondola's flight pushed into a semicircular loop. "We've got no control," Sammy yelled as the metal bucket began to spin.

Jace felt like he was on a carnival ride, rotating 360 degrees. The gondola careened west and then south again, heading under the main deck.

"Look out," Sammy shouted as they hurled toward the catwalk debris, colliding sideways with the hanging wreckage. Sammy and Jace were knocked to the floor as an eight-inch girder ripped a hole in the gondola's side, puncturing the aluminum wall.

The gondola had come to a complete stop and hung sideways, rocking in place like a baby cradle.

"Son of a bitch," Sammy shouted.

"Are you guys all right?" Dave responded.

"No injuries. But we're stuck in the wreckage," Sammy replied.

"Can I do anything?"

"No, not yet," Jace broke in. "We'd like to look things over."

Above their heads, the winch cable had gone slack. Most of the gondola's weight was supported at a rakish angle by the sharp spar that had ruptured the aluminum siding and protruded into the compartment a good two feet.

Sammy took a step toward the winch engine, and the girder creaked as the gondola tipped laterally. Jace and Sammy hugged the insides of the car.

Sammy carefully edged to his knees. Even the smallest motion caused the gondola to sway.

Under the shadow of the upper deck, Jace used his flashlight to examine their predicament: The twisted scaffolding of the catwalk staircase hung above. The girder upon which they rested was a seven-foot-long steel stub connected to a vertical pylon that joined the platform thirty feet above. A portion of the pipe deck had been taken out by the explosion and was now an open void.

Jace and Sammy were suspended two hundred feet above the raging surf that pounded the *Aurora's* frame below.

"I wouldn't do a hell of a lot of moving around until we figure this out," Jace cautioned as he gripped the car's rail.

Sammy nervously reached for the gears. "I've got to get us off this thing. Let me see if I can budge it."

"All right, but go easy."

Sammy tripped a lever.

The winch spindle turned but came to a grinding halt as the cable tightened and then resisted. Smoke and the odor of burning grease vented from the engine.

In an attempt to shake things loose, Sammy reversed gears. The gondola lurched back, tipping wildly.

"Hold it." Jace pointed. "Look up there."

Sammy craned his neck. "Oh shit."

A section of cable just above the winch buckle had stretched to its limits. A few of the bound wires had popped away. The cable showed signs of shredding.

Dave, the crane operator, had apparently contacted Stewart, who now voiced his irritation on the radio. "Sammy, what the hell's going on down there?"

"We got spun around and cracked up. We're okay, but we're stuck."

"Can you get loose?"

Sammy looked over the side at the tangled mess. "I'm not sure yet. We're really jammed in."

"What can we do?" Stewart asked. "Pull up on the crane?"

"No moves," Jace yelled. The thought occurred that Stewart might know who Jace was and end his quest with the push of one wrong button. Jace shook off the paranoia. No way Stewart would have a clue. "Don't budge an inch until we're ready."

Rain-filled gusts swayed the suspended gondola back and forth. Its aluminum frame creaked and scraped against the girder that had punctured the container. Sammy hunched next to the gearbox with one hand on the shift lever, ready to use it.

Jace clung to the railing, stooped on one knee, his back to the wind, shouting into the radio that Sammy had removed from his sleeve. Jace could barely hear Stewart over the receiver as the deluge pelted the hood of his orange windbreaker.

For lack of a viable rescue for Sammy and himself, Jace's thoughts had turned to the safety of the other men on deck, and Jace wanted to make certain that Stewart understood him clearly. He repeated the words again, slowly and carefully. "You don't have much time. Take your men out now."

"I read you," Stewart answered.

"From what I see, the rig won't stand forty-foot seas," Jace continued. "When the south tension leg takes more water and the wind picks up, pounding wave action could pull the leg away from the main frame. She'll collapse."

"Hold on a second."

Jace waited while an empty buzz sounded from the speaker.

Another strong gust of wind caused the gondola to jerk and shift.

Jace's eyes met Sammy's.

Sammy looked like he wanted to say something, but he bit his lip instead. The rain droplets streaking down his frustrated face made it appear as if he were crying. Sammy's earlier communication with Dave, the crane operator, yielded no options. Though the *Aurora*'s crew could descend to sea level by climbing down through the tension legs, they would have no access to Jace and Sammy who were suspended thirty feet under the main deck and two hundred feet above the water. No other rescue efforts could come from above. The *Aurora* had only one working crane since its other boat crane had been damaged in the blast. Word had reached Stewart that the hurricane was now a Category 5, packing 180-mile-an-hour winds, tracking toward the Texas coast. Faced with what he believed was a life-and-death situation, Jace demanded Stewart stay near the radio. Foremost, he wanted to track Stewart's every move.

"Stewart, are you still there?" Jace shouted over the storm.

"Yes, I'm back. I was just checking to see what we've got available."

"Can you hear me? Have you sent an SOS?"

"We've contacted the mainland. They're sending choppers ASAP. In the meantime, I'd like to concentrate on getting you two up here. I was just checking to see if we could lash extra cable to a wood spar and lower it to you."

"You'd never get it pushed in our direction."

Stewart couldn't see them, since Jace and Sammy were tucked up under the main deck. "How far are you from the platform edge?"

"We're some twenty-five feet to the south."

"Well, since the wind's coming from that direction, wouldn't a cable lowered over that side blow your way?"

"It's a crapshoot."

Stewart sounded like his nerves were wearing thin. "Well, goddamn it, I have to do something." Amazing. Ironically, the man who may have killed the father was concerned about saving the son.

Jace searched Sammy's face. Careful examination of their perch showed that the gondola made contact with the vertical spire at two points: where the winch basket touched a hollow catwalk banister dangling from above and where the eight-inch girder penetrated the gondola's center. It was *there* that the weight was supported, the point at which they were held in place. If they were to free themselves, the entire gondola would have to move laterally toward the blast hole. The only way of accomplishing that would be by means of the winch cable, which had showed signs of splaying.

Jace pressed his lips to the radio. "Give us a minute." Jace turned and tried to read Sammy's eyes as he chose his words carefully. "This is our decision, not his," Jace said, gesturing up with a forefinger.

Sammy gasped. "Shit, for a minute I thought you were pointing to God."

"Well, maybe I am. We're going to need somebody's help down here. And we've got no time. You know this gondola better than I do—what do you think?"

Sammy's eyes darted back and forth. "I think we ought to let Dave yank us free."

Jace shook his head. "Ain't gonna happen unless we get some leverage." He gestured toward the protruding girder. "If one of us gets out onto that girder and pushes while the winch puts tension on the cable, we might be able to jiggle loose."

Sammy pointed. "You're going out there?"

"Unless you want to."

Sammy looked down at the waves, which had grown to well over twenty feet in height. "I'm not that good a swimmer."

"You picked a hell of a place to work."

"Who knew . . ."

"Forget it. The two of us are getting out of here. Count on it." Jace handed him the radio. "Here, you explain to Stewart. I'll climb out there and shove on the gondola, while you work the gears. If we get our timing perfect, maybe we can shake loose. What do you say?"

Sammy lashed the radio to his sleeve. "How are you going to get back in if we start to move?"

"Leave that to me. I'll grab the rail and hang on if she goes. You run the controls."

Sammy shrugged. "I don't know about this."

"We can't sit this out and hope for a rescue. Hannah's coming with better than forty-foot seas, and I think the *Aurora* is going down. Stuck here, we're dead either way." Anything to get back on deck and confront Stewart. "I'd rather die trying."

While Sammy explained their plan to Dave and Stewart, Jace removed his wind-breaker. He carefully lifted his right leg over the rail and sat on the edge. Sammy watched nervously as Jace inched onto the girder butt first, still hanging on to the gondola. He wrapped his legs around the beam and leaned forward, getting a good grip on the gondola railing.

Out in the open, soaked to the skin, with the wind licking his backside, Jace felt like a circus performer without a net. He looked over the side of the gondola at the white water churning below. One slip and he would plummet. He was struck by the thought of having to swim for his life if he were lucky enough to survive the fall.

He shook the image from his mind. "You ready, Sammy?" he shouted. "Reel in every time I count to three."

Sammy swallowed and gripped the gear lever.

Jace braced himself. "Here we go . . . one, two, three."

Sammy tugged on the controls. The winch heaved and the engine screeched, struggling to spool the cable.

Nothing happened.

"Again," Jace said. "I don't think we timed that quite right. It takes a while for those gears to engage. You trip your lever on two, and by three I'll push. Ready. One, two, three." Jace put all his weight into it.

Amazingly, this time the gondola scraped forward on the girder. It had budged a full inch.

"Again—one, two, three."

Once again Sammy shifted. The engine ground for roughly ten seconds as Jace strained with all his strength. The gondola slid another two inches.

"Hold it," Jace shouted. Smoke had again emerged from the motor. The gears smelled hot. Jace looked up. The cable above the winch buckle had frayed some more, though 90 percent of it was still intact. "What's with the engine?"

"I think it's burning up. She might have a couple of tries left in her, but after that I don't know."

"All right, the cable looks okay. Tell Dave to rotate his crane jib out and away from our position so the angle of stress is sideways not so vertical. What do you say?"

Sammy nodded, and after explaining their request to Dave, Sammy relaxed the cable tension and spooled out some slack.

As Dave swung the crane toward the north, it flattened the cable's rise some fifteen degrees toward horizontal.

"That's good," Jace said, sliding his butt toward the gondola a bit. "I think we've got a shot now." He clamped his legs around the girder again and took a few deep breaths. "Okay, let's go for it. Ready, one, two, now!"

Sammy hauled back on the lever and as the cable tensed, the engine strained. Thick smoke blossomed from the engine's radiator screen as the gondola began to scrape along the girder. One inch, then another. Then a third. Jace's face reddened with exertion. "She's going, Sammy. Keep it up." An ugly rasping noise reverberated through the engine. Smoke billowed steadily into the passing wind.

"I think the flywheel's gone," Sammy shouted.

The gondola moved yet a fourth inch.

"Don't stop!" Jace heaved forward as hard as he could.

Sammy's face twisted with anxiety. "Be ready, Jace. Jump on," he yelled.

Then all hell broke loose.

Like a gunshot, the cotter pin on the winch gave away. With a metallic zing, the winch spindle spun out of its housing, knocking the cable into loops as it went. The cable smacked into Sammy's left shoulder, knocking him to the gondola floor.

The gondola shifted forward, held only by the girder and the quickly unraveling spindle, which had been hindered for a fraction of a second, tangling in the metal rods of the winch basket.

In the blink of an eye, Jace realized the winch spindle would be snarled only momentarily. Gravity would win out, and the gondola would unhinge from the girder any second.

As the gondola tipped, Jace hunched forward over the rail, grabbing Sammy by the hood of his windbreaker. The gondola rotated forty-five degrees, lost its hold on the girder, and fell sideways from Sammy, disappearing below.

"Sammy, for God's sake, grab me," Jace shouted.

Blood poured from a cut on Sammy's face as he fumbled for Jace's arms with his right hand.

Even as he struggled to hold on, Jace was fully aware of the gondola's descent. It tumbled one hundred feet, finally reaching the end of the cable where it jerked, bouncing like a yo-yo, snapping the wire. Spinning crazily end-over-end, it splashed into the heaving sea.

4

The Northern Star
At Sea off Southampton

THE SEAS WERE CALM AND the cruise ship rode steady, steaming toward the English coast. A sooty aroma from the ocean liner's stacks wafted through the night air.

Strains of music filtered through the companionways from the ballroom as Harold Berlinger took a stroll on the aft deck.

He paused at the rail, staring at the moonlight glistening on the wake, and took a final puff of his cigar before chucking it off the stern. He swirled the brandy snifter in his left hand, warming the amber liquid. As if toasting the stars, he lifted the glass and drank, savoring the final sips of Courvoisier.

It was the last night of a Mediterranean cruise, and soon he would retire to his first-class cabin, remove his dinner jacket, and go to sleep. The ship would dock in the morning. Within forty-eight hours, Berlinger would be back at his lab in Carnforth.

A renowned physicist, he had taken a holiday from work and from grief. His wife, Candice, had passed away a fortnight before, and he desperately needed a change of scene. Only a year ago, Candice had contracted pancreatic cancer. She had deteriorated before his eyes under the stress of chemotherapy. At the end, she was bedridden at their small country estate, immobilized by pain, and Berlinger had been at her side.

Berlinger regretted the manic dedication to his experiments he'd had throughout their years together: the many international conferences he had attended, the seminars, classes, and the meetings that had taken him away from his wife.

If he'd had it to do over again, he would have balanced his life differently.

Looking back, he marveled that he had been so driven, partially by altruism but mostly by greed, operating as part of a research group under a veil of secrecy. He had disliked the cloak-and-dagger feeling of that arrangement and wouldn't have considered it at all, if it hadn't been for the massive salary he'd been paid by two industrialists who headed the association.

The international energy quest had been the brainchild of Norman Scalbania, the Canadian, though Berlinger believed that Mason Marro, the American automotive giant, had his hand on the purse strings. Berlinger and his six other colleagues were never quite certain about finance. After all, it was their job to conduct experiments. The Scalbania Seven—or S-7, as they were called— were working under a grant, paid well, and promised immense profits if the research succeeded.

According to yesterday's satellite TV news coverage from England, one of Berlinger's Canadian colleagues, Hector Walsh, had met with an untimely end . . . a freak explosion in Walsh's lab. Berlinger had seen Walsh and the other S-7 scientists on many occasions when Berlinger traveled to labs in Leipzig, Edinburgh, and Oslo working on propulsion methods for weeks on end.

Though he had enjoyed moments of hope and brilliance, nothing permanent had come of the effort, even while his relationship with Candice suffered.

Now, nothing was left of his marriage.

Berlinger's challenge would be to make something of his life.

As he mused about the past, he noticed another man dressed in a white dinner jacket descending the steps from the upper decks. He had seen the Asian at other social events and had casually spoken with him on several occasions, since he, like Berlinger, traveled alone.

The middle-aged man looked muscular even in his tux, which made sense, as Berlinger had observed him on the decks at sunrise practicing Tai Chi. Yet oddly enough, the man smoked. He puffed on a cigarette now as he strolled casually down the deck.

Berlinger set his brandy glass on the rail and extended a hand. "Mr. Xi," he said smiling. "Did you decide to forgo the last dance?"

"I saw you from up there." Xi pointed to the promenade. "I thought I would bid you farewell."

"Very kind indeed. But I've just finished my drink. Perhaps we should join the others at the bar and have another."

"Excellent idea," Xi said, reaching out. "But you've smudged your jacket with cigar ashes." Xi's fingers touched his lapel.

Berlinger looked down and was surprised as Xi's hand suddenly flattened, became rigid as a board, and slammed upward into Berlinger's neck, crushing his Adam's apple.

Berlinger was staggered by the blow, his face swollen with a futile effort to inhale. He bent forward in pain, and Xi was suddenly at his side, gripping his wrist and elbow. In one deft move, Xi utilized his leverage and lifted him.

Bug-eyed with terror, Berlinger flailed wildly in the air. His arms knocked his brandy snifter off the rail as he bounced over. Then he was in free fall, the wind rushing past his face as he dropped hundreds of feet off the stern, splashing into the churning wake of the ship.

Moments later, Xi stepped back into the main ballroom, wandering through the crowd. The well-wishers danced between the tables as the band blared an upbeat rendition of "Auld Lang Syne."

Since Xi had been raised in China, he felt no sentiment for the traditional British ode to times gone by; but the music put him in a festive mood, and he felt elated that he had followed Shag's orders and completed the mission. Cho would be pleased.

5

The Aurora

AS WIND AND RAIN SWIRLED around their perch, Jace and Sammy sat astride the eight-inch girder like two men on a horse. Sammy, in his orange windbreaker, was slumped back against Jace, who now wore only his flannel shirt and jeans, since his windbreaker and flashlight had been lost when the gondola fell.

The moment the gondola tipped away, Jace had scissor-clenched the girder with both his legs and hunched over the end of the beam, clutching Sammy to prevent his fall.

Numbed by the crushing blow of the cable, Sammy still had the presence of mind to grab Jace's collar with his right hand.

As he'd sat up, Jace had used all his upper-body strength to lift Sammy—a dangerous and strenuous maneuver. Jace had leaned hard to his left as he hoisted Sammy onto his right thigh. Only the disparity in their body weight, with Jace at 200 pounds versus Sammy at 145, had prevented them from both tumbling into the ocean.

Sammy had screamed in pain, particularly when Jace was forced to grab under his arms.

Finally, as Jace inched backward, Sammy had clutched the girder with his right arm, and Jace managed to get him onto his stomach, straddling the beam at right angles.

While gripping his belt and talking Sammy through the moves, Jace had scooted Sammy farther back, guiding his left leg up and over the beam so that he wound up slouched on Jace's chest facing forward.

Breathing hard, Sammy whimpered that he felt something loose in his sternum. Jace wasn't surprised after the way the cable had struck him. Sammy might have several broken ribs or a separated shoulder. His left arm hung limply at his side.

Sammy mumbled something about swelling under his left ear, and Jace could see the lump. Good reason to believe that the lump was a sign of a muscle tear. Checking Sammy's neck, Jace's fingers came away drenched in red. Blood oozed from a deep gash that had occurred when the unraveling cable sliced Sammy's jaw.

After removing the radio from Sammy's sleeve and strapping it to his own, Jace had reinitiated a conversation with the crane cab, where Stewart had overheard the sounds of the accident.

Once Sammy was secure, Jace took a few deep breaths and shouted a brief report into the radio, describing their predicament.

Stewart initially suggested that the crane lower a cargo hook off the south side of the platform, believing that the wind had grown strong enough to blow a rescue cable in their direction. But Jace pointed out that Sammy's condition negated the possibility of Jace stepping into the hook in seventy-mile-an-hour wind gusts while holding Sammy.

It had occurred to Jace that he and Sammy might be stuck below for good and that Stewart might escape in the evacuation. He vowed to get back on deck with Sammy or die trying.

Scrambling for ideas, Jace suggested another recovery method: the cargo net. The webbing would catch the wind more easily, and the net would be easier to snag. It could potentially hold Sammy; if nothing else, Sammy might be tied to the outside of the net once it arrived. Jace asked Stewart to lash a coil of half-inch line to the net for that purpose.

Stewart agreed, and Jace and Sammy were left to huddle together on the girder while the men on deck retooled the crane. The longer they waited, the heavier Sammy's weight became, and Jace had to readjust his center of gravity several times to keep his own back muscles from cramping. Blood continued to stream down Sammy's chin onto the front of his windbreaker and over Jace's hands, which were clenched at Sammy's waist.

Sammy coughed several times. Then he moaned. "Jace, I think I'm losing it."

Jace placed his mouth next to Sammy's left ear. "You're fine. The net's on its way." Sammy was in shock. He might faint. Jace gave him a gentle nudge.

"You've got one job, and that's to keep awake. I told you, you're getting out of here. Just think about positive things. The place where you'll go for your R & R. Somewhere you love. Your favorite." He had to keep him talking. "Where is that for you?"

"Bay area," Sammy replied. "Marin County."

"Oh yeah? Well, I'm from San Antonio now, but I was originally from California. You got family there?" Jace asked, with the realization that Cory was all that he had left.

"My dad. He runs a Chinese restaurant near Fisherman's Wharf, but he lives across the bay. Near Tiburon."

"Pretty country. How old's your dad?"

"Sixty-one. He's cool."

Jace remembered the last time he'd seen his father. He was six years old the night Arthur Kelton left home. As one of NASA's key telemetry experts, Arthur had duty in Pasadena, tracking an undercover *Mars Observer* mission in August of 1993. Two days later he was dead, mysteriously killed on an Arkansas back road. Jace's mother, Jane, died of cancer two-and-a-half years later. With no other living relatives, Jace became a ward of the state at St. Catherine's Foster Home for Boys, where he met Cory Jackson. It was Cory's air force career and his connections with NASA that had eventually provided Jace the means to investigate his father's infamous death. He hadn't spoken to Cory in the last four days. Had Cory monitored the hurricane's turn to the north? Jace was supposed to call him after confronting Stewart . . . if he lived that long.

Sammy groaned. "My whole left side's numb. You think I'm dying?"

"Hell no." Jace gazed off toward the southern ocean, where clouds on the horizon had turned black. "You're not leaving me on this rail alone." Jace paused, gratified that something else had appeared in the dark skies to his left. "Here's our ride, cowboy. Look up there."

Stewart's voice crackled over the radio. "You should be seeing that net, Jace."

"We do." Dangling below the platform lip above their heads to the south, the eight-foot cargo net had appeared, swaying in the wind. Stewart had remembered to lash a coil of half-inch line at the top.

"How we doin'? How low do you want it?" Stewart asked.

"Try another twenty feet," Jace instructed.

Following Jace's directions, Dave lowered the net to Jace's eye level. The strength of the south wind began to work in their favor as heavy gusts blew the fluttering net under the platform.

Jace and Sammy watched, waiting for the perfect blast of wind to buffet the net even closer. But the gusts weren't strong enough and the cable's length was too short, constrained by the platform's edge. Even the more powerful gusts moved the cable a mere fifteen feet from vertical, still ten feet short of Jace's reach.

"It's not working," Sammy whined. The pain and loss of blood were getting to him. "We're not going anywhere."

"Yes we are, goddamn it." Jace barked into the radio, "Stewart, listen. We don't have enough arc on the cable. You have to pay out more line to increase the radius of the swing."

A moment of silence.

"You copy?"

"I do. But if the net is equal to your height right now . . . if we lower it, won't it sway beneath you?"

"Right."

"Then how the hell are you going to grab it?"

"I'm not. I'm going to jump for it."

"No," Sammy said. "We can't do that."

Another moment of silence.

Muffled background conversation on the radio was followed by Stewart's nervous cough. "There's no other way?"

"There's got to be," Sammy begged. "You'll fall."

"Stewart," Jace said. "Tell Sammy about the rescue."

"What?"

"Tell Sammy how we're getting home after we join you on deck."

"Well, if that's what—"

"Stewart. Lower the goddamned net while you tell him."

"All right. Sammy, there are five Bell & Howell choppers on their way from Galveston."

"Will they be able to land?" Sammy asked as the net began to descend.

"They should, and they're less than forty-five minutes away."

Jace nudged him. "See, we're headed for the mainland. Before you know it, you'll see your dad."

Stewart continued to describe the helicopter mission as Jace craned his neck, gazing at the pylon some three feet behind his back. He gauged the necessary maneuvers and then, as Stewart finished, said calmly in Sammy's ear, "Now listen, both of us are going to inch back to create room at the end of the beam. After we've moved as far as we can, I want you to lie forward and hug this girder for dear life with your good arm and both legs. You got that? I'm going to climb over you like a baby possum on its mother's back. You just hang on. I'll bring the net back to you. You understand?"

"But how—"

"Do what I tell you. Are you with me?"

"No. You'll never make it."

"Yes I will. Did I tell you about my college days? Did I tell you how in the summers I worked a carney show that played small towns all over the south? Did I? Scoot your butt back, that's right. In this carney show, I did a trapeze act three summers running."

"You did?"

"Sure. I was what they called a 'catcher.' Beautiful young women would do somersaults in midair, and then I'd catch them while I swung on a trapeze bar."

"Come on. Bullshit."

"No. No bullshit. Just keep moving. At the end of the show, I'd do a one-and-a-half forward pike into the net forty feet below and the goddamned circus tent would go ape shit. We're almost there. Two shows a day, three on Saturday. All summer long. Now, do you think jumping for that net without even doing a flip is going to be a problem for a crazy ass like me?"

Sammy had wriggled backward as best he could while Jace spoke in his ear, gently pulling him along.

When Jace felt the cold steel pylon at his buttocks, he asked Sammy to lean forward and clamp onto the beam. Hugging his arms around Sammy's body and keeping contact with the girder's lower flange with both hands, Jace kept his weight off Sammy as he inchwormed himself over Sammy's body.

"Aaaa," Sammy cried out, "my chest."

"Sorry." Jace grunted as he pushed forward, trying to avoid crushing Sammy's injured face. Finally Jace cleared Sammy's head. He sat up and straddled the beam, rolling his sleeves up as the wind buffeted his hair wildly.

On the increased cable length, the net had floated more in their direction and swayed erratically below.

"How'd we do? Is the net okay?" Stewart asked over the radio.

"Good as it's going to get," Jace shouted. "I'm coming up to see you,

Stewart." Then he turned. "You okay, Sammy?"

Sammy nodded.

Jace reached down and unlaced his canvas deck shoes.

"What are you doing?" Sammy asked nervously.

"I always worked barefoot in the carney show." Jace kicked the shoes off and watched them fall. The wind carried them laterally to the north—one bounced off a pipe deck girder, while the other shot cleanly into breaking waves.

"Oh, Jesus. Am I really doing this?" Jace whispered to himself, strapping the radio tighter on his left arm. He brought his right foot up over the girder, crossing it next to his left knee. He leaned into the wind and, holding on to the girder with both hands, he pivoted his weight onto the ball of his right foot, curling his toes over the beam's top flange. He waited for just the right moment.

"Jace . . ."

"Not now, Sammy."

A gust of wind lofted the net to its most favorable proximity, ten feet out and twelve feet down.

Jace swallowed hard. "Don't move, you son of a bitch," he said between clenched teeth.

He brought his left foot up quickly and, ignoring the butterflies in his gut, leaned out and uncoiled, pushing off from his toes.

Jace took off from the girder like a competitive swimmer leaving a racing block. Praying for good distance and a safe landing, he dove headfirst into the wind.

6

The Klakamas Inn

MADDY CURLED THE PAY-PHONE cord around her forefinger as she watched Foley shuffle around the lobby. The amiable old guy chuckled as he brought another beer to the logger at the pool table. Nodding and smiling, he checked with the couple by the window.

Maddy glanced at her watch—5:43. This was her fifth call.

The first to Christine had assured Maddy that everything was fine at home. Maddy had a menagerie of orphaned animals she kept in pens behind her house, and Christine had been there to feed them only an hour before.

The second call was distressing . . . she had reached the personnel department at the University of Washington and found no Dr. Bellamy listed in the Ecology Department.

The third call went to the Leavenworth Sheriff's office. Ms. Barnes, the receptionist, told her that all the officers were out but that a deputy named Shukson would call her back.

The fourth call to her answering service showed two messages: The *first* she would ignore. It was from Kit, long distance from Chicago, wanting to "chat." Her high school boyfriend from her Ann Arbor neighborhood had recently resumed his crusade to resurrect their relationship. The *second* message, from Father Navarro, was disconcerting for a different reason.

Navarro's anxious tone made her respond immediately.

She dialed the parish number and was frustrated by the delay, on hold for several minutes while one of the sisters went to find the father. Finally, the phone rustled as if it were being rubbed on the coarse cloth of a nun's habit, and Maddy was prepared to have the sister tell her Father Navarro wasn't available.

But after furiously clearing his throat, Navarro came on the line. She could visualize his round face and short-cropped black hair. "Hello, Madison Anne." He had insisted on using her full name since she was a small child. "I'm sorry I took so long. I was just saying good-bye to a parishioner."

Maddy smiled. Or nipping at your port. She remembered Navarro's penchant for sweet after-dinner wines. "Father, I'm sorry to bother you, but your message sounded urgent."

"I'm afraid it is. I tried reaching your uncle Robert and couldn't."

Maddy tensed up. "It's that serious?"

"Well, it's troubling. Your father's remains have been disturbed."

"Disturbed?"

"I should say 'vandalized.' I hate to use that word, but it's a more appropriate description."

"I don't understand."

"Someone broke the lock on the mausoleum door late last night and shattered poor Mason's urn. His remains were there on the floor when we discovered the crime. We did what we could, of course, and handled the ashes with great dignity. I've already chosen another vessel for him, and he's at peace again next to your mother."

"My mother's ashes were all right?"

"Tenille's seemed untouched."

Maddy was suddenly struck by latent guilt. She had felt greater concern for her mother's remains. Her condemnation of her father had lasted beyond the grave, largely because Maddy felt that Mason had been the force behind the lifestyle that he and Tenille shared.

"Any idea who—"

"None whatsoever, though the police believe it wasn't a random act. The lock was torched by a professional. Naturally, I thought you should be informed. If you wish to choose a different urn—"

"No. I'm sure you made an excellent choice." The word "professional" rang in her mind. The one thing her dad had been, more than anything else, was a consummate professional, even at the risk of neglecting his family. After a few exchanged words about her activities out west and her lack of plans to return to Ann Arbor, Maddy closed the conversation by thanking Navarro, adding,

"Please let me know if anything else comes up."

"Oh, I will. We're obviously very concerned. God bless you, Madison Anne."

Maddy felt a chill as she hung up.

The father's blessing had been added as if he thought she would need it. She had a sudden urge to call Christine again. The image of her dad's ashes strewn on the ground began to disturb her—the indignity of it.

By disrupting the dead, someone had invaded her life.

7

The Aurora

THE HALF-INCH NYLON LINE SAILED, uncoiling like a pencil line of fate, fragile on the wind. The end landed on Sammy's buttocks and fell away.

Sammy had stirred slightly when the lasso loop grazed his jeans, but he wouldn't move much for fear of losing his hold on the girder.

"Sammy, you've got to help me," Jace shouted.

Jace swung back and forth, his left arm clenched around the cable above the cargo net's topknot, his bare feet gripping the four-inch rope latticework below.

The half-inch line Stewart had sent down had been meant to bind Jace and Sammy together, but now it served as a snare.

Jace had tried three unsuccessful times to toss it toward the girder.

Once again, he gathered the twenty-five-foot rope, using his left hand to collect the coils.

Jace had envisioned this critical step in the rescue, but what he had *not* envisioned was Sammy's inability to snag the line.

"I'm too low," Jace yelled. "I've got to get above you so the line drops as I throw it. Give me a second."

Sammy simply waved his right hand. His left arm hung limply at his side, and his right was hooked under the end of the beam as he huddled facedown with his legs wrapped around the girder.

"Did you hear me, Stewart?" Jace shouted as the wind threatened to take his breath away. To make sure he was being heard, he tucked his chin into his shoulder and turned his head toward the radio strapped to his left wrist.

"Stewart, have Dave take me up."

"How high?"

"Try ten feet."

As if the hand of God responded, the cable began to rise.

"Say when."

"That's good right there, hold it." Jace was now above Sammy's position. Jace's two-hundred-pound weight had altered the sway of the net, and the wind no longer lofted the limp webbing as close to the girder as it had before. The cable and Jace hovered between sixteen and twenty feet away to the south.

In his attempt to recover Sammy, Jace's adrenaline was running at its peak. He had forced his own brush with death out of his mind and had nearly forgotten that ten minutes ago his dive off the girder had almost failed.

Although his body had made contact with the cargo net, the flimsiness of the webbing gave way under his weight and he slid down the mesh. Only the grasping fingers of his right hand, snagging the rectangular cross-strands of the rope-weave near the bottom of the net, had broken his fall. In that split second, he clutched with his left hand and got a firm grip. With his bare feet dangling in space, he pulled himself up, hand over hand, until his toes felt the rope mesh.

While the net bobbed and swayed in the fury of the storm, Jace had continued his wobbly climb until he reached the round topknot where Stewart's coiled half-inch line was tied.

Recovering, Jace swung back and forth in the wind, making a lasso loop at the end of the twenty-five-foot line while he shouted instructions to Sammy to catch the rope and fasten it to the end of the beam.

Sammy's curled, bloody fingers, stretched a few inches beyond the spar of twisted metal, had become the target Jace was to hit from twenty feet away.

A sudden gust of wind tossed the net, causing it to swing violently, but it brought Jace closer to Sammy than before. Feeling the strength of the gale, Jace realized Hurricane Hannah was on final approach.

"Jace," Stewart was back. "We just got word. We have a thirty-minute window before the brunt of the storm hits. We've lost radio contact with the mainland, but the choppers are a few minutes out. I can't hold them a second longer than it takes to load. You've got to get up here."

Stewart might well board a chopper and be gone.

Jace's line was ready. There wasn't time for more misses.

"Sammy," Jace yelled. "The choppers are here."

Sammy's eyes were closed.

"Sammy, I'm not leaving without you. Do you hear me? You're going to have to suck up your guts. Tighten your legs around the girder and sit up. Catch the rope and loop it around the end of the beam."

Sammy's eyes opened and then shut again. His right hand flopped weakly.

"Sammy, goddamn it, sit up! You're worried about dying? Falling off? You'll be dead if we can't get you off that perch. Now try. Try so you can see your dad again. They'll put a cast on your arm, and you'll be eating dinner at your dad's restaurant in three days. Come on, buddy, don't make me a liar. I promised you. Help me keep that promise."

Agonizing moments passed. Sammy's face was tilted toward Jace, dried blood crusted around his mouth and chin.

Suddenly, over the howl of the wind the unmistakable whine of helicopter engines cut through, followed by the wop-wop-wop of their blades somewhere above.

"Jace," Stewart shouted on the radio. "What's it going to be?"

"You hear that, Sammy? That's our bus."

Sammy's eyes opened once more.

Jace made his preparations fully visible to Sammy: he clasped the coil of line in his right hand, clutched the cable with his left, jockeying his position on the net, leaning out for a better throw. "I'm ready, Sammy, are you? Next big gust of wind and I'm tossing."

Sammy grimaced as he brought his right forearm up over the girder.

"That's it, Sammy. Fight through it." Jace cheered him as Sammy's battle with gravity continued in slow motion. His right hand gripped the girder flange. "You got it, man." Sammy's head tilted to his left, his mouth stretched open in a bellow of agony that drowned out the sound of the helicopters as he braced off his right hand and straightened his elbow. His body shook with pain as he pushed to a sitting position.

"Okay, Sammy. Perfect. Now hang on to the girder with your right hand and look at me. Watch me, Sammy." Jace swayed back and forth, waving the coil of rope. "When I toss, you've got to catch the loop. I'll pay out the line, and you stick that loop over the end of the girder, okay? That way I can pull myself to you, and you can climb on. You got it?"

Jace was interrupted by Stewart's nervous voice on the radio. "We've got a chopper on the pad, Jace. Loading now."

"I want dead air for a few minutes, Stewart. We've got only one shot at this. No offense, but if you don't mind, don't call us, we'll call you."

"All right. I'll let you know when the last chopper—"

"You'll stay off the goddamned air until I've got this guy in my hands. Clear?"

"Copy."

The net swayed and Jace took two deep breaths, settling himself down, praying for the right gust of wind. Seconds passed. Jace made a last-minute decision and tied the end of his line to the cable near his left hand, realizing how vital it would be that he not lose contact with the rope, whether Sammy caught it or not. While he secured the bow-line knot, he called to Sammy a few times to keep him focused. As he worked, Jace heard the first chopper lift off and a second land on the platform above. The wind kicked up a steady pressure at Jace's back, but it was not until the third chopper set down that Jace was suddenly thrust forward on the force of a huge gust.

"Sammy, look up," Jace shouted as he swung in his direction. "Reach out!"

Sammy raised his bloody chin and extended his right hand as Jace hit the peak of the cable's arc, some sixteen feet away and twelve feet over Sammy's hunched frame. To make sure he didn't fall short, Jace tossed the line with an underhand throw that caught in the wind. The open lasso loop flew a bit too far, past Sammy's outstretched fingers, dropping over his arm to his shoulder and encompassing his head.

By the time Jace was on the backswing, Sammy had tried to clutch the line but couldn't. The momentum tightened the noose around Sammy's triceps and neck. Sammy screamed as the line went taut around the base of his skull and, to Jace's horror, pulled him off the beam.

"Oh Jesus, Sammy, hold on," Jace shouted as Sammy fell and jerked as he hit the end of the line, dangling in space. Fortunately, the lasso noose had snagged Sammy's upper arm and neck at the same time, and the bend of Sammy's elbow acted as a hook to prevent the rope from sliding off. Momentarily, the line held, and Sammy appeared to be conscious, crimping his elbow to save his life.

"Up," Jace shouted into the radio. "Take us up now."

"Affirmative," Dave responded. "I'll be pulling you all the way up on deck. Stewart will be waiting."

The cable slowly began its ascent.

The wind drove puddles across the oil rig platform as the crane maneuvered Jace and Sammy over the listing metal deck. As the crane lowered them both, the fourth helicopter waited on the pad with blades spinning.

Jace frantically looked around to make sure that Stewart hadn't boarded the chopper and was gratified to see him with two other men rushing toward Sammy, carrying a stretcher.

Still hanging on the net, Jace watched from above as the men cut the line and laid Sammy down on the canvas gurney. The oil rig medic gave Sammy an injection while Jace was lowered.

The cargo net slumped limply to the deck, and Jace stepped off as Stewart hustled over.

"You've got a decision to make," Stewart shouted over the whine of the chopper engine. "There's limited seats left on that one."

"Which one are you taking?" Jace asked, jockeying for position.

"I can't go yet."

"Then I'll wait for the next one with you," Jace said.

"You don't understand. There may not be another."

Jace glanced incredulously at Stewart. "What? You said there were five."

"Number five broke radio contact. They don't know where he is. He may be down. There may not be any more rides, Jace. The wind speeds are going to hit well over one hundred twenty miles an hour *before* anyone else can get here. We've got five men and a weight limit for three. You're not a member of my crew, and I owe you the courtesy of a seat. It's you or Sammy."

"What about you?"

Stewart's brown eyes clouded as he shook his head. "Some bullshit about a captain and his ship, I guess." The gallantry floored Jace. What was Stewart's motive? Anything to avoid Jace's ultimate confrontation?

"Well ain't this a crock." Jace stared past Stewart at the glass cockpit of the chopper. The pilot waved his arms impatiently. Jace's destiny was about to be jammed through a dwindling crevice of opportunity. If he left, he would survive and remain unfulfilled—if he stayed, he might find resolution and perhaps die doing it. Jace glanced at Stewart. The man had altered Jace's life. Now that he'd found him, nothing would tear him away.

Jace walked to Sammy's side and knelt down. He was conscious, panting with the pain. "I bet your dad serves great food," Jace said, taking Sammy's good hand. Through lips crusted with blood, Sammy managed a smile. "When you get there, do me a favor." Jace gave him a squeeze. "Order a chicken chow mein for me."

Sammy's brow furrowed with concern. "Jace?"

Jace looked up at the two rig hands who stood by the stretcher. "Get him aboard." As the men lifted Sammy and carried him off, Jace gave him a thumbs-up.

The stretcher and Sammy disappeared into the chopper.

The moment the door closed, the helicopter lifted off, wobbling erratically in the turbulence, shooting sideways with the wind, and finally straightening out with its nose low and tail high, being carried toward the mainland by the heaving gusts.

Stewart stepped forward and joined Jace on the deck, gazing up in the rain.

Jace looked over, finally able to key on his face.

Stewart's gray hair lashed his forehead in the storm. He had a painfully resigned expression like a guy waiting for a root canal. It wasn't the face of coward—a killer perhaps—but not one wrinkle showed a lack of resolve.

Stewart spoke with his eyes on the helicopter. "I nearly split a gut listening to you guys on the radio. That was pretty amazing, what you did down there. And you never had any damned trapeze act in college either, did you, cowboy?"

"No," Jace said, staring as the chopper disappeared into the clouds. "Matter of fact, I grew up afraid of heights."

8

Leavenworth

MADDY ENJOYED ROUGHING IT IN the wild, but she also loved the comforts of home. She could have afforded to live anywhere, having inherited her parents' estate, but she chose what she considered the most beautiful place in the world—a site in the Cascade foothills fifteen minutes outside Leavenworth, Washington—a thousand feet above the Wenatchee River, overlooking Cashmere Mountain.

She had designed the floor plan of her three-bedroom, A-frame cedar home in such a way that sunrise would warm the breakfast nook off her back porch and sunset would appear over snowcapped peaks to the west, painting the vaulted ceilings of her living room with shades of fire.

Now, as she drove up her gravel driveway, she was especially grateful to see that Christine had thoughtfully left the lights on in the living room. She didn't like to admit it, but today Maddy needed the assurance of familiar surroundings.

She parked her Suzuki, climbed the stairs of her wooden front porch, unlocked the door, and entered the house, promptly walking through to check each room.

Everything seemed in order: her wildlife photo collection hung in her loft bedroom; her small library of leather-bound books sat undisturbed in the den; and most importantly, her authentic 1927 baby grand piano stood unmarred next to the couches that surrounded the woodstove in the living room.

After looking out back to verify that her animals were safe, Maddy poured herself a cup of coffee and checked her voice mail. Kit had called again, pressing for a response.

She erased the message and phoned the Leavenworth Sheriff's office again. This time, Deputy Shukson was in.

"Is this an emergency?" the deputy asked.

Maddy explained that she'd been stalked by two men at Stag Lake and had been robbed but was unharmed.

"Can you describe these guys?"

"No," she said, "but I'd like to see the sheriff."

Shukson responded, "Petty theft cases like yours usually don't merit a personal interview with my boss." He took down a description of her backpack and cell phone and promised to file a report.

Maddy hung up, dissatisfied. The futility of the conversation left her depressed. Fortunately, Christine then called, announcing she wanted to drop by.

Fifteen minutes later, Maddy was happy to see Christine standing on the front porch in her denim jacket and matching pants—a chrysanthemum pot under one arm and a large plastic feed bag under the other—smiling her dark-eyed, dimpled smile.

The women had an almost telepathic understanding. Over their two-year friendship, when either had problems, the other would make it a point to be immediately available for commiseration.

Christine handed Maddy the chrysanthemum. "A little flora, and . . ." she patted the plastic bag, "something for the fawna."

Maddy smiled. Christine had brought some fresh feed for Maddy's mule deer fawn, Einstein.

"Besides," Christine continued, "I believe in gifts when leaving on trips." She was leaving for Hawaii the next morning. "One never knows when short good-byes might turn into long ones."

"You silly. You'll only be gone a week."

"I know. But I'm paranoid about flying over water," Christine said with dramatic flourish as they walked down the corridor, "so I ritualize both the departure and the re-turn. It's my tribal heritage." Christine's pantheistic views stemmed from her Samoan origins on her mother's side.

"What's this?" Maddy pointed to the large plastic bag she discovered when they reached the kitchen.

"I think Einstein has a problem. Yesterday when I gave him his bottle, I felt his legs. I think he might have a calcium deficiency. These assorted grains—corn, oats, barley, and some alfalfa—will help to build up bone density as he matures."

Maddy could only smile.

As the owner of the largest pet store in Leavenworth, Christine was a veritable veterinarian without a degree.

Christine made a beeline for the back door. "Let's see how he likes it." Maddy followed down the back stairs to the small shed with its chain-link cages.

Over the years, Maddy had made a habit of caring for orphaned animals, releasing them back into the wild when they were healed or old enough to manage on their own. When she first began, she was a bit surprised how much they affected her emotionally. And she took what some people might consider extreme measures to assure their comfort—giving them the best food, providing heated spaces in the wintertime, adopting them as a part of her family.

Park rangers in the vicinity came to recognize her as a willing nurse. She had even hung posters around Leavenworth depicting her bottle-feeding a baby raccoon, encouraging local residents to send orphaned animals her way. Christine had three of Maddy's large photos in her pet store.

Maddy had adopted Einstein after one of her research trips. His mother had been shot in the North Cascades and Maddy succeeded in getting the wobbly legged baby home, where he became her "pet project."

Maddy had named all her animals after historically renowned scientists: the owl was "Edison," the possum "Pasteur," the mother raccoon had been dubbed "Madame Curie," and her babies, "the little rads," and finally her two cats—a large white male, "Marconi," and a calico called "Da Vinci."

Marconi was an aging Persian mongrel that required daily medicines for severe arthritis, but he had the heart of an angel and was allowed in the house on cold nights. Da Vinci, a free-spirited five-year-old, had the run of the land, a three-acre forested plot that topped the hill.

As Christine and Maddy approached the cages, Einstein rose from his straw bed and pranced impatiently toward the chain-link fence. Maddy opened the cage, and his deep-brown eyes widened with recognition as she stepped inside. He came to her side and pushed his square black nose against her thigh. Christine knelt down and pushed a handful of the grain feed under his nose. He nuzzled it several times but wouldn't eat.

"Well, you stubborn little shit," Christine playfully tugged his ear. "Maybe he's not hungry enough. He took a whole bottle of sugar milk this afternoon."

"Is there anything else we can give him?"

"Pills of course. But I thought this would be more pleasant. If he hasn't taken to the feed by the time I get back, I'll get you some calcium additives. That'll do the trick. You could phone Dr. Simpson in Wenatchee. He'll undoubtedly have—"

She was interrupted by the phone ringing in the kitchen.

Maddy pointed at the feed bag. "Keep shoving that under his nose, I'll be right back." She hustled up the stairs and walked past the large butcher block and the brass cookware that hung overhead to answer the phone on the white tile counter.

Immediately relieved it wasn't Kit, she was surprised to hear her uncle Robert's voice on the other end of the line; they hadn't spoken in months. Hearing the background sounds of an airport, she visualized Robert, his salt-and-pepper beard and blue eyes gleaming through his gold-rimmed glasses.

"Thank God you're there," he said. "I tried your number earlier and reached your service. I didn't feel right about leaving a message."

"I'm sorry, I only just got back." She immediately suspected he was calling because of Father Navarro. "Did you hear from—?"

"Maddy, please listen. I don't have much time. I'm changing planes in Atlanta."

Why was he so nervous? Robert normally displayed an indomitable spirit, much like her father's. An accomplished astronomer at Brown University, Robert had been the utopian, while his brother, her father Mason, had been the businessman.

"Listen. I've discovered something miraculous. Something that will change your life," he said, breathing rapidly. "It may impact the way all people think, Maddy. The way they live. I think I've found the key to connectivity between ancient cultures. I can't say much more on the phone, but I know you'll want to be a part of this."

"Uncle Robert, what are you talking about? I'm very satisfied with my—"

Robert continued, "If Hector Walsh hadn't been vaporized in his lab yesterday, I wouldn't have called you so soon. I was going to work with him, but he was so opinionated and self-serving. Thank God I have someone else I trust."

"Who's Hector Walsh?"

"An associate of your father's. I can't explain now. I just need to know you'll be there for me. I need people, family and close friends. I've asked Kit Lassiter to join us."

Us? Maddy couldn't believe her ears. "Kit? I ended that relationship." All Kit needed was another excuse to pester her.

"I know, but this is strictly business. I'm seeing him in Chicago on my way out west. The work he and I did at MIT convinced me that he'd be a valuable member to the team. What do you say, Maddy, can I count on you?"

"Just a minute. I thought you were calling about my father—"

"So you knew about that? Well of course, he started it all, years ago."

"Started what?" Maddy lost patience with his chatter. "Uncle Robert, I'm referring to the call from Father Navarro. Haven't you checked your messages?"

"No. I called you first. What about Navarro?"

"Someone vandalized Mason's ashes."

For the first time in the conversation, Robert fell silent. Then, he began to stutter. "Oh good Christ . . . they know."

"What? Who knows?"

"Listen. This puts me in grave danger. I've got to get to a Fed Ex office . . ."

"You're not making any sense."

"I'm sending you something. You hide it. I'll keep the other half just in case."

"In case of what? Uncle Robert, you're scaring me. What the hell—?" Maddy noticed Christine standing on the back porch, looking out into the trees beyond the back-yard.

"This will all work out," Robert continued. "You'll see. What Mason started and what I've found is more precious than all the gems ever mined. You deserve it. I need your loyalty now. After all, you and I are the last of the Marros, aren't we? I'll visit you in three days. Then I promise I'll explain everything. Until I see you, keep it secret."

"You can't leave me hanging like this," Maddy said just as Christine walked into the kitchen. Overhearing Maddy's tone, she had a concerned look on her face.

"I can't say any more," Robert said hurriedly. "Watch for my package. It'll come overnight. Put it somewhere safe. What they have won't help them unless they have what I'm sending you, so be careful. Watch out for strangers."

"Strangers? Who is 'they'?" Maddy cast a frustrated glance at Christine. "Uncle Robert, what does this mean? Explain yourself."

"I know this sounds crazy, but trust me," Robert said. "You have to. And I have to catch a plane."

"Uncle Robert!" The line was dead. Maddy hung up.

"What's going on?" Christine asked.

"Insanity."

She thought back to Robert's last warning. Strangers? His own behavior made him sound like a stranger. Then she wondered—had he meant the mysterious strangers at Stag Lake?

9

The Aurora

HURRICANE HANNAH'S WINDS HOWLED ACROSS the decks as Jace fought the weather, staggering around the turret that housed the control room.

The moment the fourth helicopter lifted off, Stewart had rushed to the radio, desperately trying to hail the fifth chopper, asking Jace to stay on deck with a flare gun to attempt to make visual contact with any boat or plane that might be near.

As much as confronting Stewart was imperative, so was survival, and Jace had decided to forgo his planned conversation to focus on the chance of rescue.

Now, rain tore at his shirt as he stumbled against the wind's fury, clutching the steel banister.

Beyond, in the darkness, the ocean boiled. Huge crests of white foam topped the black waves that towered one-third the height of the rig. Thousands of tons of surf crashed through the tension legs, and the pounding caused the floater's upper deck to shudder.

The Coast Guard wouldn't come out here, Jace thought. A full-sized battle ship couldn't handle seas like this. Yet if the chopper were somehow within a few hundred yards, the pilot might spot the brightly lit rig.

Floodlights on the crane cab and the top of the jib were glowing. Lights beamed from poles that were spaced every twenty feet along the platform. Navigation bulbs glimmered on the perimeter of the helipad. Rain-driven spray splashed from each light fixture, creating a sparkling display.

As Jace gazed across the deck at the moisture-streaked windows of the illuminated living quarters, he was caught in a timeless freeze-frame. The rig's platform lights transformed into the dripping floodlights that lit the exterior halls of St. Catherine's School for Boys in Amarillo. One winter night, while rain fell in buckets, nine-year-old Jace had lain in the darkness of his lower bunk at the foster home. Missing his father and mother, he could no longer suppress his sobs.

In that desperate moment, when words couldn't heal, a hand had reached down from the top bunk and hung there. When Jace finally accepted it, the hand squeezed hard and Jace hung on. It had happened more than once. Jace's eleven-year-old roommate, Cory Jackson, had not only saved his life, pulling him out of a frozen pond when they met, he'd been there for him in the years that followed, never questioning, always supportive until Jace grew old enough to handle his feelings.

As Jace looked around the windblown decks of the *Aurora*, he realized he might not see Cory again—precisely because Jace had successfully located the man he and Cory had sworn to find.

Jace's boyhood tales of astronauts, rockets, and other aspects of Arthur Kelton's career so enchanted an already sci-fi oriented Cory, that Cory had chosen a career path into the air force and NASA, joking about "something big out there" that he would find. Jace, on the other hand, had been unable to pursue a similar calling, shamed by the accusations of his father's alleged pilfering of classified material. After Cory became a special air force liaison to the space agency, Jace hounded him to seek answers, largely because Jace's own investigation with the Alabama Sheriff's office led nowhere. Cory finally yielded to Jace's prodding and began to use what resources he had to locate a man who might have been Arthur's murderer—Carville, the last one to see him alive. With help from an old college friend in Air Force Intelligence, Cory's search paid off. Carville, now named Stewart, had isolated himself at sea on an inaccessible Texaco oil rig. Determined to flush him out of his hiding place, Jace found a way: as an occupational safety consultant, Jace could gain access to oil rigs. Jace's initial education and his year of work as a civic engineer in Houston gave him some rudimentary knowledge, but he needed further accreditation. Plotting his strategy, Jace acquired his occupational safety and health degree at the University of Texas at Austin, and after months of trying, landed a position with the Protection and Consultant Division of Southland Insurance in New Orleans.

Now, on a tour of duty, Jace had closed on his target; he and Stewart were alone without working cell phones or any other form of communication; the only two human beings in a thousand square miles of ocean, unless of course, the chopper was near.

Jace tucked the flare gun into his belt and glanced at his diving watch . . . he'd been out in the storm for forty-five minutes with no sign of recovery.

It was time to confront Stewart.

Jace clung to the rail, struggling to reach the control room door, and exploded into the warmth of the cabin. He found Stewart huddled on a folding chair near a two-way radio on a metal table strewn with navigational charts and computer printouts.

Stewart's eyes were moist with excitement. "Jace, did you see anything just now?"

"What? No."

"I swear to God, it was faint, but a few seconds ago, a guy on the radio asked for our position." Stewart almost smiled. "I think it's the pilot of the *Bell Ranger.*"

Jace was stunned by the good news. After three hours, how could a helicopter still be airborne in this storm? He grabbed a towel off the khaki-colored file cabinet and watched Stewart, waiting for an opening.

Stewart's knuckles were white as he clenched the microphone. "Come in, *Bell Ranger.* Come in please, this is *Aurora* calling. Over. *Bell Ranger,* do you read?"

The control room floor shook. Another huge wave had pounded the damaged oil rig.

Stewart seemed mesmerized by the transmission. "Come in, any aircraft or boat. Any aircraft or boat. This is the oil rig *Aurora,* sending from coordinates twenty-seven degrees forty-three minutes west, by ninety-three degrees, eighty-nine minutes north. Come in, over." Stewart listened intently, but the receiver crackled into a sustained hiss.

Jace dabbed his face and then tossed the towel over a chair. "Stewart, we need to talk."

"Talk?" Stewart was riveted on the microphone. "Come in, anyone—anyone at all. This is *Aurora.*" He glanced up at Jace with an anxious, hungry look. "Half an hour ago our other choppers sent a transmission. Our crew was about to set down in Galveston." He nervously shifted in his chair. "But this latest voice. . . *that* had to be the missing pilot." He pressed the send button. "Come in, *Bell Ranger.*"

Jace realized contact with the chopper was a matter of life and death, but with the likelihood of the rig's collapse growing every second, he had to press. As he sat down at the table, moisture from his green flannel shirt seeped onto the paperwork. "Stewart. Look at me. Why am I here? Have you asked yourself?"

"Asked? This is *Aurora*. Come in please."

"Yes. Odd, isn't it?"

"Odd?" Stewart's dull gaze fixed on Jace. "You gave your seat to Sammy."

"And *why?*"

"You made a choice."

"Yes, but I'm no fool. My work was done when I determined this bucket was going to the bottom."

Stewart stared at him.

Jace leaned forward. "I stayed because of you."

"What?"

Jace braced himself. "I've been looking for you." He pulled the flare gun from his belt and laid it on his lap.

Stewart's gaze darted back and forth between Jace's face and the flare gun. "What do you mean?"

"I know who you are . . ."

Stewart began to fidget. "What are you talking about?"

"The night you disappeared, you left your name behind. But you couldn't change your fingerprints. Texaco's security clearance being as thorough as it is, we found a computer match in their employee files." Stewart shot to his feet as if to bolt from the room, but Jace reached out, clutching him by the wrist. "Sit down, Carville. There's nowhere to run."

Glancing about nervously, Stewart slumped back into the chair. "Who are you? FBI?"

"Hardly. No government agency would hire the son of a traitor."

"Son?"

"That's right. Jace Kelton. Ring a bell?"

Stewart blanched in shock. "You're Arthur's kid."

Jace leveled the flare gun at Stewart's face. "And you killed him. Did you think I'd forget?"

"Jesus Christ. It wasn't me. He was after both of us. The tree came down, and when we hit the ditch, your dad went one way and I flew the other, thrown from the jeep." Stewart hoisted his gray hair from his forehead, revealing a jagged scar. "I was knocked cold, lying in the cattails. When I came to, I looked back and there he was, standing over your dad."

"He?"

"Narrow-faced guy. Broad shoulders and blond hair, holding a gun. Arthur handed him an envelope and then . . ." Stewart hesitated.

"He shot him."

"No. It was hard for me to see, but as the guy bent down, Arthur somehow reached up with a knife in his hand. There was a brief struggle, but Arthur slashed at the guy's neck before taking two bullets in the head."

Jace flinched. The Alabama Sheriff's report had described most of the face having been blown away. "Goddamn it." Stewart's account made sense. A sizable and yet untraceable blood sample other than Arthur's had been found at the scene. "How well did you know my dad?"

"I never laid eyes on Arthur until our two-hour drive from Birmingham. I was on my annual two-week stint as a National Guardsman. I just happened to be at the motor pool that night and pulled the duty."

"If you were innocent, why run?"

"I panicked. I knew the killer would be searching for me. When the killer got stabbed, he fell to the ground. I thought I could get away, so I was up, ready to dash into the woods. But then this guy looks *right* at me. . His expression was wild, but his eyes were cool as death. He raised his gun in my direction and I didn't wait. I was back in the cattails on my knees, crawling like a son of a bitch for the trees."

"And then?"

"Then the bad press on your dad, describing an espionage deal gone bad. I never believed he'd sold out to the Russians, but that was the party line. And the papers never talked about finding the killer *or* his body. Just the blood. Proof, they said, that Arthur had somehow bungled the exchange."

"Bullshit. You saw him fight for his life."

"He did. But I knew the killer had survived. He'd seen my face, and I kept seeing his in my nightmares. I got the hell out. That morning. The MPs and cops swarmed my apartment. My daughter was questioned by all of them. I had her move to Orlando."

"So she knew where you were."

"Only later. I went to Mexico for about a year. Changed my identity. Picked up on the Spanish, became a wildcatter in Venezuela. Learned the trade, became a tool pusher. Finally wound up in the gulf. Got to see my daughter . . . real quietly, once in a while."

Jace shook his head. "That's all you know?"

"I didn't *want* to know." Stewart squinted in anguish. "But I couldn't help keeping track. Things were real quiet for a couple of years. Then in 1996, when the Russian's Mars mission aborted, a scientist named Robert Marro made some comments in the press. He claimed that NASA and Moscow had misinformed the public and, without naming names, claimed there had been casualties in a worldwide cover-up . . . I assumed he meant your dad, among others."

"Did you try to contact this guy?"

"Are you kidding? I wouldn't touch Marro with a ten-foot pole. I had just gotten comfortable being a nonentity."

"Where's Marro now?"

"I don't know. He travels. Pops up in the press once in a while." Stewart turned from the microphone, folding his hands as if in penance. "You believe me, don't you? I swear I was thrown into this—" Stewart jerked his head back toward the receiver. "My God, listen."

Smatterings of a voice broke through the intermittent static. "Aurora . . . do you read? Heading change . . . low gas . . ."

"It's him. I told you. We've got a shot." Stewart wheeled toward the table and clutched the mic. "This is *Aurora*. Is that you, chopper? Over."

Then came the ragged reply. "Affirmative . . ."

Silence followed.

Stewart's face flooded with hope. "I think he's very close."

"Well if he is, he's in bigger trouble than we are. How the hell is he going to land?" He visualized the pilot of the lone helicopter, lost in the storm with a windshield spattered by water.

"He's not a quitter, this guy," Stewart said.

Jace stood up. "How many flares have you got?"

"The gun in your hand and some sticks. But they won't do you any good. They'll just blow away."

Jace vaulted to the control room door and opened it a crack. Somewhere over-head, filtered by the scream of the wind, he heard the sputtering cough of a machine struggling to maintain altitude. As impossible as it seemed, the *Bell Ranger* had found them.

Jace turned and yelled, "Stewart, it's him. If he lands we'll have to lash him to the deck."

Stewart jumped from his chair, but then in an undecided dance, retreated to the microphone. "Chopper, this is *Aurora*. Do you see us?"

The weak, broken reply hissed through the airwaves. "Roger . . . gauge empty . . . landing."

"Pilot, we're just two men here. When you touch down, deplane immediately and help us tie you down." Stewart tossed Jace a flashlight and grabbed another as he lurched for the door. "Downstairs, the supply room," he shouted as he charged out into the wind. "We'll get some line."

The grind of the helicopter was still audible above the deck as Stewart and Jace rushed into the open, carrying coils of rope as their lights panned the sky.

As they reached the helipad, the helicopter bucked some 150 feet above their heads, its silver belly reflecting their beams, assuming a dangerously awkward attitude, nose pushed down, tilted into the wind. The pilot fought to steady the aircraft, and the chopper shuttled from side to side, trying to avoid the control room turret and other buildings on deck.

The engine strained as the chopper began to descend, one hundred feet, then ninety. A strong gust buffeted the craft. It settled once more, down to eighty feet, seventy . . .

The chopper engine coughed, the tail section bobbed and weaved. Jace grabbed Stewart's shoulder. "Gas," he shouted. "He's out of gas."

The engine went dead. There was nothing to do but get out of the way.

Jace and Stewart scrambled toward the control room, but there would was no need. With its blades slowing in a dying flutter, the helicopter blew backward past the helipad, traveling laterally. It tipped sideways in a tottering loop and descended toward the far end of the platform where, with a gut-wrenching sound of crunching metal, it smashed into the platform's edge, teetered for a moment, and then plunged over the side.

Jace took off at a run, stumbling occasionally from the force of the wind. Stewart was close behind trying to keep up. Jace grabbed him by the arm as they reached the deck's perimeter, where they stared into a black void of sea and sky.

It was as if the helicopter and its pilot had fallen off the edge of the world.

Nothing remained. Not one piece of debris. The seething cauldron of crashing waves had swallowed everything.

10

Leavenworth

MADDY SIPPED A CUP OF coffee as she sat on a hard wooden chair across from Sheriff Davis's desk. The clock above the door read 11:43.

Davis was nearly forty-five minutes late.

Through the glass partition facing the outer lobby, Maddy watched Ms. Barnes, the thin-lipped receptionist in street clothes, shuffle forms at her desk while Shukson, the kindly looking deputy who had spoken with Maddy on the phone, grabbed some keys on his way out the door, apparently responding to a tavern brawl.

A square-jawed deputy named Hargrove spoke with a dejected couple seated in the lobby—farmers from nearby Wenatchee, who, from what Maddy overheard, had been called to pick up their jailed drunken son.

Maddy would have much rather been in her garden or hiking. The sun was shining outside the barred window. She looked around the shoddy interior of the cluttered sheriff's office, with its bulletin board of wanted posters, pondering how her life could change so much in one day.

Yesterday afternoon, after the phone call from Uncle Robert, Christine had cautiously asked if Maddy had hired a gardener. While Maddy was on the phone, Christine had noticed a man's footprints in the flowerbeds near the animal cages—depressions in the soft bark under the windowsill. The tracks looked so fresh, Maddy found herself gazing off into the woods to see if anyone was there.

Maddy immediately called the sheriff's office, this time reaching Deputy Shukson in his car. Was she in immediate danger? Maddy had felt awkward about the nebulous reply. She didn't know. Shukson apologized, but since the two officers on duty were both assisting Sheriff Davis with a serious chemical spill on Highway 2, they couldn't do much for her tonight. Shukson suggested that if she wanted to see Davis in person, she might come by the office in the morning.

Christine had been considerate enough to stay the night, even though she had an early flight at six in the morning.

After dinner, they sat by the woodstove looking through some of Maddy's photo albums. Robert's call had prompted questions about Maddy's family. She showed Christine old photographs: Maddy as a little girl in the backyard of her parents' Michigan mansion with her pet collie, Minuet—on her father's Chris Craft yacht on Lake Huron—with her mother on a ski lift in Beaver Creek, Colorado.

After the day's events, Maddy felt vulnerable sitting by the living room's undraped windows, fully visible to anyone who might be standing outside. She was grateful Christine had stayed and equally disappointed when she left for the airport in the morning.

After Christine's departure, Maddy checked with the lab to see that her tadpole sample had arrived safely.

As she put the phone down, a Fed Ex truck pulled into Maddy's driveway. Maddy had been so preoccupied, she had almost forgotten about Uncle Robert's package.

When she opened the overnight wrapper, she found a single sheet of Xeroxed paper, fourteen by seventeen inches, folded in half. A series of vertical lines ran at odd tangents with no particular geometric logic. Where they crossed, there were numbers: 28, 45, 16, and others, 98, 22, 71. On the right, the grid appeared incomplete, consistent with Robert's remark that he would send only half of an image.

Remembering Robert's plea for secrecy, Maddy felt uncomfortable leaving the paper at the house, so she brought it with her. Whoever had made those footprints might be planning to break in.

She was contemplating how much more detail to put down on the theft report when Sheriff Davis lumbered into the lobby, smoking a cigar.

The moment Maddy saw him, she decided to keep the report as simple as possible. His full, fleshy face and his gruff manner convinced Maddy that he was not a man who would relate well to abstractions.

Ms. Barnes handed the sheriff a file, nodding toward Maddy through the glass partition. Davis entered his office with an impatient expression and shook her hand.

"So you think someone's after you." Davis removed his uniform jacket, hanging it on a coat rack in the corner.

"I can't be sure of that," Maddy replied. "But I can tell you I've been robbed."

With his crew-cut hair, chewed-up face, and stocky physique, Davis resembled a caricature of a US Marine recruiting poster. "In your report you used the word 'stalked.' That usually means being followed." He smiled for the first time, a patronizing grin. "Is that what happened?"

"That's what I assumed. Otherwise why would they be in that remote area? They stole my cell phone and broke up my equipment."

"But you didn't see anybody."

"Yes, I did, but only in silhouette."

Davis sat down at his desk and pointed to the wanted posters on the wall. "We don't deal in silhouettes." Leaning back, Davis revealed two damp patches of perspiration as he threw his arms over his head. "I need identifying features."

"There were also the footprints around the house." Maddy suddenly realized the futility of the conversation.

"I heard. And I took a look."

Maddy was amazed. "You—"

"Shukson told me this morning. I drove by your place on my way here."

"If I'd known that, I would have stayed home."

"Last-minute deal. I didn't take your call too seriously." Davis sighed as if he had been forced into doing just that. He reached into his khaki breast pocket. "That is, until I found this." He took a small folded photograph and handed it to Maddy.

She was stunned. It was a black-and-white copy of her driver's license photo. "You found this?"

"On a dead man."

"Where?"

"Shukson may have mentioned the problem we had last night. A truck carrying two tons of sulfur dioxide down Tumwater Canyon tipped over when it tried to avoid hitting a body lying in the road. I didn't know about your picture until this morning when the morgue called. Jack Fiery, the undertaker, recognized you from those animal posters in the pet store—that's what you get in a small town. Anyway, the dead man had the photo in his back pants pocket."

"My God. Who is this guy?"

"He had no ID."

"How did he die?"

"With his multiple contusions and scrapes, looks like he fell out of a car."

"You think he was the one who left the footprints at my house?" she asked, hoping that it might mean her problems were over.

Davis shrugged. "Possibly. I can't get a cast off the impressions in that bark, but I'd guess a size eight shoe."

"Size eight?" Were the footprints she'd seen at the lake that small?

"The guy on the road was short, five foot nine. Not unusual for someone of his extraction."

"Extraction?"

"Oh, I forgot to mention. He was Chinese."

11

The Aurora

THE SEA AND THE WIND had declared war on the oil rig.

One-hundred-eighty-mile-an-hour gusts drove colossal breakers against the *Aurora's* shuddering frame. As each new wave breached the pylons of the floater, the impact sent vibrations through the super structure, which were clearly felt in the tables and chairs of the control room.

Imprisoned between four gray walls, dressed in orange life vests, Jace and Stewart huddled near the two-way receiver.

Jace knew full well that the storm's incredible power would soon affect the rig's scaffolding, further damaging the southeastern tension leg. By now, the main frame of the upper deck would be separating from the top of the tension leg tube, and there was nothing that could be done. Stepping on deck could mean being swept overboard by the fierce force of the wind. Jace was further frustrated by the impossibility of contacting Cory Jackson, who would by now wonder why he hadn't been called. But since the downed chopper pilot's last words, the radio only hissed weakly on the table, with no response to Stewart's repeated transmissions. There was nothing to do but sit, wait, and—with Jace's prompting—talk.

Stewart had revealed all he knew about Arthur's death . . . that the killer was tall, blond, had a narrow face, and wore a three-piece suit and a raincoat. That wasn't much. Stewart repeated his references to the man named Robert Marro, whose accusations against NASA made him a primary lead for Jace to follow . . . provided of course, Jace survived. Jace took the rig supervisor at his word and settled with Stewart's innocence. He was obviously a victim of circumstance, frightened into anonymity for fear of his life.

They had become acquainted under duress and now, as comrades in the crisis of an impending disaster, they turned their conversation to lighter matters.

"You married?" Stewart asked.

"Naw. Had a girlfriend once. Rachel Conrad, out of El Paso." Jace envisioned the long black hair, shining in the Texas sun. What had been a warm romance slowly lost its passion, transforming into a lasting friendship instead. "I see her about once a month. She's the administrator for Easter Seals camps in south Texas. I coach track and field for disabled kids."

"Track and field? You've got the shoulders of a football player."

"Never played. I was a triathlete in college." He had medaled in the decathlon at the Pan American Games.

"Aaaah," Stewart smiled. "That explains your acrobatics during Sammy's rescue."

"I did what I had to do."

"Regardless of the risk?"

"The risk," Jace said, "would have been to do nothing."

Stewart seemed humbled by the statement. He hunched his shoulders and dropped his gaze, folding his hands in his lap.

"I guess that's kind of what I did?"

"You were on deck."

"No. I'm talking about the day your dad died."

Without blaming Stewart, Jace pondered what might have happened had Stewart been carrying a gun. "Look, I accept your explanation. You might have been killed yourself."

"Maybe . . . but it tortured me. Still does." Stewart's eyes softened, almost helpless. "You won't tell anyone where I am."

"I would check with you. If I catch up to the killer, you might have to testify."

"At that point, I would." Stewart looked relieved and then sad once again. "All those years, things must have been tough . . ."

Jace stared at the floor, remembering the nights of pain, the days of humiliation about being an orphan.

He looked up at Stewart and was about to respond, when a strange rumble shook the control room. An ear-piercing shriek of tearing metal penetrated the walls.

Jace's chair vibrated out from under him as he jumped to his feet. "Son of a bitch. I think she's going."

"Oh God." Stewart's voice trembled. He charged the door.

"Wait." Jace realized they would be blown away like leaves in a tempest. "Let's see what happens."

As Stewart retreated, the grind of metal against metal continued, occasionally punctuated by the ping of popping rivets as iron struts and beams sounded their stresses. Stewart's hands went white-knuckled as he gripped his chair. The room's grated metal floor had listed an additional five degrees to the south.

Jace hustled to the bulwark and put his ear to an iron girder. He strained to listen. "I think we lost the southeastern quadrant of the platform. Thank God we're afloat."

"For how long?"

"No way of telling." With one tension leg gone, the force of the waves and wind would invade the inner braces. The platform would come apart. "It could be any minute now. We just have to ride it out."

"Oh Jesus."

In the moments that followed, the sight of Stewart falling to his knees in whispered prayer struck home with Jace. He hadn't really faced up to the immediacy of his own death, having been preoccupied with the will to survive. But as Stewart knelt on the metal floor, Jace recalled the nights when his mother had crept into his room. Believing Jace was asleep, she would kneel at his bedside, burying her face in the bedspread as she uttered her prayers: pleas for her own healing, for the soul of her dead husband, and an appeal for Jace, that he might grow up in God's care.

Jace held on to the gray metal table waiting for the deck to list even further and possibly collapse. He had never been a devoutly religious man, but now the idea formed in his mind that providence might soon unite him with his parents in some benevolent afterlife. He looked around the iron-framed chamber that would become his tomb. The storm would tear at the platform, and as it disintegrated one section at time, the cables that held the oil rig to the ocean floor would lose their grip and the structure would topple into the sea.

Ironically, Jace now grasped that he and Stewart would probably die together on this day. He visualized the moment when gravity would take the upper deck. The room would tilt, and he and Stewart would be flung against the wall as their section of the platform slid into the ocean.

What a waste it would be if, after all this, he were to die here, failing to find his father's killer and squandering Stewart's information—the first fresh and meaningful lead he'd had in years.

He was suddenly overwhelmed with the will to survive.

Not like this. And not here, Jace thought. If I'm going, I'm not going sitting down. He vowed to make it to the door, to climb the walls if need be, to scale the gauges and alarm knobs, fighting toward the doorway into the open air, where he would hurl himself into the wind and the waves. He would swim. Swim until he drowned. "There's always a chance," he mumbled.

"What?" Stewart lifted his face.

"I said there's always a chance," Jace repeated loud enough to be heard over the roar outside. As he said it, something changed. His words echoed unchallenged between the hard metal wall, and he realized why. The howl outside the door had abated.

Stewart's eyes grew round with wonder. He rose to his feet.

Jace couldn't believe his ears. They heard nothing.

No wind.

The sound of the storm was gone.

A gentle breeze caressed Jace's face as he and Stewart stepped from the control turret onto the second-floor walkway.

The air was faintly aromatic. The sky was hushed in an uneasy tranquility. Rays of sunshine streamed through a thin layer of streaked white haze.

The ocean's relentless onslaught from the south had ceased, though the sea kicked up smaller, confused swells that seemed to come from all directions. Nothing moved on the *Aurora's* ravaged decks save the water that trickled calmly down the building walls.

Stewart shielded his eyes against the sunlight that glinted off the deck's puddles. "What happened?"

Jace checked the wall of sooty clouds proceeding north toward Louisiana. An approaching dark band peeked over the southern horizon. They were surrounded by darkness with a blue sky overhead. "I don't believe it. The hurricane hit us dead center. We're in the eye."

Stewart clutched the rail. "We might make it."

Jace laid a hand on his shoulder. "Think about it . . . the leading edge of this storm damn near took us down. Hannah's tail will probably finish the job." Jace pointed at the depression in the main deck. "Look at the warp in those cross braces. How much more can they take?"

Stewart's eyes searched his. "Maybe the trailing portion of the storm is less powerful."

"Anything's possible. But these storms usually don't blow themselves out until they hit land. I'd made arrangements with my friend Cory Jackson to try and pull me out of this mess if things got rough. With you, I mean. We had no idea how you might react, being exposed."

"You thought I might kill you?"

"Maybe. I was supposed to call him after we talked. Impossible with the hurricane. Even with the storm, I hoped he might somehow send help." Jace pointed to the four corners of the horizon. "No boat could make it through. You've seen what happens to a helicopter. And if a fixed-wing aircraft survived, what good would it do? How would they pick us up?" As Stewart stared despondently out to sea, Jace's attention turned to the gaping hole in the platform created by the absent tension leg. "I better check things out. Wait here."

He left Stewart standing at the rail and walked along the second-floor gangway to the southernmost corner of the communications tower.

To his left, the overturned crane cab lay on its side. The crane turret and jib had tipped over with some force, trashing a portion of the living quarters. A ragged gash in the wall revealed bizarre remnants of domesticity—a shattered dresser with underwear strewn on the ground and crushed bunk beds with white sheets glaring in the sun.

The warped platform between Jace and the far side of the rig hung on the three remaining tension legs. And where the deck had fallen away, a cross section of struts and braces within the deck structure were visible, barely supporting the weight of the buildings above, defying gravity for the time being.

And that could change at any moment.

Jace walked back toward the control room door. "Stewart," he said quietly as he approached. "Let's go down the stairs."

"What's the problem?"

"We're relocating."

Jace pointed toward the helipad and the small equipment shed on the deck's north side. "Let's sit over there awhile."

Stewart's eyes betrayed his apprehension. "What's going on?"

Jace glanced at the horizon where a new wall of darkness was fast approaching. "From what I can see, the communications tower, a section of the living quarters, and the warped section of deck where the crane lies could easily have collapsed. I don't know what's keeping them up now. That's why we'll wait over here."

"But if we leave the control room, we won't hear the radio. How can we call for help?"

"We can't." He guided Stewart to the edge of the slightly elevated helipad. "But I'm not setting foot in there again. We were lucky."

As Stewart sat down on the edge, Jace hustled over to the nearby equipment shed.

Inside he found toolboxes, pipe joints, and an endless array of nuts, bolts, washers, caulk, glue, and paint. He retrieved two razor knives from the toolboxes. In the shadow of the far corner, he located what he'd hoped for: lengths of chain, rope, and a roll of bungee cord—strong, yet easily severed with a knife. Jace grabbed it and brought it into the sunlight, where he began to cut the cord into usable lengths.

Stewart looked on. "What are you doing?"

"We're going to fasten together and tie ourselves to the deck, right here." Jace pointed to the braces that held the helipad. "If we lie down when the wind hits, we might not be blown overboard."

"What if the rig collapses?"

Jace handed Stewart several lengths of line and a razor knife. "If this whole section goes, when you hit the water, cut yourself away from the braces. If I'm hurt or dead, cut me loose. With your life vest, you can at least stay afloat. Maybe you'll make it."

"Is this our only option?"

Jace pointed to the horizon. "See that? The hurricane's eye is typically about ten miles wide. With the storm moving north at thirty miles an hour, we have twenty minutes of peace. Not much more. I'd say we've already used up half of that. Get ready." Jace busied himself with the bungee lines, looping them around his ankles, around an upright helipad brace, and through his belt. Stewart watched and did the same. Then, having tied an umbilical between themselves, they sat with their backs to the helipad and stared at the black gloom of the approaching storm front.

Neither man spoke. There was nothing left to say.

Faced with the inevitability of his death, Jace contemplated the things he loved most. He visualized his waterfront two-bedroom townhouse in San

Antonio—the upstairs lanai that overlooked the river, the lights of the city to the south. He would never see his home again, the rooms he had decorated himself with touches of the southwest, or his small mahogany-trimmed home office, with his collection of trophies: high school championships, athletic medals from college track meets, the decathlon bronze, and the ring he wore from the Pan American Games. The medallions told his story, an orphaned young man's battle against obscurity.

Strange that he had almost drowned as a boy, and now his life would end the same way.

He suddenly felt barren, realizing that he had no heirs, no other family . . . except Cory, his best friend and foster brother.

Jace wondered where Cory was . . . probably at Randolph Air Force Base, expecing to hear from Jace . . . never knowing the results of Jace's meeting with Stewart. Cory would pick up where Jace left off—he'd continue to try and find Arthur's killer. They had sworn support for one another.

The day after Cory saved Jace's life, pulling him from the ice pond behind St. Catherine's, Cory had been so psyched he suggested they take an oath. The two boys had sneaked into the bowels of the foster home basement, where they stood beneath the ancient steaming pipes of a musty boiler. Jace could still remember Cory's eyes, round with significance, as he took a razor blade and cut into his own thumb. He placed it against the dripping laceration Jace had inflicted on himself.

"We're blood forever," Cory had said, penetrating Jace with a glare. "Not me, not you, not the devil can take that away."

He was right. They had been like brothers until age had separated them— with the older Cory going off to the Air Force Academy and Jace remaining in his native California. Now, ironically, Cory was working with people like Jace's father at NASA as an air force liaison to the space agency in Houston, happily married to Jamilla, the feisty, fun-loving daughter of a minister. Their son, Jacel, was Jace's namesake. Even while searching for Carville, Jace had established a residence in San Antonio to be closer to Cory and his family.

Kids.

He would desperately miss the kids. After all the glories he had experienced on various renowned athletic fields, none matched the emotional lift he got from being on some renovated cow pasture, setting up poles and pits, laying the chalk for sprints, and managing the event. He remembered the wheelchairs lined up under the hot Texas sun; how he'd hoist some one-legged kid out of the sawdust after an aborted hop-skip-and-jump. Some of them made it; some of them didn't. But they had fun trying.

The dusty heat of Texas faded away as Jace felt the first moisture spatter his face. The rain was returning and the sky was getting dark.

Stewart tugged at Jace's pant leg. "Hey. Do you hear that?"

A growing roar echoed between the buildings on the platform deck as the storm front moved in.

"I guess it's time to lie down," Jace said. He began to adjust himself, but then he paused.

On the howl of the returning gale, Jace heard something else—a high-pitched whine.

A shiny cylinder hung in the sky.

"Son of a bitch, Stewart. It's a plane."

12

Timaru, New Zealand

PROFESSOR MICHAEL GRANVILLE'S HANDS WERE dirty . . . Mud and shreds of hair washed away under the kitchen sink faucet as the soap cut through the oily residue on his fingers.

He had just come from the barn, where he had been engaged in one of his favorite activities, the shearing of his sheep—handling the animals, the bleating of the lambs, the warmth of the ewe's skin as he guided the electric trimmer through the thick waves of fleece. And although he gathered the wool from the knotty pine boards of the barn floor and packed it into burlap bags for sale at the market, he never kept the profits. Instead, he gave the money to the vicar at the Presbyterian ministry for whatever good it might do.

Michael Granville was financially independent, retired and content, occupied with the mundane tasks at his farm. He had spent many years as a successful research scientist in Canada and returned to New Zealand to spend the twilight years of his life on the small estate he purchased after his divorce from his wife, Carla.

Today, as was his habit, he had finished his chores: sprinkled feed for the chickens in the coop, flushed the pig trough with fresh water, and put the mare and the gelding out to pasture.

He wiped his hands on the small kitchen towel and walked over to the round breakfast table, where he'd stacked today's mail.

His latest issue of *Science Horizons* had arrived . . . There was an assortment of junk mail, brochures from companies selling goods, and a bill from the feed store.

Then he spotted a letter, a rarity for Michael since he didn't get much personal correspondence anymore. The blue finely bonded envelope was emblazoned with "par avion," the international airmail insignia. This was not the style used by his sister, Lilith, who wrote from Auckland once a month.

Michael was curious. No return address. He examined the postmark.

Hong Kong.

Good Lord.

The only person he knew from Hong Kong was Jinseng Ma, a fellow researcher he'd seen during the years when he and six other scientists worked internationally for those industrialists—Marro and Scalbania. Egomaniacs.

They were both dead now...like so many of his past associates. Everyone was aging and slowly fading away.

Michael opened the letter with his whalebone letter opener, set the envelope aside, and unfolded the paper—a reprint of an article from the *Honolulu Examiner*. The headline read: KAHALA GOLF COURSE MURDER. A terrible Xerox copy, very messy. The black ink smudged his fingers.

He was shocked that the first few sentences announced the passing of Jinseng Ma...in Hawaii, of all places.

Michael had difficulty fathoming what had happened. Jinseng Ma had been shot by someone using a scope rifle from the hills above Kahala, a rich residential neighborhood on the main island of Oahu.

As he continued to read, Michael's fingers suddenly felt numb. Strange. The ink on his hands seemed to deaden the skin.

He suddenly felt weak and was forced to sit down on the pleated cushion of the dinette chair.

Odd, how the numbing sensation seemed to climb his wrists.

It reached his elbows, rose to his shoulders, and now the taste of something strangely aromatic blossomed under his tongue.

Garlic, he thought. Then Michael simply slumped to his right and fell to the floor.

Clutching the letter to his chest, he lay limp on the linoleum as the life seeped from him. The Xerox copy, with its smudged ink, was laced with Solozene, a powerful, undetectable nerve agent so osmotic that it penetrated the skin on contact and traveled to the heart in a matter of a few beats.

13

Leavenworth

DRESSED IN A TANK TOP and shorts, her auburn hair tied back with a black hair band, Maddy sat barefoot on the kitchen barstool with the phone propped against her ear.

On the other end of the line, Kevin Gold—a brilliant EPA lab technician in Seattle—recited a list of stats from the pollywog blood tests.

While she listened, Maddy couldn't help glancing at Robert's grid that lay on the kitchen counter. Kevin droned his figures, and Maddy's gaze ran along the grid's strange intersecting lines and the five compact groupings of numbers that appeared where the triangulations met. She was eager for Robert to explain things upon his arrival.

Outside her kitchen window, the early sun laid a shimmering mantle of dew on the meadow. In the animal cages, Einstein, the fawn, pranced about on his hay while Madame Curie and the baby raccoons celebrated the morning with wrestling matches.

Sipping her coffee, Maddy felt a bit more relaxed.

Yesterday's meeting with Sheriff Davis would have seemed like a dream if she hadn't seen a patrol car drive past her house this morning. Pledging to send an officer by twice a day, Davis had launched his investigation, forwarding a description of the John Doe to national law enforcement agencies. The fact that the dead stranger had a copy of her driver's license photo was disconcerting to say the least. But the fact that he *was* dead was a positive, according to Davis's pragmatic assessment—it might indicate the end of the matter. Maddy reminded him that she had seen *two* men at the lake, and the sheriff agreed that was reason enough to patrol the area.

Maddy normally enjoyed Kevin's company, while gently deflecting his romantic intentions, being careful not to offend him. And she was amused by his quick wit.

Kevin reached his summation.

"The chemistries fall right in line with the last four samples, though larva number five shows rather heavy concentrations of carbonates in the digestive tract."

"That's due to limestone and dolomite deposits around the lake," she said. "What about the DNA?"

"The strands are elongated slightly, but complete. I don't think we have a congenital aberration here, more likely something endemic."

"Environmental, in other words."

"You're leading me, but yes, I'd go with that."

"And you see no sign of parasitic infection?" Maddy asked, her eyes still focused on the map. Robert's numbers were undoubtedly in his own small handwriting.

"Your sample is rich with the usual amoebic forms, paramecia, protozoa of the aquatic variety, but no noxious specimens at all."

"So what do you think?" Maddy felt comfortable asking his opinion, since they had crossed the line of formality with a couple of evenings of takeout and beer working late at the lab. Kevin had even succeeded in getting her out on a date . . . Thai food.

"Well," Kevin chuckled. "I know you, and I know where you're headed with this, so my response would be biased."

"Take off your lab coat and talk to me. Do you feel there's enough here to take it to committee?"

"Alright, lab coat is coming off. You hear that snapping sound? That's the buttons of my clean white tunic falling away."

"Kevin. Please."

Kevin whistled two bars of "The Stripper" and then laughed. "I'm now attired in a rumpled cashmere V-neck."

"Okay, now you're a civilian. So tell me straight."

"Well, frankly I think you need a lot more samples. If you had more of them, you'd win. The Trumpeter Swan Study that compared Washington State's birds with Minnesota's had over fifty deformed specimens as evidence. That gives you some idea of the work involved."

"But they were trying to *prove* parasitic infection. I'm *dis*proving it. If high altitude water with no pollution runoff shows genetic deformity in frogs, then lack of ozone would account for DNA alteration at any altitude."

"Sure. But you know how it goes. The ozone question is a battle. The sheer weight of paper sometimes tips the scales, and right now I think you're light about two pounds."

"Fine. I'll ask Dr. Corbett for three more people, and we'll comb the territory. Will you send Corbett a copy so I can get his help?"

"He'll have it tomorrow afternoon."

"I appreciate it."

"No problem. And when you . . . uh, come to Seattle, maybe you'll let me take you to dinner." More whistling from "The Stripper" was followed by, "What do you say?"

"Not Thai again."

"Why not? I just want to sit across from you in the candlelight and stare into those beautiful brown eyes."

"Watery eyes, you sadist. That soup was so hot, my eyes stung."

"Naw, your eyes were irrigated by tears of joy."

Kevin was entertaining, but his boyish enthusiasm reminded her of a younger brother—not fuel for romance.

"Kevin, I'm not eating that lava in a bowl."

"Okay, we'll make it Italian then."

"I'll let you know. Good-bye." She hung up.

Maddy was satisfied with the test results . . . good foundation for further work. Her boss, Corbett, would listen. He believed in her.

She took a sip of coffee and smiled. Kevin, you weirdo. You're an oddball specimen yourself. She had met men she respected in the EPA, but none that attracted her. Science professionals often looked like they needed their heads sharpened along with their pencils.

Of course, for lack of anything better, there was always Kit . . . slick, smooth, and supercilious Kit. This morning he had left a third message on her answering machine, laying claim to his potential partnership with Uncle Robert. Good reason for us to see more of each other, he'd said. Kit meant well, but he'd been a high school sweetheart whom she'd outgrown.

As opposed to Kit's plasticity, she'd envisaged someone strong who would fill out a parka, who was comfortable with a hint of stubble on his chin. She wanted a rugged guy with a gentle soul, as cheesy as it sounded. Was that possible?

There had been one. A park ranger. Todd. He had a broad, friendly face and a lifestyle she admired. He seemed to warm up to her both times they happened to meet. But then he moved to Wyoming.

Maddy rinsed her coffee cup in the sink and walked to the counter. She picked up Robert's grid.

He was due to visit in two days. If this strange piece of paper was as valuable as he'd implied, she'd better hide it somewhere—outside the house. Where no thief would ever find it. But where?

Maddy gazed through her kitchen window toward the backyard. Einstein pranced on the other side of the chain-link fence. Madame Curie, the mother raccoon, sat on her doghouse while the little rads cavorted in the dirt, crab-walking toward one another and then jumping in the air. Edison, the injured owl, sat on his perch.

She could hide the grid in one of the animal shelters. Who'd bother with that? Her gaze rose beyond the cages, past the meadow, to the spruce grove. Now, *that* was an even better place, farther away from the house. Through the low-slung boughs of a blue California spruce, Maddy could just make out the frame of the arbor she'd built. The red roof of a birdhouse hung below. She had bored round openings some two inches in diameter for the wrens and swallows to enter.

She eased her feet into a pair of moccasins and placed Robert's grid in a brown envelope. She would roll the envelope in a sturdy tube and slide it into one of the round windows of her birdhouse. Yes, the birdhouse.

No one would ever think to look there.

14

The Aurora

AN AIRCRAFT UNLIKE ANY JACE had ever seen hovered above the crippled oil rig with its jets blaring. The quad engine jet-and-rotor combination was swiveled downward off the wing, and the plane floated on its own vertical thrust.

"What the hell is that?" Stewart grunted as he cut his bungee cords. Jace severed his, and both men scampered away from the helipad as they watched the fighter plane descend. The jet settled on the pad, the engines throttled down, and with a whir, the cockpit canopy slid back.

A lone pilot, wearing gloves, a flight suit, and a darkly tinted helmet, gestured for Jace and Stewart to approach. He stepped out on the wing and pointed toward handholds on the fuselage undercarriage. Stewart was the first to get there. He grabbed onto the rungs, clambering upward as the pilot helped him up. Stewart jumped into the cockpit, and the pilot bent down and took Jace's wrist. As Jace got aboard, the pilot smacked his shoulder with the flat of his hand.

Surprised, Jace turned as the pilot tugged at his jacket collar, loosing the straps, removing his helmet.

Jace grinned as he recognized the strong, angular features. "My God, Cory."

"Who else would come out here to save your ass?" Cory said as they embraced. "Who's that? Carville?"

"It is. But he's not the killer. I'll fill you in. And we've come to an understanding—he'll remain 'Stewart' for now." Jace held Cory at arm's length, nearly losing his balance on the wing's unsteady footing, pointing to the plane's fuselage. "This? How?"

"I kept waiting for your call. When the storm turned north, I knew you were in deep shit. Then the choppers arrived in Galveston without you. I had my boys at satellite imaging give me hourly updates. I knew the eye was tracking over the Aurora, so I pulled rank and commandeered this baby."

"You can do that?"

"Hey, I've got special dispensation from the Pentagon, man."

"What's this plane called?"

"A Y-23 Jayhawk, an air force experimental model, kind of like the navy's Osprey. I knew it was the only way." Cory looked back at the burgeoning cloud bank. "I'd love to stay and chat, but there's some wild ass weather right there." He stepped over to the cockpit, handed Stewart a helmet, and pointed to the rear compartment. "Mr. Stewart, I should introduce myself. I'm Major Jackson. You'll have to slide back and lie down in the gear rack behind the seat. I apologize this is just a two-seater, but we'll make do."

Stewart didn't seem to mind and quickly made room for himself.

Jace put his helmet on and strapped in. Cory settled into the pilot seat, hit the controls, and lifted off vertically. As the plane ascended the first hundred feet, Jace was amazed how the wind caused them to bob and weave. Cory changed the plane's altitude, and the engines swiveled to horizontal. As he throttled up and accelerated, the force thrust Jace back into his seat.

Cory aimed the Jayhawk into the northern sky, headed for a patch of blue.

HOUSTON'S RANDOLPH AIR BASE WAS well out of the storm's range, and after landing the jet safely, Cory saw to it that both Jace and Stewart were registered as civilian guests and provided with warm food and dry clothes.

Less than an hour later, Stewart left on an eastbound transport plane for Florida, anxious to see his daughter and to be reassigned to another Texaco post.

With Stewart gone and because Jace was starving, Jace and Cory decided to debrief one another over lunch.

Jace was pleased just to be indoors, dry and safe, and he delighted in even the smallest things—the taste of a hot bowl of chili, the cheeriness of the cafeteria, which echoed with laughter and small talk as a late lunch crowd filed through under bright neon lights. As Jace and Cory sat, Cory was greeted by a flyer or two who knew him, and he enjoyed retelling Jace's story as others paused to listen.

It was not until Jace and Cory had finished their meals and were left alone in the back corner of the hall that Jace noticed Cory's smile fade. He seemed suddenly morose.

"What's up?" Jace asked.

Cory looked around to make sure no one was within earshot. His voice dropped into a whisper. "I'm going to move my family to Memphis."

"What are you talking about?"

"Day before yesterday when I came out of the PX, someone tried to run me down."

"You're sure?"

Cory's eyes narrowed. "Well, I'd say so. I jumped four feet to avoid the car and it still grazed my ass."

"What kind of car was it?"

"Light-blue Buick. Official-looking air force car. I couldn't see the driver."

"So you told the Air Police?"

Cory shook his head. "I was about to . . . and then something made my skin crawl. I called DC instead and got in touch with Dixon." Cory's Air Academy roommate in Air Force Intelligence had helped to locate Stewart. "I used a safe phone to call and demanded that he tell me his best guess."

"About?"

"Somebody trying to snuff me. At first he clammed up like he'd been hit with a shovel, which pissed me off. And I told him as much. He finally broke down and admitted I was getting into somebody's shit."

"How? What have you got?"

"I'm not sure yet, but there's something nasty coming down. Twisted stuff. I can feel it in my gut."

Jace took a sip of coffee. "Talk to me."

"Well, unfortunately, I did *more* than you asked. Maybe I was too jazzed, but I got curious. I was doing routine research on *Mir* mission records and Jupiter flights, when I decided I might as well hash over old unmanned mission records too. I was dicking around with some ancient computer files when I came across a code name that didn't make sense. I should have left it alone, but I just couldn't. A particular set of Mars mission computer stats had been reclassified, not only in 1993 but in '98 as well. I questioned the protocol. As air force liaison to NASA, why shouldn't I have access to everything? Anyway, I e-mailed an official inquiry."

"Isn't that terribly risky?"

Cory shrugged. "Too gung ho maybe, but hey, I felt it was within my job description. Anyway, my e-mail was apparently forwarded up the chain of command all the way to General Purdom, who's one notch under the joint chiefs. Four days ago, while I was over at Nellis in Nevada, I received an official reply, denying the Phobia File's existence."

"That's what they call it? The—"

"Phobia File. I tried to find answers by tapping NASA's computer banks through their administrative office at Langley. Nothing. So I dropped that little gem on Dixon. Reluctantly, he admitted this Phobia File is part of a set of secret papers that came around during the Mars missions in the nineties."

"What?"

"Yeah. Around your dad's time . . . 1993."

Cory's expression shook Jace. "I don't understand."

Cory heaved a sigh. "I think your dad was killed as part of a cover-up."

There it was. Cory reinforcing Stewart's own conjecture. "Can we prove that?"

"I'm not sure. But I think there's someone who might know. When I was going through the files, I came across a two-year-old memo that named a *particular* scientist as a national security risk—a guy who had made comments the press picked up. This guy has repeatedly accused NASA of suppressing data from their Mars Observer satellite they claim they lost on August 22, 1993."

The date hit Jace like a punch in the stomach. His father had died the next day. "Wait a minute. Are you talking about a guy named Marro?"

"How'd you know that?"

"Stewart mentioned him. Seems Marro doesn't mind stirring things up."

Cory smiled. "I told you there was something big out there. I suppose you'd like to know where to find this dude." He pulled a newspaper clipping from his breast pocket. "He's the guest speaker at a science conference tomorrow." The article included a photograph of a woman and two men at a podium, holding a plaque.

Jace could use Cory's office to e-mail an abbreviated accident report to Southland Insurance about the *Aurora,* and then he could be hot on the trail of a man whose past was tied with his father. "Where's this conference?"

Cory handed Jace the article. "Vancouver, BC."

Jace took the clipping. The headline referred to a seminar to be held at the Pan Pacific Hotel, featuring several different speakers on the new field of "extraterrestrial archeology."

Looking over Jace's shoulder, Cory pointed to the article's photo, showing a bearded man wearing glasses. "That's him. The guy's heavy into offbeat astronomy."

PART TWO

15

Pan Pacific Hotel
Vancouver, British Columbia

HAVING WRESTLED THE BEDSHEETS INTO submission during his nightmare, Jace was drenched in sweat as he lay on a bare mattress. He stared at the white cottage-cheese ceiling of the hotel room, haunted by the anguish of the fading dream.

The reoccurring nightmare was still the same: he was nine years old, desperately alone, searching a vacuous black-and-white geometric landscape worthy of Picasso.

He would wander through the misty void, calling his parents' names. Then from nowhere, his mother's distorted whisper would dart like a mosquito past his ear and he would whirl around to find . . . no one.

The dream's emptiness and frustration left him exhausted.

Leaving Randolph Air Base after expediting his accident report, Jace had flown to San Antonio, stopping at his townhouse for only an hour to pack. Then he had rushed back to the airport to catch a flight to Vancouver. If he wanted to be present for Robert Marro's speech the next morning, he had to connect on a flight from Dallas.

Arriving at Vancouver's Pan Pacific Hotel after eleven o'clock at night, Jace discovered that Robert Marro had checked in, but because of hotel policies, Jace could only leave phone messages on Marro's voice mail.

There had been no response, and Jace decided he would try again early this morning, fearing that if he didn't corner Marro prior to his appearance, as evasive as the man was, he might disappear.

Jace rolled over and dialed the hotel operator, asking for Marro's room.

No answer. Jace chose to leave another message, pondering how to imply urgency without scaring the elusive professor away. "Dr. Marro, this is Jace Kelton again. As I mentioned earlier, I'm in town for a limited time and I must speak with you. It concerns vital issues regarding your work. You can reach me in room 1133. Please call."

Hoping that Marro would find the mention of his own work a nonthreatening hook, Jace hung up, got out of bed, and walked over to the large plateglass window. He opened the drapes and admired the view that he hadn't seen in the dark.

His eleventh floor room overlooked the Vancouver waterfront, where smoke drifted off the stack of a freighter across the bay and mountains flanking the city began to emerge from light cloud cover.

Once the fog lifted, it would be a beautiful, sunny day.

Jace took a deep breath and checked his watch: the digital dial read 5:49. Marro was scheduled to speak at 10:00 a.m. There was still plenty of time to locate him.

Jace decided to recharge his batteries with a morning jog. After breakfast, he'd track Marro down.

He headed for the closet. Catching his own reflection in the mirror, he was surprised to see how exhausted he looked. The siege on the *Aurora* had drained him. He hadn't gotten much sleep since.

Jace leaned closer, staring hard into his own eyes. Old family photographs showed that his eyes were much like his father's. He had tried to recapture memories of Arthur before—there were few—playing catch in the backyard, a fishing trip to a lake, where Jace had been startled by a water snake swimming through the reeds. Beyond that, there was just the sense that Arthur had been a kindhearted man. After Arthur died, Jace had understandably clung to his mother. The lasting impression of Jane Kelton—being cuddled amid a smell of sweetness, her singing him to sleep at bedtime. He remembered the day that contentment ended—the exact moment—the afternoon of his seventh birthday.

He was to have a party with friends.

The midday California sun had streamed through the windows of their rambler tract home. Jace had wandered into the kitchen for a glass of milk. His mother stood at the sink, distracted, staring at the lemon trees. Jace had tugged at the hem of her dress. With the billowing of blue taffeta, Jane had knelt down, tears streaming down her face. She sobbed, unable to speak, gripping him in a yearning embrace.

Months later, after she began to wither, she had told him. That had been the day the lab results had come in. She'd just been informed she had leukemia.

Jace cast the ghosts away as he gazed out the window. The jog would do him good.

He pulled his small leather suitcase from the rack and rummaged through the clothes, finding his athletic gear and running shoes. As he pulled a blue tank top over his head, the phone on the nightstand pulsed. The nearby clock radio read 6:00 a.m. He had asked for a wake-up call.

Jace tucked the top into his black shorts and answered, "Thank you, I'm up."

"Mr. Kelton?"

"Yes."

"This is Robert Marro." The tone was cautious. "You called?"

Jace eased onto the bed. "Yes, Dr. Marro. I've just flown in from Texas. I need to see you."

"May I ask why?"

"I'd have to speak to you face-to-face."

"I don't think that's going to be possible."

Jace was about to lose him. "Okay, but just give me a minute to explain. A personal friend of mine is a special air force attaché to NASA. He and I have common interests that concern your claims regarding the Mars missions."

A long silence followed. He heard Marro clear his throat. "You're going back a few years. I haven't discussed that lately."

"Perhaps there's reason to."

"For you maybe, not for me. I don't want to seem rude, but I'm very busy."

"This is a highly personal matter to me, Doctor. And my friend, the major, believes he's in danger."

"That *he's* in danger, you say? And his name?"

"Jackson. Cory Jackson."

Another long silence. "How about you? What's your stake in this?"

"My father paid the ultimate price for his involvement."

"Your..." Marro gasped on the other end of the line. "Dear God. That Kelton?"

"Huntsville, Alabama. 1993."

"You." Marro's breathing fell into short, nervous bursts. "But why now? Who contacted you?"

"Jackson." Jace thought momentarily about Stewart and decided not to mention his name.

"No one from the embassy?"

"Embassy? No. I was just trying to reach you. I felt you might know—"

"Let's not talk on the phone." Marro clipped the words. "If we must, we'll talk in person."

"Your room?"

"Certainly not. Outside the hotel. I'm supposed to attend a welcome break-fast at eight. Let's do it by the water's edge. There's a promenade."

"Fine. I was about to take a jog."

"A jog? You're certainly nonchalant. Don't you realize what you've gotten yourself into?" Taken aback, Jace was about to reply, but Marro continued, "I have one other matter to attend to, so wait fifteen or twenty minutes. I'll be waiting for you past the exhibition halls, standing at the railing by the bay some two hundred yards east. I have a beard and glasses."

Pondering Marro's anxiety, Jace walked through the hotel lobby, keeping an eye on the people around him. A young man cleaned ashtrays by the elevator; a middle-aged woman in a white apron vacuumed; another polished the brass handles on the conference room's glass doors. Near the escalator, a sign over the grand ballroom read: WELCOME NEW EARTH CONFERENCE.

Jace emerged from the hotel's back door into the brisk salty air of Vancou-ver Bay. The fog had lifted and clear blue sky hung over the city. The bright morning seemed full of expectation, though Jace had mixed feelings, consider-ing what Marro had said. What *had* he gotten himself into?

With engines rumbling, two pleasure boats meandered along the shoreline. Few people were out this early.

Dressed in a set of gray warm-ups he had pulled over his tank top and shorts, Jace headed east on a walkway flanked by shrubbery and approached a pink-cheeked woman in a fur coat walking her toy poodle. She gave him an embarrassed smile as the dog defecated in a flowerbed. Through her open coat Jace noticed pajamas, oddly coupled with a pearl necklace.

Beyond the woman, a series of exhibition halls lined the hotel's exterior. And farther still, there were shops and meeting rooms.

Eager to find Marro, Jace broke into a slow trot along the green railing, feel-ing the sun's rays on his face as he skirted the water's edge. He passed some ivy bushes and descended a flight of stairs, where he reached the lower level of the large promenade.

Marro should be visible any moment.

Jace glanced north. A large number of seagulls circled over the bay to his left like a mobile, spinning around the vortex of some fishy feast. In the distance across the water in a park, dotted colors danced across the gray canvas of the waterfront. Parents and kids and kites. Out early, playing. He had a kite once— a box kite that his father had made in the garage before he died . . . bright red.

Jace came to the end of the walkway. To his right, a passageway led away from the shore toward downtown. The narrow walk was shaded from the morning sun.

Jace stopped and felt his gut churn. Some forty yards away, where the passage-way took a sharp right turn, a dark shapeless mass huddled on the cement. Jace heard a muffled cry as he walked tentatively toward the dark mound. Another cry—more of a wail.

"Hey!" Jace shouted. The shape moved abruptly at his call. The brim of a hat appeared. The dark mound was a square-jawed man in a raincoat and a white scarf. A rain-coat? In this weather? Something else moved beneath. Kicking legs—the heels of shoes driving into the pavement.

Jace broke into a run. "What the hell are you doing?"

On his knees, the man in the coat made a jerk with his right arm and pulled what appeared to be a manila envelope from the body. Déjà vu shuddered through Jace as he stared into the man's expressionless pale eyes. The man whirled, and with long blond hair flying, broke into a full run toward town, leaving the squirming body on the pavement.

Jace had to either help the victim or give chase to the attacker, who rounded a corner of one of the exhibition buildings and disappeared.

A pitiful moan convinced him to let the assailant go. He turned toward the man on the ground, who wore a rumpled blue three-piece suit, narrow gold-rimmed glasses, and a trimmed gray beard. His eyes were wide with disbelief, his face contorted by panic.

With horror, Jace realized . . . it was Robert Marro.

Marro's bloody hands gripped his own throat. A crimson opening gurgled air that hissed through the larynx. Marro gripped the wound, fighting to keep it closed. Blood seeped onto the pavement as Jace knelt and held Marro by the shoulder.

"Easy. I've got to get help," Jace said.

Marro's right hand leapt from his throat to Jace's collar as he tried to speak.

Desperately, Jace looked down the pathway and saw the woman with the poodle, gawking in their direction. "Help!" Jace yelled. "Call an ambulance!"

The woman, apparently frightened, turned abruptly back toward the hotel with her poodle in tow.

Marro's hand tugged at Jace's face.

Jace looked down. Marro's lips formed soundless words.

"What is it?" Jace asked. "You can tell me. I'm Kelton."

Marro's hand worked its way past Jace's collar and grabbed the back of his neck.

Jace leaned down, placing his ear to Marro's straining mouth. He tried to make out the words.

"What?" Jace asked. "Say it again."

"NASA."

Jace could hardly hear the faint whisper. "NASA? What do you mean?"

Marro struggled and Jace tried to make eye contact, but Marro again forced his head into place. "Tell Maddy . . ."

"Maddy?"

"NASA . . . the stone."

Jace struggled to understand. "A stone? What stone?" Jace was so close that his own face brushed Marro's beard, and he felt the moisture of tears rolling down Marro's cheeks.

Marro was able to form another syllable. "Ease." He'd spent the last of his energy, and his final attempts dissipated into a series of unintelligible muttering.

Jace lifted his head and stared at Marro's face. "Dr. Marro. Who did this to you?"

Marro's body went into a spasm. Jace clutched his shoulders, hoping for more, but Marro's mouth opened and closed like a salmon out of water. A last hiss of a syllable formed on his lips, "aaoorrg." He went limp as the spark of life left him.

Jace studied his face; the wide set, slightly crossed eyes stared blankly through gold-rimmed glasses. He let Marro's head fall gently back into the pool of blood that had formed beneath.

Here he was, alone with a dead man in a strange town.

The seconds ticked by.

A young blonde woman in green slacks with a little girl suddenly appeared in the passageway, walking in Jace's direction.

Relieved to see someone else, Jace got to his feet.

The woman saw him and screamed, hiding the child's eyes, ushering her back in the direction they'd come.

Jace suddenly realized how grotesque he must look. Blood had splattered across his warm-ups, covering his chest. His pants were soaked with a dark-red stain at the knees. He reached up and felt the sticky smear up the side of his neck where Marro had collared him.

Jace began to remove his blood-stained clothes as he walked toward the hotel. He stripped off the gray warm-ups, rolled the pants into his jacket, and tucked them under his arm. Then he broke into a run.

Nearing the water's edge, he rounded the corner and trotted onto the hotel grounds.

"Halt!" A voice shouted. Two Vancouver police, a man and a woman with guns drawn, had suddenly appeared behind him.

"You there," the man shouted. "Stop where you stand!"

Jace obeyed and turned slowly. Both RCMPs were crouched in a firing stance.

"Drop the bundle!" the female cop yelled.

The blonde woman and her little girl rushed up behind the police, their faces contorted with fear. "That's him!" the woman screamed. "That's the man."

"Lose that bundle *now!*" the burly male cop shouted.

Jace let go and raised his hands. The cops approached cautiously, moving toward him with guns high.

"Officer." Jace pointed to his right. "There's a body—"

"Get on your face!" the male cop yelled.

Jace dropped into a push-up, feeling the chill of the pavement on his belly as the cops jumped on him.

"Put both hands behind your back!" the woman said.

Jace craned his neck. The female cop's name tag read JENKINS.

The male cop—FERGUSON, according to his name tag—closed the handcuffs on Jace's wrists. Jace was yanked to his knees. "You're a bit bloody, friend," Ferguson said.

"The dead man." Jace stumbled to his feet.

"Yes. We saw your handiwork," Ferguson replied.

"My handiwork? Are you crazy? Someone killed him." Jace found himself searching for explanations. "I found him while I was running."

"From the scene of a crime?" Jenkins asked as she picked up Jace's bloody warm-ups and shook them. "No knife here."

"Okay," Ferguson mumbled. "Jenkins, go back and check the promenade for a blade." The woman and child stood off by the rail, nervously clutching each other's hands. "And get that woman's name," Ferguson barked, pointing at the mother. "She'll have to make a statement."

Jace looked up at the hotel. People had gathered near the glass windows of the rear entrance.

Officer Ferguson propelled him toward the rear doors of the Pan Pacific.

"Where the hell are you taking me?" Jace asked.

"Hell's a good word for it," Ferguson said, shoving him. "You're going to jail."

16

Leavenworth

THIS WAS THE THIRD RESTLESS night since Uncle Robert's frantic call. The waiting had been frustrating, but this evening's news from Vancouver had made her physically ill.

As a midnight windstorm rolled through the east slopes of the Cascade foothills, a resounding explosion of thunder shook Maddy from a fitful sleep.

She rolled over in bed and looked past the pine branches that scraped her bedroom window. A new flash of lightning lit the sky over Cashmere Mountain.

She still felt like hell.

She'd been dumbfounded by the call from Vancouver from an Inspector Orville, which came via Brown University—via Father Navarro in Ann Arbor. The inspector seemed to sense her shock and thankfully described the crime without graphic detail.

But she was struck by the surreal nature of the conversation . . . as if she were playing a part in a TV show, suddenly informed of a relative passing in some distant land. She hadn't cried at the news, but rather she found herself wandering aimlessly through the house some moments later.

Robert had mentioned he might be in danger, but the brutality was overwhelming. Bewildered, Maddy had taken a bottle of Merlot from the pantry and retired to her bedroom. Alone in the dark, she'd sipped the wine until she'd gradually fallen asleep.

The bottle was there, next to the bedside lamp. Maddy reached up and tried the switch. Nothing. The electricity had gone out in the storm.

She sat up and swung her bare feet onto the weave rug next to her bed and then fumbled for a match in her nightstand. She walked over and lit the candle on her bedroom dresser.

The feeble glow of the flickering flame washed across pictures she'd hung on the wall—a collage of family photos.

In one, her father toasted her high school graduation; in another, her mother sat in their backyard gazebo; in yet another, her parents relaxed on the rear deck of their yacht.

Next to those, a photo taken in Ann Arbor at Christmas twenty-four years ago of Uncle Robert holding Maddy on his lap. She had been just three years old, wearing a lace party dress and black patent leather shoes. Her hair was tied with festive red ribbons. Against blurred splotches of tree lights in the slightly overexposed blush of the flashbulb, Maddy held the Pooh Bear that Robert had given her that morning. That was the day Robert coined the nickname "Maddy" for Madison, and it stuck.

Seeing Robert in that picture—that freeze-frame of joy—finally brought the tears. "We're the last of the Marros," he had said to her. How true. And now, she was alone. That jovial eccentric, who visited on those distant cherished holidays, was just a blend of color in a snapshot.

Tears continued to stream down her face as she sat on her bed, staring out the lanai window, watching departing traces of lightning through sheets of rain. Is that all we are as well—brief flashes of light? What's left behind—a few distant rolls of thunder that echo then fade?

Poor Robert had no children. His legacy . . . perhaps nothing but that ridiculous scrap of paper she had hidden in the birdhouse. Had that scribbled ink caused his death? If so, she was snarled in its complications. The mystery had compounded: why had her father's remains been desecrated; why had Maddy been stalked; why had Robert been killed? The murderer might have the answers, and whether she liked it or not, she'd be involved in Jace Kelton's prosecution.

She gazed out at the forested expanse, realizing that her peace in this mountain paradise had been shattered. Who was this Kelton—one of the men at Stag Lake, or the fictional Dr. Bellamy? And how did it all relate to the dead Asian man who'd been found on the road?

Her sadness slowly ebbed into a rising appetite for retribution. A seething anger swelled inside as she contemplated the brutality that Robert endured and the audacity of the maniacs who taunted her.

She'd be on a plane to Vancouver tomorrow. She wanted to see the face of the bastard who butchered her uncle.

17

Downtown RCMP Precinct, Vancouver

JACE LEANED AGAINST THE RADIATOR, looking out the open window of Inspector Orville's office. Pigeons cooed in the eaves of a stone office building across the way, while spires and cornices of the city rose beyond.

Marro's assassin could be out there.

Jace replayed the murder in his mind, plagued by visions of the killer's face. There was something oddly familiar about the man who had slaughtered Marro. The broad-shouldered, blond fellow had a distinctive fluid gait as he fled. What were the words? "Blond panther in a trap." And the killer's eyes, "cool as death." Coincidence? Or was it possible that after more than twenty years, Jace had confronted a man who resembled Stewart's description of Arthur Kelton's killer?

The implications were devastating. In the heat of Orville's initial interrogation, Jace had hinted at his suspicion. Orville's reaction had been clinical, like a condescending doctor listening to rantings of a madman. Fortunately, Orville had allowed Jace a brief phone call to Cory. Cory was the only one who could justify Jace's motive for being at the murder scene. Jace's desperation caused Cory to take emergency leave and catch the next northbound transport. When Cory arrived, he was not allowed to see Jace but was, instead, immediately questioned by Orville alone in an outer office. They had been at it for over twenty minutes.

Jace sighed and gazed back at the wall clock. The delay was unnerving.

Although emotionally drained, Jace felt better physically now that he was dressed in jeans and a blazer the police had retrieved from his hotel room. At least he was waiting in Orville's quarters rather than a cell. The office conveyed an academic professionalism like Orville, himself. It smelled of pipe smoke and was furnished with a dark wooden desk, walnut file cabinets, and bookshelves.

Jace finally heard voices outside the opaque glass door.

A key turned in the lock, and Orville entered. He was a dark-haired man with a bushy mustache, dressed in a tweed coat and a maroon sweater-vest. Jace was delighted to see that he was followed by Cory, who gave a sympathetic smile and warmly gripped Jace's hand. But as Orville turned his back, Cory caught Jace's gaze and rolled his eyes, shaking his head as if to indicate his misgivings.

Orville tossed a computer printout on his desk, offering Cory and Jace the two round leather chairs opposite. Jace declined and chose to stand while Cory took a seat.

"I'm sorry you had to wait, Mr. Kelton. But Major Jackson and I have become acquainted. We took a few moments to legitimize his identity, among other things." The inspector settled into his chair. "He's basically corroborated your story. Though, I must admit, some of its implications are a bit fanciful for my taste."

Jace hopes started to slide. He'd heard Cory engage in a myriad of sci-fi theories when he had an audience.

"I explained about your dad," Cory volunteered, "and the connection to Marro. Not much more than that."

"Okay," Jace said, hesitantly. "So where are we?"

Orville leaned back and took an apple from the wicker basket on the credenza. "Well, the primary issue is whether there was another man at the crime scene. We're waiting for Mrs. Albrighton's testimony."

"Albrighton?" Cory gave Jace an inquiring look.

"The poodle woman." Jace visualized her pajamas and pearls. "They found her. She lives in a condo near the hotel."

Orville took a bite of apple; a small piece landed on his wool tie and clung to the rough fabric. "If Albrighton confirms with a written statement that there was another man," he swiveled around to Cory, "I might consider accepting Mr. Kelton's motives, though they still sound rather obtuse."

Cory shrugged. "What else would you like to know?"

Orville looked out from under bushy, graying eyebrows. "Well, this Mars business is a bit beyond me. Yet, you both maintain its significance."

Jace leaned against the radiator. "Yes. Marro claimed—"

Orville interrupted. "The major explained Dr. Marro's speculation about

NASA. But as I looked into your family history, Mr. Kelton," Orville picked up the printout, "I came upon your father's questionable reputation."

"That was bad press."

"Allegedly part of a covert operation?"

"That was a lie."

Orville raised the file. "Not according to the FBI."

Jace's hated the age-old accusations and being put on the defense. "I intend to force the FBI to rescind that. I was trying to contact Marro to see what he knew. Why would I kill him?"

"Precisely the issue." The inspector tugged on his mustache, took another bite of apple, chewed, and contemplated, swallowing before he spoke. "Yet you insist that some reincarnated assassin from the past—"

"Yes. I'm . . . that's what I believe."

Cory's eyes narrowed. "You're sure, Jace?"

"I'm sure of the description."

"Sure? Based on an eyewitness in 1993, whom you can't produce, and who's not mentioned in any files?"

"He'll come forward when the time comes."

"This may well be the time."

Jace glanced nervously at Cory.

Orville shrugged. "We'll see. For now I'm left to assume that Marro knew something vital. And that Major Jackson's findings added some urgency."

Cory sat in silence.

"Well, Major?"

"What?"

"What was so important about Marro's claims?"

"That's . . . a tough one. Certain NASA files remain top secret because they affect the security of the United States."

Orville frowned and patronizingly cocked his head. "Really? Well, they also affect your credibility and the integrity of Mr. Kelton's argument." He leaned forward and glared at Jace. "You should know that Madison Marro, Robert's niece, arrived in Vancouver today. I've invited her to come to my office later this morning to discuss the circumstances of her uncle's death. Having met with the coroner, she's concluding arrangements to fly her uncle's remains to Rhode Island for a funeral." He wagged a finger at Jace. "Madison could easily bring charges against you." The inspector stroked his chin. "And I may well be put in the awkward position of having to explain away your overzealous curiosity about Marro."

Jace looked expectantly at Cory, who had begun to study the spit shine on his shoes. "Tell him what you know, Cory. The facts."

Orville nodded. "Yes, do. By all means."

"You're asking for privileged information."

"And it will remain privileged, Major, as long as charges levied against Kelton don't force testimony in open court."

Cory looked up. "And no court case if—"

"Vancouver authorities, namely myself, are convinced of Kelton's innocence." Orville wiped his mouth, sweeping the apple fragments away. He threw the core into a wicker wastebasket.

Cory remained silent for a moment, as if formulating his strategy. He sighed and puffed his cheeks like a trumpet player, placing his air force cap in his lap. "Okay. Regarding Marro's accusations about NASA: have you ever been aware that there were theories that NASA was not exactly open about the reason why some of their missions failed?"

"Actually I haven't been. Though I know some failed."

Cory nodded. "Yes. And they claim that their data from those failed missions was irretrievable."

"If they say so, it probably was. I don't see the point."

"Well, Marro was a champion of these claims. He took a lot of heat for stating that both NASA and the Russians repeatedly withheld information from unmanned Mars missions starting in the late seventies and continuing through the eighties and beyond."

Orville frowned. "What's that got to do with this murder?"

Jace couldn't help himself. "That's what I'm trying to figure out."

"I see. So Marro severely criticized a reputable government agency. If that made him unpopular ..." Orville reached for a meerschaum pipe in a mahogany pipe holder on his desk, "... why would he do that?" Orville tamped the pipe with the silver tool he had taken from his breast pocket.

"I don't know. Maybe because NASA shot back with such nebulous explanations. In any case, this was awhile back. His most recent criticisms of NASA happened over a year ago." Cory produced several newspaper articles and laid them on the desk. "Here are his statements that NASA's '93 satellite, which they claimed exploded, actually got excellent shots of the planet and its moons."

The inspector lit his pipe and examined the newspaper clippings. A strong cherry tobacco fragrance permeated the office.

"Notice, on August 22 of '93," Cory pointed, "the Jet Propulsion Laboratory in Pasadena lost contact with the one-billion-dollar *Observer* four hundred thousand miles from Mars. This satellite was intended to circle the planet for a Martian year. It would have taken thousands of pictures, covering every square mile of the surface."

"And you claim it had?"

"Marro did—as he did about another NASA mission in '98. Although, to be precise, Marro claimed the materials released from *that* mission were censored."

"But even if NASA's photographs were somehow incomplete . . . so what?" Orville asked. "There have been several missions since which covered images of the planet surface quite comprehensively from what I've seen in the news."

"No. You saw news the agency wanted you to see."

"Is there some charter that obligates them to share every bit of data they acquire?"

"No. But I think they're morally obligated to reveal facts that might influence the future of civilization."

The pipe dropped from Orville's lips. "I don't follow."

"Marro was fixated on the idea that the '93 mission had been more targeted to the Martian moons than the planet surface."

"What of it?"

"He believed that data had been suppressed because it may have shown evidence that an ancient civilization had once colonized the planet."

"Civilization?" Orville's mustache twitched. "You realize what you're implying?"

"I fully understand the conclusion. Yes, sir."

"All right. But even if that were the case, why not make this knowledge public?"

"Proof of an alien civilization thousands of years old on a neighboring planet would pose a threat to conservative elements in our society, like business and religious leaders who don't want to rattle our belief system."

Noting the growing skepticism on Orville's face, Jace interjected. "Of course, we're not claiming any of this alien stuff ourselves."

"Just a minute." Orville exhaled a large cloud. "Major, your concerns here seem overblown. Conjecture about aliens is common."

"Right. Conjecture," Cory repeated. "But conjecture about a monster is quite different than having one at your door. The US government doesn't want proof of alien cultures at our door."

Orville looked unconvinced. "But with science fiction books and movies, every five-year-old child has been indoctrinated with the potential of finding something out there. Surely the government would admit it."

Jace was somewhat relieved. Perhaps Orville would elevate the conversation to a philosophical debate.

Cory raised a warning finger. "Well they haven't. Not since Roswell in 1947."

"Roswell?" Orville cradled the bowl of the pipe in his hand. "That's well-known science fiction bunk."

Cory smiled. "Maybe so, but the 'science fiction' Marro was trying to expose to the world was the government's *fiction* about our space missions."

"And you believed him?"

"I thought there was a chance he had something."

"Why didn't you take official action with your superiors?"

Jace wondered if Cory would reveal the attempt on his own life. Cory seemed to contemplate it. He straightened up and placed his cap on one knee but then fell into a military monotone. "I won't elaborate on my duty as an officer, Inspector."

"I see. How convenient." Orville clamped down on his pipe as someone knocked at the door.

Officer Ferguson stuck his head inside. "Inspector, excuse me. May I see you?"

Orville rose slowly, brushing ashes from the front of his speckled coat. "Give me a moment, gentlemen." He joined Ferguson in the hallway, closing the door behind.

Jace took the other leather chair next to Cory. "Marro's killer. Cory, I swear, it's him—the guy Stewart described."

"How the hell is that possible?"

"I don't know. I've got to get out of here."

"I'm working on it. How am I doing?"

"Lay off the sci-fi shit," Jace whispered.

"I think he's tuned in."

"Not to *War of the Worlds*. Tone it down or he'll send us both to a mental hospital."

Cory glanced at the door. "I've gotta tell you something before he gets back . . . in case you don't get out."

"Thanks for the assurance."

"Listen." Veins stood out on Cory's forehead. "My intelligence buddy, Randal Dixon, is back from Germany. He located a NASA official he thinks I should see—a guy named Higgins, who went on record a few years back requesting public disclosure of NASA's files. See, there's a five star general who—"

They were interrupted as Orville reentered, holding a pink piece of paper. He walked to the walnut file cabinet by the window giving Cory a sidelong glance. "I think we're more prepared for extraterrestrial revelations than you think, Major. But then I don't see those issues from your perspective. What I do find pertinent," Orville opened the drawer and pulled out a form, "is that you and Mr. Kelton were motivated by your convictions. I won't pry any further into your security concerns."

Cory smiled broadly. "I'm appreciative, sir."

Orville walked back to his desk and faced Jace. "Perhaps most importantly," he held the pink piece of paper in the air, "this statement from Mrs. Albrighton corroborates your story." Orville bent over the desk and cleared his throat. "As a result," he put a pen to the paper, "I'm signing off on your arrest report. But I caution you, this may not be over."

"I'm free to go?" Jace rose to his feet.

"For now." Orville handed the form to Jace. "I'm waiving any criminal charges at this time. But whether you'll be lucky enough to evade a civil complaint lies in the hands of Madison Marro, Robert's niece . . ."

18

Bern, Switzerland

AS DARKNESS FELL, THE THREE-TIERED fountain at the intersection of Königsrue and Victorstrasse came to life. Floodlights set in the stone border of the large concrete catch basin beamed high into the multiple apertures as spraying water shimmered down the twenty-eight statues.

A herd of unicorns circled the lowest level; a bevy of porcupines ran in the opposite direction on the second; and on the third, three black bears stood on their hind legs joining forepaws at the pinnacle, where the spouting water originated.

Bern was renowned for its aquatic art. This piece—certainly one of the most elaborate displays in town—was overlooked by Dr. Emma Hoffman's second-floor corner apartment.

As usual, during these twilight hours, Emma sat in her study at her computer. But unlike other evenings when she had watched the water dance, tonight the fountain didn't hold her attention. Instead, she stared blankly into space, hardly noticing the splashing or the street noises below. She was troubled, having come to the conclusion that she faced the imminent probability of her own death.

Emma had just seen an Internet news brief reporting Robert Marro's murder in Vancouver. On her desk, yesterday's copy of *USA Today* contained a small article describing the shooting of Jinseng Ma on the island of Oahu. A few days prior, Hector Walsh had been vaporized by an explosion in his Toronto laboratory. Two weeks ago, Dean Sutwith had died in an auto accident in South Africa.

The press seemed to draw no correlation between these ostensibly random and distant obituaries. But to Emma they were devastating, not only because she knew each of these men, but also because, like herself, each had been a member of a secret organization known as the Scalbania Seven, or S-7 as it came to be called.

The founder of the group, Norman Scalbania, and his successor, Mason Marro, had both passed away due to justifiable causes, of old age and cancer, respectively. But the seven scientists they had enlisted in their cabal had remained hardy and active until a few days ago. Now the list was rapidly shrinking; Walsh, Sutwith, and Jinseng Ma had died violently. And though Robert Marro wasn't one of the original seven, he was a scientist, and he was Mason Marro's brother, a coincidence that stretched the odds beyond reasonable limits.

As for the other still-living members of the S-7 . . . Emma hadn't spoken with Harold Berlinger in some time, not since November of the prior year at the Munich Twenty-First Century Symposium. And the last she'd heard, he'd moved from his long-time home in Surrey. She would have to locate Berlinger somewhere else in England. Michael Granville, she'd been told, lived on a farm in New Zealand, but he was incredibly difficult to reach, having become somewhat of a hermit in his retirement.

She did have contact with Torbald Ürg, however, in Sweden. They had corresponded late last year, and she knew how to reach him at the University of Oslo.

If there was a reason to sound an alarm, Torbald was an excellent way to begin. She had known him better than the others, and like her, he was a physicist, though he also excelled in geology. Emma respected his staunch ethics, and she remembered him fondly for his kind manner and his calming effect on those around him.

Emma decided to e-mail, since phone calls might be monitored, but would keep the missive general in nature, simply suggesting a meeting in case the e-mail could be hacked. She knew Torbald would agree to gather the surviving members of the S-7 to discuss options.

As she turned from the window, Emma shuffled the materials on her desk. The leather pad was piled high with books and papers, but fortunately, she had set Torbald's most recent letter aside. She used a straight edge to scroll down the lines until she came to the paragraph that specified Torbald's e-mail address.

Her Mac computer went through its routine flashes and screen wipes and logged on to her mailbox.

Adjusting her reading glasses, she moved the cursor to the "To:" line. Then carefully, she typed the recipient's address: the letters t u r g @ u n i v o s l o...

Her vision suddenly blurred as a strange odor emanated from the computer keyboard.

Emma reached up, responding to the sudden pain behind both eyes.

Her face seemed aflame as her sinuses filled with blood. She slumped forward on the desk. As her head smacked down on the keyboard, her glasses fell onto the leather pad, and she slid like a rag doll off the chair onto the floor.

Lying on her side on the Persian rug, Emma's body convulsed several times as a severe brain hemorrhage disconnected her kinetic functions.

A last breath caught in her throat, and her heart—after slowing to a sluggish, futile rhythm—finally stopped beating.

19

Vancouver, British Columbia

"THERE YOU ARE, MR. KELTON." A stoic Officer Ferguson reached through the white grating of the cage window and handed Jace his effects. With his duffel bag in hand, Jace took the small tan envelope and checked its contents: money, a watch, and his commemorative Pan American Games ring.

Orville and Cory stood by, exchanging final words, and Jace looked around the precinct lobby, attempting to center himself. Questions about NASA and Cory, about Marro and his connections with Jace's father reeled in his mind. Life had become a good deal more complicated; he should have been headed back to San Antonio by now.

Orville shook Cory's hand and turned to Jace. "Let's hope I won't need to see you again, Mr. Kelton. Good luck to you both." With a final wave, the inspector began to walk down the hall toward his office.

"You and I need to talk," Jace said.

"Not here." Cory whispered, watching Jace fasten his wristwatch. "Let's do it outside."

Smiling at Ferguson, Jace tucked his loose change into his pants. He adjusted his belt, and looking up, became mildly distracted by a woman who had entered the precinct and now stood at the reception desk.

As Cory donned his cap, his eyes seemed drawn to her as well. As Jace and Cory walked shoulder to shoulder toward the large frosted windows at the precinct entrance, the beautiful woman headed in their direction.

Jace couldn't help noticing details about her. Dressed in a pair of black slacks and a teal blazer, she strolled easily through the sunlight-dappled lobby, her shiny auburn hair bobbing with each stride.

"Too bad we're leaving," Cory mumbled, admiring her as she approached.

Jace focused on her face as she passed. Her amber eyes shone like brass in the light.

"Mr. Kelton! Just a moment," someone called.

Jace turned as Ferguson emerged from behind the cage.

The woman in the teal blazer stopped and turned as well. With an intense expression, she watched Ferguson hustle over to Jace.

"Sorry to hold you up," Ferguson said, "but the inspector just buzzed me. He's asked you both to wait while he retrieves an urgent message from our operators . . . for Major Jackson, I believe."

"A message?" Jace gave Cory a curious glance.

Ferguson smiled apologetically. "Yes. From another air force gentleman."

Over Ferguson's shoulder, Jace saw the woman's expression change. Her soft amber eyes hardened. "You're Jace Kelton?" she asked, advancing.

"Yes." Jace intuitively retreated a step. "And, you're—"

"Madison Marro." She turned to Ferguson. "Why is this man walking around?"

"Beg pardon, miss?"

"Why isn't he in a cell?"

"Ms. Marro—" Jace ventured forward.

She recoiled. "I was talking to the officer. Where's Inspector Orville?"

"He's . . . I'll get him." Ferguson hurried toward the hall.

As Maddy followed him with her gaze, Jace made the mistake of touching her arm. "If I could—"

She pulled away. "Take your murdering hands off me."

"I'm not a murderer."

"In that case, you're a coward. You left my uncle to die in the street."

Jace glanced at Cory, who seemed suddenly content to let Jace defend himself. "No. By the time I—"

"I don't want to hear it. You left instead of helping him."

"That's not true. He was—"

"I *don't* want to talk to you. I came here to talk with the inspector, where is he?" She began to pace, hailing the desk sergeant. "You have ten seconds to get the inspector out here."

Cory removed his cap. "Ms. Marro, there's been a complete misunderstanding."

"Who are you?"

"I'm Mr. Kelton's friend. I respected your uncle's work."

"Really? Is that the connection here?"

"There's no connection," Cory said, "Jace was just trying—"

"I can't take this. I'm leaving." Maddy turned toward the front door just as Orville scurried from the hallway. "I'm bitterly sorry, Ms. Marro, I had no idea you'd arrived."

"Apparently not," she nodded at Jace, "with this convict on the loose. How could you let him go?"

"The evidence—"

"Evidence?" Maddy's eyes flashed.

"My investigation . . ."

She pointed at Jace. "Your investigation is obviously a joke."

"I'm sure if I explain," Orville tried again.

"Explain it to my lawyer." She spun and walked away.

"Please come into my office," Orville called.

"No way." Maddy's shoes clicked an angry cadence as she spoke over her shoulder. "Not without my attorney—you'll be hearing from him."

"Ms. Marro . . ." Jace called, but it was too late. She disappeared through the front door, leaving the three men to stare out the window as she entered a waiting taxicab.

"Wow." Cory looked over at Jace. "You know, I think she *will* press charges."

Jace suddenly envisioned an opportunity. Madison Marro was the "Maddy" Robert had mentioned in his dying breath, someone who would know volumes about Marro—his life and, perhaps, even his death. Maddy might even have insights that would lead to clues about Arthur Kelton's killer. "I've got to talk to her." Jace lurched forward.

Orville restrained him. "Where are you going?"

"To the airport."

"I wouldn't confront her," Orville said. "She'll only make a scene."

"Right," Cory frowned, "you'd have to sneak up on her."

"If that's what it takes."

"I almost forgot." Orville thrust a yellow piece of paper at Cory. "This just came in."

Cory unfolded the slip, read a few lines, and smiled disarmingly at Orville. "My office, they're always in touch. Thanks for everything, Inspector. We'll talk soon."

Orville nodded. "Very good, let me know if I can be of help."

Cory watched the inspector leave, replaced his cap, and gave Jace a nervous glance.

"What's up?" Jace asked as they made for the door.

They descended the precinct stairs, stepping onto the Vancouver street. Cory took a quick look around and handed Jace the note. "It's from Dixon."

Jace read the words. DAVENPORT'S ALIVE. MORNING STAR RETIREMENT HOME, SANTA FE, NEW MEXICO.

"Davenport," Cory said intensely. "The mission director on space flight in 1993. Your dad's boss."

"God. I should talk to him . . ."

Cory shook his head. "You can't be two places at once. Besides, you're a 'civi.' I'm the one with credentials. You chase Madison, get some answers."

"I thought you were tied up at the base."

Cory had taken a pen out of his pocket. "I was. But . . ." he grabbed the yellow slip of paper, "when the inspector called me, I realized both of us were up to our necks. So . . ." Cory scribbled something on the back. "I'm on emergency leave." He gave Jace a mischievous grin. "A dying aunt I never had."

"You're basically AWOL."

Cory ignored the comment and thrust the yellow note into Jace's hands. "See that top number? That's my new cell. It's so new it's probably secure. After you see Madison, use a landline and tell me what you plan to do. I'll call you when I can and report what I've found, but I may just leave messages on your San Antonio landline."

"You think there's surveillance on my cell?"

"By now, probably." Cory pointed to the slip once more. "That bottom number is Dixon's phone. He's very low profile, so use it only if you're in monstrously deep shit."

20

*A Hunting Lodge
Outside Kamloops, British Columbia*

THE LARGE MOOSE HEAD OVER the fireplace stared down at the three men huddled in the glow of a single light bulb hanging from a brown cord. The small table at which they stood had been nicked repeatedly by Shag's combat knife.

Shag held the blade that had sliced Robert Marro's throat in his right hand. He stabbed the air with it, venting his frustration, pleased to see that San and Ji followed the tip of the knife with apprehension.

San and Ji, both Chinese agents, who had been imported into Canada three weeks earlier, were well indoctrinated in Western culture, speaking English in a flawless American slang.

They were aware that Shag could kill them if they disappointed him. As the senior North American Chinese operative, Shag was coded with that privilege.

East German born, and as the finest and youngest American-based Soviet agent to be stranded in America after the Cold War, Shag had defected to the Chinese. Now he carried Beijing's confidence with pride, like he carried his scars—the worst of which was hidden by the white silk scarf he wore.

San's squad was part of an international team formed to acquire what the Chinese believed could be a powerful tactical device and an economic weapon—ostensibly an energy source—discovered by Robert Marro. And though Shag was marginally pleased with the performance of agents in England, New Zealand, and Switzerland, one of San's men, Lee Chou, had died mysteriously while on his mission in the United States. Lee now lay embalmed in a Leavenworth morgue, and Shag was angry and concerned about the attention it might bring.

Shag took a swig of schnapps from his silver flask. He stuck his knife in the wood tabletop and laid a scaly, battered hand on the scrap of paper that lay before him. As part of their training, Shag addressed the men in English. "I e-mailed this last night," he glared at the two others. "Cho had plenty of time to examine it. He tells me the coordinates are incomplete—only one-half of a grid that shows where to find Marro's discovery. It doesn't tell us enough." Shag pushed his long blond hair aside. "Cho is getting impatient. He's due here in three days, and he wants answers. And we don't have them."

"But you have Mason Marro's Peruvian Prize," San said.

"That was evidence that an energy source exists, not directions where to find it. We need the rest of the instructions."

"But we went through the house—"

"Shut up." With his flask in one hand and his knife in the other, Shag slinked back and forth like a cat in front of the feldspar fireplace. "Why do you think I'm here?" he asked, stopping to nick the fox hide on the back of a rocking chair with the tip of his blade. "I fooled Robert Marro into thinking he was meeting some Russian scientist, and I killed him because I thought this," he said as he pointed to the paper, "was all of it. But it's only half."

Speechless, San and Ji stared.

"Right?" Shag slammed the flask on the table and shouted, "And you couldn't find the other half?"

San chose his answer carefully. "I tell you, we searched her house."

"Then where the fuck is the rest of this?" Shag picked up the grid and held it in his hand. "Did Lee have it?"

"I don't know."

"There's *too much* you don't know." Shag continued to pace. "You leave Lee at the house while you track her at the lake. Then he disappears. Twenty-four hours later, he's found like a crash test dummy abandoned on a highway." Shag pulled his hair back from his face. "Who killed him? It wasn't Madison Marro."

San made the mistake of smiling.

"Funny? You think so? One of China's best operatives dies in a backwoods town? Where does that leave us?"

San forced an answer. "Why not kidnap the woman?"

"Really? Where would you suggest? At her uncle's funeral? En route to the airport? You want to blow this wide open and cause an international incident? Take a couple of men, go back to her house, and search again."

San still seemed confused. "But what about the woman?"

"Hopefully she'll show up. Secure her, force her to tell you where to find the grid."

"And if she doesn't cooperate?"

"Bring her here." Shag preferred to work alone. Burdened with this command, Shag was a general who hated having to consult foot soldiers on global strategy.

"Can I call you? How do I contact you?" San asked.

"No cell phones while I'm away. Damned surveillance." Shag was due in Sweden to oversee another hit that had gone badly. "I'll meet you here in two days."

Shag had the manpower to track Madison, but he preferred not chancing the exposure. He made up his mind to gamble on her returning home. When she did, San and his people could finish the job away from surveillance cameras and the prying eyes of the police. With their off-road bikes and the wide-open Canadian border, his men had had no problem getting into Washington State from Canada.

They would easily do it again.

21

Over Alberta, Canada

GOLDEN FLASHES FROM A TRAILING sunset splashed across the forward bulkhead of Canada Air 747. The first-class cabin was mercifully almost empty, and Maddy closed her eyes, leaning back in her sixth-row window seat as the voice from the flight deck droned its welcome.

With the aisle seat next to Maddy's unoccupied, she had plenty of room. She slipped her shoes off, breathed deeply, and attempted to clear her mind, though images of the day persistently flashed back; she kept visualizing her visit to the Vancouver Morgue, where she'd been forced to identify Robert's body. She wondered if she could ever forget his pale, lifeless form on the slab and the jagged laceration on his neck.

Perhaps tomorrow's funeral would bring an end to this nightmare. She'd arranged a small service that included a group of Robert's friends, plus his colleagues from Brown University.

She had also been disturbed by her conversation with Kit Lassiter, who was to fly in from Chicago.

Kit had heard about the murder before Maddy called. He naturally expressed regrets, citing his years of friendship with Robert. But then he fell silent. Maddy had tried to draw information out of him, on account that Robert had chosen him as a confidant. Only after she insisted on a response, Kit relented, stating intentions to finish the work Robert had begun.

"And what work was that?" Maddy had asked. Kit seemed surprised she didn't know.

He'd refused to discuss it on the phone, intimating that it might be dangerous.

The exchange left Maddy with familiar suspicions about Kit and his motives. Attractive, very bright, and egotistical, Kit was a poster child of the postmillennial "me" generation. He chose to leverage relationships rather than respect them, something Maddy noticed when they were young. Kit's narrow views had stifled any lasting relationships with women, which Maddy understood. After all, her own association with him was impermanent by her own doing. On the other hand, Kit had related very well to certain men, like Maddy's father, who had treated Kit like the son he'd never had. Kit was the neighborhood kid from a broken home who hung around the Marro house on holidays, which inevitably led him toward Maddy, months of adolescent bonding, and their dates in high school.

As graduation approached, Maddy grew tired of his grandstanding, and their teenage infatuation ended by default when Maddy left for the University of Michigan. Kit went on to MIT. She'd seen little of him during their college years, though he hounded her during summer vacations until she made it clear to him that she had outgrown his game.

Even after her rejection, Kit occasionally pursued her, and he was difficult to ignore. Kit had remained close to Mason, and the two reveled in their manly pursuits: hunting and sporting events, mainly. When Mason passed on, Robert seemed to step in, becoming the object of Kit's sentimentality.

Robert's phone comments indicated why Robert had chosen to confide in Kit: he was not only a family friend, but also an excellent mathematician and an electronics whiz, operating a highly successful computer programming company in Chicago, handling large corporate projects and government work.

As to Kit's stated intentions to complete Robert's work? Maddy remained undecided about that. Robert's outlandish claims had caused his colleagues occasional embarrassment. And now there were too many unanswered questions about his death—particularly about his murderer. Jace Kelton was a puzzle. He didn't act like a blood-thirsty killer.

Maddy had called her Seattle attorney, Sarah Eisenstern, about the incident at the precinct. Sarah had assured her that she would question Orville and quantify potential claims Maddy could make against the Vancouver police and Kelton himself.

Maddy adjusted the pillow under her neck, trying to relax. She imagined herself back home with her animals—Einstein, Edison, Madame Curie, and the little rads. Hopefully, Mrs. Dubin, an elderly innkeeper, was taking good care of her pets in Christine's absence.

Maddy took a deep breath and pictured a sunrise over her back porch, the animals waiting for their breakfast. She dropped into a restless slumber. Several minutes passed before she became aware of a voice that invaded her rest.

"Ms. Marro," someone said softly. "Would you like a cocktail?"

"No, thank you," she said with her eyes closed.

Why would a flight attendant disturb her nap? "How about some champagne?"

Her brows furrowed. "No. I'm fine, thanks."

The leather seat next to hers creaked as someone sat down. She opened her eyes, shocked to find the man named Jace Kelton seated to her right holding two full champagne glasses.

"My God!" The champagne spilled as she pushed him away. "Are you crazy?"

"Don't be angry." Jace's pale blue eyes pleaded as he set the dripping glasses on the armrest. "I realize this is a surprise . . ."

"A surprise? Goddamn you." Maddy couldn't believe the audacity. She glanced down the aisle. "Where's the attendant?"

"I convinced him to give us a couple of minutes." He nodded to the drinks. "This is a peace offering."

"Like hell." Maddy unbuckled her seat belt and tried to rise, but Jace grabbed her wrist, forcing her to sit. She struggled to pull free. "Stop it."

A balding man in the seat ahead of hers had turned, glancing over his shoulder. "Is something wrong?"

"Yes," Maddy said.

"No," Jace replied, still holding her arm. "Look. I spent thirteen hundred dollars on this first-class ticket—the least you can do is listen. I swear to God I won't hurt you."

"Hurt me? You've already done that." Her anger over Robert's senseless death had boiled over. "Just leave me alone," she snapped, and because Jace refused to let go, she instinctively swung her free hand, landing a resounding slap on his cheek.

Jace was stunned. "Holy shit, lady."

The balding man had turned again. "Shall I call the steward?"

"Yes," Maddy said. "I want this asshole out of here."

"Asshole?" Jace glared at her as he backed into the aisle. "All right. Fine. I guess you don't care what your uncle said to me before he died. I suppose you can live without that." Jace turned, moved forward, and sat down in the second row.

"Can I be of help?" the balding man asked over the seats.

"No. Thank you." Maddy shook off the overture. "Please, don't bother." Maddy caught her breath and pondered Jace's comment. It hadn't occurred to her that Robert might have said something.

The steward, a young man with short-cropped red hair appeared with a towel in hand, apparently having noticed the commotion, but Maddy dismissed the incident as trivial and asked him to take the glasses away.

As the flight attendant returned to his bulkhead workstation, Jace's words continued to echo in her mind. Why would a crime suspect risk confronting her in full view of witnesses? He'd actually looked distraught when she smacked him, something she wouldn't expect from an amoral killer. She dabbed the champagne off her slacks with the towel, contemplating what to do.

Jace's presence on the plane challenged her.

Maddy slipped on her shoes and, giving the balding man in 5A a sheepish smile, crept down the aisle. Jace was in seat 2A with no one seated next to him.

She put a hand on the seat back. "Mr. Kelton," she said, as pragmatically as she could, "I apologize. I've been quite upset."

Jace looked over his shoulder. "Of course you have."

She moved a step closer. "Seeing you here thoroughly confused me," she said, unsmiling. "I'd like to sit. Do you mind?"

"Just don't ask me to turn the other cheek."

"I think I've finished venting." Maddy eased into the seat and looked around the cabin for unwanted listeners. She adjusted herself and faced him. "I don't understand why you followed me."

Jace placed his strong-looking hands on the thighs of his khaki pants. "I . . ." he managed a cautious smile, "among other things, I hoped you wouldn't press charges."

Maddy stiffened. "Don't get your hopes up. I notified my lawyer about what happened. There's nothing friendly about this conversation."

Jace doused the grin. "All right." He looked into her eyes, as if reassessing his strategy. "I regret all of this, of course . . . what you must be going through. But I was caught in the middle. I just wanted to talk to your uncle. Cory, my friend whom you met at the precinct, was fascinated by his research."

"The black officer?"

"Yes. He's been studying Robert's work. I followed Robert to Vancouver, spoke to him on the phone in the morning. We set up the meeting, but then I found him—"

"Please, no details. I don't think I can handle it."

"It's difficult to know what to say." Jace kept his eyes riveted on hers. "Forgive me."

She was impressed how controlled he appeared. His sincerity floored her. She kept telling herself to dislike him. "I suppose I should apologize too, for hitting you. But you can see why. I was upset—"

"Of course. And the last thing I want to do is cause you further discomfort. I'm genuinely sorry." He absentmindedly touched her wrist.

She pulled her hand away. As if embarrassed, he lowered his eyes. She noticed the straight, almost noble cut of his nose, his strong jaw line, the width of his shoulders, and his well-muscled neck. He was a handsome man, in a rugged sort of way, with steel-blue eyes that burned with determination. And though she chastised herself for allowing details about him to affect her, she continued to study him. His hands rubbed together in contemplation, and she was shocked to notice what appeared to be rope burns between the thumb and forefinger of each one.

"What's that?" She pointed.

He opened his palms. "Oh, I was involved in a rescue on an oil rig. Chewed me up a little."

"An oil rig? You're in the petroleum business?" She tried not to frown.

"Sometimes."

"I see," she said, disguising her disappointment. "Why aren't you at work?"

"I'm a consultant. I've put work off until these problems are resolved."

Had Kelton been commissioned by oil people? She remembered the cigar-smoking oil men her father used to bring around the house. She wanted to get on with the questions and get out. "Back there"—she motioned to her own seat—"you mentioned that Robert said something?"

"He did. Not a lot. I tried to remember what I could."

"Well?"

"The first thing he said was . . . 'NASA.'"

Odd, those words from her uncle's past, not at all what she might have expected. It had been years since Robert's public claims about conspiracies within the space agency. She had found his press coverage embarrassing. "What else?"

"Then, he said 'the stone.' Does that mean anything to you?"

She shook her head.

"And he mentioned your name. He said 'tell Maddy.'"

She visualized the photo of herself sitting on Robert's lap by the Christmas tree. Though she tried to suppress it, a sob rose from somewhere deep inside. She cupped a hand up over her mouth. "He mentioned me?"

"Yes," he said, gently. "'NASA,' 'the stone,' and your name. I've replayed it in my mind. He did say the word 'ease,' or something like it, just before he moaned for the last time. He was having . . . difficulty."

She fought the tears. Jace handed her a cocktail napkin, and she dabbed her face. Whether she liked it or not, Robert had emotionally burdened her with his dying words. She tried to regain her composure as Jace waited silently.

The 747's engines changed pitch as the plane reached cruising altitude. The aroma of dinner wafted forward from the amidships bulkhead, and the flight attendant worked his way up the aisle with trays in hand. Jace craned his neck, and seeing service was underway, said, "Would you sit here while we eat? There's so much I'd like to ask."

Maddy debated. She could almost imagine the odor of petroleum on Jace's clothes. If she stayed, she'd be pinned into the seat by the fold-down dinner tray. Before she could find the words to excuse herself, the steward had arrived and placed a filet in front of Jace. The steward smiled. "Your special vegetarian order here, Ms. Marro?" he asked.

She nodded and the steward poured them each a glass of red wine, giving them a grin. Then he disappeared toward the rear of the plane.

Jace took a sip of the cabernet. He turned toward her, his voice dropping to a whisper. "When Robert said 'NASA,' it meant a lot to me. My father worked for the space agency until he was murdered. It happened over twenty years ago, not unlike Robert . . . on the street. They never found the killer." Jace stopped, reluctant to say more, as if he were holding back.

Amazed by the grisly coincidence, Maddy asked him to elaborate. As they began to eat, Jace told his tale: a detailed account of how Arthur Kelton died on a lonely Alabama back road; how, after the jeep had overturned in a storm, the driver had disappeared, and how Arthur had been killed with a handgun.

Jace explained his frustrations over how he'd made no headway with local authorities and how NASA had dismissed the incident but never squelched the rumor that Kelton had died in a secrets-for-money deal gone bad. Jace described how, two years after college graduation, Cory Jackson had agreed to help him in his search. Through Randal Dixon's intelligence resources, they located a man who matched the description of the missing driver. Jace had spent five years, changing his profession, manipulating himself into a position to get to an oil rig in the gulf. Maddy was touched by Jace's expression as he spoke. His eyes burned with deep passion as he described his years of humiliation and sacrifice and his now renewed determination to catch his father's killer.

"Cory felt that, based on Robert's comments to the press, he knew of a cover-up—what Cory describes as a misinformation campaign, reflected by secret air force documents. Does the name 'Phobia File' mean anything to you?"

"Not a thing." Maddy was puzzled. She had viewed Robert as an eccentric astronomer, astrologer, and visionary, not an infiltrator. "I hadn't seen Robert in some time."

Jace seemed to interpret her pensiveness as grief. "I'm very sorry. Forgive me for putting you through this."

Maddy watched the kindness surface behind the self-assurance in his eyes. She found herself empathizing with him and admiring him. Jace seemed to fill the airline cabin with his presence, as if sheer willpower could occupy space. Every word, every action carried with it a sense of purpose.

"The real reason I came to see you . . ." He paused. "Although it sounds amazing, I believe my father's killer and Robert's are one and the same. I saw his face, and from the description—"

"Are you sure?"

"I'm not sure of anything right now." Jace's tension seemed to ease as he leaned forward. "Except that you and I have a lot of reasons to talk."

In that moment, she sensed a strange synergy. Yet in light of his story, she also felt a foreboding, the unpleasant notion that something beyond her control had propelled this man into her life.

The flight attendant interrupted. He poured coffee, chatting with both of them, visibly amused that the two prior combatants were getting along. As the small talk faded and the attendant left, Maddy weighed the connectivity: Jace's mysteries from the past were only a portion of a riddle in which Robert had played a part. And now, because she had Robert's grid, she had inherited the enigma and whatever it might bring.

"Robert," she said wistfully, looking out at the full moon that hung over high clouds, "with his wild dreams—somehow he created all this."

Jace's questioning expression caused her to explain further: how she'd been stalked by strangers, the mysterious death of the Asian man, and the tracks around her home.

"I'm sure it all happened because of Robert . . . that paper he sent."

"Paper?"

"A bunch of lines and numbers, at least the half in my possession. Robert kept the other half. He said he was in danger because of it."

Jace's eyes flooded with intensity. "You think he had it on him?"

"He might have . . ."

"The man who killed Robert pulled an envelope from his body."

Maddy was stunned. "Orville didn't mention that on the phone."

"He should have."

"All he said was that Robert had been robbed."

"And he had. His wallet was missing."

"But an *envelope* . . . that's the first I'd heard."

"I suppose the inspector assumed the motive was robbery." Jace's eyes narrowed. "You think that paper was what he wanted?"

"Yes," Maddy said, visualizing the geometric lines. "He'll be surprised to find half of it missing."

Jace's next words summarized her own concerns. "That means the killer will be looking for you."

22

*Aerospace Research Center
Langley, Virginia*

CORY ROSE TO HIS FEET and tossed the magazine he'd been browsing through onto the table as Ms. Benning emerged from the office. The perfectly groomed forty-year-old secretary walked across the carpet past the receptionist, crossing her arms as she chattered in a peevish staccato, "Major, I'm afraid Mr. Higgins is somewhat confused by your appearance here this morning. He doesn't remember having an appointment with you."

"He wouldn't. I came unannounced."

Benning pursed her lips. "Well he's quite preoccupied—"

"My apologies for the short notice." Cory fingered the brim of his cap. "But this is very important."

Benning gave the receptionist a nervous glance. "Perhaps we could find an opening for you this afternoon."

Cory tucked his cap under his left arm, pulled a pen from his breast pocket, and rummaged for a business card. "Here." He wrote a single word on the back of the card and handed it to her. "Give that to Mr. Higgins, and tell him I've got ten minutes before I have to get back to the airfield."

Ms. Benning stared at the word. "Is this supposed to—"

"Just give it to him."

Looking bewildered, Benning retreated to the office.

Cory saw no reason to be seated since he'd either be joining Higgins or leaving, so he paced around the reception area, gazing at the color photographs on the wall. The large wood-framed pictures showed a series of historic events:

a shot of pad 39A at the Kennedy Space Center with a space shuttle in launch position, a shot of the Apollo 11 astronauts in the ocean during recovery of their capsule, an in-flight picture of the shuttle Columbia deploying a communications satellite. Unable to suppress an inner pride, Cory read the plaque of John F. Kennedy's words to Congress: "this nation should commit itself to achieving the goal, before this decade is out, of landing a man on the moon . . ." He was interrupted when the door opened and a chunky, balding man in shortsleeves emerged from the rear office. Cory advanced a few steps but the man rejected the handshake with a skeptical look.

"I'm Higgins," he said, squinting through heavy black glasses, "let me walk you to your car."

This was the brush-off Cory had feared. "Please give me a few minutes."

"Follow me." Higgins smiled at the receptionist as he opened the outer office door. "Back in a moment, Marsha."

They were out in the hall headed for the elevator, with Higgins walking briskly and Cory keeping pace. "Look, Higgins, I—"

"One moment, Major, if you don't mind." Higgins had passed the elevators and pushed through the backstairs exit door. His shoes echoed in the concrete stairwell as he vaulted down the two flights, never looking back. He pushed on the silver bar and then burst through the metal fire door into the sunshine.

Cory was on his heels as they walked across the lawn toward the eight-foot fence that bordered the freeway. Higgins reached the chain link first, and amid the rushing sound of the traffic below he spun around, gripping the wire with a pudgy hand.

"What the hell are you after?" Higgins asked angrily. Cory could barely hear him over the hum of the traffic.

"I'm a special liaison to NASA—"

"I know *who* the fuck you are. Your name's on the security ledger. I was aware of you years ago." Higgins pulled Cory's card out of his pocket. "I want to know why you're bothering me with this." He pointed to the scribble.

"So the term 'phobia' means something to you."

"Why do you think I'm talking to you out here?" Higgins pointed to the freeway. "Away from audio surveillance."

"The '93 *Orbiter* mission," Cory said, cupping his hand by his mouth. "You were a shift boss on the monitoring deck."

"So I was."

"And you made an inquiry into the COMSAT relay tables."

"That was a mistake. As far as I'm concerned, it never happened." Higgins squirmed and made a move to return to his office.

"Just a minute." Cory grabbed his elbow. "I can no longer assume that my family is safe when I'm away, do you understand? I'm in danger, and I want to know why."

Higgins angrily retrieved his arm. "You keep shoving the word 'phobia' at the wrong people, and you won't just be in danger—you'll be dead."

"Why? Is NASA covering up the Mars missions?"

Higgins's gray eyes squinted curiously behind his black-framed glasses. "It's not NASA, Major. Don't you know that?"

"What? Who then? The air force?"

Higgins shook his head. "You don't have a clue, do you? It's much bigger than that. The code name 'Phobia' was a reactive measure by the joint chiefs to comply with our foreign policy."

"Foreign? So the Russians are in on it. Marro was right."

"From what I read, Marro is dead." Higgins cocked his head as if awed by Cory's naiveté. "Let it go. You're in no position to do anything."

"I can't let it go. It involves others. What do you know about the 1993 *Orbiter* mission? Do you remember Arthur Kelton? He was killed in '93. How about his boss, Carl Davenport?"

Higgins body went rigid. "This interview is over." He turned and began walking back.

"So Davenport knew something?" Cory followed.

"Good-bye, Major."

"My life may depend on it." Cory hustled along. "Is the Phobia File tied to the Russian mission in 1988? The Martian moon, Phobos?"

Higgins whirled, red faced. "Get in your car and leave. I can't help you."

Cory pressed on. "Phobia. Why the name?"

Higgins squared his shoulders and faced him. "The name's appropriate, Major. 'Phobia' as in 'fear.' He pointed at the sky. "Personally, I *fear* the future. And unless you stop digging, you may not have one."

23

Providence, Rhode Island

THE THIRD-FLOOR DEN OF ROBERT'S University Avenue home contained hundreds of books. The west wall was stacked with volumes of architectural digests, blueprints and photos of the mammoth architecture of ancient civilizations, including the pyramids, the Mayan ruins, Greek temples, and Buddhist shrines.

After shuffling through the shelves, Maddy and Jace had located what appeared to be two pertinent items: a loose-leaf compilation of theses, articles, and art examining the potential relationships between new and old-world architecture along with a scrapbook six inches thick, filled with press clippings.

Maddy leafed through the press book while Jace sat at a small desk and paged through a series of drawings that were meant to correlate the geometric parity between Egyptian and Mayan pyramids.

"Why was Robert obsessed with the connection between Egypt and the Mayans?"

"He spoke of the prehistory of the human race," Maddy said as she turned the album's pages, "the theory that all cultures were influenced by a universal technology long before recorded time. Ever since I was a little girl, he talked about the cosmic connection between all peoples. He often talked about the newspaper coverage of alleged structures on Mars that resembled monuments; of course, they were only truly covered in the underground press, but based on some of those claims, Robert beat his drum, attempting to establish proof that there might be an extraterrestrial connection. He became obsessed, writing letters to NASA, demanding they release all their Mars photographs."

She continued to study the articles as Jace captured her in a mental photograph of his own.

Dressed in a peach-colored blouse and blue jeans, she sat barefoot on the tan leather couch, her shiny auburn hair pulled back in two barrettes, her face framed by a sliver of sunlight that shone through the east window.

He was struck by the smoothness of the skin around her neck, her hands, and her feet. She was a remarkable woman—mentally tough and tawny, yet delicate at the same time.

Jace enjoyed the moment. He relished the peace in the privacy of her uncle's home, happy that they'd somehow bonded on the plane.

During the flight, Maddy had come to accept him. In fact, once he told his story, she even expressed the belief that Cory's problems and Jace's quest for answers might well align with her own. By the time they landed in New York, Maddy had asked Jace to join her in Providence. She had gone ahead with Robert's casket by train. After an overnight layover in Manhattan, Jace had flown to Rhode Island and met her at the house.

Seeing her like this in the serenity of the den, gave him a different sense of her essence, a coziness he hadn't expected. It was the lull before the storm . . . Maddy's friend Kit Lassiter was due to arrive anytime, and soon she would be surrounded by people at the wake this afternoon.

"Look how many articles there are," she said, sitting cross-legged. "He kept track of Mars for two decades."

Jace left the desk and joined her, looking over her shoulder. "Anything important?" The leather-bound book was filled with scores of newspaper clippings from the *New York Times,* the *Washington Post,* the *San Francisco Examiner,* and other major papers.

"I'd have to study these more carefully." She turned the pages. Many of the yellowed articles were highlighted in grease pencil, where Robert had noted comments by NASA officials.

Suddenly, Maddy paused and pointed to a small rectangular excerpt from the *Birmingham Herald.* "My God, look."

Jace followed her finger to the headline: NASA EXECUTIVE KILLED NEAR HUNTSVILLE.

"It's your father, Jace. Here it is in black and white. Robert noted it, all those years ago."

Without a word, Jace took a seat next to her. Maddy handed him the album. He read the small article, dated August 26, 1993, that briefly described the discovery of a body on a lonely stretch of Highway 79, footprints in the mud and an untraceable splotch of blood, the only clues. He read on. A NASA official at Huntsville verified that Arthur Kelton had been expected for a meeting the morning he was killed. The article ended with a mention of the local sheriff's office turning the case over to federal authorities.

A familiar hollow longing settled in his gut. "I wish Robert was alive to tell me what he knew."

"So do I."

For the first time, Maddy touched him, laying her hand on his. She smiled warmly, her amber eyes glowing. "There's a reason we came together like this; it's to help each other."

Jace wanted to pledge his loyalty to her—his help. He fumbled for the right words, cursing himself for not having them ready. I'll give you anything you need, he thought, immediately hating the banality of it. He was trying to find the phrasing when a buzz from the stairwell drew her attention and broke the spell.

"It's probably Kit," Maddy said. "Would you mind waiting while I let him in?"

Yes, I mind. I'd rather talk to you. "Of course not."

She slipped into her loafers. "I need to brief Kit alone for a few minutes."

Did he know you, the way I want to? "Take all the time you need," Jace said.

Maddy patted him on the shoulder and left.

Jace stared at the photo album, wondering how much Robert knew about his father. Had they ever spoken? Why was Robert interested in Arthur's untimely death? There must have been a reason.

He decided to call Cory tonight to solidify his plans, which at this point were totally unresolved.

The creaking of the old stairs sounded as Maddy descended the stairwell, followed by the clack of her leather soles on the hardwood as she reached the first-floor landing.

He heard her fuss with the front door latch.

As the stained-glass door swung open, revealing Kit Lassiter's buoyant smile, Maddy was surprised to see how good he looked. He had dropped ten to fifteen pounds, wore a black leather blazer that offset his prematurely gray hair, and, as usual, his dark eyes penetrated her with voracious intensity.

"Maddy! You look fantastic." Kit stepped across the threshold and caught her in a bear hug.

"Hello, Kit." She tried to pull away.

"It's been far too long." He pressed her close enough to feel her breasts against his body, but she succeeded in escaping.

"You're sure wired for a guy who's attending a funeral."

Kit feigned remorse as he closed the door. "Oh. I'm sorry. I was just happy to see you."

"Well, I'm . . . happy to see you." Maddy wasn't sure for how long, but then again it was somewhat gratifying to see his familiar face. "Come upstairs. There's someone I want you to meet."

"One of the Brown professors?"

"No." Maddy edged toward the banister. "I've made a new friend."

"Christ, you just arrived. Who is it, the gardener?"

She started up the stairs. "Just follow me."

"Lead the way." Kit was right behind her. "Man, you've really stayed in shape."

Sensing his eyes on her backside and expecting to feel his hands there any moment, she launched into conversation. "I'm anxious to have you tell me about Robert's work."

"If you promise to do the same."

"Of course, whatever I can." They had reached the second-floor landing, and she turned to confront him. "I want to understand how and why you're involved." She climbed again.

"The 'how' is easy. Robert asked me to come along. The 'why' is something I hope to discuss with you. There's an incredible amount of money at stake, if Robert was right."

She stopped. "Right about what?"

"What the S-7 were after."

Maddy was completely in the dark. "The S-7?"

Kit stared at her. "Jesus Christ. He did tell you, didn't he?"

"Tell me what?"

Kit looked nervously up to the third floor. "Where's this new friend of yours?"

"He's in the den."

"Alone with Robert's papers?"

"Yes, why not?"

Kit clutched the banister as if to lock himself to the rail. "I want to know who he is."

"Relax, Kit. He just wants to help." Kit's skeptical grimace prompted her. "He was there when Robert died."

"A witness?"

"You might say. Robert died in his arms."

"Shit. Not the Kelton guy."

Maddy shushed him. "He's innocent. They released him."

"And what do you know about him?"

"Quiet. He'll hear."

"What the fuck do I care. I asked if you know him."

"I've started to . . ."

"Christ, Maddy, this is a family thing. You can't bring a complete stranger—"

The voice at the top of the stairs interrupted him.

"We won't be strangers once we're introduced." Jace leaned on the landing rail.

Kit squinted up at him. "Well. You're about the last person I expected to see. You've got a lot of balls, friend."

"Thanks, but who's counting?"

Determined to seize control, Maddy climbed the rest of the stairs gesturing for Kit to follow. "Jace . . . this is Kit Lassiter. Kit . . . this is Jace . . . strangers no more."

Kit hadn't budged.

Maddy retreated to fetch him, and Kit reluctantly followed up the stairs. Jace met them at the top on the third-floor landing, and Maddy watched their icy handshake. Maddy moved quickly to separate them, leading them both into Robert's den, where Kit slumped into the leather couch while Jace distanced himself, sitting on the windowsill. Maddy leaned against the desk situated between them. Since neither man spoke up, she initiated the conversation, explaining Jace's involvement—through Robert's NASA connection and Jace's father's death.

She showed Kit the clipping in Robert's scrapbook as justification, and Kit seemed mildly interested at the coincidence.

Maddy reinforced her intentions to involve Jace in the investigation because of Jace's obvious interest in Robert's final words, which were "NASA," "the stone," and "ease," in that order.

While Maddy talked, Jace stared at Kit's reflection in the window and Kit glared back at him without uttering a sound. To break the ice, Maddy chose the same question she'd asked on the stairs.

"Kit. Tell me . . . What exactly is the S-7?"

Kit bit his lip without reply.

"Kit, let me make something clear to you." She gestured at Jace. "He's here because I want him here. You spoke of family, and you were absolutely right. Robert was my uncle. I am the last remaining member of the family, and I will decide what becomes of Robert's research. Now if you want to play in the game, I suggest you start cooperating."

"Well, first of all," Kit pointed spitefully at Jace, "he's wrong—"

Maddy raised her voice. "Let's begin with my question, do you mind? What is the S-7?"

Kit answered reluctantly. "A group of researchers. The 'S' stood for Scalbania, an industrialist who came up with the idea."

"The idea?"

"Of scientists secretly trying to find a new energy source to replace fossil fuels. After Scalbania died, your father, Mason, funded the effort."

Maddy tried not to appear rattled. "My father? To replace fossil—"

"Yes. Your family, remember?"

Her father, a dyed-in-the-wool petroleum advocate, involved in an enterprise she would have applauded? Why hadn't she been told?

Kit seemed revitalized by her stunned expression. "If you want to call the shots, you've got a lot to learn," he said triumphantly. "Your parents never told you."

Maddy was dumbfounded. "Why the hell wouldn't they?"

"Robert told me that Mason's dying wish to your mother was that an important document called the Peruvian Prize be buried with him so you'd never find it."

"But why?" Maddy's assumptions about her parents began to unravel, and Father Navarro's phone call gained incredible importance. "My God. Do you realize someone vandalized my father's remains last week?"

"Of course. That's why Robert panicked. Someone else knew about this prize."

Maddy was stung by the realization that her Uncle Robert had revealed everything to her arrogant ex-boyfriend. She suddenly felt orphaned. "My mother never said a word," she mumbled, thinking back on the two years after her father had passed away.

"But she did tell Robert," Kit continued. "On her deathbed. She gave him a copy of that Peruvian document. It changed his ambitions." The leather couch creaked under Kit's weight as he reached forward and paged through the photo album on the coffee table. "Robert had been fascinated with Mars as a potential seat of an ancient civilization. But after Tenille died, his interests became more earthbound and he began to travel, searching for archeological clues."

"You're saying that after my parents died, Robert chased around the world, and that he found some 'stone'—a mythical energy source?"

"Or the instructions to find one. Based on what the Peruvian Prize revealed, he took a sabbatical from Brown University. When he felt he had gathered enough clues, he called me and asked me to get involved."

"Was this 'Peruvian Prize' the map Robert sent to me?"

"No." Kit seemed to revel in her confusion. "From what Robert told me, the Peruvian Prize was a stone rubbing, a series of pictoglyphs. What he sent to you was a grid Robert made on his own, after years of calculations."

Maddy's world had turned upside down. Kit had bested her. "Then why did Robert even call me?"

"Because when he finally conjured up the grid, Maddy, he realized he needed support. Mine and yours. To be honest, he felt guilty about excluding you."

"How considerate."

Kit seemed fully in control. He crossed his legs and directed his next volley at Jace. "And as far as your belief that one of Robert's last words was 'NASA' . . ." Kit chuckled. "You're dead wrong. It's more likely that he was hinting at his summer home in 'Nassau,' in the Bahamas."

Maddy glanced at Jace, whose face had flooded with doubt.

"N a s s a u?" Jace asked, looking as if he'd been punched. "He had—"

"A condominium in *Nassau*." Kit smiled nonchalantly. "He had acquired it just this year, because he was interested in the Bahamian Islands as part of his research."

24

Santa Fe, New Mexico

MS. WELLS, THE NURSING HOME administrator, showed a tan, thin woman in braids into the lime-colored office.

Cory turned from the window as the braided woman approached, and she cautiously offering a handshake. "Hello. I'm Heidi Plumber."

"Thanks for seeing me." Cory took her hand, nodding to the administrator. "Could you give us a few minutes, Ms. Wells?" To which Heidi nodded her permission.

"Okay. You take your time, Heidi," Ms. Wells said, retreating through the door. "If this doesn't feel right, don't do it." Wells, ruddy and rosy-cheeked in her plum-colored suit, had been downright nasty when Cory arrived at the Morning Star Retirement Home. Cory's request to speak with Carl Davenport would have to be sanctioned by his daughter. Wells had studied Cory from head to foot, since "it's quite apparent you're not a member of the family."

The racial slur bothered Cory a lot less than the delay; he would be AWOL in a few hours.

"Why do you want to see my dad?" Heidi rejected Cory's gesture to sit down and hooked her thumbs in her jeans.

Cory tried to be considerate. "First, I'm sorry you're missing your garden show." He noted the soil-stained gloves tucked into her lizard skin belt.

"My assistant is covering for me."

"I won't keep you then. But I just need five minutes with your father."

"Why?" she asked sharply. "He's hardly fit for visitors."

"I wasn't told that until I arrived. I had no idea. I'm sorry about his stroke. Ms. Wells *did* say he can talk."

"Barely. He's paralyzed from the neck down. I hate to put him through it. What's the point?"

"It's very important." Hesitantly, Cory reached for his wallet, feeling like a turtle with its neck stuck out. He handed his identity card to Heidi. "I'm special attachéto NASA, Ms. Plumber. This concerns a matter of security."

"Dad's been retired for years."

"I know. But I'd like to ask him a couple of questions. It concerns something that happened twenty years ago."

Heidi grimaced. "Surely there's someone else."

Cory brought both hands to his chest in a prayerlike position. "But he's the only one who would know."

Heidi walked over to the window and looked out into the hills. "To be honest, I find this disrespectful." She turned. "It seems to me that official business of this nature would demand some notice. An official letter. Something."

"I tried calling yesterday, but I was told there's no phone in room 333."

"At my request."

"A few minutes with him. You could be with me in the room if it makes you feel better."

Heidi appeared fidgety. "I think I better discuss this with June . . . Ms. Wells. Why don't you have a seat."

Cory moved to block her exit. "Please, it's a matter of life and death."

"So is my father's condition. If you'll excuse me." Heidi sidestepped, opened the door just far enough to squeeze through. "Just wait. I'll be back." Then she disappeared.

Cory looked around the room. Two chairs, one couch, a magazine rack. How long would she be gone? He fussed with the magazines and was about to sit down when a nurse came in.

"Major Jackson?"

"Yes."

"Ms. Wells asks that you wait on the back veranda. There's a pleasant view of the valley."

"Would you tell Ms. Wells—"

"Please." She gestured to the hall. "Mrs. Plumber is checking on her father."

"Oh. All right." With his hopes renewed and with hat in hand, Cory followed the nurse past several patient rooms and through a set of swinging doors onto the veranda. The nurse gestured to some wicker chairs by the rail, where a gray-haired woman sat knitting. Two elderly men played checkers in the shade of the porch.

The nurse disappeared. Cory walked over and sat on the rail. He nodded pleasantly to the old folks and stared off past the green lawn to the beige desert sands beyond. The Morning Star Retirement Home was located on a ridge that overlooked an expanse of rolling hills.

Cory's attention was captured by a speck in the bright-blue sky. Beyond the greenbelt above the sage and cactus, a prairie hawk hovered, flapping its wings. The bird apparently stalked some unsuspecting prey.

Suddenly, the hawk folded its wings and collapsed its body into a wedge, dropping from the sky like a rock. Cory strained to see, but it disappeared into a hollow.

After a few seconds, it emerged with what appeared to be a small rattle-snake in its talons.

Cory looked over his shoulder. No sign of Ms. Wells. He checked his watch. He'd wait another ten minutes.

Hopping off the rail, he moved to a white wicker chair, nodding hello to the kindly looking white-haired woman busy with her knitting needles. She seemed preoccupied, and he turned back toward the prairie hawk as it flew toward the horizon with the snake writhing beneath.

Cory remembered reading that certain desert hawks hunted snakes for sport. They didn't kill them for food. They killed snakes as if to get rid of them. No one knew exactly why.

"Major Jackson . . ."

He turned. "Yes."

The nurse reappeared, smiling apologetically. "I'm afraid Ms. Wells feels Mr. Davenport should not be disturbed." She began to walk away.

Cory rose to his feet. "Can I speak with Mrs. Plumber again?"

"No. She's gone."

He stepped forward. "Then I'd like to see Ms. Wells."

The nurse blocked his path. "I'm afraid that's impossible. She asked that you leave. You can take the path to the front parking lot. Ms. Wells prefers you not reenter the building."

"I see," Cory said, with his hat in hand. "So I've received a final shovelful of her hospitality, is that it?"

The nurse led Cory to the stairs. "I'm sorry, sir," she said sympathetically as Cory began to descend.

Cory looked over his shoulder. "It's not your fault."

He stepped out onto the lawn. Above, on the porch, the kindly old woman with the knitting needles waved. "Good-bye, good-bye," she said. "Visiting hours are from nine to five Monday through Friday, ten to four on Saturday . . ."

Her voice trailed off as Cory donned his hat and headed down the cement walkway toward the parking lot. In the shadow of the retirement home, he gazed up at the third floor.

Davenport was up there somewhere . . . room 333.

Cory passed a metal screen door that led to the basement. He was struck by the sound of several washers and dryers rumbling; a strong, moist smell of laundry powder emanated from the cavernous room.

He stopped and stared into the darkness.

In the dim light, he saw a lone tall African American man in a white smock tending the wash loads. The man strolled back and forth between a large laundry bin and the machines, rolling a canvas laundry cart filled with sheets and towels.

A tall black man . . . alone, dressed in a white smock

25

Providence

KIT SAT ON THE LEATHER couch chuckling to himself. The arch of his neck reminded Jace of a fighting cock, a banty rooster who needed his feathers clipped.

Kit seemed reassured by Maddy and Jace's reactions to his revelations: they were both speechless when he finished. In the silence, Kit looked from one to the other and finally relented. "Look. I'm sorry." He suppressed another laugh as he gazed at Maddy. "But if Kelton joined you on this trip because he thought Robert's last words referred to NASA as opposed to 'Nassau,' it's an incredibly stupid mistake."

Maddy refused to reply as she slowly paced the floor.

"And don't pout, Maddy. I can't help it if your parents excluded you from the family secret."

Maddy seemed to gather herself. "Ultimately, that secret remains my business."

"I suppose. Although Robert made it mine as well. When we met in Chicago, he insisted that he wanted me to have a major interest in the coming expedition."

"When he called, he did mention you."

"So it's clear I have reason to pursue this. But I don't see why Jace should be involved."

Jace didn't react. Still off balance from the "NASA" mix-up, he leaned back on the windowsill as Maddy stopped pacing to face Kit.

"Jace's father and Robert had common interests."

"On the basis of one newspaper clipping?" Kit's shrugged shoulders conveyed his skepticism, and Maddy shot Jace a pleading glance as Kit continued. "Robert's work was intensely focused on issues beyond NASA as of last year. He had planned to explain everything at a meeting between you—me—and one other colleague." He nodded in Jace's direction. "No one else."

Maddy ignored the slam. "This other colleague, any idea who?"

"One of the S-7, I would guess."

"So Robert had approached them."

"Not as a group. He sought out two different individuals on two separate occasions. Robert made it clear that he needed expertise beyond his own— thermodynamics, electromagnetism, and quantum physics. An S-7 member named Hector Walsh had those credentials. But I guess Robert chose not to reveal much to Walsh, because he was turned off by the guy's attitude. So Robert found someone else he could trust among the S-7 group."

"But you don't really know."

"Like I said, Robert was careful. Maybe he was smart, considering that Walsh is dead."

"How?"

"An explosion in his Toronto laboratory. Took out the entire building."

"What about the others?" Maddy asked. "Where are they?"

"Others?"

"The S-7?"

"I'm not sure. Robert avoided them. He felt they might have conflicting interests. Many of them were foreigners."

"Can't you remember names?"

"Besides your father, Scalbania, and Walsh . . . I remember a Swiss woman named Hoffman . . . Robert felt good about her. There was a Chinese guy whose name I don't remember, and a Swedish scientist, who had a guttural-sounding name. Oh, Org, or Urg."

The comment caught Jace's interest. He pushed off the windowsill. "What did you say?"

"Urg. U R G, I think."

"That's it," Jace said slowly, stepping toward the coffee table. "Robert said 'Nassau,' 'the stone,' 'ease,' and then he *moaned* something unintelligible. I think he was actually saying the name of that scientist. Urg. I'm sure of it."

Maddy turned. "And my name. He was asking you to tell *me*, wasn't he?"

Jace nodded.

Her eyes burned with renewed intensity. "Perhaps he was saying that the energy source was a jewel, located in Nassau . . . and that Urg was someone he trusted."

"What makes you think it's a jewel?" Kit asked.

"Robert's comments on the phone. He said he had discovered something 'more precious than all the gems ever mined.'"

"I don't think so." The couch creaked as Kit rose to his feet. He walked over to Robert's desk and toyed with a letter opener. "I think it's bigger than that."

"Oil?" Maddy dreaded the possibility.

"No. Something that would make oil and electricity obsolete."

"But he never specified," Maddy added. She looked up at Robert's book-case. She seemed to be studying the volumes of books. "Hundreds of thousands of cubic yards of pollution lofted into the atmosphere from gasoline and oil consumption. Huge quantities of toxic waste emptying into rivers, the deso-lation of oil spills at sea," she added wistfully. "What if Robert's vision could help turn the tide? Since petroleum fuels will likely dry up in 2043, alternative energy sources are rapidly becoming the most important issue of the day. Rob-ert's ideas might be the answer." She turned to Jace with a mischievous twinkle in her eye. "Besides, Robert said 'tell Maddy.' He didn't say 'tell Kit' with his dying breath." She seemed suddenly empowered and spun around. "Since Rob-ert wanted us to work together, you will help me, won't you?"

"Help *you*?" Kit asked. "I . . . of course."

"And what about you?" She stepped over to Jace.

On first impulse Jace wanted to agree, but he was reminded of the "Nas-sau" mix-up and angered by Kit's overbearing attitude. His thoughts had already drifted to getting back on the murderer's trail. He looked her straight in the eyes. "I think it's time I move along. You've got Kit's help."

"I need you as well. I'm going to Nassau to Robert's apartment. There must be a reason he wanted me to. But at this point, I need you to go back."

"Back?" Kit asked.

"The grid. The map. Whatever it is." Maddy continued to stare at Jace. "What's hidden in my birdhouse must be just as important as what Robert found in Nassau."

At that, Kit jumped in. "Well, then maybe I better go get it."

"No," she said calmly over her shoulder. "You're coming with me." She appeared suspicious that Kit might take possession of the map himself.

"It's so nice to be wanted," Kit said, smiling.

"Will you help me, Jace?" Maddy's eyes softened.

Jace intended to help, but another glance at Kit's smirk made him feel detached. "I've got some thinking to do."

The doubt on Maddy's face was replaced by determination. She turned. "Kit, use the kitchen phone to make our airlines reservations, would you please? A flight tonight after the wake. After five preferably."

Kit pulled a cell phone from his pocket. "I can do it right here."

"I prefer you do it downstairs."

Kit seemed reluctant to leave, but Maddy ushered him to the door. "I'll finish and be down in a minute." After fumbling with the door handle, Kit left.

Maddy closed the door behind and turned, her eyes aglow with resolve.

Feeling like a naked man about to be examined in a hospital smock, Jace watched as Maddy walked toward him.

She stepped closer than she ever had before and placed a hand on his chest. "I meant what I said before Kit arrived. There's no doubt in my mind that we were meant to help each other. My survival may depend on it. It appears Cory's does. I think we're in a race of hours, not days."

Her face relaxed and her voice fell into a soothing whisper. "I don't want Robert's death to be meaningless. Do this one thing for me." Jace felt the back of his neck redden as she touched his shirt collar. "I need your strength. With Christine gone to Hawaii, there's no one else I trust. Please. Get the grid from my birdhouse and then decide. Bring it to me in the Bahamas or send it. But help me."

26

Santa Fe, New Mexico

CORY ARRIVED AT THE THIRD floor wearing a white smock over his uniform. With his face obscured by a white hairnet and a surgical mask, he pushed the empty laundry cart through the elevator door and stopped in the center of the hall, checking the room numbers on the opposite wall. Room 333 was to his left.

In the basement next to the bin where a large laundry chute emptied, a gagged hospital attendant named Willis lay on the floor. He wasn't hurt, just had a bump on the head, possibly a slight loss of circulation where his wrists and ankles were bound with strips of bedding.

Cory was sorry he'd had to take such drastic steps, but the way he'd been treated was ridiculous. And now Cory looked pretty ridiculous himself, pushing the cart down the hall, aware of his own breathing through the puffy surgical mask, wondering who would be the first to point a finger to accuse him of being an impostor.

At the far end of the passageway, a nurse clad in white casually glanced in Cory's direction and then returned her gaze to a chart that hung on the wall outside one of the patient's rooms. She seemed preoccupied enough, and after examining the chart, she entered a room and disappeared.

Grateful, Cory hustled along.

The third floor was apparently reserved for patients requiring constant medical supervision. He passed the doorways one by one and smelled as much as saw the occupants' infirmity. In room 328, a TV soap opera droned. In 329, a shriveled woman had fallen asleep listening to a Christian preacher on the radio. In 331, a frizzy-haired man in a wheelchair hunched, staring out a window.

Perhaps because he had been an orphan with no older relatives, Cory had never seen a convalescent center. He was struck by the futility; these poor people all waiting to die.

He was relieved to reach the door that read 333—Davenport's room.

Cory left the cart in the hall and stepped in, gently pushing aside a cream-colored curtain.

A man in navy-blue pajamas in his midseventies lay in bed; his face was contorted with the legacy of a stroke, the right side of his mouth drawn into a paralytic crimp under the cheekbone. His eyes were trained on a shopping channel program on a TV suspended from the far corner ceiling.

Cory leaned back outside, checking the hallway for the nurse. No sign of her.

He ducked back into the room and removed his surgical mask and cap. He approached the bed. "Mr. Davenport," he whispered.

In slow motion, the man's eyes rolled in his direction.

"Don't be concerned, I'm Major Cory Jackson, USAF." Cory knelt by his head.

The man's eyes were moist with age, his gray hair stuck to his forehead. The crooked mouth formed a word, hissing through teeth mismatched by an apparently nerveless jaw. "Willis?"

Perhaps he couldn't hear. "He's on break. You are Carl Davenport aren't you?" Cory was gratified to see recognition in the eyes. "Forgive me. I need to ask about some-thing that happened many years ago on one of your NASA missions."

"NASA," the stiff tongue jammed the word.

"Right, when you were missions director at Pasadena."

Davenport's eyes lit up. "Pasa . . ."

"Exciting time, wasn't it," Cory said, leaning an elbow on the white sheet. "A proud time."

The moisture in Davenport's left eye was squeezed by a pained half-smile.

"I know this may be something you haven't thought about in a while." Cory realized he didn't have time for formality, so he leaned close to Davenport's ear. "My best buddy grew up an orphan. His dad was killed. My friend never knew why." Cory leaned back. Davenport's eyes had blanked in a perplexed expression. His head rotated a few degrees toward Cory. "My friend's name is Jace Kelton. His father was Arthur Kelton, who worked with you."

Davenport's gaze searched the ceiling and then settled on Cory's face. The moisture at the corner of Davenport's left eye had formed into a tear.

"Do you know why Kelton died?"

The tear tracked down the cheekbone and fell onto the sheet.

"Were you in charge that night?"

"Mi . . . shun," Davenport said.

"Yes. Mission Control. Why did Kelton leave?"

"Or . . . der."

"Yours? Your orders?"

"No."

"Someone above you?"

The frequency of Davenport's panting increased. He appeared visibly agitated.

Cory nodded sympathetically. "I know this is hard."

Davenport's eyes darted back and forth. His left hand emerged from beneath the sheet, gripping the mattress. Cory worried about his state of mind, but he was determined to get answers.

"Why did Kelton leave Pasadena that night?"

"Pic . . . tures."

"He had them?"

"Yes." Davenport twitched.

Cory began to fear for the man's welfare. Davenport's face contorted in frustration. "I'm sorry if this bothers you." Cory put a hand on Davenport's shoulder. "But, do you know who killed him?"

"See . . ."

"See? See what? Something on Mars?"

"I . . ."

"Yes, go on . . . you what?"

"Aay." A trickle of saliva appeared as the mouth struggled to continue. Nothing more followed.

Cory felt compelled to help. "See," he said, prompting him. "I" . . . Cory said in awe. "A? Holy shit, you're saying the CIA was involved at Mission Control?"

"No." Davenport wheezed. His fingers clawed the sheet, and his glances flew frantically toward the door. "Now. Wells."

"The administrator?"

"More . . ."

"Oh, God. You're here because they want to watch you, is that it? Wells is an agent."

Davenport exhaled in resignation. His eyes blinked repeatedly. Yes. They were saying. Yes.

Cory understood. He got to his feet. "Shit. I'm sorry man. You're scared to death."

Davenport's eyes continued to blink. Suddenly it became clear—something Dixon must not have known—there were other patients under surveillance here. Could this entire complex be a storage tank for security risks?

Affirmative, Cory thought as he heard the squeal of tires in the parking lot. He left Davenport's side and jumped to the window in time to see a black sedan stop at the front of the building. The woman named Wells ran off the front porch to meet the car. Four men jumped out as she pointed to the front and back entrances. The men split up; two climbed the front stairs . . . two ran toward the rear.

Escape. Cory's only thought.

He leapt back around the bed and put a hand on Davenport's shoulder. "I never saw you man, don't worry. And they sure as hell ain't gonna see me." He replaced the surgical mask and cap and was out the door.

The hallway was quiet. The elderly man with the walker still stared from the entrance of the locker room.

Cory checked the elevator. Lights on the overhead register told him that a car was on its way. He spun and headed in the other direction. As he approached the back stairs, footsteps echoed up the stairwell. They had cut off every exit.

He suddenly knew his only remaining option.

Darting back toward Davenport's room, he passed the door marked LAUNDRY. He opened it and stepped into a closet containing shelves filled with hand towels, toilet paper, and rags.

A small sign hung over a two-by-two metal door waist-high on the far wall: CAUTION, LAUNDRY CHUTE. DEPOSIT TOWELS AND SHEETS ONLY.

It was big enough . . . had to be, for all the bulky sheets.

Cory yanked on the handle, pulling on the hinged door. Hanging onto one of the shelves, he was able to jam his feet into the funnel-like opening. Wriggling his torso and shoulders inside and with one hand holding either side of the door frame, he was ready.

Oh Christ, this is fucked, he thought. He let go.

Twenty-four feet of silver sheet metal passed before his eyes as he hurtled down the chute. He was in the open air for a fraction of a second and landed on a mound of sheets and towels in the basement bin.

Fortunately his mandatory parachute exercises in the air force had taught him to absorb the shock, and he took the impact evenly from his feet to his buttocks.

A wide-eyed Willis watched as Cory rolled onto the concrete floor.

Cory got to his feet without a word and strode out the metal screen door. As he reached the sidewalk, Cory knew not to run or look back.

Still dressed in his white smock, he walked briskly across the hot asphalt through the parked cars and found his rental. Without a glance toward the building, he got in and drove away.

As he pulled onto the two-lane road that led into the New Mexico desert, he removed the surgical cap and looked into the rearview mirror. No car followed.

Wells and the others were still searching the building, never considering someone would jump down the laundry chute.

Cory smiled.

He could hardly believe it himself.

27

Leavenworth

THE DRIVE UP THE HILL to Maddy's house was exactly as she had described it—a series of hairpin curves that opened onto a plateau.

Jace kept the dusty 4x4 in second gear, grinding up the steep road, moving as fast as he could to reach the house before the sun sank in the west.

According to Maddy, the birdhouse that contained Robert's map was easy enough to find, but Jace preferred not to stumble through the underbrush in the dusky twilight.

Catching glimpses of the panorama as he guided the car through the turns, Jace enjoyed the country music station on the Jeep Cherokee's radio. He could remember the twang of Hank Williams' and Patsy Cline's music echoing around his father's California ranch home as a small boy. And now, alone in the countryside, Jace hummed along with the songs, trying to take his mind off the problems he and Cory might face in the near future—the troublesome issues that Cory had intimated during his brief message.

On Jace's morning layover in Chicago, he had called Southland Insurance in New Orleans and lobbied for at least an extra week to file the *Aurora's* accident report, though that obligation paled next to his current investigation. He'd checked his voice mail at his San Antonio apartment and heard Cory's message. In rather nondescript terms, Cory hinted that things were getting much more complicated and that he felt he was in over his head.

Jace called back on a landline, reached Cory's cell phone voice mail, leaving a message of his own, asking for a response.

Finally, as Jace changed planes in Spokane, Cory returned the call. Jace found a quiet corner near his Horizon Airlines boarding gate and they exchanged guarded information, well aware of the lack of security on Jace's cell.

"Who is this Kit guy?" Cory had asked.

"A family friend. Maddy seems to trust him."

"Well, the important thing is, she trusts you. We need answers *fast*. There's something nasty at work in the government, and I stirred up a hornet's nest in Santa Fe. "

"Any damage to you?"

"No. I got away. But if they didn't know what I was doing before, they sure as hell do now."

Jace didn't like the sound of it. It seemed Cory had opened Pandora's box and wasn't sure how to shut the lid again. "Just watch your ass."

"Don't worry. I'm not even going home. What if somebody's tailing me?" Jace remembered that Cory had sent his wife and son to visit Jamilla's mother in Memphis until things calmed down. "I'll swing over to Pasadena to recon with Dixon for an update. Then I'm headed your way. I wangled an excuse to visit Fort Lewis to pick up some of General Simpson's Boeing Aerospace archives. I'll probably roll into Leavenworth sometime late tonight."

"Good. I'll check things at Madison's place and meet you back at the motel," Jace said. Minutes later, his flight took off with Jace feeling edgy and restless, consumed by an uncertain future.

At the Leavenworth airport, Jace had rented a Jeep and taken a short drive through the mountainous neighborhoods toward the outskirts of town. There, he located the quaintly provincial "Cascadian Inn and Trailer Park." The mousy but pleasant Mrs. Dubin, the innkeeper, was surrounded by racks of sightseeing brochures in her small office. The wiry old woman gave Jace directions to the house. She'd been up there that morning to feed the pets, she'd said, in light of Christine's absence.

Mrs. Dubin's directions were quite clear. A two-lane road would dead-end at Maddy's land a thousand feet above the Wenatchee River.

As he drove, Jace began to understand why Maddy had spoken with such affection about this 360 degree view. Under a rose-colored, cloud-dotted sky, massive buttes shouldered up to the Cascade Mountain Range to the north and south. To the east, hundreds of square miles of rangeland stretched as far as the eye could see. To the west, beyond Cashmere Mountain, the jagged Cascades cut into a gleaming sunset.

As Jace rounded a final bend, he saw the house.

Maddy's A-frame reminded him of a wilderness getaway brochure. Set on a rise between several tall pines, the house jutted into the sky.

The Jeep followed the gravel driveway through a lazy curve up to the front porch.

Jace brought the vehicle to a stop at the steps. Awed by the beauty of the place, he exited the car and was immediately struck by the serenity. He was miles from civilization. The stark silence was almost shocking, interrupted occasionally by the soft chirping of a bird. Swallows cavorted under the deep cedar leaves, and the large black windows under the peak reflected the sunset.

Jace left the car and walked along the south side of the house, boots crunching on the gravel path.

Suddenly, a cacophony arose from the rear yard. Maddy's animals heard him coming. He peeked around a juniper bush that nestled under the east corner of the house and spotted six raccoon cubs and their mother gathered at the fence in a center pen. To their left, a yearling fawn stood with its black eyes wide with anticipation. To the right, an owl with a splint on its wing perched on a twig suspended in a cage that held a small doghouse.

Amused, Jace walked toward the enclosure and was greeted by two cats meowing their welcome as they appeared from an adjacent flowerbed. Jace squatted to pet them. The particularly friendly white Persian rubbed its face along the ridge of Jace's boot, while the calico plopped on its back in a submissive pose. Jace reached out and rubbed the spotted cat's belly, and the playful feline purred and softly kicked Jace's hand with its hind feet.

As if jealous of Jace's attention, the baby raccoons put on a tumbling exhibition inside the pen, using the chain-link fence as a springboard, chattering as they ran up the wire, acrobatically vaulting back to the ground.

The fawn stomped its feet, nudging the feed trough.

Jace noticed the pointed snout of a possum protruding from the doorway of the doghouse. Jace whistled a greeting and the nose disappeared. In the shade of the opening, two beady little eyes glared from within. Not to be outdone, the calico cat began its own gymnastics, wriggling from side to side on its back, begging for affection, as the white Persian curled around Jace's right foot.

Jace could imagine Maddy playing with these characters, caressing them with her delicate hands. He stroked the friendly Persian behind its ear, gave the calico one last pat, and stood up to look around.

Beyond the chain-link pens and the shed to which they were attached, diffused sunlight played on the treetops of several spruces Maddy had described. According to her, it was that grove to the east that shaded the arbor where the birdhouse hung with a scrolled paper tucked inside.

Jace glanced at his watch. It was almost seven. Time to get on with the search.

He gave the house a final glance. It was evident that Mrs. Dubin had been there earlier in the day—a small mound of dry food remained in a cat dish on the back porch.

Jace did a double take.

He hadn't noticed it at first, but now he could make out a dark slit where the glass-paneled back door met the jamb. Had Mrs. Dubin been inside the house?

The back door was open just a crack.

28

Emerald Bay
Outside Nassau, Bahamas

JIMMY, THE APARTMENT HOUSE MANAGER, held the news clipping in a chunky black hand. "God. Mr. Robert was killed?" His heavily creased face twisted in confusion.

"Yes, I'm afraid so." Maddy was surprised at his apparent sadness.

"How well did you know him?" Kit asked, suspiciously.

"Not well," Jimmy replied in a Bahamian accent, "but he was a gentleman and always had a kind thing to say. I'm terribly sorry."

"Will you let me into his apartment? I have identification."

Jimmy shrugged, challenged by the request. "Normally when someone dies, isn't it necessary that an attorney—?"

"I understand," Maddy said gently, pulling her Washington State driver's license from her wallet. "But I've come such a long, long way. It's important that I get in. I have reason to believe he left something for me."

Jimmy squinted at the license. "Oh my, Washington State. Mount Saint Helens. That mountain was no saint."

"No." Maddy smiled at the association. People outside the country often knew Washington best for its volcanic activity. "But you'd be a saint if you let me in."

"Miss . . ." Jimmy shook his head, "the regulations."

Kit impatiently pulled a one hundred dollar bill out of his pants pocket and held it in the air. "Maybe we could make up some new rules?"

Jimmy broke into a broad smile. "Perhaps if that one had a twin brother, yes sir." Maddy was amazed at Jimmy's sudden affinity for cash, considering how grieved he'd been only moments before.

Kit dug out another bill and Jimmy accepted it with a nod. "I will go and get you an extra key. Please wait a moment."

As Jimmy disappeared into a back office, Kit drew close to Maddy and whispered, "We could both stay here tonight, you know. I don't think he would care."

Maddy cringed. "Kit, give it a rest." She walked across the room and gazed out the window of the manager's office. Under a row of opaque globe lamps lining the street, several bicyclists rode by. A group of scantily clad teenage girls walked along the white-curbed boulevard in the evening heat.

Kit's reflection shone in the darkened windowpane.

He leaned against the desk, studying Maddy's rear end, which was a bit more exposed than she preferred after she'd changed into shorts at the airport.

"Nice view from here."

Kit's suggestive innuendoes had begun during the flight. After takeoff from Rhode Island, he had talked mostly about himself with the buoyancy of three piña coladas floating in his eyes.

Maddy didn't mind drinking, but she hated a drunk. And Kit began to qualify. His insecurities about her past rejection brought him to a new low. With prurient delight, he mentioned their teenage sexual experimentation, reminding Maddy that he had found their coupling uncommonly fascinating. He proposed that, for comparison, he and Maddy might try an encore.

When she changed the subject to matters at hand, Kit assumed the ridiculous stance of a jealous suitor, asking annoying questions about Jace.

"I think you made a big mistake back there," Kit had said, leaning on the armrest.

"What?"

"Sending him to get Robert's grid. What if he disappears?"

"He won't."

Kit chuckled. "We'll see. Personally I didn't buy into his 'do-or-die for my dad' act."

"Act? He's obsessed by it."

"No, no." Kit wagged a finger. "I saw the way you looked at him. You're the one who's obsessed . . . you find him attractive."

Had her fascination with Jace been that evident? It was none of Kit's business in any case. "Kit. You're way off base. It's starting to piss me off."

"Come on, Maddy. This is Kit you're talkin' to." In response to Maddy's frown, Kit downed the last of the piña colada and, with foam still on his upper lip, said, "Okay, forget it. I was out of line. Have a drink, and let's celebrate old times. What do you say?"

Kit continued to try to sell her on what fun they might have on this trip—the farthest thing from her mind.

She now fully regretted having him along. When he wasn't showboating his corporate success, calling his office from the plane, he was bothering Maddy with his advances. She was torn between dumping him and needing his help. If Maddy could have traded seats with someone else, she would have. Finally feigning a nap, she survived the last half of the flight. It had been dusk when they landed at the Nassau airport.

As they rode together in a cab to Emerald Bay, Kit had resumed his monologue. She'd tried to ignore his drivel by staring out the car window at the scenery. Gradually, she managed to tune Kit out as she became captured by the beauty of the pristine beaches along the northeastern coast of New Providence Island, though the clarity of the water beyond the surf reminded her of the gradual destruction of the planet's oceans. What if Robert's secret could bring an end to the murder of the seas?

In the last remnants of an early fall twilight, teenagers snorkeled and kids laughed and chased each other among the dunes while their parents relaxed under the trees that lined the highway. Couples of various ages walked the sand.

As Maddy watched the passing lovers stroll hand in hand, her thoughts turned to Jace.

By now he should have been to her home and found the birdhouse. According to their plan, Maddy was to call him at the Cascadian Inn to give him a safe address to which he could send the map. Of course, she'd hoped he would deliver the paper to Nassau personally, but she doubted he would after seeing how preoccupied he'd been when he left Robert's house in Providence. Jace had been understandably absorbed in his own quest. Maddy admired Jace's dedication, and she regretted that she hadn't been able to talk to him at length after Kit's arrival. What stayed in her mind was their final moment alone in Robert's den—the flash in Jace's eyes when she handled his shirt collar—that hint of passion, explosive beneath his calm exterior.

Now, as she stared out of the apartment house office, she remembered how Jace had almost flinched at her touch. She couldn't help smiling at how she had shocked him at the Vancouver police station. No wonder he was gun-shy.

Thoughts of Jace lingered as Maddy saw Jimmy, the manager, reappear, holding a spare key that dangled on a chain.

Kit stepped forward and snatched the key. In response, Maddy turned and strode across the office, hoping with every step that Jace would take one more risk and join her. Feeling pumped at the possibility, she caught Kit by the wrist. "That's mine."

Kit's fist closed around the key. "I paid the man."

"I wouldn't have found it necessary. Now give it up." Using both hands, she uncurled his fingers. "My uncle, my key."

With a retiring smile, Kit relinquished the chain. "No need to get so worked up."

Maddy led the way from the office, and with Kit's gaze undoubtedly glued to her derriere, she preceded him upstairs to the second floor.

She searched along the open-air corridor and finally located apartment 29B.

Maddy pushed the key into the lock and the door swung open.

With Kit on her heels, she entered and flicked on the lights. She was impressed. The apartment decor was sparse yet tasteful. Modern art hung on the walls, and a delicate teak dining room set seemed to float over the hardwood floor near the kitchen. The sunken living room was carpeted in a champagne berber and offset with modern low-cut furniture: a slate-colored Italian leather couch, matching chair, and a small white granite coffee table.

As Kit went into the other room, Maddy sidestepped a gauze-covered easel. She pulled back a set of sheer drapes, revealing a lanai that looked out onto a kidney-shaped swimming pool one story below, glowing turquoise in the night. The white concrete that surrounded the pool was lit by overhead purple lanterns that hung from a series of black metal rods. The complex was lit by four floodlights located at the corners. Several dark-green tables and chairs lined a section of pool deck that tiered onto a rockery, descending to a white sand beach.

"He's got a small den in here," Kit yelled from the other room. "Lots more books and papers. I'll take a look around." Maddy could hear desk drawers being rifled as she turned from the lanai window and walked to a bookshelf suspended on the wall over the couch.

On the lowest shelf, next to several travel books supported by conch shell bookends, Maddy noticed a picture of Mason and Robert. Judging from the Space Needle in the background, the photo had been taken in the early sixties at the World's Fair in Seattle. Standing near a fountain, her father and uncle stood arm in arm—a couple of young rascals on vacation. They couldn't have been older than seventeen.

Nothing else on the shelves struck her as unusual—more travel books, several small Polynesian statuettes, a piece of Mayan-looking sculpture.

Turning back, she was drawn again to the lanterns and the flickering glow of the pool lights beyond the lanai window. She stepped toward the glass and, confronted by the easel, she now noticed a small hobby stand that contained a pallet, a clay jar full of brushes, and a small box with tubes of oil paint.

She raised the gauze sheet that hung on the easel, amazed to find a fresh painting. The picture depicted a bleached stucco lighthouse with blue trim, standing on a spectacular rock outcropping. White surf broke on jagged boulders that surrounded the spindly tower.

Robert had fussed with watercolors over the years, having minored in art at Yale University, but she was completely unaware that he'd graduated to oils. The seascape showed off his delicate sense of color.

Maddy reached out and touched the canvas, smudging a tiny dab of the blue pigment. Still damp—not more than a few days old.

Robert must have painted it the day he left the Bahamas for Chicago.

She rubbed her forefinger and thumb together and looked around for something to wipe it off. While stooping to grab a small rag from the hobby stand, she suddenly noticed a glinting reflection.

There it was again, playing on the canvas . . . a ghostly flash of light, shining through the lanai glass door.

Maddy rose and stepped closer to the window.

The flash reappeared and was quickly gone again.

As she looked out into the night, the glare struck her squarely in the eyes. Overcome with curiosity, she yanked the metal handle of the sliding door and stepped onto the deck.

A gentle rush of warm ocean air tousled her hair as she looked around. The lanterns by the pool swayed in the evening breeze. Several people roamed the beach beyond the pool area.

Her eyes adjusted to the darkness and neighboring silhouettes began to take shape. She noticed a lone figure seated at one of the tables on the opposite side of the rounded swimming pool. A middle-aged man wearing a lightweight business suit sat in a deck chair angled diagonally toward the beach. He seemed to be gazing out at the crashing surf. In the low light, given his age and physical type, he could have been mistaken for her uncle—sporting a short-cropped beard, though he wore no glasses.

The reflection that had called her attention emanated from an object in the man's hand—what appeared to be a square, polished cigarette case which intermittently caught the glare off one of the overhead floodlights.

The bizarre shimmer continued to play across her face in what seemed to be a pattern of flashes. Enchanted by its surreal quality, she stood alone on Robert's second-floor balcony.

With the breeze and the sound of distant surf calming her senses, she was transfixed by a complete stranger, who sat across the expanse of the swimming pool, dazzling her with his light.

29

Leavenworth

SUSPENDED IN DOUBT, JACE STARED at the glass-paneled back door of Maddy's home. It was cracked a mere three inches, but it might as well have been open a mile if someone had broken in.

Supposedly, Mrs. Dubin had been the only person to visit Maddy's house in her absence. Had the innkeeper been careless and left the door ajar? Everything else seemed in order. It was quiet except for the gentle chatter of the raccoons as they fussed in the pen.

Jace had to investigate. He crouched as he crept toward the back porch, walking softly on the grass, avoiding the noisy gravel that lined the pens. Stopping between the juniper trees that lined the porch stairs, he tiptoed across the wide cedar floorboards.

He reached the back door and peeked inside.

Maddy's kitchen had a light, airy feel, with beige Corion countertops, almond-colored appliances, and light walnut cabinets. Under each cabinet, an inordinate number of collector coffee mugs hung on hooks. A toaster and coffee maker sat on the counter by the sink. Several barstools surrounded an island, separating the kitchen from the polished wood table in a breakfast nook.

With the hum of tension in his ears, Jace gently pushed on the door. The hinges creaked as it swung open.

He stepped inside. The wood floor was beautifully polished. No sign of anything unusual.

Jace eased through the kitchen and sneaked down a cedar hallway lined with wildlife photographs that Maddy may have taken herself. He paused at the first doorway to his right—a dining room that held a colonial-style table and six chairs. An oak armoire stood against the far wall with antique dishes and glassware displayed on the top half.

Jace hesitated. In the dresser section of the armoire, one of the drawers had been left open. Given the home's neatness, that didn't make sense.

Bracing himself for surprises, Jace moved further down the hall, which opened into a large sunken living room. A grand prow of floor-to-ceiling windows faced west. On the distant horizon, the Cascade Mountains jutted against the sky.

A couch and an armchair surrounded a woodstove against the rear wall of the living room. In the far corner, a shiny antique grand piano sat near a small rolltop desk.

Several sheets of paper lay on the floor next to the desk. Like the open armoire drawer, the small mess on the floor struck him as odd. Perhaps one of the cats had been inside the house and climbed onto the desk, and yet—he glanced back at the dining room—cats couldn't open drawers.

Somewhere toward the rear of the home, wood joints creaked as the house began to cool in the evening. There was no visible sign of damage. Perhaps Mrs. Dubin could shed light on the inconsistencies.

Jace stared through the vaulted windows at the silhouetted jagged peaks in the west. The house grew perceptibly darker inside as the sunset began to fade. Outside, shadows in the yard had grown black among the shrubs. It was time to get to the business of the map.

Glancing around as he retraced his steps, Jace returned to the kitchen and, after pressing the push-button lock on the back door handle, he walked out on the back porch and pulled the door tight.

As he stepped down the stairs onto the gravel, a tingle of apprehension shot up his back. The junipers rustled behind him and someone said, "No sudden moves, Kelton."

Jace froze, raising his hands in the air.

Three men wearing ski masks and holding silenced semiautomatic handguns stepped out from between the bushes. One leveled a gun at Jace's head while the other two flanked him.

The shortest of the bunch seemed to be the spokesman. He brandished his weapon. "Step over to the fence."

All appeared to be of medium build, well under six feet. The masks made it impossible to distinguish features.

"How do you know my name?" Jace reluctantly edged toward the chain link.

The leader leaned forward. "You're famous. Ever since your Vancouver incident. Now show us the grid."

"Grid?"

The man smacked Jace on the side of the head with the gun barrel. "Smart ass. You know exactly what I mean . . . Robert Marro's grid."

Jace's temple stung from the blow. "The man who killed Marro has it," he said, wincing.

"You're only half right. We want the other half. Where is it?"

Jace glanced around for a means of escape. Chain-link fence to his left, house to his right, three guys with guns blocking both ways out. Impossible. "I'd give it to you. But I've been through the house, and I can't find it. Search me if you want."

"Show me where it is." The cold voice was unrelenting.

Jace shrugged and said nothing.

"A little bloodletting maybe?" The leader pointed his gun.

Jace envisioned a bullet plowing into his forehead, but the hooded stranger whirled instead and aimed into the pens, firing seven silenced staccato shots thk-thk-thk-thk-thk-thk-thk through the fence. In a split second, three baby raccoons were splattered against the shed wall. Another squealed, lying on its back with its hind legs kicking, as the two remaining cubs cowered behind their mother, eyes white with confusion.

Jace's first thought—Maddy's anguish. "Goddamn you, don't kill them," he shouted.

The man turned coolly. "Then show us." He pointed the handgun at the yearling fawn. "Or I'll slaughter the rest and then start on your legs."

30

Nassau

THE RIPPLING LIGHTS FROM THE pool and the roar of the surf in the darkness beyond the beach added to the mystic aura created by intermittent flashes from the stranger's cigarette case.

Perhaps it was the shadowy newcomer's resemblance to Robert, but Maddy was suddenly overcome by an irresistible urge to talk to the man. She resolved to satisfy her curiosity and stepped into the living room, where she heard Kit still fussing in the back rooms. Deciding not to disturb him, she crept quietly toward the apartment door.

Once outside, she made her way down the hall toward a green exit sign and down a set of back stairs to the main level.

Skirting the building, she followed the signs that hung over a concrete walkway and found a back gate. Soon, she was bathed in the glow of the swimming pool lights. She passed the gently gurgling filter and crossed the deck, drawing closer to the tables and the stranger beyond.

She approached the shadowy figure from behind and, not wanting to startle him, kept her distance as she stepped to his side.

The man had turned slightly, and she was struck by the kindly expression on his face. On closer examination, he was several years older than Robert; his mustache and beard were silver-blond, and his hair glowed white in the dim lantern light.

The man held the cigarette case as if to offer it to her, and in a Swedish accent asked, "Are you the one I'm waiting for?"

The oddity of the question surprised Maddy. "Am I what?"

"Wasn't that you up there?" He craned his neck toward the lanai.

"Yes."

"Then join me, won't you?" The man stood politely, and Maddy found herself looking up into his transparent blue eyes. He was at least six feet tall and immaculately dressed in a tropical cream-colored suit. His Panama hat sat on the table near a worn newspaper.

"So you know who I am?" She fumbled for the back of the canvas chair next to his.

"Unless you're the cleaning woman, I would say you must be Robert's niece, Madison. And I . . ." he extended his hand, "am Torbald Ürg, Robert's friend."

"My God." She slumped into the neighboring chair. "We were just talking about you."

He sat. "Indeed? And who is 'we'?"

"An old friend of mine and Robert's—"

"Mr. Lassiter?"

"Exactly." She pointed to the apartment. "He's up there."

"I see. And who else knows about me?"

"Another man named Kelton, who was there when Robert—"

"I know." Torbald reached for the newspaper and held it like a baton. "You don't think he's a killer? You trust him?"

"I do, completely."

Torbald opened the newspaper and, as if in deep thought, pointed to one of the articles. "Good. For this is the time for trust. We must choose our friends carefully. There are many killers, and like an evil wind, they have driven me here to find you."

"I don't understand."

"Then let me explain. In the last few days, I have been saddened by many deaths among those who were my former colleagues in the organization referred to as the S-7. Does that sound familiar?"

"The Scalbania 7."

Torbald nodded approvingly. "You know their names."

"Some. Not all."

"Then let me enlighten. They now read like the obituary column in the *New York Times* . . . Dean Sutwith in South Africa, Hector Walsh in Canada, Jinseng Ma in Hawaii, Emma Hoffman in Switzerland."

"All dead?"

"And more. When I tried to contact Michael Granville in New Zealand, I was told he had died of a stroke. Harold Berlinger of England is missing. Then of course, the ultimate blow . . . your uncle, brutally struck down."

"You were close?"

"As two professionals could be."

"Had you spoken with him recently?"

"Only days ago. Before I realized the gravity of this debacle. When I heard of his death, I dropped everything, left my field research in Sulitelma, and came straight to Nassau. That is why I am so fashionably and suitably attired. For fear of my life, I decided not to venture to my home in Göteberg to pack, so I am now the owner of a new wardrobe that can only be worn in temperatures over seventy degrees."

"And you came here assuming I would show up?"

Torbald shrugged. "To die in Sweden or wait in Nassau. I chose. I would rather act than be acted upon."

"By whom, do you think?"

"Whoever they are, my dear, they have a heartless agenda . . . to find your uncle's secret prize and kill all who stand in the way." Torbald pointed toward the beach. "That's why I have him."

On cue, a burly blond six-foot-eight giant of a man in a T-shirt and shorts climbed from the breakwater. In his left hand he carried two small travel bags, and in the crook of his well-muscled right arm, he cradled a high-tech crossbow that gleamed under the floodlight. A wicked-looking dart lay in the firing groove. The stock of the weapon glowed with a tiny fuchsia laser just under the arrow.

"Hans Ostertag, my nephew," Torbald explained as Hans crested the last of the angular boulders at the top of the rockery. "He was a commando in the army."

Hans approached and took her hand. He towered over her chair. "Hello, good lady," he said, smiling.

"He speaks little English. But he has the eye of an eagle and a heart of gold." Maddy couldn't take her eyes off the crossbow. Torbald noticed her fascination. "This collapsible, plastic alloy device circumvents airport security. Hans will go wherever I go as my protection."

"So someone's trying to kill you," she said softly, remembering the stalkers in the woods and wondering about her own safety.

"Unquestionably. The S-7's speculative vision of twenty years ago is now heightened by an impending and inevitable energy famine. We have less than three decades to find the answer, Ms. Marro. Oil reserves will be finished. And then what? How will the great emerging populations of the third world, such as India and China, satisfy their emerging appetites? This ravenous world breeds fearsome adversaries. And you and I stand in the way of their ambition. They will not rest until they have killed us and taken possession of Robert's secret."

"So you know what Robert found?"

Torbald's eyes glowed with intensity. "I can only guess. But I surmise it means limitless power."

"As in 'influence' or 'energy'?"

"Both."

Maddy's heart began to pound with unexpected excitement. "Can you find it?"

"Perhaps. But frankly, *you* should be the one to find it."

"Because I'm his niece?"

"No. Because it is your destiny. After I meet your friend Mr. Lassiter and judge his mettle, I will explain how this incredible story began with your father and why, with God's blessing, it should end with you."

31

Leavenworth

LIKE A MAN IN SEARCH of his own gallows, Jace led his three captors away from Maddy's home into the hazy woods, knowing he'd be dead the moment he handed over Robert's paper. He reasoned that the short hike would be the only way out. On open ground, he might have a fighting chance to break free.

The hooded strangers trailed him; the nearest one prodding him with his gun barrel, with the others a few yards behind as they marched a narrow path across a clearing spotted with thickets.

They tramped ankle-deep in ivy and salal as Jace's mind raced, searching for a means of escape.

In the spruce grove ahead, several dozen pine trees surrounded a small creek. Nearby he saw the wooden bench and a fire pit by the arbor that Maddy had described. In the dim light, the shape of the arbor's archway reminded Jace of a tombstone. He wondered how soon he might lie dead beneath it.

"How far?" the man behind asked, prodding Jace's buttocks with the gun.

"In those trees," Jace replied. "We might have to dig for it."

"You said nothing about digging. If there's digging to do, your bare hands will do it."

Jace envisioned himself burrowing in the soft earth on his hands and knees, being buried in the same hole by his abductors after they lost patience and shot him. Would Maddy return home to find half of her animals dead and Jace's remains rotting under the trees? He vowed not to die, to somehow find a way. He wanted to see her again, to hand her the grid that she'd sent him to find.

As he stumbled through the ground cover, he became aware of his mouth repeatedly forming the word "please." He hadn't prayed much in recent years, but realized that he was praying now, begging the almighty for the slimmest of chances. He was closing the distance between himself and the arbor . . . now down to fifty yards.

With the word "please" again on his lips, Jace stepped on a branch near a thicket.

A covey of grouse exploded out of the bushes with their wings rustling, making a sound as loud as a revving car engine.

The man at Jace's back instinctively swung his weapon across his body toward the disturbance, and Jace knew he'd been given the chance he'd prayed for.

He pivoted and locked the man's gun arm under his own, dragging him to the ground. After two quick elbow-slams to the face, Jace disarmed him. Grabbing the gun, he pulled free, jumping to his feet. Then he was on the run, zigzagging, vaulting small bushes as a hail of bullets hissed overhead.

Through a bloodied mouth the downed man screamed, "Don't kill him yet!"

The other two men stopped firing and gave chase.

Jace dashed for the grove, and his athletic speed paid off as he outdistanced the others. In a matter of seconds, he spied the birdhouse hanging from the arbor. The small eighteen-inch-high replica of Maddy's home hung on a wire, suspended from a trellis.

Sprinting at top speed and switching the gun to his left hand, Jace launched himself through the arbor, leaping high to take the birdhouse like a football under his right arm. The surrounding latticework shattered as he pulled the wire from the wood frame. He ran on, unwillingly spilling a spoor of birdseed for his pursuers as he struggled in vain to cover the holes. Fortunately, with his longer legs, Jace outpaced the others.

He had taken a long arc along the ridge of the plateau, working north and southwest, circling back toward Maddy's house. As he ran toward the west, the outlines of the A-frame roof became visible against the final pink of the day.

Slowing to a walk, Jace hugged the birdhouse in the crook of his left arm. Using the butt of the gun in his right hand, he smashed the quarter-inch plywood walls. His hands groped inside, and he located a manila envelope among what was left of the birdseed. He tucked the envelope inside his jacket pocket and, tossing the damaged miniature structure aside, dashed for the house.

Looping around the front yard, he approached the driveway, where his car was still parked.

There was no one in sight.

He had evaded his captors. He could escape to the motel.

Jace jumped into the Jeep, laid the automatic handgun on the front seat, and put the key into the ignition.

Suddenly, he caught a movement in the rearview mirror as a dark shape reared over the backseat.

"Shit," Jace tried to reach for the handgun and shield his head, but it was too late.

Everything stopped with a blunt thud as he was clubbed from behind.

32

Nassau

MADDY, KIT, AND TORBALD GATHERED around the granite coffee table to compare notes. Maddy became so immediately engrossed that she was only remotely aware of Hans Ostertag as he roamed about Robert's living room. The big blond guy insisted on being constantly in motion, checking the outer hallway, the back bedrooms, stepping out onto the lanai in the dark.

Kit was stunned when Maddy brought Dr. Ürg and his nephew to the apartment. From the first moment, it became apparent that the silver-haired Swede had knowledge about Robert's project that far exceeded Kit's.

In his hyperintensive fashion, Kit peppered Ürg with questions, asking for all the answers at once, but Torbald resisted the pressure with patient stoicism. "If you don't mind, Mr. Lassiter, I would rather learn more about you and Madison before formulating either theories or a plan."

"What's the matter? Don't you believe us?"

"It's not a question of faith, but rather of structure. Since it appears we have been thrust into this enormous undertaking together, let's begin by sharing what we know before jumping to conclusions."

This was Torbald's clinical aptitude at work, his opportunity to measure each person's potential reliability. And Maddy became his first subject. Torbald asked Maddy about her home life and her interaction with her parents. She felt mildly embarrassed by the scarcity of her own knowledge. "During college and immediately after, I was focused on my own agenda. I'd become disenchanted with my father. And frankly, my mother was dysfunctional. She drank heavily."

"Apparently she was functional enough to be of some help to your father."

"What do you mean?"

"She was fully aware of Mason's aspirations, while you were not."

The judgmental edge to Torbald's gentle voice gave Maddy pause. "That's what Kit tells me. It seems they kept me in the dark."

Torbald's tone softened. "But what did you assume your parents were doing when they went on extended trips?"

"Taking vacations. My mother loved Europe—Italy in particular."

Torbald shook his head. "What about Peru?"

Maddy was stunned. "I don't know. They always brought me souvenirs from Rome."

"A ruse, according to Robert. Mason traveled to Peru repeatedly in search of the mystical item now known as the Peruvian Prize."

Maddy rose and stepped to the lanai window, fingering the lip of the easel that held Robert's painting. Torbald continued as she gazed out at the moon, which splashed silver across the distant ocean. "Unknown to the S-7 committee, Mason searched for a legendary energy source. A nonpetroleum alternative."

She turned from the curtain. "But that's so out of character."

"Is it? Well, draw your own conclusions."

Maddy was left to contemplate the implications in the lull that followed, until Kit jumped in and petitioned Torbald on how much Robert had trusted him. "Mason and I used to go to ball games together . . . he took me fishing up north. Robert would tag along, except when we hunted. Robert couldn't stand the sight of blood. But I was over at Christmas, Thanksgiving . . . that sort of thing. They treated me like family."

Torbald threw Maddy an inquiring glance and she nodded.

"And why would Robert consider you qualified?"

Kit shrugged in self-satisfaction. "My age, I guess. I'm physically fit. And hey, computers, electronics, satellite technology. I'm good at math and I dabbled with physics at MIT. In fact, Robert and I did some research together on hyperdimensional physics when he visited me at MIT . . ."

As Kit droned on, Maddy remembered the two years before her father died—her righteous indignation and her tunnel-visioned zest for her own life . . . understandable feelings for a young woman in her early twenties. But she'd apparently missed opportunities for intimacy with her father, for sharing what appeared to have been a commendable pursuit. Considering her own ecological passion, why wouldn't her father allow her to contribute to that endeavor?

Kit concluded.

Maddy shook off her doubts, hoping the professor's details would shed light on the riddles. She moved to the couch and sat, determined to not let Torbald gloss over matters. After he recapped his own scientific history, she asked, "Do you mind if I ask you more about my dad, how he got involved?"

"Of course not." Torbald sat cross-legged. "Norman Scalbania met your father at a political fund-raiser for the Atomic Energy Commission in Washington, DC. After several meetings over the years, Mason decided to offer major funding to the S-7."

"But why would Dad do that?"

Torbald's gray eyes fixed on hers. "That is something I prefer you decide, Maddy. His motives remain somewhat cloudy, and I hope the facts will speak for themselves."

"More facts then," Kit said eagerly, leaning forward from his perch on the coffee table. "Namely, about you. Why did you do it, Professor?"

Torbald shrugged. "Like the others, I was contacted by Scalbania because of my prior work. I was best known for my revisitation to the principles of Thomas Moray, the man who discovered the 'Swedish Stone' in the northern mountains of my country. It's a scarce volcanic mineral, heavily carbon based, porous in nature much like pumice, which generates up to fifty kilowatts of electricity in laboratory conditions without external stimuli. I was able to recreate Moray's experiments, powering a bank of thirty-two light-bulbs with one three-ounce piece of the milky looking substance. Unfortunately, since the rare mineral disintegrates during the duress of experimentation, it remains most mysterious. For all its potential, I couldn't find sufficient quantities of the rock to justify my theory that it might someday illuminate a city."

"Could that be the stone Uncle Robert mentioned when he died?" Maddy asked.

"I don't think so. This mineral is exceedingly rare and unusually soft. Quite fragile really, not enduring enough. As you undoubtedly realize, Robert's vision was of something much grander and durable—perpetual, in fact."

Kit moved closer as Torbald continued. "Overall, Scalbania's idea was quite admirable. He wanted scientists like myself to reexamine discarded alternative energy theories of the twentieth and even nineteenth century. In many cases, men like Nikola Tesla, Nathan Stubblefield, and Thomas Townsend Brown were discredited too easily along with their work to develop instruments of power and light. Many of their findings were forcefully interrupted or suppressed. When I was approached, I decided to join Scalbania, because he appeared to be a philanthropist. Many of the scientists used terms like 'saving the planet,' 'ensuring our children's future,' that kind of thing. There was a new world feeling about the effort, and I was full of grand ideas."

"And you think Scalbania's motives were purely altruistic?" Maddy asked, suspecting her father's were not.

"Well, let's face it. The man was an industrialist and had a practical side. Power is power, after all. But with Scalbania's vision and your father's money, things rolled along. Imagine the consequences of a replacement fuel for gasoline, a low-cost substitute for electricity, or a safer power than nuclear fission. You can see why someone might invest in the possibilities."

"Investing," Kit said, knowingly. "I might have been born at night, sir, but it wasn't last night. Don't tell me you and the others didn't want the big bucks."

Maddy thought Torbald might take offense, but his expression didn't change. He simply uncrossed his legs. "There may have been an opportunity for 'big bucks,' Mr. Lassiter, but in case you think me to be a mercenary, please be aware that even after the S-7 effort ceased, I struggled on with my own meager funds. It was Robert Marro's revelations about Tenille's deathbed confession that changed my plans."

Torbald squinted out the lanai door into the darkness. "When Robert told me that Mason's Peruvian parchment chronicled the existence of an ancient power vortex, I decided to abandon my meager efforts and join him. Of course, the desecration of Mason's ashes changed everything."

"So the Peruvian Prize and the grid I hid at my home are two completely different pieces," Maddy said.

"Absolutely. The Peruvian Prize told of an ancient legend. Nothing more. The grid was of Robert's own geometric design."

"How would these vandals find out about Mason's urn in the first place?" Kit asked.

"I have no idea."

"Are you the only one left?" Maddy asked.

"So it appears. Look at the list: Sutwith, Jinseng, Walsh, Hoffman, and Granville. Even Berlinger is missing. It appears that, overnight, I have become an anachronism, threatened with obsolescence."

Torbald looked around the apartment uneasily, as if suddenly intimidated by his own assessment. He glanced at Kit. "Mr. Lassiter, I hope you won't mind, but I would like some moments with Maddy alone."

"May I know why?"

"Robert's disclosure about his brother was shared with me in complete confidence. No matter how much you were esteemed by Mason and Robert, I consider that a delicate family matter. If Maddy chooses to share it with you, that's her decision."

Kit couldn't disguise his disappointment. "You want me to leave?"

"That's not necessary. I'm becoming claustrophobic in here, anyway." Torbald rose and gestured to the lanai. "Maddy, perhaps we could take a walk?"

Torbald shouted something in Swedish, and in a split second, Hans appeared from the back bedroom. After a brief unintelligible exchange, Hans nodded and joined Kit in the living room while Torbald ushered Maddy out the door. As they entered the outer hallway, Torbald took her arm and led her toward the back stairs. "Don't worry about your friend," he whispered. "Hans will keep him amused."

"I'm not worried. I just can't wait to hear what you have to say."

As they walked down toward the pool, he smiled for the first time. "Let's walk on the beach. I think it's appropriate that this be told under the stars."

33

Leavenworth

AT FIRST, JACE THOUGHT HIS face was on fire. Both of his cheeks blazed with a stinging pain. With his eyes still closed and his mind reeling, he began to regain consciousness, only to realize his head was being violently pounded back and forth.

Jace opened his eyes as one of three masked assailants slapped him across the face once, then again. Blood flowed down Jace's chin. He shook his head and the man stopped swinging. Jace blinked several times, struggling to orient himself. The back of his head throbbed, and judging from the surrounding darkness, it had been some time since he'd been clubbed in the car.

Jace was naked from the waist up, spread-eagled against the chain link, with both wrists bound by rawhide to the pet cages.

The light of a pale moon revealed a finger-painted scrawl on his torso. Someone had written the word "LIAR" across his chest in the stickiness of dried blood; blood that, at first, Jace thought was his own. Then he saw the puddles at his feet and the four dead baby raccoons splayed on the ground. From what Jace could make out, the remaining animals in the pens appeared untouched, and the two cats sat on the porch steps, watching the strange goings-on.

The man who had slapped Jace hovered two feet from his face, apparently letting Jace come to his senses. "Can you hear me?" he asked as the other two masked assailants flanked Jace, hands on their hips.

"Oh, I hear you just fine." Jace spit droplets of blood through his bruised lips, looking past the spokesman, wondering which of the three men had whacked him in the car. One of them must have been bright enough to double back from the grove.

"You like games?" The spokesman took a half step closer.

Jace glared at him, confused. "What?"

The man reached into his back pocket and pulled out the brown manila envelope Jace had retrieved from the birdhouse, removing a piece of paper, which he jammed in Jace's face.

Even in the dim moonlight, Jace could see that the sheet from inside the envelope was blank.

"You're wasting our time." The man presented another sheet full of lines and numbers. "Where is the other half of this?"

Jace was shocked. "That's what I came for."

"Bullshit." The spokesman tossed the blank sheet aside. "It's a decoy. What have you done with the real grid?"

"Nothing."

The hooded man looked back at the others, shaking his head. "You're either brave or stupid," he said, pulling a serrated knife from his belt. He placed the tip of the blade on Jace's naked left breast. "Let's find out which it is . . ." The man dragged the tip of the knife across Jace's chest, cutting into the skin.

Jace winced as the blood oozed. "Untie me," Jace said, through gritted teeth, "and we'll find out whether *you're* brave or stupid."

"Tell me what you've done with the grid."

"I swear to Christ, I don't know where it is."

The spokesman placed the knife blade under Jace's right nipple. "I'll take this off. You have five seconds."

Jace had no doubt that he was about to be maimed. "Give me a minute to think."

"Five," the man said calmly. "Four, three, two . . ."

The man arched his hand in preparation to flick the blade but froze as someone behind the juniper bushes yelled, "Drop the knife and back off. Move and you're dead, asshole."

The man obeyed, and as the blade hit the dirt, a dark figure stepped from the shrubs. It was Cory in full uniform. He had a nine-millimeter Beretta trained on Jace's three captors. "Step away from him," he shouted at the spokesman. He waved the gun at the others. "Both of you get over there with Jack the Ripper.

Keep your hands high or I'll blow you away. I'd love to, believe me. Give me an excuse."

The hooded men bunched by the fence as Cory stepped over to Jace, holding the Beretta in his right hand, working the rawhide restraints with his left. "Hey," he said. "You look like shit."

Jace nodded as his left wrist came free. "This bastard thinks I'm a pot roast."

"So that's why he was carving you?"

Jace loosened the rawhide on his right wrist. "Whoever they are, they knew I'd be here."

Cory moved off a couple of feet to a better vantage point. "Get their weapons and pat them down."

Cory kept his Beretta trained at the men's heads as Jace circled them, pulling Intratec TEC-9s from their belts. He tossed two of the semiautomatic weapons into a flower bed and clutched the third gun in his right hand as he retreated to join Cory.

"Time we find out who Zorro and his friends are," Cory said. "Take off your masks."

None of the men moved.

"I said take them off."

The spokesman suddenly screamed, "San!"

Jace had no idea what the word meant.

"Shut up," shouted Cory.

"San!" the man screamed again.

Cory stepped forward with the Beretta trained at the man's forehead. "You yell again, bitch, and I'll take you out. Now take off the goddamn—"

The backyard illuminated with a flash of golden light as a deafening explosion shook the ground. Flaming pieces of Jace's rented 4x4 went flying into the air over the roofline of the house, and a fireball mushroomed into the night sky.

Seconds later, the rear window of the A-frame exploded with the blast of gunshots. Cory was spun around as a round struck him in the shoulder. He regained his balance and reared up on one knee to return fire with his Beretta.

More shots rang from the kitchen, and Jace made out the silhouette of someone just inside the door.

Focused on this latest threat, Jace trained the TEC-9 on the shape and fired repeatedly, and apparently accurately, because the man was knocked back into the darkness of the room.

Jace heard Cory cry out.

In the heat of the firefight, the hooded spokesman had dropped to his knees, recovering the knife that had lain at his feet, and now jammed the blade into Cory's chest below his sternum, twisting the hilt as he grabbed for Cory's Beretta.

Horrified at Cory's screams, Jace turned and fired point-blank, blowing a hole in the spokesman's neck. The shot jerked the man's body sideways, and he collapsed on the gravel.

The other two men had scrambled for their own weapons in the flower bed. Worried that they might turn and fire, Jace spun and sprayed three shots in their direction.

The bullets spattered into a small tree grove as the men took off. The Intratec in Jace's hand clicked empty. Brimming with rage, Jace grabbed Cory's Beretta from the gravel and fired four more times, catching one of the men in the thigh.

As his partner disappeared into the darkness, the downed man stuffed something into his mouth, immediately convulsed, and then lay still.

All firing stopped. The glow from Jace's blazing 4x4 filled the yard. In shadows thrown by the chain link, Maddy's animals cowered against the back walls of their pens. A distant wail of sirens could be heard weaving up the base of the mountain.

With an eye on the back door, Jace frantically crawled to Cory, who lay on his back, sprawled against the fence. Cory's bloody right hand gripped the knife hilt lodged in his chest just below the heart.

Tears welled in Jace's eyes as he knelt next to his friend. He reached out, wanting to remove the dagger, but Cory pushed his hand away.

"That's gotta come out of there, man." Jace choked on the words.

"Don't touch it," Cory gasped.

"I've got to call for help." Jace rose to one knee.

"Hear the sirens? They're coming." Cory clutched Jace's arm, his eyes wild. "Don't leave me. What if I die while you're gone?"

"Okay. I'm here." Jace tried to cradle Cory. A dirt bike ignition sounded on the far side of Maddy's house. "Somebody's taking off."

Cory nodded. "Good. Let him go." He grimaced. "This is bad. Everything's mushed up inside. I think I've got a hole in my heart."

Jace prayed the sirens were from an ambulance, not just a cop car. "Goddamnit. What can I do?"

Cory let go of the blade and reached out with his bloody right hand. "This time I'm the guy drowning. I don't know if you can pull me out."

Jace grasped the bloody fingers. The grip was still strong. "They'll patch you up, buddy. Just concentrate. Focus on my face."

"You couldn't come up with something more attractive?" The hint of a smile had appeared but faded as he coughed. "Listen. I heard from Dixon."

"Don't talk."

"I have to. The Phobia File was definitely named for Phobos, the Martian moon. You know, Phobos means 'fear' in Latin. And it's *not* NASA, Jace, it's Langley. The CIA put a damper on the Mars missions since 1993." Cory strained, catching something in his throat. "Higgins was scared shitless, and from what Dixon said, it's an international cover-up. The US, the Russians, they all wanted to hide something. Your dad . . . Davenport . . ."

Cory jerked forward, choking on the blood that welled from the corner of his mouth. Glistening red oozed down his chin. He seemed to lose focus as he stared past Jace toward the night sky.

"Look at me, Cory. I'm right here." The sirens on the mountain sounded closer.

Cory continued to stare blankly at the stars. His right hand climbed Jace's wrist with faltering fingers, leaving bloody imprints up Jace's forearm. He clutched the elbow and locked onto Jace's bare bicep.

Cory's face paled to ashen gray. His eyes began to glaze. "Jace. There's something big up there. I know it."

Jace followed Cory's gaze up to the stars that flickered through hazy blackness overhead.

A lump pushed against Jace's throat. "Whatever's up there, Cory, we'll find it together."

"I don't know," Cory whimpered. "I think . . ." He hung on the word. "I'm gonna get there before you do." Cory's face twisted. "Oh God," he gasped, staring at the sky. "Jamilla." He exhaled a seemingly endless sigh as his fingers loosened from Jace's arm, and his hand fell away. Cory's head rolled limply to the left. Muscles in his face relaxed.

"Jesus," Jace said in a curse that became a prayer, "don't let me lose him." He grabbed Cory and held him hard, as if to prevent him from falling. As he embraced his friend, he felt the lead weight of death settle into the body.

Cory was gone.

Jace raised his face to the sky. He bellowed a hollow, anguished cry. His voice echoed emptily through the trees.

The stars continued to twinkle above, oblivious to agony.

Sobbing, Jace buried his head in the hollow of Cory's neck. Visions of their years of friendship flashed before his eyes, and he was only remotely aware of vehicles cresting the hill, spraying gravel onto Maddy's front drive.

34

Nassau

A HARVEST MOON DAPPLED THE sea into a shimmering runway that stretched from the shoreline to the horizon. Advancing breakers assaulted the beach one by one, their emerald transparency clouded as each wave crashed into phosphorescence.

Torbald's hair appeared albino white against the black eastern sky as he and Maddy stepped off the cement stairs onto the beach.

Torbald threw his jacket over his arm, and Maddy removed her shoes. They strolled together with Maddy delighting in the soft grind of sand between her toes.

A few people wandered the strand in the distance. With the hot breeze caressing her face, Maddy felt very much alive, surrounded by incredible beauty, tingling with anticipation as Torbald prefaced his tale.

"Your family's legacy is something that should have been shared with you many years ago. I neither judge your parents for not telling you, nor do I make apologies for them. But I want you to know that everything I have to say is the truth as I understand it."

Intuitively, she had faith in Torbald, who was rapidly proving himself to be Robert's trustworthy friend.

"I met your father only a few times, but Robert told me much of this story. I must say that from Robert's account I came away with a respect for your father's initial efforts." Torbald stared out at the horizon as if seeing visions of the past.

"You must remember the tenacity Mason demonstrated. He held this secret quest close to his heart. Tenille kept that covenant until she passed Mason's findings on to Robert at the time of her death."

"I can believe that, but it's their altruistic twist," Maddy said. "What you're telling me is so unlike Dad. Something doesn't fit."

"Perhaps for you it never will. After all, you wouldn't be the first child to misinterpret her parents' motivations."

"But to me Dad was . . ." She flashed back on her father's constantly booming voice at the dinner table. "Forgive me for saying so, but he was a somewhat one-dimensional man. Loud. Proud. Business was everything."

"I understand. From what I saw, Mason was dynamic, outgoing, and perhaps a bit too boisterous. And, according to Robert, he was also secretive. What he did and what he said were frequently diametrically opposed—a tactic that made him a formidable manipulator and opponent."

"But why would he seek out Scalbania, who was into alternative energy?"

Torbald nodded. "Mason was a shrewd strategist. He looked forward to eventually being revealed as the automotive magnate who backed environmental issues. As the S-7 research moved along, Mason maintained his private agenda, having sealed an agreement with Scalbania that they alone would control any findings of the group. Your father was . . . shall we say, somewhat self-centered about things."

"You're being kind." Maddy kicked at the sand. "He had an ego that wouldn't quit."

"Well, sometimes it takes a great ego to accomplish great feats," Torbald said with a hint of admiration. "After Scalbania died, Mason took complete control, particularly since Scalbania made no provisions for his own family. Scalbania had divorced his wife some years before and disinherited his only son, who sided with his mother in a bitterly contested divorce. And so, fully in control and without consulting the other scientists—including myself—Mason explored possibilities. He didn't divulge his intentions to Robert but continued to have long talks with his brother, listening to Robert's sometimes outlandish theories about ancient, long-forgotten resources. As you may know, Robert was obsessed, documenting legendary mystical powers used to erect Egypt's pyramids; the hypothesis was that a link existed among the raising of monolithic structures all over the world."

"I saw his books. He seemed fascinated by an Egyptian–Mayan connection."

"That was just the beginning. He became convinced of the unilateral origin of other mammoth structures—among them, the statues on Easter Island, the great sunken seawall off the Bimini trench here in the Bahamas, and the over one hundred fifty huge concrete spheres that are buried in Costa Rica."

"Spheres?"

"Inexplicable ten- to twelve-foot, perfectly circular orbs of rock unearthed in Central America. They are so exact they might have been machine-tooled."

"And there's no explanation?"

"None. But the phenomena that proved the most astounding"—Torbald held his coat in one hand and opened his arms wide—"were the vast array of earth drawings around the planet; ancient shapes in the ground that measure hundreds of feet in diameter. Among them, the White Horse of Uffington and the Cerne Giant in England, figures of humanoids in Ohio, and great earth drawings in Arizona and California. They were created by the earthbound cultures of the past, invisible to someone on the ground and yet easily observed from the air." Torbald stopped walking. "The most devastatingly important of all—the earth drawings on the plain of Nazca in Peru. Are you aware of them?"

"I don't know much about them," Maddy said quietly.

"Well, you will." Torbald smiled reassuringly as he began to stroll again. "The Nazca plain hosts magnificent outlines of a hummingbird, a spider, a monkey, and several humanoid shapes hundreds of feet long, to say nothing of the many crisscrossed straight lines scratched into the earth. These massive etchings were discovered by twentieth-century visitors only when someone flew over the area in the late twenties. People walked right by them without knowing they were there. Today they are common knowledge. These geoglyphs are your legacy, Maddy, because your father focused his search on that mystical Peruvian plain." Torbald's voice intensified. "Your mother was with Mason on the eastern slopes of the Andes when he visited a monastery in the small village of Chupicchu somewhere near Nazca. There, he met a ninety-seven-year-old monk who possessed an ancient parchment."

"The Peruvian Prize."

"Precisely." Torbald stared into her eyes. "Mason knew its value. He paid a fortune to possess this tattered paper, restored over several generations. It was the last graphic reproduction of a stone rubbing that had been taken from a Nazca temple located near Pisco Bay on the Peruvian coast. The temple itself fell into the sea centuries ago."

Torbald pointed a finger at his palm as if the paper were in his hands. "The parchment, with its blend of language and hieroglyphs, revealed the fascinating legend of the god Quatel . . . a mythical figure whom I have related through research to pagan gods in other cultures, specifically Thoth in ancient Egypt and Horan, the Druid sky spirit. According to the geoglyphs, Quatel borrowed a piece of the sun that he brought to the Nazca Indians, his adopted earth children. Quatel taught the Nazcas to harness the power of this sun fragment, which he named Alca, 'fire from the stars.'"

"What a beautiful name."

"And Alca *was* beautiful. Presumably the Nazcas used this 'star fire' to build magnificent temples and burrow in the earth to make aquifers. Alca had the energy to defy gravity and move huge stones."

"Stones. Like the Egyptian pyramids I suppose." Maddy smiled.

"You're getting ahead of me."

"I'm sorry. But if Alca defied gravity, then those earth drawings, those geoglyphs . . ."

"According to the legend, the Nazcas didn't make the geoglyphs. Quatel's singular restriction was that his children should not use Alca's power to *fly*. *That* was a privilege for gods alone. The Nazcas disobeyed. One day, while Quatel busied himself with tasks on the other side of the moon, the natives defied his mandate and used Alca to rise into the heavens. Upon his return, Quatel learned of their disobedience and punished them. He took the sun fragment and hid it deep in the earth and then angrily departed for his home in the northern sky." Torbald's eyes shone. "According to the Nazcas, the continuing eruption of volcanoes in the mountains affirmed Alca's continued presence beneath the ground."

"And the geoglyphs?"

"Occurred because"—Torbald knelt and traced in the sand at his feet—"before leaving, Quatel used Alca's fiery hand to draw a map on the earth. This chart would show the Nazcas where they might find Alca at some future time— with the delicious irony that they could not view the entirety of the 'earth map' until they learned to fly themselves by other means. There have been recent theories about how one could see the individual earth drawings from surrounding hills, but without an understanding of the totality of the mural . . ."

Torbald's lines in the sand began to look familiar. Maddy knelt at his side. "That looks like Robert's grid."

"That was Robert's contribution. He interpreted the lines on the Nazca plain as geographic coordinates. When Tenille told Robert that Mason found the hummingbird and spider on the Peruvian Prize to be identical to the large earth drawings of the Nazca plain only two hundred miles away, Robert realized what Mason never had . . . that the plain of Nazca is a giant map itself. Robert had solved the riddle, which Mason would have, had he been given time. It was Mason's strong belief that Alca actually existed. He dedicated his life to finding it. He felt if he could control Alca, he would eventually hold the petroleum industry hostage, and thereby dictate the world's economic future."

"So his motive was greed after all."

"Don't judge him too harshly, Maddy." Torbald brushed sand from his knees and rose, staring into Maddy's eyes. "It's impossible to be sure what your father would have done with Alca had he found it. Robert certainly gave him the benefit of the doubt by reminding me that Mason's actions were affected by alcoholism. Who knows, perhaps finding Alca would have changed things. The pity was that Mason never had the chance. Severe complications of a stroke muddled his mind and, as if to seek a shred of immortality, Mason clung to his secret, selfishly believing that even in death he should possess the key to the ancient riddle. Tenille honored his request and buried the Peruvian Prize with him. However, she realized the waste of it and made a copy of the parchment prior to his interment. When Tenille succumbed to lung cancer three months later, she told Robert everything, confessing that Mason had used Robert's theories to pursue the legend." Torbald spoke sadly as he finished, "In a final moment of atonement, Tenille handed Robert the only copy."

Maddy could not help but be angered by her father's self-centeredness and her mother's deceit. "Why couldn't they tell me? Why would my mother exclude me?"

"Well, first of all, Maddy . . ." Torbald placed a sympathetic hand on Maddy's shoulder. "Robert deserved to know. Indirectly, he had inspired Mason's search. Secondly, as Robert told me, Mason and Tenille both recognized the dangers that Alca presented. You were very young; you had your own goals and dreams, and your parents saw no need to endanger you. Look what has happened since, with the murder of my associates and your uncle. Human life means little in the face of potential billions."

"But it's just a legend."

"A legend that has killed seven people and currently threatens my life. My position is clear. Whether Alca is real or unreal really doesn't matter. These killers are on my heels. If I can, I must find Alca before they find me. Of course I defer to you—it's your family, but you must help me to help yourself." Torbald was a man with few choices.

Maddy wondered if she had many of her own. Though she felt wronged and yearned for the comfort of her quiet lifestyle, she recognized that she might be forced to solve the mystery. If Torbald was right, the violent people involved would force the issue.

Torbald stood by as Maddy digested the problem. She stared at the ocean, watching ribbons of white waves crash in from the Atlantic. A flock of pelicans flew past, wings shining under a halo that ringed the moon. Maddy glanced back at Robert's apartment complex, glowing like a small castle on the shoulder of the beach. She imagined Robert walking these sands, contemplating his quest on nights like this.

Away from the buildings' light, the sky had deepened into an inky star-speckled blanket. Maddy felt small, gazing into the infinity of space. Then, among the galactic haze, Maddy envisioned Quatel, a ghostly astrological figure striding across the skies with a flaming ember in his hand, bringing a piece of fire to the earth.

"Star fire," she said softly, envisioning her father at the Peruvian monastery. "An eternally burning light, like the sun? Or a dynamo of perpetual energy, somehow contained. Do you think that's possible?"

"Of course—look up there." Torbald pointed at the heavens. "We stand in our atmospheric bubble witnessing the energies that rage beyond. Should our limited experience on this earthly speck of dust prevent us from recognizing the marvels that surround us? Who are we to say what is or is not possible? Alca isn't just a theoretical fragment of the sun, it represents the stuff of unlimited imagination . . . a power that molds stars."

"But if Alca exists, could it be some natural phenomenon hidden on our own world that could only be explained by a myth? Or are we to believe that this 'star fire' is something left behind by an alien visitation?"

Torbald shrugged. "What of atomic power? Nuclear marvels existed before we imagined them, Maddy. The fringe of our sun exploded thousands of nuclear bombs every day for millions of years. Then it became news. Humans captured its capacity. Would Alca be any different?"

"You're not answering me. Is it something from beyond our earth?"

"We can't think like that any longer, Maddy. *Everything* on this earth is from beyond. Atomic particles from our own solar system bombard our bodies every day. We have pieces of the stars inside us. The earth itself is simply a chunk of cooled star. Every school child knows that."

"But what do *you* believe?"

"As a man of faith, I believe God is the origin of all things."

"Even alien visitations?"

"Why not?"

"But you profess a Christian faith, and you're fascinated with pagan architecture."

Torbald's fervor thawed into a kindly smile. "God is the ultimate architect. In glorifying their accomplishments, humans fail to recognize that *all* creativity flows from a universal stream of consciousness. That stream originates from the rushing river of God's creation. As thinking beings, the moment humans looked into the heavens, we wanted to rush toward the cosmos, to fly, to bond with it, a destined joining with the heavens by osmosis, if nothing else. Yes, a cosmosis, our oneness with space and God's river of creation as our rightful inheritance." He spread his arms. "As a believer, I ride that river. As a scientist, I occasionally climb onto a raft full of facts." He stabbed the air with a forefinger. "But as a man who wants to stay alive . . . I am *forced* to solve Robert's mystery. And, from the look in your eyes, that's what you must do." Torbald pointed to her heart. "You can't turn your back on something potentially magnificent. Especially when *you* are the one who is meant to find it."

Robert's dying words to Jace reentered her mind, his final instructions to "tell Maddy." After several detours, her family's legacy had refused to pass her by.

She could only smile and nod.

Torbald grabbed her by the shoulders. "Good, Maddy. Let yourself go. Find your cosmosis, share it with the world, and put every ounce of energy into this hunt."

35

*The Cascadian Inn
Leavenworth*

JACE PLACED A HAND AGAINST the tile wall of the motel shower to steady himself. He'd had no rest since the gunfight at Maddy's house and felt drained, grateful for the streams of warmth that splashed his face. Blood still oozed from several cuts inside his cheeks, and as the taste of salinity filled his mouth, he spat some red into the drain.

The paramedic who attended to Jace had cleaned around the gash in his chest before stitching the wound. During the shower, Jace had succeeded in scrubbing the blood and grime from the rest of his body, but somehow he still didn't feel clean. He chose to let the hot water continue to pour, as if it could wash away the pain.

Jace's conversation with the police had been confused. He marveled that he'd been able to communicate at all.

In the glow of Jace's flaming rental car, Sheriff Davis and his deputies had driven into Maddy's gravel driveway. They had charged into the night with guns drawn, having noticed one of the hooded men lying by the side of the house.

As Sheriff Davis told Jace, he had followed the trail of blood toward the rear of the home, where he was shocked to see the carnage. Davis thought everyone was dead, including Jace, who was covered in red and lay sprawled across Cory, hugging his body.

It was only after Davis drew closer that he realized Jace was alive, only superficially wounded. But Jace was more injured in another way, nearly speechless with grief. He'd had trouble focusing, leaning against the sheriff's car, wrapped in a blanket while Davis debriefed him.

The revelation of a dead man in the kitchen didn't surprise the sheriff; the fact that all the corpses were Asian did. Davis told Jace that another Chinese corpse had been found only days ago on the highway nearby. These men carried no identification.

The deputies' subsequent search in the backwoods behind Maddy's home revealed three dirt bikes hidden in the brush. Tire tracks of a fourth led off the plateau to the north toward Highway 87. But as Davis had pointed out, a search to the east or west on the interstate might be pointless if Jace's assailant had made his escape off road. Even the State Police chopper Davis had recruited would have trouble spotting a single rider under tree cover at night. Nevertheless, Davis had issued an APB on his car radio.

Jace rolled his neck back and squinted, letting the full force of the shower hit his eyes. They were sore from the beating he'd taken and from tears he'd shed when he called Cory's wife.

After Davis dropped Jace at his motel room, Jace phoned Jamilla to personally break the news. As Jace described Cory's death, the reality of their loss sunk in all the more. It was agonizing to hear Jamilla cry. Their conversation was interrupted several times as they wept together. Jace didn't elaborate on details: the hole in Cory's chest, the dark pool of blood on the gravel, the ambulance drivers placing the limp form in a black body bag, and the chilling sound of the zipper closing. But during the rehash, the reality took hold—Cory was gone forever. They'd had their last reunion. The idea of an autopsy upset Jamilla even more, and the conversation ended when she begged Jace to understand why she was forced to hang up.

Jace hadn't bothered her with the subject of Cory's funeral—military personnel would get in touch with the sheriff. According to Davis, Cory's autopsy would be complete by morning and Cory's body would be flown to an air base in Houston. Jace was told he would have to meet with a board of inquiry the morning of the funeral to explain the circumstances of Cory's murder.

Memories of Cory poured through his mind like old movie scenes: their early years, the many nights discussing their shared ill-fate at the foster home.

Jace remembered one windy evening when a summer storm brought sand pelting against the dormitory windows. During that unsettled night, Jace had bemoaned his parents' deaths. Cory had comforted him with tales of his own misfortune, insisting that as horrible as Jace's losses might have been, Cory had never even known who his parents were. Jace at least had photographs to remember. Cory's eyes had grown wide as he explained the significance of their blood-brother ritual in the furnace room. As a black orphan in a predominantly white area, Cory had chosen to begin his own bloodline with Jace. Tears welled in Jace's eyes as he recalled that statement. He remembered lonely Christmases, snowball fights, the laughter and the pain; Cory and he somehow knew their misfortune had become a mold for the greater strength of character that was being formed in its crush. Now, two decades later, misfortune had finally crushed Cory.

As Jace stood in the shower, his pain began to crystallize into resentment—and thoughts of revenge. Like Jace's father, Cory had died at the hands of strangers, and Jace vowed to find out who these maniacs were. A word floated forward in his mind, something he had completely forgotten and neglected to mention during his interview with Davis.

San. Wasn't that it? Of course, the word yelled by the spokesman. A Chinese name? Or could it have another meaning?

Jace used his fingers to trace the grout between the shower tiles, crosshatching up the wall, connecting pieces much like the puzzle in his mind. Robert Marro's killer—his father's killer—was Aryan in appearance. Maddy's house was searched by Asian men. Davis had found a nameless Asian man on the highway days before. And though Robert's murderer was assuredly Caucasian, there had to be a Chinese connection. A Chinese connection to his father? Could that make sense?

Whatever the word "San" meant, he had to tell Davis.

Jace nearly slipped on the slick shower pan as he whirled to turn off the water. He tore open the shower stall door, grabbed a towel off the rack, and then ran into the bedroom. Rubbing himself absentmindedly, dripping on the shag rug, he yanked the phone off the nightstand and dialed 0.

Mrs. Dubin came on the line and patched Jace through to Davis, who was at the lab, following up the investigation with his forensics people.

"Why aren't you asleep, Kelton?" the sheriff asked over the sound of other background voices.

"I couldn't."

"I don't blame you. You okay?"

"There's something I remembered. Just before all hell broke loose tonight, the guy who cut me yelled a word. It was 'san' or possibly 'sand,' something I thought you should know."

"Good." Davis sounded beat. "We don't know much else. Deputy Hargrove tracked the dirt bike tracks north to Highway 2. He lost the trail on the asphalt. The license plates on the bikes at the house came up on our computers. They were stolen from Winthrop two days ago . . . no witnesses. The guns they carried had their serial numbers filed off." Davis coughed and then recovered. "These guys weren't fucking around. Forensics did an analysis on the guy you tagged with the Beretta. Throat cultures show he killed himself with an arsenic cocktail. This was a suicide squad. You're sure that note you described was all they were after?"

Jace was reluctant to elaborate on Maddy's grid. He'd played down the paper as being a missing letter she'd wanted retrieved. "I can't be sure."

"Well, we may never know unless we come up with better leads. One odd thing—remind me, how many men did you see up there tonight?"

"Four. Three that chased me, and one in the kitchen."

"That would make five, including you. But my forensics people were able to isolate six distinct shoe prints near the house."

"What about Cory?"

"No, his military shoes were smooth soled. Your attackers wore crosstrainers. The extra set of prints came from a pair of climbing boots. Someone else was there. We'll put that 'san' or 'sand' business in the computer and run a check. Try to remember anything else."

A knock at the motel room door interrupted the conversation.

Jace wanted to finish the conversation, so he asked the sheriff to hold while he went to the door. After a second thought, he decided to peer out the window.

Under the porch light, Mrs. Dubin fidgeted on the cement walk in her bathrobe. She looked up and, noticing him peeking past the drapes, shouted through the glass, "You need to hang up, Mr. Kelton." She mimed the action with her hands. "There's a call holding for you. It's Madison, long distance from Nassau."

36

*Robert's Apartment
Nassau*

MADDY STOOD ON THE LANAI, gazing at the ocean. She found the quiet moment she desperately needed using Kit's cell phone while the others waited in the living room.

She maintained her composure at first as Jace shared his tragic report, but then the realization set in, and her tears began to flow. What was to have been an update on the retrieval of the grid took an unexpected turn, and she was stunned into silence by Jace's brutal account. Even in his own grief, he seemed concerned about the slaughter of Maddy's baby raccoons and the destruction of her property.

Momentarily overwhelmed, Maddy had been unable to reply. When Jace softly asked if she preferred to speak at a later time, she felt oddly close to him, as if their mutual suffering spanned the miles. She whispered her strong desire to speak to him face-to-face and suggested she fly out to Cory's funeral in order to obtain Robert's grid.

That's when Jace shared a final shocker: someone had removed the map from its hiding place prior to his arrival. Jace warned that his attackers were disguised, carried no ID, and were Asian like the man Sheriff Davis had found earlier, indicating a highly organized campaign against her.

Gaining her resolve, Maddy told Jace about Torbald's list of overseas casualties. The news seemed to steel Jace into renewed focus. Enemies seemed to be everywhere. They had to be. A single law enforcement agency would have difficulty confronting such a huge international effort. Jace agreed that approaching the FBI might not be only futile, but also dangerous. Cory had cautioned there was something "nasty" at work within the US government, and with other nations involved, there were few options.

Maddy didn't know where to turn.

As they said good-bye, Jace had reassured Maddy that prior to Jace's departure for Houston he would leave Mrs. Dubin in charge of her animals.

Maddy turned from the lanai rail, heaved a deep sigh, and wiped away what was left of her tears. It was after two o'clock in the morning. The moon had arced on its course over the apartment complex. It was time to get some sleep. She was about to go back inside when she heard a thud.

Maddy turned to see Hans Ostertag wrestling with Robert's fallen easel. The big man stooped to recover the painting he had apparently knocked to the floor.

Maddy opened the lanai door and entered as Torbald came to his nephew's aid, straightening the tripod's legs.

Hans sheepishly replaced the painting as Kit looked on.

"Oh, Miss Marro, sorry," Hans stuttered, blushing.

"What happened?" Maddy closed the glass.

"He was coming to get you when he tripped," Kit said, derisively.

Hans pointed to the canvas, reverting to Swedish, obviously apologizing.

Torbald rallied to his defense. "He feels terrible that he has marred Robert's painting."

"It's okay." Maddy noticed a rent at the lower right-hand corner of the canvas. Dabs of blue and white streaked Hans's elbow where he'd made contact with the still-wet oils.

"Not okay." Hans scooped the pigment from his arm with his fingers, making the awkward gesture to try to replace it.

Maddy gestured to the kitchen. "Go clean up. There must be a towel by the sink."

Hans shrugged, and while Torbald led him past the couch toward the counter, Kit stepped over, whispering, "The clumsy idiot tripped and then fell into the easel."

"Don't make a big thing of it." Maddy glanced at the rent in the oils. "Robert's probably the only one who would care." She hesitated, focusing on the smudge. "What's that?" She bent down to get a closer look at the smeared paint and noticed several ink marks visible on the canvas beneath. "Kit, hand me that palette knife."

Kit passed Maddy the small blade.

"There's something here," she said, scraping. The ink marks extended beyond the rent. She carefully removed an inch-long strip of the oils horizontally following the marks. The knife lifted a dab of blue, revealing a small number "7" and the letter N. Maddy turned toward the kitchen. "Torbald, there's something under this paint."

Torbald hurried into the living room with Hans in his wake. He stooped to look. "Dear God, it looks very much like the grid."

"Could it be?" Maddy asked excitedly. "What do you think the "7" means—Scalbania 7?"

"I don't know yet," Torbald replied.

"Well, let's remove the rest," Maddy said.

"Not yet. Consider how Robert chose to hide this beneath the painting. We mustn't destroy his intent."

"What do you mean?" Kit grabbed the knife.

"Think it through." Torbald restrained him, gripping his wrist. "What covers the clue might be as important as the clue itself."

"What? This lighthouse?"

"Precisely. Why would Robert choose that as his subject?" Torbald turned to Hans and spoke in Swedish, and as Hans left, Torbald explained. "He's going to wake the building manager."

Kit rolled his eyes. "Why are we getting this Jimmy guy involved?"

"We are going to ask him about the lighthouse," Torbald said patiently.

"You'll have to bribe the greedy son of a bitch." Kit flopped down on the couch.

It was only a few minutes before Hans returned. Jimmy followed, wearing striped pajamas.

Hans lingered outside the apartment front door as Torbald apologized about the late hour and questioned Jimmy about Robert's art.

Jimmy yawned, rubbing his eyes. "Did Mr. Robert really paint that?"

"He did," Maddy said. "Can you tell us, is this a local landmark?"

"That's not a Nassau lighthouse." Jimmy folded his arms. "But I've seen it."

Everyone looked on expectantly.

"Well?" Torbald followed.

"I'm trying to remember. I'm tired."

"I told you." Kit rose from the couch. "How much this time?"

"Good things come in threes."

"Shit." Kit rummaged in his pants pocket and handed Jimmy his third one hundred dollar bill.

Jimmy smiled. "You'll find that lighthouse on Cat Island."

"Where's Cat Island?"

"East of here, Ms. Marro. Half-a-day's boat ride. Cat's one of the other islands in the Bahama chain." Jimmy tilted his head, peering at the picture. "Painting's got a hole in it."

"Thank you for your time." Torbald stepped forward.

"What are those marks there?" Jimmy asked.

Torbald ushered Jimmy toward the door. "Hans will take you back."

Jimmy looked over his shoulder, but Hans towered over him, ushering him from the room.

The moment Jimmy was gone, Torbald scraped the rest of the oils away, depositing the paint on the palette Maddy held. Soon the canvas showed the expected series of lines and numbers.

Torbald stood back from the easel. "My God, Maddy, this is the original. Not one half—both halves. These lines show the geometric tangents of the Nazca plain.

Look . . ." He stepped forward and turned the canvas on its side. "This is north. See how the lines converge here in the eastern quadrant? That's the point of the equinox. That's the fulcrum from which we can make other calculations." Torbald's explanation was cut short as Hans, his crossbow in hand, burst through the door shouting in Swedish.

Torbald frowned. "We must leave immediately." He grabbed the canvas and handed it to Hans, who began to break down the wood frame, rolling the cloth into a scroll.

"What happened?" Maddy asked.

"We are being watched."

Kit leapt to his feet. "Why would he say that?"

"There is a white van parked across the street. The engine is running, and the man sitting in the front seat is wearing a hood."

Maddy remembered Jace's description of his attackers. "How can we leave?"

A rapid-fire reply from Hans caused Torbald to snatch his briefcase. "Hans knows a way."

Kit grabbed Maddy's travel bag plus his own. Torbald and Hans were already out the door.

As Kit pushed Maddy into the hall, she resisted, pausing at the doorjamb for one last look at Robert's apartment.

"Maddy, let's go," Kit whispered.

Saying a silent good-bye, as if to Robert himself, she pulled away.

They were on the run, and she intuitively knew that they would be for the foreseeable future.

PART THREE

37

Cat Island, Bahamas

UNDER A CLEAR BLUE MIDDAY sky, the Toyota Corolla sped through the underbrush, passing palm groves, raising a cloud of dust on the southern flatlands of Cat Island.

"Kit, could you bring it down a notch?" Maddy hung onto the overhead strap of the rented car's backseat.

"What are you worried about? We're the only ones out here." Kit negotiated a tight curve on the one lane dirt road as ferns and fronds battered the side of the small car.

"That's not the issue." Maddy glanced over at Torbald, who sat at her side, leaning hard to his left with the momentum of the turn. In the passenger seat, Hans's head bumped the roof liner. "We're all taking a beating. It's uncomfortable at this speed."

Kit looked over his shoulder. "I thought we were in a hurry."

"We are, but not at the risk of losing our lunch," Maddy replied.

Slowing down, Kit made eye contact in the rearview mirror. "How's this?"

Torbald nodded his approval and went back to studying a dog-eared chart he had borrowed from the tiny Cat Island Marina. He carried twenty odd maps in his briefcase, including Robert's canvas ink drawing, now cleansed of the oil paint.

"Six kilometers to the town of Clemmons." Torbald squinted into the folds. "There should be a large rock outcropping at the shoreline, and then a left turn onto a small peninsula. The lighthouse should be visible from there."

"I still don't see why Captain Atwood couldn't just drop us off," Kit said over his shoulder. "He had a good-sized dinghy."

"Submerged reefs," Maddy answered. "Hence the lighthouse."

"Bullshit. He was just lazy."

Maddy shook her head and chose not to respond.

The heavyset Captain Atwood had been cooperative enough, considering that Kit, ill-tempered from lack of sleep, had haggled the poor man to death.

Maddy found Kit's behavior annoying, especially because *her* credit card was the one to be used to charter Atwood's ancient fifty-two-foot Hatteras. As it was, she paid a thousand dollars a day plus gas to get from Nassau to Cat Island, which was located to the southeast some two hundred miles. Fortunately, Atwood's tri-cabin boat with its fifteen-foot beam had accommodated Maddy's weary party quite well; they had slept little during their evasive action the night before.

During their 2:00 a.m. escape from Robert's place, Maddy had gained an appreciation for Hans's reconnoiter routine. He led their retreat, ushering them to the apartment basement where he'd located an escape route through a swimming-pool maintenance room. They burst into the breezy night onto the beach without being seen.

After a fifteen-minute sandy hike toward the north, they cut across a beach frontage road and tried to find a cab. With little traffic and no pay phones in the sparsely populated area, it quickly became apparent they would have no luck. Continuing their trek another mile, they woke the manager of a small beach-front cabana. They had slept there for four hours. At daybreak, a taxi brought them to the Nassau docks. Fortunately, they'd found Captain Atwood, whose boat had been the only charter available, because it was a pleasure craft and not a deep-sea fishing boat.

During their ride on the gently rolling swells, Captain Atwood had told them what he knew of their destination.

Cat was small, L-shaped, and out of the way. The lighthouse Robert had painted sat on the southeastern tip on a spit called Governor's Point, which Atwood explained was also called "triangle point" by the locals.

Torbald's eyebrows had knit with interest. "Why triangle?" he had asked.

"Because one corner of the Bermuda Triangle rests almost exactly at those coordinates," Atwood had explained.

As Maddy recalled the ruddy, almost mystical expression on Atwood's face as he talked about the ships that had disappeared off the coast, the distant ocean became visible through the windshield.

"We're very close," Torbald said, pointing. His landmarks began to appear one by one. They had already passed through the tiny ramshackle township of Clemmons.

Kit steered the Toyota past a boulder-covered crag and turned left. The Toyota's tires crunched on the crushed clamshells that covered a road, which crowned the peninsula. The spectacular promontory was bordered by water on three sides. At the island's easternmost tip, Robert's now familiar lighthouse crested a mound of gray rock. The white tower gleamed against the barren eternity of the Atlantic.

Kit brought the overheated car to a stop at the base of a path that led up to the lighthouse cylinder. The roar of the surf greeted Maddy as she exited the vehicle with the others. All around, huge waves crashed onto gnarled rock formations, blowing plumes of spray into the hollows.

Maddy's gaze rose to the glass lantern room at the top of the lighthouse.

Torbald mumbled that he estimated the building to be well over a hundred years old; it certainly looked its age, with its weathered walls. While Maddy led Kit and Torbald up the steep lighthouse path, Hans took his usual flanking route, clambering over the boulders further to the south. As they finished their climb, Maddy stepped to the threshold and tried the handle of the main door.

It was locked.

Winded, Torbald folded his arms around his satchel, leaned against a metal banister, and suggested that, while he caught his breath, Kit and Maddy should scout the perimeter of the whitewashed building.

They agreed. Climbing over the rocky terrain, Maddy and Kit circled the tower but found no other access. As they returned to the front step, Maddy's disappointment was short-lived. She saw Hans standing downhill some fifty yards away, waving and pointing at the ocean.

"What's he saying?" She brushed the hair from her eyes.

"There's a man fishing on the rocks below." Torbald said as he headed in that direction. Kit and Maddy quickly caught up, and as they crested a large boulder, Maddy saw the man to whom Hans had referred.

A leathery-faced, middle-aged fellow set his fishing pole aside and climbed forty feet of rough rock to greet them. He was barefoot, dressed in torn Levi's and a fuchsia T-shirt that burned bright against his black skin. Speaking in heavily accented English, the smiling man shook hands all around and introduced himself as "Satch, the keeper of the flame"—a name he'd acquired because the beam of the lighthouse operated on an antiquated gas system.

Torbald asked, "Do you remember a man about my age who came here some days ago to paint a picture of this lighthouse?"

"Yes, sir. We spoke to one another."

"He was my uncle," Maddy interjected. "Just passed away."

"I'm so sorry. He was a very energetic man."

Torbald squinted at the lighthouse. "Did he tell you why he wanted to paint this?"

"To remember it."

"That was it?" Torbald ran his hand through his silver hair as Satch nodded. "Did he say anything else?"

Satch thought a moment. "He found the triangle fascinating."

Maddy's interest piqued. "The Bermuda Triangle?"

Satch broke into a broad semitoothless grin. "Oh no, miss. The triangle that's over there." He pointed to the other side of the lighthouse. "It's a shape that nature made in a rock at the water's edge."

"Will you show us?" Torbald seemed quite excited.

Satch agreed. He led them across the rocks toward the north side of the spit.

Tugging at Torbald's sleeve, Maddy whispered, "What's the big deal with the triangle?"

"Remember the marks on Robert's grid?" Torbald patted his briefcase. "If you'll recall, incomplete triangles are the predominant shape on the Nazca plain."

Maddy did remember. Where Nazca's long, straight earth lines converged they often formed two sides of unfinished triangles, as if a third side might be added later.

Satch came to a jagged crag and pointed to the water's edge. "There it is, as old as the sea itself, or so they say."

Satch indicated a large, rectangular black rock at least fifty feet long and twenty feet wide, which sat just above the breaking surf. The shape of a triangle was clearly visible in the gently rounded top of the rock, etched into the stone some four inches deep.

"Look at that," Torbald said in awe. "It's perfect." The wedge measured some fifteen feet at its widest point. Straight, precise edges appeared to have been cut into the stone. "Mr. Satch, thank you, thank you again." Torbald grinned broadly. "We don't want to keep you from your fishing. Please go enjoy yourself. We hope you don't mind if we stay here for a few moments?"

"No."

"Then we'll just make ourselves at home." Torbald began to usher Satch back up the incline. "Don't let us disturb you any further."

Looking nonplused, Satch shrugged and began to retreat. "Okay. I'll be over there if you need me."

Torbald smiled disarmingly, hovering near the lip of the boulder. The moment Satch left, he quickly clambered down the embankment toward the water and stepped onto the monolith.

The charcoal-colored stone bubbled air from a million tiny holes as the surf spray drenched it. The texture was highly porous, drying easily after being soaked.

Torbald handed his briefcase to Maddy and knelt down. With his pants drenched from the brine, he felt along the edge of the wedge—almost as if he were searching for a pulse. "Note the shape of this rock?" Torbald shouted above the roar of the surf. "It reminds me of a sarcophagus. It's very odd, unlike the other boulders on the shore . . . volcanic as opposed to the other rocks, which are most certainly hypabyssal."

"Hypa . . ." Kit struggled.

"Formed at the surface of the planet," Torbald said absentmindedly. "This coffin-like stone doesn't belong here." Torbald rose and indicated the angular depression in the stone. "And look how the triangle's narrow corner points toward the sea . . ." He took his briefcase from Maddy and fumbled for a compass, laying it in the palm of his hand. "The third side is pointed west."

Maddy was confused. "Is that significant?"

"It means this is the marker Robert found," Torbald said excitedly. "And rather than keep records, he painted its location in case something should happen to him." Torbald clutched a protractor in his hand, setting it into the wedge's southern apex. "Ahhh, yes." Without explanation, he began to scale the embankment from where they had just come.

"Torbald?" Maddy called.

"Let me show you something. Come up here where it's dry, all of you." Torbald had reached a flat spot, and as the others followed and gathered around, he pulled several maps plus a blank sheet of paper from his briefcase. He spread one of the maps on the ground. With his compass and protractor in hand, he began to trace on the sheet of paper that he had laid on top of a large map labeled "Le Monde."

"Look at this map of the world . . . if I connect the Bahamas with the pyramids in Giza, Egypt, to a third point where the Nazca plain sits in Peru, I form a triangle thusly, which I've marked in pencil. We'll call this triangle 'A.'" He pointed to the paper. "You'll notice that the angle of triangle 'A' at Nazca taken against its longitude is 22.5 degrees. You will also notice the angle at Giza taken against its latitude is also 22.5 degrees."

Torbald gestured to the wedge in the stone. "The tip of the triangle in the rock down there, which we'll call Triangle B"—he pointed excitedly—"has that same angle of 22.5."

Maddy stepped forward. "But your triangle 'B' in the rock is nearly at right angles to what you've just drawn on the map."

"True. Triangle A, the Nazca-Giza-Bahama triangle, is only half of the geometry. Triangle B in the rock is the other half. If we orient ourselves to Triangle B in the rock and overlay its orientation in real life to the way it would appear on a map . . ." Torbald looked across the island. "And if the lines of this wedge, as it sits, were taken to infinity, they would run toward the south and somewhere to the west. Let's trace that on the map." Checking his compass for the triangle's orientation, Torbald used his pencil to draw a line on the map from the Bahamas toward the west, across Mexico and into the Pacific.

Torbald smiled knowingly. "Now let's review Robert's final words. He said 'Nassau' . . . and there we went. He said 'the stone' . . . and here we stand. And because Robert didn't know exactly—or because he wanted to avoid naming the precise location to Mr. Kelton, a complete stranger—he verbalized the final necessary clue, but he ran out of breath. 'Ease' was not the word he intended to say but rather the first syllable of an unfinished word, which I suspect was 'Easter.' I also believe that Easter would have been followed by another word, 'Island.' If you look at the map and connect Easter Island to Nassau, that gives us our second leg . . ." Torbald ran his pencil from south to north.

Maddy was confused. "All right. You've drawn two lines that ostensibly head from our position to infinity toward the south and west. How do we determine where the third intersecting north–south line should be?"

"I can do that by taking our 22.5 degree angle at Easter Island and creating the third leg, which runs due north up the 109th longitude toward our open-ended triangle 'B.' We can see how the triangle falls across Mexico and the southern United States. And where the westerly line from Nassau meets the northerly line from Easter Island . . ." He finished the lines. "It completes the triangle. Now, Maddy, where is the northernmost point of our newly formed 'B' triangle?"

Brimming with anticipation, Maddy checked the spot on the map where the lines intersected. "There, in the American Southwest." She placed a finger where Torbald's lines met. "Near Arizona."

"Yes." Torbald handed Maddy a larger map of the United States. "And if you add 7 degrees north to that, as the grid indicates, where do you find yourself?"

Maddy squinted at the map, locating the name in a tiny font. "It says 'Monument Valley.'"

"All right, then that," Torbald said, his eyes shone with delight, "must be the hiding place of an ancient miracle."

38

Randolph Air Force Base
Houston

AS EVERYONE WAITED FOR CORY'S casket to disappear, Cory's wife, Jamilla, clutched Jace's hand so hard the ridges of his commemorative athletic ring dug into his fingers. She had sobbed into her handkerchief during Chaplain Sutherland's eulogy, while Clarissa, Jamilla's mother, moaned her sorrow. Jacel, Cory's six-year-old son, had stared up at his grandmother, his eyes wide in bewilderment.

Cory's glossy maroon coffin would be lowered into the grave any moment.

Jace's best friend would leave the surface of the earth. Little wonder some ancient Indian cultures left their dead above ground, perhaps gaining comfort from the departed loved ones remaining in the light of day.

Jace glanced up at the bright Texas sun.

An outdoor funeral created disquieting contrasts: a buoyant blue sky mocked the sobriety of the mourners' black clothes, distant sprinklers shot a cheery spray of water onto the cemetery lawns, and the military formality of the funeral seemed oddly out of place in the September sunshine.

Jace and other seated civilian mourners were surrounded by standing air force personnel—forty to fifty men and women in dress uniform—Cory's friends and coworkers. Jace recognized some faces he'd seen on his recent emergency arrival from the *Aurora*. The judge advocate general who had presided over the hearing that morning was among the officers seated in back. His ruling had been that Cory had been killed in a random civilian incident, with no bearing on his military record. As for a final report—the air force would await further findings from the sheriff's office.

In the hush of the midday heat, the anticipated moment of farewell arrived as Chaplain Sutherland gave the benediction and asked the congregation to bow their heads in prayer. Four air force officer pallbearers stepped forward, took the flag off the coffin, and folded it into a tight triangle. One young man advanced and handed it to Jamilla. Seconds later, a seven-man honor guard raised its rifles and fired three times.

In the vacuum of silence that followed, the pallbearers took hold of the white rope that cradled the casket. They lowered Cory's coffin. It came to rest at the bottom of the grave, and the men snapped to attention.

Jamilla took a handful of dirt and cast it onto the coffin. Clarissa and Jacel followed, sprinkling their handfuls.

Now it was Jace's turn. With his throat knotting with emotion, his eyes drenched with tears, he grabbed his own fistful of yellow earth and dusted the top of the shiny veneer. He uttered a prayer for Cory's soul and a last good-bye to his boyhood friend.

He turned and joined the family at the edge of the grass, taking Jacel's hand into his own, putting an arm around Jamilla. She sobbed and buried her face in his shoulder. "He was my life. They took my *life* from me.

Jace whispered, "I'll find the people who did this, Jamilla. I promise. I'm meeting Madison Marro in Phoenix tonight. While the Leavenworth police continue their investigation, I'll follow what leads I can."

Jace knelt and hugged Jacel. "Be strong, son. Help your momma. Pray for your daddy, and pray for me. I'll be back."

The small boy's hands met around his neck. "How soon, Uncle Jace?"

Jace swallowed hard. "When I can tell you that your daddy's work is done."

Jace held Jacel tight as the little boy's rib cage pulsed with sobs.

After a few moments, Jamilla's mother approached and took Jacel's hand. "Let Uncle Jace go," Clarissa said.

Jace looked up into her clouded eyes. "I'll walk you to your car."

He took Jamilla's arm, and they strode down the sloping green lawn toward the black limousines that waited at the bottom of the hill.

They had descended the asphalt path among the tombstones a few hundred feet when someone called out, "Mrs. Jackson?"

Jace turned, and what he saw sent a shiver up his back. A black air force officer emerged from the departing mourners. In the backlit glint of the sun, the man's stature seemed hauntingly reminiscent. It was as if Cory were alive, miraculously rising from the ground to declare that everything had been a terrible mistake.

Jace shaded his eyes as the officer drew near, and the fantasy faded—the man's face was fuller, the eyes deeper set, the nose a bit broader.

The officer removed his cap as he approached. "You may not remember me, Mrs. Jackson. I'm an old friend of your husband's. My name is Colonel Randal Dixon."

Jamilla took his hand. "Thank you for coming, Colonel. Cory spoke of you."

"I had great respect for the major." Dixon nodded to Clarissa and, with a riveting glance, shook Jace's hand. "You would be Jace."

"I am."

"I need a word with you." A cordial tilt of the head to Jamilla. "I'm sorry if this is inconvenient, but may I steal Jace away for a moment?"

"Of course. Won't you join us later at my home?" she added graciously.

"I would, but I'm due in Washington tonight. I'm afraid I can't stay." Dixon nudged Jace and gestured to a shady spot under neighboring trees. "Perhaps we could talk over there?"

Jace glanced at Jamilla. She nodded understandingly. "We'll find our way to the car, Jace. Say good-bye when you're ready."

Jace watched as Clarissa hobbled with her cane, holding Jamilla's arm. Little Jacel hung on as they continued down the path.

"I didn't notice you before," Jace said as they headed for the trees. Some of the officers still milled about the grave site.

"I stayed at the back." Dixon pointed to the now empty rows of metal chairs. "Officially, I'm not supposed to be here. But I had to see you."

They reached a shaded pocket under several willow trees. A desert wind blew gently through the coolness of the branches.

Dixon looked up into the filtered sunlight as if to gather his thoughts. "Besides paying my respects, I came here to tell you what I know. Cory would have wanted it that way. You'll excuse my directness, but I don't have much time." The intensity of Dixon's eyes contrasted his otherwise calm appearance: the immaculate uniform, the sculptured hair and neatly trimmed mustache. "How much did Cory tell you?"

"Not a lot. The last time I saw him, he had a hole in his chest."

"I understand. But would I be correct in saying that 'fear' is now a special part of your vocabulary?" Dixon was probing.

"Yes. He told me about the Phobia File—that it was coded because of an international mandate. The Russians were in on it."

"That's right."

"Apparently Robert Marro's claims about a cover-up were legitimate."

"Marro was a key player, but he didn't realize how deep it went." Dixon leaned forward and lowered his voice. "Over the years, our trajectory experts did elaborate studies on Mars. They found serious anomalies in the elliptical patterns of the Martian moons, particularly, Phobos. It turns out that, over time, Phobos had an orbit that accelerated closer to the planet Mars. In a natural body, that's indicative of a lack of mass."

"I don't follow."

"The orbital pattern showed Phobos might be porous, perhaps even hollow. Phobos has a radius of 7 miles. The other Martian moon, Deimos, is 3.9 miles across. They're two of the smallest moons in the solar system."

"You're implying—"

"I'm not implying anything. When Cory asked, I was able to access top-secret material. According to the files, Phobos seems to be an artificial body."

"That's insanity. I thought Robert Marro was embellishing—"

"Jace. I'm not making this up."

Jace remembered Cory's theories. "You mean . . . Cory wasn't just blowing smoke."

"I know why you'd think that. I remember how he was in college."

"He was a sci-fi freak."

Dixon leaned in. "But when Chuck Armstrong played golf on our moon's surface in 1969, you remember seeing coverage of that on TV?"

"Sure."

"Was that sci-fi?"

"That's different," Jace said.

"Why?"

"Because we're suddenly faced with the possibility of an alien intelligence."

Dixon's expression hardened. "People found it totally acceptable for the US government to spend millions of tax dollars to find intelligence in space. Remember the *Voyager* satellite, the one with a picture of two humans, a description of our race, and an invitation to contact us? No one batted an eye. What about SETI, 'The Search for Extraterrestrial Intelligence'? Giant dishes trained on the sky, continually listening for radio waves from space. Was it ludicrous to anticipate an answer? Are we all crazy?"

"I mean no disrespect."

"Well, I do. I disrespect our government's misinformation campaign. From the atom bomb to stealth fighters to Area 51 and now the Phobia File. We've had a history of denial. The Phobia File shows that after decreasing for centuries, the Phobos moon orbit began to *expand* again four years ago. What does that tell you?"

"It's controlled?"

"Bingo." Dixon nodded. "Get used to it. This ain't no bullshit."

"But surely the astronomy community would be aware of that data."

"Not if the astronomy community was fooled because data had been falsified."

Cory would have loved it. Jace had been pummeled into silence, and though it was hard to believe what he'd just heard, Dixon's words sent him scrambling. "So you believe Phobos is some kind of satellite?"

"Maybe. I don't know. But something . . . some kind of *energy* is steering that rock. Among the intellectual elite in the intelligence community there's been a lot of talk about hyperdimensional physics."

"Explain."

"Physics that deal with multidimensions where Newtonian principles no longer apply. Some scientists believe the planets in our solar system are guided by a gyroscopic effect based on the tetrahedron triangle. The tetrahedron is the natural triangular vortex within any sphere. It's also the key geometric element in the pyramids of Egypt and, as a matter of fact, in a pyramid that NASA photographed on the Cydonia plain on Mars in 1976."

"I thought those 'ruins on Mars' rumors were refuted as tabloid journalism."

Dixon shrugged. "Let's say NASA gave the press a new 'ruins' photograph that they, themselves, disqualify as incomplete information. They made no further mention of other pyramids that stand nearby."

"So these monuments that Robert believed in were real?"

"They weren't proven not to be."

"And now you're saying that this supposed Martian pyramid has the identical geometry as some of ours?"

Dixon clicked his tongue. "That's right."

"I'm meeting Marro's niece in Phoenix. She's convinced that there's a vortex of some kind—a power center that Robert Marro discovered." Jace was struck by the irony. "Oddly enough, through a set of triangles."

Dixon looked uneasy. "Run that by me again?"

"She mentioned something about matching northern and southern triangles with a common angle of 22.5 degrees."

Dixon's eyes narrowed. "A tetrahedron triangle is based on a pure 45 degrees. But when it's cut in half by an axis . . ."

"It's 22.5."

"There's something to that." Dixon moved out from under the willow, and they walked down the hill toward the cars.

Jace glanced at the limos where Jacel, Jamilla, and her mother waited in the sun. "What about them? Are they in danger?"

Dixon's eyes clouded with concern. He shook his head. "I don't think so. But I'll keep tabs on them." Dixon extended a hand. "In the meantime, I look forward to your findings."

"How would I let you know?"

"Don't worry. If you guys score, I'll hear about it."

Jace shook Dixon's hand and felt his camaraderie.

Dixon hesitated. "Jace. One last thing." He stepped closer. "The Phobia File contained the names of several men instrumental in advancing the Phobos theories. I thought you should know . . . your dad was one of them."

39

The Hunting Lodge
Near Abbotsford, Canada

BRUSHING A LOCK OF LONG blond hair back from his face, Shag tucked his white silk scarf into his shirt collar and reached for the deck of cards. He poised them on his fingertips. "How many cards, Mr. Cho?"

Cho's slicked-back black hair glinted electric blue as he leaned forward. His watery eyes were set like a badger's, walleyed and expressionless, bulging above the skin that stretched over his cheekbones. He spoke immaculate English, though he hadn't said a word in some time. Instead, he patiently chewed some of the sunflower seeds he carried in his vest pocket. After some contemplation, he used his delicate fingers to slide a single card facedown toward Shag.

Shag dealt him another, and then he glared at the next player.

With his back to the moose head that hung over the fireplace, Hector Walsh cleared his throat, looking quite unlike himself, disguised in his bleached hair and a full mustache. "I hate to be obvious, gentlemen, but I'll take three." He tapped the knife-marred table with his left hand, which was still bandaged from the sulfur burn he had suffered while setting the explosion in his Toronto lab. Walsh had arrived last night, traveling safely after having been resurrected by Cho's network with a set of fresh IDs.

Shag turned to the chubby man in the lambskin vest. "And you?"

Vincent Scalbania's pouty mouth twisted spitefully. "I don't give a shit."

"That's impolite." Cho's green eyes fixed on Norman Scalbania's stepson. "I had it in my mind not to kill anyone today, but you might change that."

Vincent slapped his cards on the table. "I came here to talk business, not to gamble."

"You're gambling with your life," Cho said coolly.

"In that case, I intend to win."

Cho gave Shag a quick glance before turning to Vincent. "Some people win. Others die trying. But if you check the cemetery, you'll find there are no dead winners."

Shag took a swig of schnapps from his flask. "It's Mr. Cho's game, Vincent," he said. "Play the game. You're lucky your ass is still warm."

Vincent's thick lips pressed into a scowl. "Give me three, for Christ's sake."

The poker was a fabrication of course, but the game served Cho's purpose: allowing him to stall and reassess, to cool hot tempers that had reached a boiling point, to detract from Vincent Scalbania's dramatic demands. What was to have been a final planning meeting had suddenly become a power struggle within Cho's ranks.

Vincent Scalbania had arrived bristling with paranoia, fearing that he would either be left out of Cho's operation or killed like the other members of the S-7. He had blurted his ultimatum before anyone else could say a word. The pudgy bastard had even stunned Shag when he admitted that—under a false identity of "Dr. Bellamy"—he had checked at the Klakamas Inn for Madison Marro, located her during her fieldwork at Stag Lake, and watched the drama unfold as Shag's men had stalked her. Vincent had followed Madison back to the lodge and tailed her to her home. There, Vincent had surprised Lee Chou, who had been left to keep an eye on things, and clubbed him from behind. Shag was impressed that Vincent had overcome a trained Chinese agent, stashing his body in the trunk of his car and later chucking it on the highway. Vincent's break finally came when Madison stashed something in her birdhouse. Vincent had discovered that the birdhouse contained one-half of Robert Marro's grid, which Vincent removed, leaving the envelope stuffed with a blank sheet to make the theft less obvious.

The story made sense to Shag, who had been debriefed by Nang, the lone survivor of the gun battle at Madison's home. The account explained why the American named Kelton hadn't relinquished the grid under the duress of torture. He couldn't.

Vincent, armed with sole possession of the half-grid, pointed out that even though Shag had recovered one-half of Robert Marro's grid in Vancouver, without *Vincent's* half, Cho couldn't do a thing. Consequently, Vincent demanded a third of the potential profits as opposed to the 5 percent he had been offered.

With Vincent's heated words still echoing in the room, Cho had surprised everyone by suggesting things could be best resolved during a card game. Vincent had refused at first, but after Shag placed his combat knife next to Vincent's ear, he agreed to sit down.

Shag took one card from the top of the deck and examined his hand. He had dealt himself a king of spades, which was no help to his pair of tens. "I'll fold," he said, quietly.

To Shag's left, Cho raised his bet to two hundred dollars, and while Walsh considered his wager, Shag glanced out the window, checking two of his men, who stood in their black parkas under the eaves of the woodshed. From their vantage point overlooking the rolling hills of western Canada, they could spot a car approaching on the one-lane road six miles out.

Shag had asked that his guards remain armed. He wasn't nervous; he simply understood that there was a remote possibility that his people could be traced, even though they had died without ID.

Walsh's raspy cough shook Shag from his thoughts.

"I'll see your two hundred, Cho." Walsh placed several wrinkled bills on the already substantial pile.

Vincent Scalbania contemplated his bet, and Shag again stared at the rain. He pondered how best to use his task force going forward. Du and Kwan waited in Nassau for further instructions. Xi and Chang, the two men by the woodshed, had arrived with Cho. Nang, the lone Leavenworth survivor, and Wo guarded the lodge entrances, with Wo on the front porch and Nang at the rear door. All were armed with Intratec TEC-9 semiautomatic handguns with the mandate to protect Cho at all costs. Normally, Cho traveled with ease, carrying the credentials of a Chinese diplomat, but as the chase for Robert Marro's prize deepened, so had the risks. Cho's safety was now in Shag's hands.

As an intelligence master of the Communist regime in Beijing for two decades, Cho wielded the power of the Chinese government, particularly the Ministry of Technology, which had heavily endorsed his plan as early as 1986 when China pursued what it called its 863 Program—an accelerated development of space technology and internal energy needs. Cho believed that the answer to his country's ravenous energy requirements lay within the province of other nations' space programs, and Cho had been instrumental in convincing his superiors that cyber theft and technological espionage accomplished more than research. It had been Cho's prying into his cousin Jinseng Ma's scientific work in Hong Kong that tipped Cho off to the existence of the S-7 and ultimately led to a diligent surveillance of all S-7 members, including Mason Marro.

The subsequent investigation of Mason Marro's travel to Peru brought attention to all aspects of Mason's life and his death. This resulted in the mysterious disappearance of the funeral director who had presided over Mason's remains and the cultivation of a financial relationship with Norman Scalbania's disinherited stepson, Vincent.

Vincent Scalbania had been disowned in Norman's will and was vindictive and eager to garner profits from his estranged stepfather's project.

Cho had also plied Hector Walsh with large sums of money after Walsh was approached by Robert Marro. Walsh was a brilliant scientist and essential to Cho's effort, having helped interpret the Peruvian Prize with its elaborate legend of Alca and the origin of the Nazca plain.

Vincent had become expendable, and he had sensed it. That's why Vincent had decided to make his move now, before someone might terminate him.

Shag never liked Vincent, though the fat little fuck showed some balls, all pompous storming into the lodge. He was still huffy, fanning his cards and smiling at Cho.

"I think I'll see your two hundred, Cho." Vincent stacked the bills. "And I'll raise you another two."

Cho glared, nodded, and reached for his money. He laid the matching hundreds on the pile and placed a hand over the kitty. "Before I see your cards, Vincent, a question."

"I know what you're going to ask."

"Do you?"

"You think I've betrayed you, and you don't understand why."

"No. I want you to tell me why I shouldn't kill you."

"I was worried you might. But without my half of the grid, you're stuck."

"So now it's 'your' half?" Cho bit into another sunflower seed and spit the shell onto the hardwood floor. Cho seemed disturbed by Vincent's confidence. "Suppose I don't need it? Perhaps the answers lie in Nassau," he said, chewing.

"You've lost track of the Marro party."

"Only temporarily."

Cho pulled Shag's half of the grid from his jacket pocket. He toyed with it, held it up to the light, squinting at the lines and numbers. He nodded across the table at Walsh. "What do *you* have to say?"

Walsh phrased his answer carefully. "The Peruvian Prize documented Alca's existence, but I believe Robert's grid is a clarification of the Nazca plain, a series of coordinates on an overlay, if you will. We need a reference point to align the topography—a meridian of some kind. That's the missing key."

Cho's green eyes narrowed. "That's a lot of speculation from someone who hasn't seen the missing half."

"Well, I assumed—"

"No more assumptions." Cho gave Shag a nod and in Chinese said, "Ask Wo and Nang to join us, weapons cocked and ready to fire, trained on the fat one."

Shag got to his feet. As he sauntered toward the front door, he heard Vincent's voice. "What are you doing?"

Cho didn't answer.

"I think you better think this through," Vincent said, his voice rising. "You won't find a thing without the grid."

Shag opened the front door and summoned Wo.

As Shag walked back through the living room, Wo cocked his weapon and took a flanking position to Vincent, who now began to stutter. "Goddamn it, Cho, let's talk."

Cho leaned forward in his chair. "Why? When a pig is sufficiently fattened, it's time for slaughter."

Shag opened the back door. Nang followed him to the table. In Chinese, Cho told the two gunmen to aim at Vincent's head.

They obeyed, and Vincent began to crack. "Cho, stop it. Goddamn it, Walsh, you've got to back me up."

Walsh's mustache twitched. His eyes flitted nervously between Cho and the gunmen. "Cho, wait. I think there's something you should know."

"Ahhh." Cho hooked his thumbs in his vest and leaned back in his chair. "A collaboration." At Cho's command, Nang pivoted and pointed his weapon at Walsh.

"Never against you," Walsh said, with a firmer tone than Shag expected. "It's just that once you find Alca, Vincent and I are worthless. We need some insurance."

"And you left me to pay the premium?"

"No, it's not like that," Walsh said. "But I felt I'd better keep a record of our activities. My report is stored with Vincent's will, to be mailed to the FBI by his attorney at Vincent's request, or in the event of his death."

Shag remembered that in his early years, Walsh had been hired by the United States government, working in Washington on several research projects. Cho glanced at Shag, who nodded affirmation. Walsh could be telling the truth.

"I see. So *your* motive is fear. And his," he nodded at Vincent, "is greed."

"No, damn it." Vincent pointed at Walsh. "Ask him. We were going to split the money."

Cho's ragged smile revealed remnants of sunflower seeds between his teeth. "Vincent's thirty-three percent plus your five, Walsh? I'm surprised."

"It's business, after all," Walsh pleaded.

"I don't think you have much choice in the matter," Vincent added caustically.

Cho folded his narrow hands. "Vincent, I commend you for your initiative." A glance at Shag. "You duped our men. Well done. Give up the grid and I'll guarantee you ten percent apiece, plus a bonus . . . your life."

Vincent's face clouded with confusion.

Walsh tossed his cards on the table.

Cho smiled, glancing at Vincent. "I believe it was my call, Vincent. What do you have?"

Vincent absentmindedly clutched his cards. He blinked several times and refocused on his hand. "Why? Is this winner take all?"

"What do the bandits say? 'Your money or your life.'"

"Jesus, Cho. I'll take the deal. Ten percent."

"Show me your cards."

Vincent's hands shook as he laid his hand over. "Three queens."

Cho's expression remained unchanged, his gaze riveted on Vincent. "Shag leaves for Nassau this afternoon to track Madison Marro." Cho glanced at Shag and nodded amiably as he finished in Chinese, "Leave Nang behind to locate Vincent's attorney. Get that letter at any cost."

"What did you say to him?" Vincent stuttered.

40

Sky Harbor Airport
Phoenix, Arizona

JACE SET HIS SUITCASE down. "Hello, there."

Golden highlights flashed through Maddy's hair as slivers of sun blazed through the windows above baggage claim.

"Hello, yourself." She extended a hand and studied his bruised face, her eyes warming with empathy. "Glad you made it." Instead of being killed like Cory, she meant.

"I was lucky," he said dryly.

She picked up on the bitterness and squeezed his hand sympathetically. "I'm glad you're here in one piece. I thought about you yesterday . . . what you went through in Houston. I'm deeply sorry."

The degree of compassion on her face caught him off guard. He was suddenly at a loss for words. As if sensitive to his ambivalence, she took the opportunity to turn and hail two of her companions. Two men broke off their search for their luggage and came over. As they approached, Maddy explained that Kit was busy roaming the outside drive, looking for ground transportation.

Jace was introduced to Torbald Ürg, the silver-haired scientist with his calm, ingratiating manner, and his nephew, Hans, a grinning giant. Jace liked both men immediately. While Hans and Torbald returned to the slowly turning carousels to gather their bags, Jace again had Maddy to himself.

She became more animated, relating their boat trip to Miami and elaborating on Torbald's interpretation of Robert's grid.

"Can you imagine?" Her amber eyes danced with excitement. "The Nazca plain is a living map of a patch of ground in Arizona."

"Arizona?" he asked, dumbfounded. "Who'd have guessed?"

"I think Robert did. I think he understood the connection all along."

Jace remembered her as dynamic, but now, in anticipation of a coming expedition, she glowed with enthusiasm. Jace wanted to tell her about Dixon's comments at the funeral, the immensity of the mystery surrounding the Phobia File, but he chose to wait. He'd been dulled by the fury and pain of the last few days and for the moment preferred Maddy's exuberance, uplifted by her buoyant smile.

He sensed new warmth from her, the way she touched his arm, drawing near as she told her story in a hushed voice.

Maddy glanced about for eavesdroppers and edged even closer. "During our layover in Miami," she said, "Torbald bought a bunch of reference books he felt might be helpful. He and Kit went to a photo lab and had the grid on Robert's canvas scanned. Kit found a computer workshop where he purchased geographic software. He and Torbald rented a powerful Mac computer and, using an Adobe graphics package, Torbald matched Robert's Nazca overlay with topographical maps of Arizona and New Mexico."

Hans Ostertag reappeared, easily carrying three travel bags under one arm and a canvas sheath in his other hand.

Torbald brought up the rear with his briefcase in hand, and Maddy acknowledged him with a smile. "It took Torbald two hours of experimentation, trying various sizes and combinations, but he made a match."

Torbald gave Jace a nod. "We made a printout once we secured the coordinates."

Jace checked for watchers over his shoulder. "May I see it?"

"Of course." Torbald tugged on Hans's sleeve to pull him into the circle as Maddy, Jace, and Torbald huddled in the middle of the concourse to block the view of passersby.

Torbald opened his case and extracted a laser print of a topographical map he had aligned with Robert's geometry. He adjusted one sheet over the other, matching Robert's geometric lines to the topographical map, pointing to the tracings as he said, just loud enough for Jace to hear, "These are the lines of the Nazca plain. As you see, some are broken; some form angles. On the overlay, they align themselves with these topographical impressions." Jace watched with interest as Robert Marro's Nazca tangents fell into place over Arizona's delineated mountain ranges.

Torbald pointed to the chart. "The map encompasses a huge area: the entire four corner region where the states of Utah, Colorado, Arizona, and New Mexico meet . . . over one hundred sixty thousand square kilometers. What interests me most is this spot." Torbald indicated the apex where two lines met at a severe angle. "Where these lines cross, we have a meaningful juncture. The angle formed is exactly 22.5 degrees, which is the same angle as the wedge at the lighthouse at Cat Island, and of the larger triangles on a world map formed by Giza–Bahamas–Nazca, and Easter Island–Arizona–Nassau."

Jace strained to read the marker. "Looks like a Navajo Indian Reservation."

"Yes," Maddy added, "near the northeastern corner of Arizona, only a few miles from the Utah border—a place called Monument Valley."

Jace remembered seeing pictures of large buttes in the desert.

Maddy smiled. "We can be there in six or seven hours."

Torbald cautioned, "Maddy fails to mention that if the legend holds true, Alca would be sequestered somewhere underground."

Jace appreciated Torbald's diplomatic cool. "So where do we begin?"

"Logic would dictate that we question the locals for clues visible on the earth. Surely the designer of a grand earth map at Nazca intended some means of hinting at Alca's location. I think somehow Alca will speak to those who seek it."

Jace could see why Maddy put so much faith in Torbald. And Jace was fascinated with Hans. He carried himself like a wrestler, yet he seemed exceptionally bright. Jace pointed to Hans's sheath. "Maddy tells me you're an excellent shot." Hans's accommodating smile shaded with confusion, so Torbald translated.

Hans replied lengthily in Swedish.

Torbald nodded and turned to Jace. "He says that the word 'shot' is inappropriate, since no noise is involved. Hans prefers the stealth of the crossbow."

Hans nodded enthusiastically. "Yes." He made a sound by pursing his lips "hissssss." Then he said, "Quiet."

Jace smiled and mimicked the "sss" sound, and then he mentioned that his own weapon was much louder. He had just recovered a hastily arranged shipment from Jamilla in Houston via military airfreight—Cory's Model 92Fs Beretta Parabellum pistol, complete with a fifteen-shot magazine and some spare rounds, which Jamilla gladly wanted Jace to keep for protection.

Maddy interrupted, pointing.

Kit had pulled up to the curb in a white Ford Expedition and beckoned wildly.

As they exited baggage claim and piled into the vehicle, Kit remained in the driver's seat, babbling about having handpicked the car from the Thrifty Rental lot. Maddy interrupted him in midsentence and, making reference to Kit's erratic driving, insisted Jace take the wheel.

Kit objected to his downgrade and tried to slide into the passenger seat, but Maddy now demanded that *she* sit there and asked Kit to move to the rear.

Responding to Maddy's wishes, Jace walked around the car and took the wheel while Torbald and Hans shuffled into the middle seats, leaving Kit to ride with the luggage on a third bench in back.

Jace put the 4x4 in gear, guiding the vehicle out of the airport as Kit began to suggest places to stay for the night. Maddy was openly indifferent and calmly suggested which freeways to take. But Kit objected, stating that he wanted to drive through Sedona and Flagstaff. As if to reestablish her role as team leader, and obviously tiring of Kit's argumentative nature, Maddy firmly insisted they stop in Winslow for the night. They would initiate their search the next morning from the town of Red Rock, a small community in Navajo country. Finally, Kit relented and, with their itinerary set, they left Phoenix on Highway 87, speeding into the dry heat of the afternoon.

Jace was struck by Maddy's attitude, remembering her lack of resolution when Kit had dictated his terms at Robert's Providence apartment. He wondered if Maddy and Kit had somehow had a falling out. Jace glanced back and caught sight of Kit's brooding dark eyes, glaring from the backseat. He was no longer the center of attention. With Torbald assuming the role of scientific counsel, Maddy had taken command of the group, and Jace wondered how well Kit's ego would survive the demotion.

As they drove, Maddy showed trust in her companions by inquiring about Cory's findings. Momentarily reluctant, Jace nevertheless decided to share information, even in the presence of strangers. Jace explained Cory's earlier suspicions and elaborated on Dixon's opinions regarding the Phobia File and its implications.

Torbald seemed enthralled by the moon story. He mused that Dixon's report and the discovery of Alca's legend could indicate a pattern of miraculous events for the advent of a new science. He leaned forward and tapped Jace's shoulder. "I'm curious, Jace. Did your friend Cory or Colonel Dixon ever speculate about legendary origins as they relate to the Phobos moon—or to Mars, for that matter?"

"Not that I recall. Why?"

"Oh. It was something Robert used to say. As you remember, he was convinced that the alleged monuments on Mars and monuments here on Earth were related. Pyramids in Mexico, pyramids in Egypt, pyramids on the Red Planet. Robert was convinced that the mathematics involved in pyramid construction were the keys to the connection. The Egyptian pyramids were constructed on the universal constant of pi, which became meaningful to Robert when he discovered that the Martian pyramid in the Cydonia plain sits astride the north latitude 40.86 degrees, whose tangent equals 'e' divided by 'pi.'"

Jace looked over his shoulder. "A coincidence, perhaps?"

"Perhaps, until you realize that the word 'Cairo,' where the Egyptian pyramids sit, has the same ancient Arabic root for the word 'Mars.'"

"I had no idea."

"Very few people do. Yet the Russians made an extensive study of the possibilities. Robert believed that both the US and Russia knew precisely what they were looking at on the Martian surface and were both cooperatively suppressing information . . . even to the extent of agreeing not to send a manned mission to the planet with technological equipment capable of verifying the authenticity of Martian artifacts until they could do so simultaneously."

"But what about the current Mars missions?" Jace asked.

"Well, notably, the mission slated to explore Phobos in 2011 failed. And that was a Russian mission. What does that tell you?"

"And the US Rover missions on the surface?"

"Like a child playing with a shovel in a million-square-mile sandbox. Meaningless infinitesimal detail."

"So you think this business about the moon—"

"Doesn't surprise me. I have no trouble believing that your government would conceal findings of that nature or that the 2011 mission by the Russians was either a ruse to placate skepticism or was really the effort of a concerned nation trying to get an edge on the United States. Robert had always hoped he could make headway with the Russians. He had tried repeatedly to break the silence by convincing them to reveal what they knew."

"How do you think this relates to Alca?" Maddy asked.

"I don't know yet," Torbald said, shaking his head. "But there will be plenty to do." As Torbald addressed the tasks ahead, the conversation took a more practical turn. He and Maddy began to assess equipment needs. As Torbald viewed it, they should be fully equipped for a three-day stay. They would need food, tents, shovels, a pickax, lanterns or flashlights, and, as Jace pointed out, some dynamite and weapons. The group agreed that with all due respect to Hans and his high-tech crossbow, it would be advisable to procure guns. If handguns were unavailable, they would try for rifles or a shotgun.

The next few hours passed easily. As the sun sank low in Jace's rearview mirror, they pulled into the outskirts of Winslow, where they checked into the Golden Gecko, a quaint neon-laden motel with a small square swimming pool centered inside a rectangular green stucco courtyard.

Torbald and Hans decided to share one room, while at Maddy's suggestion, Kit, Maddy, and Jace were to each have one of their own—an idea that Jace appreciated, since having Kit as a roommate didn't appeal to him.

The moment they finished registering, Maddy encouraged Kit to accompany Torbald and Hans on an equipment scavenger hunt.

Jace made overtures to join them, but Maddy intervened, insisting that while the others searched the town, she and Jace should catch up on details. She quietly informed Jace that they should meet by the swimming pool in twenty minutes.

As Jace settled into his room, he removed his shirt and washed his face. He had just finished sorting his toiletries and was about to find a clean shirt to wear, when he was interrupted by a knock.

He opened the door and was surprised to see Maddy. "I'm sorry," she said. "I didn't mean to disturb you." Her gaze fell on his bare chest.

"I was just coming downstairs."

"I went to the lobby, but there were two beer-toting cowboys yucking it up by the swimming pool and a dreary old codger snoring in one of the rattan chairs," she said. "Could we sit on your veranda instead?"

She was on her way in as he mumbled, "I . . . sure."

Judging from a soapy scent of gardenia emanating from her blue halter top, she had freshened up, and as she brushed past it occurred to Jace that she had taken a bath.

Jace rummaged in his bag for a T-shirt, fighting to get it over his head as Maddy walked straight to the sliding-glass door that overlooked the mountains south of town.

"You have a much better view than I do," she said. "It's a lovely time of night." Warm air billowed the curtains as she stepped onto the lanai.

Jace joined her at the railing.

The evening felt soft and serene, and several small wrens cavorted through the brush in the vacant lot behind the motel.

Low light warmed the hills off to the southwest, and Maddy's face was painted a bright gold as she turned to Jace in the late sun.

"I hope you don't mind that I asked you to stay," she said softly. "Our conversation at the airport was unfinished." He was at a loss for words. She continued, "I feel an inevitability about all this . . . the way you and I were thrown together. Besides, you've had to sacrifice so much. I'm in your debt."

"You don't owe me anything."

"I feel I do, particularly with Cory's loss."

"I buried him, Maddy." He fought the lump in his throat. "It's over. I wouldn't be here if I hadn't settled with that."

"Well I haven't settled with it." A hint of moisture formed in her eyes. "Not when I look at the bruises on your jaw. I can't help but feel responsible."

He was touched by her sensitivity. "Maddy. Don't blame yourself. It's not you. It's those maniacs—what they did to your uncle—and Cory." He brushed away one of her tears. "When I saw you at the airport today, I felt as if I'd just come home from some foreign war, and you were the only sane thing left in the world."

Her eyes softened. "I'm glad to hear you say that. I hoped that somewhere inside your rage . . . inside your desire to find your own answers, you would—"

"Want to see you?"

"Something like that."

"Yes."

The tears were gone. A look of awe flooded her face. "'Yes'? One word? That's all you have to say?"

He responded with an inquiring shrug.

She smiled. "I love the simplicity of that. No conditions or qualifiers."

"There aren't *any* conditions when it comes to you," he said with a smile. "Maybe you can tell by the gash on my lip, I jumped headfirst into this mess."

"You certainly did. And are you excited?" She said it with the prospect of shared adventure.

"I think so."

Her eyes faltered at his lack of affirmation, and he realized he had understated his feelings, still reeling from the numbness of Cory's death. He immediately wanted to erase her slightest disappointment. "What I mean . . ."

She stared at him expectantly.

He marveled at how she affected him. She could reach into him, touch his pain, stir his senses. He wanted to capture her, but it was too soon, he told himself—there would be time.

As he studied the delicate lines of her face, he envisioned when they might join in body as well as spirit, and he relished the anticipation, suspecting that eventually they might truly be . . .

"Together," he said, softly. "That's how we'll finish this thing."

41

Nassau

HECTOR WALSH PEERED AHEAD, FIGHTING the glare of the windshield. He perspired freely in the humidity, uncomfortable with the facial hair he'd grown as a part of his disguise. It was ninety-two degrees in Nassau, and though the car windows were open, the rushing breeze felt like a blast furnace.

It was so hot that Shag and his men had foregone their usual uniforms of black cotton and donned colorful tropical shirts.

As the wind whipped through the passenger side window, Shag's long blond hair buffeted past his ears. Above the trim of his cream-colored scarf, Walsh caught sight of the ragged scar under Shag's left ear. Walsh didn't know how Shag had acquired the mark because Shag wouldn't tolerate questions, but Walsh remembered that Cho had once commented how the man who had inflicted the wound was dead. "How much farther?" Walsh asked.

"It's on this street." With his sinewy hands locked on the steering wheel, Du glanced back through the rearview mirror.

Walsh felt claustrophobic, having been jammed into the backseat with Kwan, one of Shag's warriors, who reeked of ginseng. Like Du, Kwan not only wore the perfumed essence under his clothes, he chewed ginseng gum incessantly. Walsh suspected that effects of the root heightened both men's hyperintensity. "Mind if I go with you, Shag?" Walsh asked, yearning for the cool air-conditioned interior of a building.

"You're in my care," Shag said sarcastically. "When you pee, I hold your dick." Shag wasn't far off. He had accompanied Walsh to every restroom.

Walsh found it ironic that Shag was to be responsible for his well-being, considering that he had previously feared Shag. Cho had asked him to accompany Shag to Nassau, ostensibly to separate Walsh from Vincent Scalbania in order to prevent their further collusion.

Walsh felt a modicum of pride that he'd been able to stir Cho into paranoia—a victory of sorts, as was the deal he'd struck. Cho seemed totally respectful that Walsh's incriminating letter to the FBI had been stored with Vincent Scalbania's will in Toronto. If there was safety in the tiger's cage, Walsh had achieved it. Walsh would survive. He was too valuable to eliminate until this project concluded. Walsh's small suitcase contained the Peruvian Prize, both halves of Robert Marro's grid, a selection of several conventional maps and historic manuals that addressed cultural anomalies of various South American cultures, plus an astronomical diagram, which had been supplied to him by the Chinese Space Ministry. This rather complex isometric printout used algorithms taken from infrared elevations that sectioned each landmass on Earth into shaded layers. The plastic overlays were color-coded to show topographical shapes as they related to one another across various continents. Walsh believed that the shapes on the Nazca plain related to other earth tracks. Walsh was the key; he had the scientific background to solve the riddles and, having kept Robert Marro's claims close to his vest, he alone could make head or tail of the clues Cho needed deciphered to complete the mission.

Cho had promised great rewards. In the end, Walsh was to move to Hong Kong, where he would enjoy 10 percent of the profits from the venture and live like a king. Yet he pondered how things might play out in the long run.

If the acquisition of Alca's new technology belonged to China, and Alca answered the world's energy needs, all industrial and economic power would swing to Beijing. And for good reason: as fossil fuels dwindled in the new century and nuclear power continued to prove unwieldy, China would hold the rest of the world hostage and rapidly become the *only* superpower.

Of course, Walsh knew that his security in Hong Kong would eventually erode. He had discussed those realities with Vincent Scalbania, and it was Walsh's plan to take his profits and escape Cho's influence as soon as possible. Where could they go? Vincent had discussed Switzerland.

Walsh's thoughts were brought to a halt with the van as Du pulled into a parking space. Du gestured to a three-story stucco apartment complex on the beach side of the avenue.

"The office is on the first floor," Du said calmly. "The manager's name is Jimmy."

"Walsh," Shag barked as he leapt out of the van, "stay on my hip."

Walsh noted the spring in Shag's step. He was incredibly agile for a man in his late forties.

Shag led the way up the paved ramp to the main floor of the complex, where he easily located the manager's suite. Walsh followed as Shag waltzed into the air-conditioned foyer. A black man in a colorful shirt sorted receipts behind a counter.

"You're Jimmy," Shag said, catching him unaware.

"I am. And you are?"

"Interested in seeing an apartment."

"I don't have a vacancy."

"Robert Marro's place is vacant, from what we understand."

Jimmy's eyes faltered at the mention of the name. "Well, not yet."

Shag reached into the back pocket of his pewter slacks and pulled out a wad of bills. "I'd like to see the unit." He shoved a stack of money across the counter. "Consider this a nonrefundable deposit."

Jimmy tried to maintain his composure. "You wouldn't be able to occupy it until the end of the month."

"No problem. I'm window-shopping."

"You just want to see it?"

"And ask a few questions."

Jimmy's gnarled hand slowly closed around the money. He stuffed it into his pants. After retrieving his master keys, he led Shag and Walsh to the second floor to unit 29B. Once inside, Shag made a cursory visual search of the place, feigning interest in its view, while Jimmy glanced nervously at Walsh, as if to glean some hint as to what was really going on.

Shag ambushed Jimmy in the small hallway between the kitchen and the bedroom. "You had visitors here," he said quietly.

"What do you mean?"

"A day ago. You had people in this unit. They're friends of mine."

"It was completely proper. Robert Marro's relatives."

Shag handled another large wad of money in both hands. Separating the bundle, he raised a fist filled with cash next to Jimmy's face. "I want to know where they went. Tell me and I'll give this to you."

Jimmy's eyes darted back and forth between Shag's eyes and the fist of bills, which hovered a mere six inches from his chin. "They went sightseeing."

"That's a lie."

"No, they went to Cat Island."

"For what reason?"

"To see the lighthouse in Mr. Robert's painting."

"What's so important about the lighthouse?"

Jimmy shrugged.

"And where is it?"

"The painting or the lighthouse?"

"Both."

"The lighthouse is on the eastern cliffs of Cat, on Governor's Point." Jimmy glanced down at Shag's other hand, which still held the money. "I'll tell you more," he said with a smirk, eyeing the bills. "Since you're interested."

"Good." Shag handed him the remainder of the wad, which Jimmy grabbed with a sigh of relief.

"They took the painting along. There was something under the paint," Jimmy said.

"Under?"

"Ink lines that they were excited about . . ."

"Did you see the ink lines?"

"No."

Shag backed away and Jimmy made a move for the door, but Shag restrained him.

"Is there something else?" Jimmy asked.

"Of course. The lease."

Jimmy chuckled nervously. "You mean you really want this place?"

"I do." Shag put an arm around Jimmy's shoulders. "Let's go in the living room and talk." Shag glanced back at Walsh and waved him off. "Walsh, wait outside while I discuss a contract with this gentleman."

WALSH'S FEARS WERE VINDICATED ROUGHLY twenty minutes later. He had joined Du and Kwan celebrating their ginseng festival, vigorously chewing their gum, gabbing about an island prostitute they'd met at a bar the previous night. Their description of a tag-team ménage à trois in the back of the van caused Walsh to disgustedly remove his hand from the stickiness of the vinyl seat.

Through the window, Walsh's attention was drawn to the flash of Shag's long blond hair. Shag ambled across the boulevard with his lithe, easy gait and climbed into the front passenger seat. "Sorry it took so long. I had to wash up. Take me to the marina." He tossed Jimmy's set of manager's keys to Du.

"What happened?" Walsh asked softly as the van began to roll.

"No one will go to that apartment for a while. At least not until the stink starts to seep out into the hall." Shag stuffed the wad of blood-stained money into the glove compartment. He retrieved his flask of schnapps and took a sip.

"He's dead then?" Walsh asked.

"And happy. He's wearing a new smile under his chin, from ear to ear." Shag held his combat knife in the air. He had taken time to wipe the blade clean.

42

The Chinle Wash
Near Rock Point, Arizona

WARM WIND WHIPPED DUST DEVILS into the air as Jace drove the 4x4 up the eastern edge of the Chinle Wash gorge.

Feeling comfortable in her shorts and sneakers, Maddy sat in the passenger seat gazing out at the canyon floor.

The aspen trees that hugged the shallow creek bed several hundred feet below had begun to turn fall colors, shimmering gold and crimson against red sandstone cliffs.

"I see it," Torbald said from the backseat.

Maddy gazed ahead as the house came into view. Surrounded by turrets of jagged stone and windblown sage, the shoddy structure hung perilously above the ravine. It appeared as if the house might break loose at any moment, leaving Maddy to ponder the logic of building that close to a crevasse.

"Surely she doesn't live there by herself," Jace said as he negotiated the Ford up the bumpy wagon trail.

"Some of these older Indian woman are pretty tough," Maddy answered.

Dust and sand swirled around the six-sided wood-and-mud structure that locals called a "hogan." A stick-frame barn with a sod roof sat across the road, and a buckskin horse grazed in a fenced corral. With no vehicles in sight, it appeared that horse and buggy might have been the primary means of transportation down the mesa. Maddy spied someone on the porch. A lone figure sat rocking in the shade, staring into the immensity of the canyon.

"That must be her," Jace said. "Strange she hasn't moved."

"Perhaps she's deaf," Torbald added. "She could be, at ninety-four."

"They said she was quite coherent." Maddy sat up straighter. They were about to meet the oldest woman in the territory, according to the locals at the general store. While Kit and Hans foraged for provisions in the nearby town of Ganado, Maddy, Jace, and Torbald had spent the morning scouring the small community of Red Rock, inquiring as to who might best know the history of Monument Valley.

The answer was universal . . . the person who knew the most was one who had lived her whole life in northeastern Arizona: an American Navajo woman named Sara Tupi, also known to some by her Indian name, Wind Woman.

Jace pulled the 4x4 to a horse rail near the front porch steps. The elderly figure near the peeled-post banister at the side of the house hadn't stirred. But the moment Jace killed the car engine, a fifty-something woman in jeans and a cut up sweatshirt glared from the front door.

"Maddy, you greet her alone," Jace said. "That'd be better than all of us piling out at once."

Maddy was grateful Torbald had insisted only the three of them seek out Mrs. Tupi, in order to be less intimidating. Kit, in particular, was left behind with Hans to ostensibly gather fresh food for their mission.

Maddy opened the door slowly, smiling as she stepped from the car.

"Hello," she called, advancing across the rust-colored sand toward the porch steps. "I hope you don't mind us just dropping by. We wondered if we might have a word with Mrs. Tupi." A glance toward the rocking chair left some doubt. The elderly woman in the floor-length cotton dress hadn't budged.

The woman at the door edged forward. "What do you want?"

She reminded Maddy of Christine, with her long black hair and smooth, deeply tanned skin.

Maddy felt it best to introduce herself. She put one foot on the bottom stair. "I'm Madison Marro."

"I'm Darla. One of Mrs. Tupi's daughters."

Maddy climbed the three remaining steps, extending a hand.

Darla shook reluctantly. "My mother is old and tired. She doesn't have visitors."

Maddy scrambled for the right words. "But my friends and I traveled thousands of miles to find this place."

"Here?"

"Well, actually Monument Valley. We're looking for something quite extraordinary . . . something magnificent."

"The valley is magnificent, Ms. Marro, but you won't have trouble finding it."

"I'm not making myself clear. We're looking for a legendary place." Darla's confused expression forced Maddy to elaborate. "Could you ask your mother if she would talk to us?" Maddy pointed at the Ford. "Tell her that the man with white hair in the backseat is a person of great wisdom who has come from Sweden to speak with her. He searches for a spiritual place."

The elderly figure stirred. The gray head turned, and a pair of startling light-blue eyes focused on Maddy's face. Maddy smiled and nodded in recognition, but the frigid countenance remained unchanged.

Darla appeared unimpressed. "You seem like nice folks, lady. But we don't want to buy whatever you're selling. Now please leave us alone."

"I'm not selling, Darla. We're scientists."

"You're a long way from your laboratory."

"For good reason. We've sacrificed a great deal to come here," she directed the next words toward Wind Woman, "to find a place of miracles."

Suddenly, the desert breeze was cut by the old woman's raspy voice. "Darla."

Darla looked around. Wind Woman's gnarled hand beckoned. Darla went to her side and knelt.

Maddy found the sight of the two of them timeless; it was like witnessing a scene from the turn of the twentieth century as mother and daughter conferred. Wind Woman made halting gestures, chewing words through aged lips; Darla objecting, though obviously bowing to her authority. The old one's whispers reminded Maddy of the brush of lizard skin sliding over rock.

After an animated exchange, Wind Woman asserted her will. Darla finally shrugged and returned to the steps.

"She wants to know if your white-haired friend is a man of spirits."

Maddy pondered briefly and responded, "He is. He often talks to God."

Darla said something in the Indian language to the old woman, who nodded.

"She wants to speak to him." Darla's brow furrowed. "My mother is a woman of great feeling. She is the daughter of a Navajo chief and can still remember when renegade tribesman fought the American cavalry in these canyons."

"Don't worry," Maddy replied. "We'll treat her with respect."

Maddy summoned Jace and Torbald. After briefing them about Darla's concerns, Maddy ushered Torbald ahead while Jace brought up the rear.

Torbald was wonderful. His body language projected his sincerity and reverence. He knelt at Wind Woman's side, placing his hands in hers. "Good afternoon, Mrs. Tupi. Or do you prefer we address you by your ancient name?"

"Those who know me, call me what I am."

Torbald smiled. "Indeed. And so we shall. My name is Torbald Ürg. I'm honored to know you." He looked back over his shoulder. "This is Madison Marro, the leader of our group. She is a scientist who cares much for the land and its animals."

Wind Woman nodded courteously, and then her eyes drifted toward Jace.

"And this is Jace Kelton—a man who has sacrificed a great deal to make this journey."

"I see that on his face," Wind Woman said.

Leaning back against the porch rail, Jace smiled at what he perceived to be a reference to his bruises, but Maddy wondered whether the old Native American had read things deeper than skin.

The introductions having been made, Torbald adjusted himself, and with red dust spotting his khaki shirt and pants, he sat at Wind Woman's moccasin-covered feet while Darla held the back of her mother's chair.

Wind Woman folded her hands in her lap as she listened to Torbald's brief explanation of why they had sought her out. Her thin fingers clutched the folds of her pumpkin-colored caftan dress. She watched Torbald carefully, occasionally looked up at Jace, and then at Maddy. Her windbeaten, furrowed face looked as rugged as the land, yet her eyes burned with passion as she began her story. Unburdened by the weighty phonetics of her native tongue, Wind Woman toothlessly articulated phrases in perfect English, explaining that she had been raised in a small village near Red Rock.

She told of the reservation, the lives of the people, the battles against the sun and the cold. She explained that this hogan was her summer home and that she had another in the depths of the canyon near the aspen groves, where she and Darla went to escape the fierce winter winds that ravaged the mesas.

Wind Woman became more animated, spreading her arms as she described the day when the reservation land had been rezoned and shrunk to its present size, how the government had robbed the Navajo of territory. She spoke of her land's history, of President Taft and his dealings with the Navajo, and the statehood of Arizona, plus other events that affected her as a small girl.

Torbald appeared to empathize with her appreciation of things past. "In the days when you were small, what were you told of Monument Valley?" he asked.

"Were there stories of holy places, of unusual occurrences?"

Wind Woman's hand shook as she pointed to the horizon. "In the time before I was a child, there was a place where our elders went to seek the spirits." Her eyes glazed with the vision. "The wise men of my father's tribe called this place the 'cavern of infinity,' where the land sang a song."

"A song?" Torbald asked.

"A sound from the earth. When the elders came near, they felt a gateway to the edge of existence."

Maddy had to interrupt. "What do you mean 'felt'?"

Wind Woman's transparent blue eyes met Maddy's. "An invisible door would beckon to those who could sense the world on the other side. This would happen at the change of seasons."

"At the summer and winter solstice?" Torbald asked excitedly.

"Yes. On the day when the sun turned, the elders sat before the invisible doorway and witnessed the movement of stones."

"What movement?" Maddy asked.

"When the land sang, the rocks on the desert floor would slide across the sand toward the doorway. The elders could feel the power. Their cheeks would flap as if blown by the wind and their hair would rise into the air."

"Electromagnetic energy," Torbald said, to no one in particular.

"If you wish to call it that," Wind Woman said. "To me all energy comes from a place that has no name."

"Why does it have no name?" Maddy asked, surprised at the concept.

"It is invisible, like the hole in your heart when you have a need. Or the haven in your head from which feelings come. I know of no names for those places."

Maddy contemplated the analogy as Torbald continued with a question. "What happened to this doorway to infinity?"

"After a time, it was said to be bad. The men whose skin shook when the rocks moved were unable to think. The place became forbidden to all those but the shaman, who kept it sacred. It was a worrisome place of afflicted spirits."

"Navajo spirits?" Torbald asked.

"Not Navajo. It was said that the doorway must be the final place of the long heads of the Anasazi tribe . . . that it was *they* who entered the cavern."

"The Anasazi tribe disappeared," Jace spoke for the first time. "Where do you say they went?"

Wind Woman looked up at Jace, her eyes clear with conviction. "I like you. You say little, but you ask important questions."

Torbald couldn't contain himself. "I'm sorry, could you clarify where the legend says that the Anasazi went?"

Wind Woman pointed a finger to the clouds.

"What? To heaven?" Torbald asked.

She shrugged and nodded. "To heaven without dying. But *only* the long heads—only *one* of the two Anasazi tribes. The Anasazi were 'the ancient ones.' The *round* heads were basket makers who went to New Mexico to become the Pueblos, and the *long* heads were those who walked the world and settled in Arizona in Monument Valley." She glanced at Jace. "Until one day when they disappeared. It is said that they found a bridge to the sky and walked across. The cavern of infinity is the place from which they left."

Torbald looked at Maddy and Jace, beaming. "That's it. Some of the ancient Nazca skulls were oddly long as well. We may have something here. This cavern of infinity must be the grid's destination." He turned back to Wind Woman. "Will you show us this place?"

Wind Woman stared at her lap and didn't answer, folding her gnarled hands in contemplation.

"It's very important," Maddy added. "Can you help us find it?"

Wind Woman sighed and Darla interjected. "She's tired now. I think that's enough."

"Please," Torbald said, "we need a guide and would be happy to pay for the information." Torbald reached for the money in his wallet, but Wind Woman raised a hand in protest.

"I am too old," Wind Woman said, "but my great-grandson Akita will take you. He has not grown up in the ancient ways, but someday he will feel the dance of the souls. He will be your spirit guide."

Torbald seemed at odds with the cash in his hands. "I'd like to give you some of this, if I may."

"No." Wind Woman shook her head. "Give it to Akita. I will make sure he is waiting at dawn at the gas station on the east side of Kayenta, a small town to the north."

Torbald got to one knee. "Well, I thank you. If there were something I could do for you . . ."

"I don't need money," Wind Woman said toothlessly, "but I ask a favor." She reached out, took Torbald's hand, and after glancing at Jace, riveted her gaze on Maddy. "Will you promise me?"

"What is it?" Maddy hoped to grant her some special gift.

"Come closer." Wind Woman gestured that Maddy approach and grasped Maddy's hand as well.

"When you go to Monument Valley," Wind Woman said, clutching Maddy with a surprisingly strong grip, "if you find the bridge across the sky . . . will you let me come?"

43

Cat Island

LIKE A GREAT DARK FINGER pointed toward the sky, the silhouette of the lighthouse stood out against the stars. The cupola's gas flame flashed off rotating mirrors, which launched a beam of light into the darkness.

The surrounding ocean was surprisingly calm. What had been whitecaps in the late afternoon had flattened into a gentle series of rollers that lapped the rocky shore.

Hector Walsh stood on one end of the great boulder, lit by the pulsing glow of the lighthouse.

He tried to fathom why this particular location on the planet surface had relevance to Nazca. The monolith's triangular wedge of 22.5 degrees pointed south, which might equate to a tangent toward Nazca. With Cat Island as ground zero, Walsh had used a sextant to view the constellations, particularly Orion's Belt, which had so intensely interested Robert Marro. Egypt's great pyramids had been constructed on an axis that faced directly toward that constellation. And as Walsh had found during prior computations, one of the median lines of the Nazca plain centered on Orion's Belt.

Walsh pondered if perhaps the triangular shape in the great beach rock reflected a galactic relationship that translated to earth-map coordinates.

The lighthouse keeper, Satch, had mentioned how animated Torbald Ürg became at the discovery of the wedge. Satch had described how, after having been ushered away, he had peeked over the rocks and watched Torbald explain his calculations to the rest of his party but had been unable to hear over the ocean's roar.

It was a shame the wiry little lighthouse keeper had to die.

Even now, Shag and Kwan were down on the other side of the point dissecting his corpse. They were to throw Satch's remains into the ocean from a fifteen-foot rowboat they had stolen from a carport in nearby Clemmons. The ocean was calm, and it was Shag's inspiration to dump the body parts beyond the reef. Night-feeding sharks and the reef crabs would eliminate any trace of the carcass.

In the meantime, Du had remained in Nassau, checking for traces left by Madison Marro's party. One of the native boys at the tiny Cat Island Marina had seen Madison's group arrive from Nassau by boat. Du meant to locate the captain to ascertain Madison's next destination.

Walsh heaved a sigh. Setting his sextant aside, he adjusted the bandage on his left hand. In the glow of his flashlight, he checked the coordinates in an atlas, occasionally glancing at the triangle in the rock at his feet. The shape itself was a mystery. Even though the great black boulder had been worn by time, the indentation remained incredibly precise and geometrically flawless.

Walsh heard a noise above him on the boulders and glanced over his shoulder. Holding his flask of schnapps and a lit cigarette, Shag made his way down the incline.

"What's taking you so long?" Shag's typical straightforward question.

"I'm doing what I can." Walsh stared at the map. "But I haven't found anything yet." Then he did a double take. Shag wore nothing save his briefs and a stained towel around his neck. His forearms were covered with dried blood.

"You better find something. Madison's people did."

"We don't know that." Walsh tried not to stare at the scars on Shag's chest and arms. "Somehow this . . ." Walsh held up Robert's grid, "relates to that." He pointed to the triangle.

"It has to," Shag said. "There's nothing else here. We went through the entire lighthouse—turned the place upside down."

"What?"

"I said we—"

"You said, 'upside down.'" Walsh grabbed Robert's grid and scanned it, turning it slowly in his hands. Triangles. Nazca showed several. The image of a triangle turning on its axis entered his mind. "That's it."

"What?"

"We need to change the angle of the triangle to fit. As long as Nazca is one point on the triangle, we should find destinations that fit the other two points. I would guess that Nassau is one of them. Here. Hold this." Walsh handed Shag the flashlight and continued to fuss with the maps.

Struggling with the stack of paperwork, he successfully traced the dimensions of the Nassau triangle onto the world map, using Nazca as an apex.

"Look." He showed Shag. "When I fit the shape of the triangle in the rock with Nassau and Nazca as two points, the third point lands on Egypt."

Shag took a drag off his cigarette and tossed it into the ocean. "So they've gone to Egypt?"

"No, no. There might be a thematic significance to Egypt, but that's not the objective. I must turn the triangle with Nassau as the point of origination. If I do, we wind up in the middle of the Pacific. Something's missing." Walsh stared at the boulder. "We need to have the satellite analysts in Beijing involved. Matching Robert's land maps to some tangent that runs north." He stared at the map and traced more lines. Suddenly the geometric shape made sense. "Holy God. That's it." Walsh was seeing what surely Torbald Ürg must have seen only days before. With some awe, Walsh stared at Shag's bloody face. "The northernmost tangent runs through the American Southwest."

44

Deke's Texaco
Kayenta, Arizona

JACE WAS FORCED TO SQUINT as bright sunlight glinted off the dusty front window of Deke's Texaco. The two-pump relic from the fifties was sided with rippled aluminum dotted with rusted rivets. The Texaco Star atop the pole by the roadside had faded long ago, bleached by ultraviolet rays and pelted by sand.

Dressed in gray jeans and a black T-shirt, Jace leaned against the fender of the rented Ford Expedition, savoring the last few drops of Maddy's coffee. She looked beautiful in her shorts and red blouse this morning, *and* she she made a great cup of joe. She had arisen early to painstakingly grind her own beans at a convenience store in Rock Point.

As Maddy wandered in his direction with a refill, Jace hoped for another opportunity to talk to her; however, when Kit sidled over mouthing off, wired on too much caffeine, Jace excused himself and strolled around the service station.

Jace hadn't seen Maddy alone since last night's short conversation on the lanai, and that had been interrupted when Torbald and the others returned. They'd been quite worked up, triumphant with their loads of equipment plus Torbald's gift to Maddy—a small green fanny pack to hold her personal items. She thanked him for his kindness and, at Torbald's suggestion, they all went to dinner together. During a tasty meal at a Mexican restaurant, Maddy updated Kit and Hans on Wind Woman's revelations, which took time, since Hans had to have everything translated.

After a few hours of sleep, they arose to a wake-up call at 4:00 a.m. Chewing on donuts, they hurried to catch the dawn only to find the gas station deserted. There was nothing to do but watch the sun rise and wait for the arrival of Akita, Wind Woman's mystery grandson.

Gradually, the sky began to brighten. The colors of the land changed dramatically as the sun peeked over distant haze-shrouded mountains, splashing light across the valley, laying long shadows between the cacti.

Deke's Texaco still looked naked in the bright sunlight, and Jace wondered when someone might appear to flip the "closed" sign to "open."

He glanced back at the rest of the crew.

In the shadow of the locked two-door garage, Maddy, Kit, Hans, and Torbald had gathered, chatting to pass the time. Jace watched as Maddy shared more coffee, strolling from man to man. Her fluid movements were feminine and yet limber at the same time, a testament to her innate athleticism.

Jace was tempted to wander over to the group, but with Kit's continued guffaws, he decided to wait. Instead, he decided to busy himself with a careful inventory of the gear in the rear compartment of the 4x4.

He opened the rear gate of the SUV and sorted through the bags. Dust popped off several large backpacks as he tugged on their straps. He dug through the equipment, making a mental list: flashlights with spare batteries, a small tool kit, two shovels, two pick-axes, a crowbar, fourteen sticks of tan-colored dynamite with twelve blasting caps that Hans had acquired, plus two days of food supplies, a tent and some blankets, and perhaps the most important item—sun hats for everyone.

A separate duffel bag contained weapons: two hunting knives, a shotgun that Kit had purchased from a farmer in Ganado, a hunting rifle, and Cory's nine-millimeter handgun that Jamilla had shipped.

Hans kept the canvas sheath containing his crossbow with him at all times. Through Torbald's translation, Hans informed Jace that he had learned to shoot in the Swedish Army; that he was an expert marksman with virtually all guns; but that he had learned to fire a crossbow during commando training, specifically because the weapon was virtually silent, making it an excellent choice for infiltration and recovery missions.

Jace pushed aside several bags of luggage, Torbald's briefcase among them. Torbald's luggage contained some reference books that he had purchased in Miami, volumes on the Indian cultures of South America: the Incas, Mayans, and Nazcas. Torbald had expounded on his beliefs relating to the Nazca culture, how they had been worshippers of water in their parched homeland, something he related to the Anasazi Indians as well. He'd been fascinated that Wind Woman had called some of the Anasazi "long heads," because many of the Nazca skulls that had been excavated had strange oblong shapes. Torbald suspected that there had to be some intrinsic connection between the two civilizations.

Jace slammed the Ford's tailgate as Maddy once again broke away from the group and walked toward him, coffee cup in hand. He wasn't surprised that she'd chosen to escape Kit's boisterous laughter, which still echoed near the garage.

As she drew near, Jace nodded to the others. "What's Mr. Buzzkill up to now?"

"Telling his favorite jokes." Maddy shook her head. "I was too embarrassed to stick around. Hans doesn't understand English well enough to get the point, and I had to bail when Torbald asked me what the word 'roids' meant."

Jace smiled. "Did you explain?"

Maddy glared at him and then smiled.

Jace gazed over at Kit. Jace had unsuccessfully tried to find things about the loudmouth he might like. "He's kind of a ball and chain, isn't he?"

"Believe me, if he hadn't been my dad's darling and my uncle's adopted companion—"

"You would have ditched him?"

"But I really can't. He knows too much. He'd be dangerous out there. Besides, we were good friends at one time."

Jace squinted at the horizon. "Well, with any luck this will end in two days and we can go home." She seemed taken aback by the comment, and he realized that it might have sounded uncaring. "You know what I mean."

"I do." Maddy took another sip of coffee. "We do have our own lives, after all."

"We'll see. I just hope we . . ." Jace hesitated, gazing up the road toward Kayenta. A distant cloud of dust had formed on the horizon. "Somebody's in a hurry."

Maddy shaded her eyes. "You think that's one car?"

"Hard to tell."

The dust cloud moved along rapidly in the distance.

"Hey," Kit shouted. "What's that?" He ran over to Jace and Maddy as Torbald followed. The small dust tornado now revealed itself to be a truck, hurtling toward them.

"What do you think?" Torbald asked Jace.

"Whoever it is, they're moving with purpose. Let's be ready." Jace stepped back and lifted the tailgate on the 4x4 to retrieve Cory's Beretta. Unholstering the weapon, he stuck it barrel first in the back of his jeans.

Hans looked over at Jace, pursed his lips and made the "sss" sound, unslinging his crossbow sheath, moving to the rear. Jace understood Hans's intent. "Torbald, ask him to stay low. He'll be backup."

Torbald translated, and Hans gave Jace a thumbs-up as he took his position at the tailgate of the Ford.

Jace gestured to Maddy. "Stay with me, Maddy." Then a look over at Kit. "Grab the shotgun and hunker down with Hans. If there's trouble, scatter them with some high shots."

Kit grimaced. "Who died and made you God?"

Jace stared at him. "My best friend did. Do what I say."

Mumbling to himself, Kit rummaged around in the gear and then joined Hans.

The dust cloud on the horizon grew considerably larger, and moments later, a candy-apple-red pickup raced into the gas station with its stereo blasting. The deep rumble of a bass rhythm sounded from the open windows.

Billows of dust settled on the group as the truck came to a grinding halt. A young Indian man, about eighteen, jumped out of the cab. Dressed in oversized pants and a yellow tank top and sporting a brush cut, he strutted toward Jace.

"Hey, y'all." The youth grinned. "I'm Sparky."

"Sparky?" Maddy responded. "Where's Akita?"

"Oh, that's what GG Tupi calls me. Don't mind her."

"GG?" Torbald approached. "Great-grandmother?"

"Yeah. Wind Woman. She says you guys want a guide." Sparky pointed to the northeast. "GG wants me to show you the valley where the elders used to get spooked. It's like forty-five miles out that way." Sparky eagerly surveyed their faces for a response, but he became distracted as Hans and Kit stepped out from the rear of the Ford. "GG said there were three of you."

"Our friends," Maddy responded. "We're all together."

The shotgun in Kit's hand caught Sparky's eye. "Planning to do some hunting? There's not much game out there."

"We're just careful," Jace said, wishing Kit had had the sense to hide the weapon. "Snakes. That sort of thing."

Akita shrugged. "No snakes in this heat. They come out at night—something you ought to know if you plan to camp. You guys follow me in your vehicle." Sparky grinned at Torbald. "Since you're the dude with the cash, you can ride with me."

Hans and Kit piled into the backseat of the Ford, and as Maddy joined Jace in front, she nudged his elbow. "So *this* is our spirit guide?"

Sparky revved his engine, and the big bass speakers in his truck blared.

Kit said, "He's a punk."

Jace smiled and donned his shades. "Wind Woman talked about moving rock, but who knew she meant heavy metal."

Maddy looked back at Kit. "She told us that cheeks flapped and hair stood on end." Maddy laughed. "That's what Torbald's experiencing about *now*."

As Sparky peeled out, Jace closed his window to avoid the speeding truck's dusty wake. They drove several miles in their private sand storm before they reached asphalt and began their caravan north on Highway 163.

As they approached the greater Monument Valley, Maddy studied the map, keeping Jace apprised of their location. The road wound through great stretches of flat desert pierced by jutting buttes. Where creases in a mesa afforded shade, Indian homes were occasionally nestled among the cliffs. In the valleys, rare bits of greenery appeared: corn and gourds grew in the furrowed, irrigated land and livestock thrived in the midst of the brutal desert. On a distant hillside, sheep grazed under the watchful eye of a lone woman whose frisky dog ran circles around the flock.

Suddenly, without signaling, Sparky took a left turn.

Dust rose again as the one-lane road deteriorated into an old wagon trail—two soft ruts that led west. Then even the ruts disappeared into open rangeland, and Sparky brought his truck to stop at the lip of a ridge. He jumped out, and everyone climbed onto a knoll. Sparky gestured toward a series of buttes.

"It's out there somewhere," Sparky said.

"What do you mean 'somewhere'?" Jace removed his sunglasses. "Can you be more specific?"

"I'll try. But this place is hard to find. It's a valley they call 'Denava.' A patch of ground where they say the legends happened."

"How far?" Maddy asked.

"I'd say . . . a six-mile hike." He gestured. "You can't drive over that terrain."

"On foot? Dear God." Torbald wiped his moist brow with a handkerchief and glanced at Maddy.

She patted his shoulder. "We'll take our time."

45

Miami

THE MIAMI MARINA COVERED EIGHT square miles of shoreline. A sea of masts spiked the bright-blue Florida sky as far as the eye could see.

Perched at the helm of the Hatteras, Shag watched the movement on the docks. He had been sailing only twice as a boy in East Germany and hadn't done any pleasure boating in America, having been much too preoccupied with undercover work since age twenty. With his blond hair tucked under a seaman's cap, Shag took a pull on the schnapps from his silver flask, surveying what he considered floating decadence. Only in the United States could money be spent for such little benefit; millions of dollars sunk into extravagant hulls, used mainly for sightseeing or socializing.

Droves of well-dressed people strolled up and down the pier. A few chartered deep-sea fishing boats arrived with their catch, and boaters lingered on their decks drinking and laughing, while marina personnel scurried to supervise marine traffic.

Some of the passersby smiled at Shag, assuming he was the captain, not realizing that the real Captain Atwood was tied up below decks.

Under the assumption that he had been hired for a week and would take his foreign guests on an assortment of sightseeing cruises along the Florida coastline, Atwood had been quite jovial, making reference to his visit to the marina only two days earlier. In fact, he'd talked about the Marro party freely, expressing how pleasant they'd been.

That was the last time the captain saw the light of day. Now he was tied to a bunk in the aft cabin, his mouth taped shut. Du was keeping an eye on the fat fuck while Shag stood watch to make sure no one came aboard. Shag gave a casual wave to an overweight bikini-clad woman on the stern of a passing Bayliner. He turned into the sun and stared up the pier.

He spied Kwan and Walsh working themselves up the gangplank. Shag had been impressed with Walsh's poise. Playing the role of a wealthy Canadian businessman on holiday with his Chinese assistant, Walsh came off quite sophisticated.

As they approached the stern of the Hatteras, Kwan gave Walsh a boost and he joined Shag on deck. Walsh appeared enthusiastic, and Shag noticed he had removed the bandage from his left hand.

"Well," Shag said expectantly. "Did you get your e-mail?"

"I did." Walsh pulled a slip of paper from his shirt pocket. "Beijing made the match. Properly interpreted, Robert's Nazca grid fits coordinates on the Arizona–New Mexico border. It must be where Madison's people have gone."

Shag turned to Kwan. "Go below and tell Du we're leaving in half an hour. Kill Atwood, stow his body in the cabin, and lock the door."

Kwan hesitated. "You want to leave his body rotting down below?"

"Why not? No one will notice the stench until we're gone." Shag headed for the rail.

"Where are you going?" Walsh called.

"I'm going to use a pay phone to call Cho."

"I've done that," Walsh said. "He's chartering a plane, flying into New Mexico."

Shag turned. A rush of anger spread through his chest as he leapt toward Walsh, grabbing him by the collar. "I should slit your fucking throat."

Walsh's eyes bulged as he clutched Shag's wrists. "What's the problem?"

Shag wanted to tear him apart but remembered that Walsh was in his care. Rather than hurt Walsh, he shook him as he emphasized key words. "This may be your free ride, jaggoff. But it's my *job*, goddamn it. Talk to Cho without my permission again and I'll kill you."

46

Monument Valley

UNLIKE THE LUSH SPLENDOR OF Maddy's hometown Cascades, Monument Valley's cliffs spoke of nature's relentless ferocity. Millions of tons of earth had been torn away, leaving hardy towers of rock as a testament to nature's power. Maddy reveled in this natural museum, commenting to Torbald on the geological display—quartz, feldspar, and granite sheaths thrust through the dusty desert.

Sparky led the group onto the valley floor. Jace, Hans, and Kit were right behind, hauling backpacks full of equipment. And Maddy followed, wearing her fanny pack and toting the weapons bag. Torbald walked at her side, carrying his briefcase. Maddy took Torbald's arm as they navigated the steep terrain, venturing down the slope, leaving Sparky's truck and the white Ford on the ridge.

The morning sun hung low over the horizon when they began their hike with a temperature of a mere seventy-five degrees, but as time passed, it grew brutally hot. Thankfully, they had been prepared with their water jugs and hats.

After an hour, Maddy began to worry about Torbald.

He seemed more sensitive to heat than the others, probably because of his age and his Nordic upbringing. He began to lag a bit, and Maddy hung back, giving him moral support. Maddy reasoned that as long as Torbald carried on a conversation, he was probably all right. And so far, he talked while hiking, sharing occasional thoughts about the geography. He pointed out anomalies in the rock, commented on the coarseness of the sand, related stories about other desert climates he'd seen. Maddy hoped the older man's endurance would last.

Sparky had promised they would reach their destination prior to the full heat of the day, but that was one of the *few* things of which Sparky seemed certain. The spunky young man kept sidestepping their questions, saying that he was simply following Wind Woman's directions.

His waffling made Maddy a bit uneasy, particularly when Sparky admitted that he had only been to the general area once, when he was a twelve-year-old participant in a reservation-sponsored wilderness quest.

The group's conversation soon dwindled due to exertion, and they walked in silence. Torbald now seemed to falter badly, frequently swigging water. Maddy began to feel the strain of the march. What had begun as an ambitious trek through open country became an unbearable ordeal. Maddy's legs burned. She wore a tank top drenched with perspiration. Her discomfort was intensified by a gnawing at her insides—the eerie feeling that they were being watched. She'd noticed Jace had looked back over his shoulder several times.

Maddy shouted ahead and asked if Jace thought everything was all right.

He had pointed to the top of a neighboring mesa and said, "I don't know. I saw some people up there. Three or four, moving along the ridge."

Sparky responded. "Climbers, probably. Sometimes a few folks like to scale those rocks."

Jace shrugged back at Maddy and no more was said, but perhaps Jace's concern was justified. From up there, anyone could see them.

She imagined a sniper with a riflescope picking them off. She told herself to calm down.

Jace looked back and gave her an encouraging smile.

With no wind, the air hung heavy over the tablelands, and the only sound that broke the monotony was the crunch of their shoes and their heavy breathing.

Maddy was so preoccupied with her own laborious trudging that she barely noticed Sparky come to a stop. As the others caught up, he stood on a small mound overlooking a spectacular basin, bounded on all sides by buttes, and creased by gouges in the earth, where rampaging water had run off from El Ninõs cloudbursts.

Sparky pointed ahead. "See how these four buttes surround that arroyo? If this is the place, it was called 'Denava' by the elders. It means the 'corners of the earth.' Kinda cool, huh?"

"Cool it's not." Maddy wiped her brow.

Torbald had doubled up, panting, bracing his hands on both knees. As he recovered his wind, he stood upright and gazed at the spectacular scenery. "I can see where the elders might be impressed. The symmetry of those buttes is quite unique."

Breathing hard, Kit dropped his backpack to the ground. "Unique? Like a furnace is unique. There can't be any place hotter than this."

"And lonely," Hans added. His first English words all day.

Maddy smiled at the big man's comment. Their thirty-mile drive on the dirt road plus a six-mile hike had put them literally in the middle of nowhere.

"Now what?" Jace asked as Hans lowered his sack.

"We search." Torbald said.

"For what?" Kit wheezed.

"Something in the cliffs. I suspect we should examine those walls." Torbald pointed to a huge butte that faced east. "Wind Woman's reference to the equinox."

"Right." Maddy sat down. "The wall facing the sun."

"To save time, why not split up?" Torbald asked. "Hans can accompany Kit and Sparky, searching to that eastern face, while the rest of us look there." Torbald pointed west.

"No," Hans said, and then he finished in Swedish.

"All right. Hans insists he stays with me. Sparky you go with Maddy and Jace."

Maddy remembered her feelings of being watched. "I think that's a mistake. Let's stay together."

Sparky stared at everyone. "What are you guys so nervous about?"

"Other people might be out here searching," Jace said.

"For what?" Sparky asked.

"Christ, Jace." Kit put his hands on his hips. "Go ahead and spill your guts."

"Kit. Chill, okay?" Jace said.

Kit fumed. "Maddy, he's doing it again. Who the hell is he to tell me what to do?"

Jace turned, dropping his pack to the ground. "If you're off the edge, someone has to tell you."

"You're a fucking guest here," Kit snarled. "I was the one Robert chose, not you."

Maddy had heard enough. "Stop it, both of you."

"What are they talking about, Maddy?" Sparky asked quietly.

"I'll tell you later." Maddy stepped between Jace and Kit. She glanced at her watch. "Look, we're all tired. It's just after twelve thirty. Let's head for those boulders and have lunch in the shade. Then we'll decide what to do."

No one argued with her suggestion, and Maddy led the way to the large rock formation.

In the shaded west side of the boulders, Sparky shared their sandwiches and bottled water. Over Kit's objections, as they sat together, Maddy told Sparky enough to satisfy his curiosity—that the ancient holy place might possess physical properties of scientific merit. Fortunately, Sparky didn't seem overly impressed with that clinical explanation and, like the others, he gave in to the heat and took a two-hour nap.

When Maddy awoke, Sparky had reinitiated their search by climbing up a large rock mound to look around. In his absence, Torbald speculated how long the search might take, addressing issues about camping.

Jace suggested they pitch their tent precisely where they sat, using the rock out-cropping as a base of operations from which to venture out on short expeditions.

"We can't keep the boy here." Jace wiped his forehead with the back of his hand.

"Who needs him?" Kit asked. "He's taking us for a ride. He doesn't know any more about this country than we do."

Maddy ignored the remark. "Let's scout around. What exactly should we look for?" she asked Torbald.

"Good question," Torbald replied. "Some kind of continuity to Nazca . . ." Sparky had climbed down the last few nearby boulders as Torbald finished his thought. "Some marking in the ground, no matter how subtle, should stand away from other natural formations. I suggest we look for artwork, or even a straight line among the natural configurations . . . any marker or sign."

"Sign?" Sparky asked as he approached, having overheard. "Why didn't you say so? There's a lot of cool shapes in the desert rocks."

"In this place?" Torbald gestured toward the desert.

"No. The ones I remember are all over Monument Valley. Naturally there's big stuff, like the elephant butte. But, I've seen a hawk's claw, a round rock with a hole in it that they call the bride's ring, the arrowhead boulder, the hanging snake, and there's a deep hole in—"

"Just a minute," Maddy said. "Where's the arrowhead boulder?"

"North of here. See that butte?" He pointed to the northernmost of the four. "It's on the other side of that."

Torbald seemed to realize what Maddy suspected. "Is the arrowhead a rock?"

"No, it's been dug out of the rock," Sparky said. "Fills up with water when there's flash floods."

"Sounds like Cat Island," Jace said. "There's your continuity, Torbald."

"Can you take us, Sparky?" Torbald got to his feet.

"Sure. We can hike around the east side and drop down into a draw." Sparky indicated a saddlelike scoop just off the shoulder of the butte.

"I don't think there's any need to stay in this valley." Torbald turned to Sparky. "Take us to that marker."

Forty-five minutes later, Sparky had led the party over the crest of a sandy embankment and down a wash that emerged onto the flatland on the far side. As they descended the hillside, a dark shape on the ground stood out against the light-colored redness of the desert floor—a flattened ellipse resembling a fat, partially buried cigar.

"God, look at that," Torbald exclaimed. "It's black. Like the other one."

Jace took the lead, and a few minutes later they climbed onto the eight-foot-high boulder. They stood together staring amazed at a triangular wedge at their feet.

Maddy felt the chill of excitement as she realized it was identical to the one at the lighthouse.

Torbald danced with delight as he fussed with his briefcase, pulling out his compass. "Fifty feet of porous volcanic rock." He checked the magnetic heading. "And again, this triangle points due south toward Easter Island."

Maddy checked the horizon. "Not another scrap of this perforated granitic material around. This doesn't belong in the valley."

"You're right." Torbald knelt and touched the foamlike surface. "And what does this monolith remind you of?"

Maddy gazed from one end of the fifty-by-twenty-foot stone to the other. "A sarcophagus, like the one on Cat Island."

"Yes, but think of our map and the corners of the triangle in the Pacific. Don't these behemoths remind you of those massive stone blocks on Easter Island? You know, before they've been carved with faces?"

"Are you suggesting that this huge stone and the one on Cat Island were somehow hewn from the same quarry as the headstones in the Pacific, thousands of miles away?"

Torbald shrugged. "They're volcanic. What other explanation could there be?"

Maddy remembered Robert's dying words and wished that he were alive to share what he knew. She stared at the triangle and followed the direction of the arrow that pointed toward the butte they had just circumvented. Its red stone pedestal sat due south, and the setting sun threw shadows in relief on the cliff wall.

"My God," Maddy exclaimed.

In a depression in the cliff, a shadow thrown by the descending sun had formed the beginnings of a subtle, yet defined triangle that pointed down the face of the cliff.

"Look! The ultimate sign," Torbald said.

The shaded triangle pointed straight toward the base of the butte cluttered by a ramp of rock; the pile of fragments had ostensibly tumbled from the cliffs above.

"That rockfall makes a fine stairway," Jace said.

"The ascent to Wind Woman's cavern?" Maddy asked.

"Maybe. Or rubble from an initial excavation. In any case," Torbald turned to Sparky, "you've served us well. And unless you have a strong desire to stay, I think you can go home."

"Cool." Sparky smiled all around. "I got places to hang. But what about you guys?"

"Tonight we camp at the base of that butte. And with any luck, tomorrow we begin the search for your great-grandmother's legendary doorway."

47

Anderson Heights, New Mexico

IN THE DEEPENING TWILIGHT, THE Learjet touched down on the small private airfield that serviced the mountain community near the Arizona border. The absentee owner of the field, Bret Anderson, had been handsomely paid for what Shag said was a visit by a Chinese jewelry wholesaler. This wealthy merchant was to arrive to seal a manufacturing agreement with several native turquoise craftsmen in the nearby town of Thoreau, bringing tooling equipment to set up shop.

Having secured the airfield with his men, Shag stepped from the shadows of a hanger as the jet taxied and came to a stop.

Cho had acquired the Learjet from a large American corporation that had benefited from trade deals with China over the last few years. The host company had no idea the aircraft would be used for intelligence operations. Its management simply made the plane available to Chinese dignitaries as part of a diplomatic exchange.

The forward door of the jet swung open, and a hydraulic stairway unfolded. Dressed in body-hugging black T-shirts, Wo and Nang stepped out, followed by Xi and Chang who surveyed the tarmac's perimeter. As they spotted Shag, they seemed to relax, and Chang stuck his head back into the fuselage. Moments later Vincent Scalbania emerged with Cho on his heels, and they both descended to the asphalt below.

Shag took a swig from his stainless steel flask, tucked it away, and glanced back at the chain-link fence. Placing two fingers between his lips, he whistled sharply three times—the prearranged "all clear" signal that summoned two black Hummers driven by Du and Kwan. Shag had purchased the wide-bodied all-terrain vehicles with cash in Albuquerque only hours before.

As they rolled toward the plane, Shag strolled casually in their direction. The moment the Hummers pulled to a stop, Hector Walsh emerged from the rear seat of the lead car.

Du and Kwan joined Wo and Nang as they began to unload cartons from the hold into the spacious all-terrain vehicles. Shag smiled as he noticed the "Standard Electric" logo on each crate. They actually contained weapons and survival gear.

As Shag and Walsh converged on Cho and Scalbania, Cho extended his hand, greeting Shag with a rare handshake.

"Things went smoothly in Miami, I assume?"

"No hitches," Shag replied, giving Walsh a quick glance.

"Not that it matters." Cho's eyes canvassed the surrounding area. "The authorities won't find you in Beijing."

Shag had spent little time in China. "Beijing? But I had some matters of—"

"The Ministry of Science demands we leave immediately for China upon recovering the device. That means *everyone*, Shag." Cho's meandering gaze settled in the vicinity of Shag's forehead. "You. Walsh and Mr. Scalbania, all our men. It's a reasonable request. Beijing requires a tidy package, no stragglers and no loose ends, until there's a comprehensive assessment of what we've procured." It was a veritable barrage of language from the normally reticent Cho. He had turned to Walsh, who hung on his every word. "Mr. Walsh, I assume the isometric charts that our technicians provided remain productive."

"They do. I have them right here." Walsh began to pull the paperwork from his briefcase, but Cho waved him off.

"I'm sure your calculations are admirable, Mr. Walsh. Simply tell me the facts."

"Well, I've had the opportunity to study our overlays very carefully. I believe our target lies in the heart of Navajo country, more specifically, a rugged area called Monument Valley."

"I see." Cho pulled several sunflower seeds from his vest pocket. "And how far is this site?"

"It's about a seven hour drive," Shag interjected. "I suggest we stay in Gallup tonight and get an early start in the morning."

"That's not an unreasonable idea." Cho chewed and spat several shells onto the tarmac, nodding toward the Hummers. "Though with the vehicles you chose, our natty little group looks a bit obtrusive, don't you think? We could paint signs on the doors that announce that we're a commando unit in search of a raid."

The reproach caught Shag unaware. "They're formidable overland vehicles, Mr. Cho. The best I could find."

"I understand. But I would have preferred vans of some kind, something more conventional. I mentioned that to Mr. Walsh during our Miami telephone conversation."

Shag glared at Walsh, who could only shrug. "I was somewhat preoccupied with my calculations."

"Never mind." Cho frowned. "I suggest we drive under the cover of night. Let's *not* caravan, but rather maintain cell-phone contact on the road. We can get a few hours of sleep at a rest stop somewhere near our destination."

Scalbania spoke for the first time. "You don't mean we're all sleeping in these trucks?"

"My men sleep standing up, if necessary, Mr. Scalbania. They are soldiers, not sightseers. We'll manage."

"What about later?" Scalbania asked. "How are we getting out?"

"Our operatives in Mexico have made arrangements to transfer us across the border near Animas. We'll be flown by helicopter to Sajinja, where we've made arrangements for a trawler to take us out to sea. Cuban helicopters will pick us up from the boat. We'll jet to China from Havana and be in Beijing in a day. First, of course, the matter of locating the Marro troop. We'll pick up their trail at first light. It shouldn't be too challenging, gentlemen. A Caucasian scouting party that includes two foreigners and a beautiful woman should leave a broad track through reservation land. They won't be hard to find."

48

The Butte

JACE WATCHED AS THE CAMPFIRE sent a crazed nebula of embers spiraling.

Under the stars, Maddy, Torbald, and Kit hunched on their backpacks as the fire's glow elongated their shadows on the slanted tent wall. Beyond, to the south, the massive shape of the mystery butte hulked in silhouette.

While the others talked, Jace hung off to the side, keeping an eye on the barren landscape, which stretched for miles in the moonlight.

Excusing himself on the pretense of stretching his legs, Jace had wandered from the campfire. In fact, he was mindful of the group's vulnerability in the vastness of the desert. Even though Hans was on watch, Jace strolled the perimeter, occasionally fingering the butt of Cory's Beretta that he now wore holstered on his belt. Jace had distributed the weapons after Sparky left, though Maddy refused to carry a firearm. Kit was left with the shotgun, Torbald the rifle, and Hans still carried his crossbow.

Jace appreciated Hans's military training. Together, they had checked their campsite. Hans, using pidgin English, had reiterated the wisdom of having the tent on a mound overlooking the surrounding desert. With sign language, Hans had suggested a two-hour sentry schedule—Hans was to take the first shift, Jace the second, and Kit the third.

Jace agreed that an outcropping of boulders flanking the camp on a neighboring knoll would be the best vantage point. As darkness fell, Hans had taken his crossbow and assumed his post, allowing the others to finish dinner.

Maddy stuck to dehydrated fruit and crackers; the others ate canned goods and dried meats. The food was hardly satisfying, but no one seemed to care. As they finished eating, Torbald lit a cigarette and he and Maddy reviewed the significance of the day's events.

Closer examination of the butte and the rockfall on its northern side had convinced Maddy that the debris was relatively recent in geological terms, probably less than a hundred years old. Judging from the shadowy triangle that had appeared on the cliff wall at sunset, Wind Woman's "cavern of infinity" might be found somewhere beneath the rubble. Jace, who had experience with dynamite during road survey work after college, volunteered to supervise the attempt to blast away the rubble in the morning.

Returning to the halo of the camp, from his vantage some fifteen feet away, Jace watched as Torbald and Maddy shared the dream, bantering viewpoints, advancing theories. She took obvious pleasure in the rhetoric, her face bright with interest, enjoying the conjecture.

"So . . . your summary, Torbald?" she asked, using a stick to draw in the sand. "What can we expect? An antigravitational device? A universal power source, capable of propulsion?"

"Wait a minute," Kit chimed in. "You're making those assumptions based on the artwork on the Nazca plain?"

Torbald took one last drag off his cigarette and exhaled a large cloud of gray smoke as he tossed the butt into the fire. "True. They're assumptions. But after all, the mystery of Nazca has never been solved. Extraterrestrial entrepreneurs like Erich von Däniken speculated that the long runwaylike shapes in the ground indicated that Nazca had been designed as a prehistoric airport. His theory was supported by the existence of another earth drawing five hundred miles to the west of Nazca near Pisco, a town on the Peruvian coast. This monstrous shape, a triad six hundred feet long on the side of a mountain, points toward the Nazca plain, much like landing lights precede a runway. Naturally, UFO addicts became quite excited."

Maddy stopped her doodling. "Pisco. Isn't that—"

"Exactly, Maddy. The location of the temple where your father's Peruvian Prize originated."

Something inside Jace rebelled against the continued extraterrestrial conjecture. Cory had risked his career because of *his* offbeat suppositions, and even though Dixon seemed convinced of the legitimacy of the Phobia File, Jace still had doubts. At the risk of being judged the eternal skeptic, he felt motivated to interrupt.

"Excuse me, Torbald," he said, smiling as he stepped forward into the light. "With all the speculation over the years, hasn't anyone given a more *conventional* interpretation to this Nazca artwork? Aren't we overlooking the obvious rational explanation that the natives carved their own earth drawings?"

"But how could they? The drawings were only viewable from the air," Maddy ventured.

Torbald nodded. "*That* was the question. Did the Nazca Indians have the ability to view their expansive artwork?" Torbald straightened up and cleared his throat. "Several years ago, a scientific expedition of English and Canadian specialists went to examine the Nazca plain. I found their official conclusion quite astounding. It engages in speculation as fanciful as any alien conjecture."

"What? Witchcraft?" Kit guffawed.

"Very close, Mr. Lassiter. The scientists studied ancient social customs, and they concluded that prehistoric Nazca shamans sucked on coca leaves as part of a tribal ceremony still common to many South American tribes. Presumably, in the resulting euphoria, the shamans engaged in out-of-body experiences that elevated their psyches into imaginary flight. Can you imagine? These scientists suggested that the shamans' projected telepathic visions from on high inspired their fellow tribal members to walk in processions along prescribed lines, which eventually formed the graphics of the animal figures on the plain."

"I don't understand," Maddy said. "The shamans' out-of-body flight led the natives to walk the outlines of figures until they were formed?"

"That was the theory," Torbald responded. "Apparently the ground is soft enough to have eventually worn into definable outlines. They called the exercise physically 'proceeding' a piece of art. Of course, what these scientists could not explain was who would have directed the precise design of the artwork in the first place."

"Particularly if, as you say, the earth drawings are proportionately so exact," Maddy said. "You mentioned that the hummingbird is quite ornate."

"And it's several hundred feet long." Torbald smiled. "Imagine us trying to go out there," he pointed into the desert, "to walk a pattern that complex. Frankly, I find the expedition's 'official' explanation of shamanic mental transference more outlandish than von Däniken's alien visitations."

"There must have been other theories," Jace said.

"There were." Torbald scratched his chin. "In the nineteen seventies, an American airline executive named Woodman took it upon himself to prove that the ancient Nazca Indians had actually *flown* in order to enjoy their own artwork. Woodman's South Dakota aviation firm built a lighter-than-air balloon using what were considered 'natural' materials indigenous to the region around four hundred BC. Woodman's people created a balloon from woven fleece and animal skins, with a wood frame for a gondola. Well, he succeeded in making an eighty-five-foot-long rickety balloon heated like this." He gestured to the flames. "With the balloon placed over a fire, the momentum of hot smoke elevated his crude craft and, believe it or not, the thing actually rose over three hundred feet off the ground."

"Ah. So what does that tell you?" Kit asked.

Torbald smiled. "Not much more than the fact that astute twentieth-century technicians could build au naturel balloons, Mr. Lassiter."

"I don't understand."

"Well, the earth drawings in Nazca are only a small fraction of the hundreds of other earth drawings that exist around the world."

"So?" Kit said.

"Don't you find it odd that there are no archeological drawings of *balloons*? If, indeed, massive art around the planet had been created in that fashion, with flight prevalent in the cultures of England, the American Southwest, and Peru, wouldn't we have discovered some remnant, a carving, some reference to the balloon itself? A flying device in a prehistoric culture would have been miraculous and noteworthy."

"I see what you mean," Maddy said. "Flight itself would have been the memorable phenomenon, not the drawings made for aerial enjoyment."

"Absolutely. The balloon would have been a *monumental* achievement, memorialized in ritual and shown in the art itself." Torbald had made his point.

"The same issue applies with the shaman theory, doesn't it?" Maddy asked. "Are we to assume that shamans' out-of-body experiences created the other earth drawings around the world?"

"Precisely. And that coca leaves were imported for the purpose." Torbald chuckled. "There's simply too much earth art on the planet to localize those ideas."

Maddy seemed even more excited now. She postulated that lacking other plausible explanations, Alca's existence was even more credible. Alca might be something beyond their wildest expectations—powerful enough to allow industrial nations to cleanse their ecological wounds—something to enable third world countries to satisfy enormous energy demands without further scarring the planet. Alca's permanent solution, she believed, could herald the end of petroleum.

Kit popped the bubble. His eyes suddenly gleamed with anticipation. "Big oil dies. And the players with the energy get richer than God." He looked from Maddy to Torbald. "Have you guys talked?"

"Talked?" Maddy asked.

"About the profits. How we're going to cut the pie."

Maddy's face fell. "Kit. This isn't the time. We don't even know what we're dealing with."

"I think we better predetermine shares." Kit eyes beaded in the firelight. "Maddy, you get consideration, with your family and all. But Robert counted on me like family, you know what I mean?"

Torbald rocked back and clutched one knee. "Money isn't the primary motive here."

Kit pointed a finger at Torbald. "Are you refusing to discuss it?"

"Not at all. But I think it's up to Madison. And I trust in her ultimate judgment."

Kit seemed momentarily put off, but then he turned to Maddy. Leaning forward over the fire, he said, "Okay. Tell us how we're dividing the spoils."

Maddy's eyes glowed with irritation. "We're not plundering a village. This is a scientific effort. Whatever benefits are derived, there'll be plenty of money for everyone."

"I'm trying to avoid any future misunderstanding," Kit said, acrimoniously. He looked up, fixing his eyes on Jace. "What do you say, Kelton?"

Detached from the moment Kit's greedy tirade began, Jace had already taken a step away from the fire. "I'm with Torbald. It's Maddy's call."

Kit shrugged. "All right, Madame Mission-Director. Make the call."

"I haven't given it a moment's thought." Maddy was clearly upset but snarled in the debate.

Having lost all interest in the conversation, Jace turned from the fire and, once again, wandered away.

Out under the moon, he found a quiet spot among the sage and cacti. After carefully checking to make sure there were no snakes in sight, he sat on a boulder and looked up into a sea of stars. He couldn't help but ponder what Torbald had said.

Cory would have found it conclusive. He had wanted to believe that "there was something out there." Judging from Torbald and Maddy's enthusiasm, Jace was in the minority. As he thought back on it, his negative feelings began when he was just a boy, not long after his father died; they were rooted in the embarrassment and innuendo he associated with the aerospace industry. It was Cory who had become the addict. As a young man, Jace had associated space exploration with his own staggering loss. And Cory's space *fantasies* had been even less palatable. Cory's death had revived Jace's bitterness.

As his eyes became more accustomed to the dark, Jace looked up and watched layer upon layer of normally unseen stars appear like a fine, distant dust.

According to Torbald, Egyptian and Mayan temples were constructed upon astronomical coordinates. If Earth were center stage, and the night sky simply a backdrop, why the fascination with a mathematical significance of the stars? And if Earth were the focal point, why wouldn't the legend of Alca and the Nazcan god Quatel have a more grounded perspective? Considering the Nazcas were worshipers of water, why wouldn't Quatel have emerged from the rivers, the ocean, or even the center of the planet?

A soft footfall sent a tingle up Jace's back. He pulled the Beretta from its holster and whirled around. Then he recognized Maddy standing in the darkness. She had approached much too quietly.

"Damn it, Maddy. I could have—"

"Sorry I startled you." She stepped forward, still glowing with enthusiasm.

"You shook me up. Of course, it's not the first time." He smiled and tucked the gun away.

"I think that's healthy." She moved even closer. "I remember how you looked in Providence when I . . ." she reached out and touched his collar, "got close to you like this."

He caught a whiff of gardenia soap. She had it stashed in that fanny pack of hers, he thought. He found himself intrigued by the vision of her sponge bathing behind some rock away from camp.

"And remember how on your motel lanai, you said that we would finish this mission *together*?" she asked softly.

The phrase meant much more than that. A sense of destiny had tugged the words out of him. "Yes. I'm committed."

"Are you really? I watched you tonight, standing there on the fringe. You're having trouble with all this, aren't you?"

"With Kit?"

"That's not what I meant."

"Did you satisfy his greed?"

"I didn't." She tossed her head. "I frankly don't know what's fair, and I chose to deal with it later. I'm talking about your resistance to Torbald's theories."

"I'm skeptical."

"And not afraid to say so. It's your calculated aloofness that challenges me." She inched closer. "You're honest, courageous, and yet, to your credit, vulnerable."

"To what?" He sounded more defensive than he'd planned.

She stood on tiptoe, easing a bare arm around his neck. "Me."

Jace couldn't help but smile as she continued. "And as vulnerable as I am out here," she glanced at the desert, "I feel completely safe with you." She tilted her head and brushed her lips across his chin.

Her touch held a luscious invitation.

Maddy was right. He *was* vulnerable, gazing into her eyes, feeling her warmth through the flimsy tank top against his rib cage.

He inhaled her sweetness as her mouth hovered an inch away from his.

"Maddy...I..."

"Yes?"

He hoisted her, taking her in an embrace. "I'm not a damned bit skeptical about *you*."

Her eyes beamed with unbridled assent.

He held her closer now, feeling her contours against him, imagining the marvels of her body.

The stars overhead seemed to suddenly fall around them as he eased his lips toward hers and kissed her deeply.

49

The Desert

HECTOR WALSH LEANED FORWARD IN the black Hummer, intent on the action unfolding in the vehicle's headlights.

Only moments ago Cho had sat in the backseat, spitting sunflower seed shells through the open rear window as he described their escape route to Mexico in greater detail. Two custom Blackhawk helicopters had already landed in Alimas, anticipating Cho's arrival. A powerful Communist underground in Mexico with strong ties to Cuba had paved the way for a smooth transition.

But in the middle of Cho's discourse, he had looked forward through the windshield, distracted by what he saw.

Sparky, the Indian boy, had been beaten into unconsciousness, his body now slumped on the ground.

Shag had unsheathed his knife, and Cho seemed concerned with the outcome. He had leaned out and asked Shag to explain what he was doing.

"The kid told me all he knows. They're out there now," Shag yelled from the edge of the ravine. "I'll cut this little shit and we can move on."

As Cho got out and walked toward the red pickup truck, Walsh followed, closing the car door behind as he checked his watch. It was after two o'clock in the morning.

The unconscious young boy now hung limp in the grasp of Xi and Chang while Shag held his knife to the lad's throat.

"That's inadvisable," Cho said, looking down at the boy. "You've beaten him within an inch of his life. Why not throw him into his truck and push the damn thing over the edge?" Cho pointed toward the deep gully.

"What's the problem?" Scalbania yelled, stepping from the other Hummer with Du and Kwan on his heels.

"We don't know how long we'll be out there." Cho nodded toward the wide expanse called Monument Valley. "If the boy's throat has been slashed, the police will have cause to search for a killer. If he's battered when his truck crashes to the bottom, his corpse will look as it should . . . bruised by the impact."

Shag was obviously disappointed by Cho's decision, but he acquiesced and grumbled something in Chinese.

Xi and Chang dragged Sparky toward the truck. Shag opened the driver's side door, and they tucked the kid behind the wheel.

On Shag's command, all four men pushed, and the pickup began to move, its tires crunching on the sand as it rolled toward the crevasse. Walsh couldn't help himself; he followed Scalbania and Cho to the edge of the embankment to view the demolition.

The vehicle lofted into the air and hit hard after an initial thirty-foot drop. Then it tumbled tailgate-over-hood as windshield glass shattered and pieces of metal tore away. A fender flew off to the side, a rear tire disengaged, the roof of the cab caved in. After another fifty feet, the truck smashed into the bottom of the arroyo, rolling twice before it disappeared in a cloud of dust.

"There, you see," Cho said, turning away. "If anyone finds him now, which is unlikely, it will look as if he fell asleep, went off the road, and killed himself."

"Dead is dead." Shag hoisted his silver flask to his lips, took a long pull, and tucked the canister into the inside breast pocket of his safari jacket.

The search around town had taken only five hours. Several people talked about the strangers: a giant blond man, a beautiful woman, and three others who had asked questions about Monument Valley. The tip-off came when Walsh overheard two elderly men in wide-brimmed hats share scuttlebutt at the general store: a young man they knew named Sparky had been playing pool at the Valley Tavern, bragging about taking the mysterious outsiders into the desert.

The rest was easy.

Shag clubbed Sparky in the tavern parking lot two hours later. The boy spilled all he could, even showing them the precise location from which he had guided Madison Marro and her group into the desert. With his face bloodied by blows, he described the approximate location that he called "the Arrowhead boulder."

This excited Walsh immensely, particularly when Sparky described the characteristics of the now familiar triangle.

"We'll take the Hummers in as far as we can." Cho looked off to the northwest.

"That won't be far," Shag said, pointing. "We're going to run into a lot of rugged rock and uneven country."

"Then we'll leave one man with the vehicles and take the rest on foot," Cho said. "They've apparently found the location. All we have to carry is some water and weapons."

50

The Butte

SECONDS TICKED AWAY. MADDY AND Jace knelt with Torbald in the gully. Kit and Hans crouched behind a large boulder. In the hush of the desert heat, everyone waited for the roar of an explosion that refused to come.

Jace's gaze met Maddy's. He nodded reassuringly. Unlike the others, who wore T-shirts and polos, Jace wore a short-sleeved khaki shirt. He had used one of the hunting knives to cut his jeans into a pair of shorts. His black hair was matted with grime, his face was dusty from prior dynamite blasts, and his forearms were covered with dirt, streaked with perspiration. He had worked hard in the heat, and Maddy loved the way he looked: intense, determined to get it done.

Everything had changed between them. Everything.

Each gesture, each word carried a reminder of their embrace the night before. One long kiss had led to several others, and the kisses would have become much more had Hans not made an appearance on the knoll, looking for Jace to relieve him on watch. In the brief moments Maddy and Jace had in the moonlight, everything in them had collided. Their bodies charged with energy; words rushed, yet soft, as they expressed their feelings.

Maddy knew that if they hadn't been unexpectedly interrupted, they would have made love, then and there, under the stars. But it wasn't meant to be. When Hans approached, Maddy pulled away from Jace.

He had touched her face with a gentle understanding and uttered a single word.

"Later," he had whispered, in a way that meant so much: a promise, a wish, an expression of future desire. She had slept sweetly with the memory.

This morning when they met in daylight, her perspective changed. Jace seemed suddenly transparent; the tough, rugged exterior peeled away in layers the moment he smiled, because today, the smile was for her.

Maddy watched as Jace checked his diving watch. The explosion was way overdue. He had preburned lengths of the old orange-colored fuse to check its timing. "It's been over ninety seconds," he said.

Kit glared from across the way. "What's the hang-up?"

"Old powder," Jace replied. "The damn things are unpredictable."

Another fifteen seconds passed. Kit squirmed, shifting the weight on his haunches. "You better check it."

"That's not wise," Jace said quietly. "Give it some time."

Everyone's patience had worn thin after three prior explosions removed only some of the rubble, revealing nothing extraordinary on the newly exposed cliff wall.

Kit edged around the boulder, stepping out onto the sand. Torbald inched upward, venturing a glance at the butte.

"Kit . . . get back. Torbald, keep your head down," Jace said calmly.

Kit caught Maddy's eye and, as if to demonstrate his bravado, he squared his shoulders and refused to move. "If you won't go, maybe I'll have a look."

Maddy glanced at Jace. "How do you know when it's safe?"

"With old equipment, you don't." Jace had mentioned his preference for a magneto detonator, which would have allowed him to set charges on the end of a wire. He'd been forced to improvise with blasting caps, stuffing a match into the frayed end of a three-foot fuse—lighting it and hoping for the right timing. "I'm working with antiquated material."

Kit frowned as he stepped forward. "Come on, Jace. It's obviously a dud. I'm—"

Kit was interrupted by a huge explosion that knocked him on his backside. Dust danced across the desert floor. A blast wave passed overhead, filling the air with sand, sending an echo from butte to butte through Monument Valley.

Tiny rock fragments peppered the surrounding area, plinking off Maddy's arms, which she'd crossed over her head.

As the shower of particles ceased, Jace asked if Maddy and Torbald were okay, then he stepped over to help Kit, who refused Jace's hand.

Instead, he wiped his face, coughing incessantly. He was covered from head to toe with dirt. Maddy suppressed a smile, though she was grateful he wasn't hurt.

Hans was already up and headed for the base of the butte with his crossbow slung over his shoulder.

Everyone dusted themselves off and, after grabbing weapons and flashlights, started for the incline. Hans was already climbing through large chunks of sandstone and granite. When he reached the lip of the chasm, he glanced into the depression. Turning, he yelled something in Swedish.

"What's he saying?" Maddy asked as they rushed forward.

"We've succeeded in clearing . . ." Torbald panted, "what he believes is the base of the cliff."

Kit broke into a run, reached the rubble first, and scurried up the rockfall. Torbald, Jace, and Maddy joined him. She was cheered by what she saw.

A good deal of the rock had been blown away, forming a V-shaped trench. Another ten vertical feet of smooth cliff surface had been revealed.

"What do you think?" Jace asked.

"We dig," Torbald replied.

Hans scrambled back down the mountain toward camp. While Jace, Kit, and Maddy clambered down the sides of the newly formed crater to give the cliff wall a cursory examination, Hans reappeared with the pickaxes and shovels slung over his shoulders.

Jace and Hans began to lift the smaller pieces of rock out to Kit, who handed them to Torbald and Maddy in chaingang fashion. It was slow going, and as the hours passed, everyone worked up a sweat.

After the group had cleared the smaller rocks from a large portion of the wall, Hans and Jace asked Kit to help budge a large piece of granite, a jagged hunk that weighed at least four hundred pounds.

They decided to try and push rather than lift the boulder while Maddy and Torbald braced the large chunk with smaller rocks. Everyone strained, and using the pickaxes, they jimmied and hoisted. Veins stood out on Jace's forehead, Hans's face shaded to a deep purple, and Kit's cheeks ran with perspiration.

Finally they managed to topple the stone off to the side.

Maddy gasped with excitement. Where the boulder had been, a gaping hole appeared.

Jace fell to his knees and shone his flashlight inside.

"There's a passageway here." He reached in. "I think we can clear a few rocks and climb through. Give me a hand."

Hans supported Jace and he rolled over, easing himself into the breach, feet first. Then he disappeared.

Soon several stones began to emerge.

Jace hoisted eight or nine pieces, roughly two feet in diameter, from the cleft. He then reappeared, perspiring freely and smiling. "That's it," he said as he regained his feet. "There's enough room for us to slide through one at a time."

"Did you *see* anything?" Maddy asked.

"There's an incline of about ten degrees, headed into the mountain. Pretty musty in there. I hope there's enough oxygen."

"Is it wide enough for him?" Torbald gestured to Hans.

"I think so." Jace smiled again.

"Good. Then there's enough room for our backpacks."

Kit stared at Torbald. "You don't mean you want to haul everything?"

"Yes. I think we should take the tools, weapons, the rest of the dynamite, lights, everything we can carry. Who knows how far this goes or what we might encounter."

Torbald's recommendation led to gathering the rest of the gear from camp, and they returned to the cave opening and took inventory. Each person had a flashlight. Maddy wore her fanny pack and carried the bag that held spare batteries, food, and several canteens. Jace brought a crowbar, two pickaxes, and a Coleman lantern, plus his Beretta. Kit had a backpack filled with blankets and the shotgun. Torbald hauled the rifle, his compass, and books. Hans carried his crossbow, a shovel, and the bag with spare dynamite, tape, plus small tools.

They were about to enter the newly discovered tunnel when Torbald asked them to pause. "I would like to say something." Removing his sun hat, he looked from one face to the next and rested his gaze on Maddy's. "I want to dedicate this to you."

She was struck by the sentiment. "Why not wait until we *discover* something?"

"We have. The Nazca earth map led us *here*." His brow furrowed with sincerity, and he blinked several times. "God knows how many people have died." Then Torbald recited the names of the S-7.

Maddy felt the weight of his somber words, and she envisioned her father's deathbed wish to her mother and Robert's tragic death in Vancouver. Her eyes moistened as she answered, "Let your dedication go to my visionary father,

Mason Marro, and his courageous brother, Robert."

"To Mason and Robert," Kit repeated as if it were a toast.

"Good for you, Maddy," Torbald said, apparently pleased with her reply.

Jace reached out and shook her hand. It gave her a rush as he said, "Lead the way."

She wiped a tear from her cheek. "You're damned right I will." Torbald nodded his approval as she dropped to her hands and knees to enter the opening. Torbald's sentimental moment faded immediately as she began to crawl forward.

Dust blossomed off the tunnel floor as she scurried forward, pushing the food bag ahead with one hand, holding her flashlight with the other.

The others followed with swaying flashlight beams, clanking tools, and scraping bags as she negotiated the shallow descent. The dankness made breathing difficult. The air was scented with the subtle smell of sulfur. The floor was covered with a fine red dust that collected on her boots. The ceiling and sandstone walls were surprisingly smooth, as if they had been rubbed by passing hands over thousands of years.

Jace called forward to ask if she was all right. She responded that she was fine, though she found the air stifling.

After the first ten yards, the passageway widened and Maddy was able to walk upright.

Judging from the thud and the exclamation toward the rear, the space was still somewhat cramped for Hans.

Several yards farther, the tunnel became wider still, now a full six feet in diameter. Maddy's flashlight beam fell upon a small alcove in the north wall. As she passed, her shoe brushed something white. She knelt and unearthed a bone. After several minutes of probing the surrounding area with the tip of a pickax, she and Torbald had gathered a pile of petrified animal bones and bits of pottery.

"These aren't that old," Torbald commented. "Late first millennium from the look of them. Around AD nine hundred."

"They're bovine," Maddy said, handling what appeared to be a carved animal tibia. "Buffalo, I think."

"And it's notched." Torbald trained his light on the fossil. "Used in some type of religious rite perhaps?"

"Makes sense, since Wind Woman talked about the cave of infinity being a place of worship," Jace added.

"Infinity? Bullshit." Everyone whirled around as Kit stepped out of the darkness. No one had noticed his absence while they had examined the artifacts. "A scam," he said cynically. "There's no infinity here. This fucking dust bowl is a dead end."

"We don't know what's around the bend," Maddy said.

"I do. I've just been there. It stops dead."

"That can't be." Maddy's heart sank as she rushed past Kit, flooding the tunnel with her light. Jace was right behind, cautioning her to slow down. After another several hundred feet of a gradual descent past curiously blackened walls, covered with the soot from what must have been a thousand torches, the tunnel once again leveled off and came to an abrupt halt.

They stood in a small fifteen-foot-square, roomlike cave. Its walls were covered with crude drawings, an assortment of desert creatures, whose style appeared to resemble Pueblo art.

Maddy faced a solid stone wall—the dead end Kit predicted.

Torbald cursed in disbelief. "I don't believe this," he said. "It's impossible."

"Stand back," Jace said as he dropped one of the pickaxes. "Something has to give." Wielding the other, he took a few hefty swings at the rock.

Maddy covered her face as chips of rock pelted the group. The concussion of metal against stone became deafening in the confined space. But after Jace's many strongly landed blows, nothing happened.

"Keep probing," Torbald pleaded. "There has to be a way through."

"Try the perimeter," Maddy added as she propped her flashlight on the food bag so that the beam flooded the wall.

Hans dropped his backpack and let fly with the other pickax.

Torbald used the shovel, while Maddy hammered the sidewalls with the crowbar.

After a few moments of pounding, Jace noticed that Kit simply stood off to the side. "Hey, you want to join the expedition?"

"What expedition? This is over."

Jace stepped over to Torbald and took his shovel, giving the older man a gentle nudge, pushing him out of the way. "You're on a break, doctor." Jace tossed the shovel at Kit who caught it by the handle. Jace pointed. "Find a place and start whacking."

Kit threw the shovel to the ground. "Fuck you. I'm not taking orders from some fat-headed prick. You think because you and Maddy had a tumble in the desert—"

Kit never had the chance to finish.

Jace launched himself and grabbed Kit by the neck, backing him up several feet. Kit's eyes bugged out as he fought for air.

Fully enraged, with his face just inches from Kit's nose, Jace's tone fell into a low growl. "If you open your wise-ass mouth one more time . . ."

Maddy clutched Jace's shoulders to restrain him. "Jace, stop. Step back, please."

Jace loosened his grip and backed away as Kit retreated to the far wall, coughing and rubbing his neck.

Maddy found Kit's attitude obnoxious, but she hated to see anyone hurt. "Are you all right?" she asked, extending a hand that Kit brushed away. Maddy faced the others. "He has a point, you know. We've pounded every square inch of this wall."

Even Jace couldn't hide his disappointment. "I don't know what to tell you, Maddy."

Torbald shook his head. "But the triangle on the desert floor, the shadow on the cliff wall . . . it all made sense. Dear God, it can't end like this."

51

The Cave

MADDY'S EXPEDITIONARY FORCE HUDDLED IN the dark. Swirling particles of dust drifted through the flashlight beams that cut the gloom.

While the others sat together exhausted, Kit had moved to a corner, nursing his bruised ego.

Jace hadn't given Kit a second thought, but he was seriously concerned about Maddy. She looked utterly depressed, seated across from him on a backpack, fussing with a food bag. She had handed out some sandwiches and beef jerky, which everyone wolfed down, and broke out a canteen, passing the container to Torbald who was the first to take a drink.

"Maybe there's a second opening in the cliff." Jace wiped his face with the fringe of his shirt. "We could start over and blast away more of the rockfall."

No one replied.

Jace accepted the canteen from Torbald. He took a swig. The water was warm but satisfying.

"You know, I'd regret any damage we might cause to unknown buried artifacts," Maddy said softly, "but how about blasting in here? What would happen?"

"Impossible to tell without knowing the lay of the land above us." Jace paused to take a second swallow and then passed the water to Hans. "In a confined space, the force flows toward the point of least resistance. If that's over our heads, we'll have a cave-in."

Hans mishandled the canteen, and it fell to the cave floor with a clank. "Sorry," he said. He bent down to retrieve the canister.

"There's more water." Maddy reached for another canteen. "Kit, you need some of this." It was apparent she felt badly for him. Kit hadn't said a word since Jace's reprimand.

Maddy fidgeted in the food bag for another bottle. As she handed it to Kit, Hans began to jabber in Swedish.

Torbald responded instantly, training his flashlight on Hans. After a quick verbal exchange, Jace was surprised to see Torbald drop to his hands and knees.

"What's happening?" Jace asked.

"Look." Torbald's finger pointed to the puddle. "And observe." Hans splashed more water on the floor. Bubbling in the dust, the small pool slowly shrank in size and dissipated in a matter of seconds.

"What's going on?" Maddy asked.

"It's draining." Torbald listened to the dripping sound below. "The floor must be porous."

Even Kit came to his feet.

"It looks solid enough," Jace said.

"There's something beneath," Torbald replied as Hans reached for one of the pickaxes.

Gesturing for the others to stand back, the big man took a mighty overhead swing and hammered the stone floor.

Dust rose and sparks flew, but after several blows, Hans had made little headway.

Jace grabbed one of the backpacks and rummaged through it. When he turned to the others, he was holding the dynamite.

"I thought you said we'd cave this place in," Maddy said.

"Maybe." Jace pointed to the floor. "If it's porous down there, the rest of this place might be honeycombed. Let's blow a hole in something and find out." He turned to Maddy. "Why don't you take the others and wait outside while I set the charge?"

"No. I'm staying with you."

The look in her eyes convinced him not to argue, and while the others gathered their equipment, Jace began to prep a dynamite bundle. He had six sticks left. He laid two on the ground and wrapped the other four with tape.

As Hans, Kit, and Torbald headed for the passageway, Maddy slumped to her knees next to Jace and aimed the flashlight on Jace's work.

"Why are you doing that?" she asked as he frayed one end of the string.

"I'm loosening the fuse so I can stuff a match inside," he answered. "Then I'll strike it on a rock, and we'll run like hell."

"What about these?" She pointed to the two remaining dynamite sticks.

"Put them away," he said as he tied a small band of tape around the match head and the frayed end of the string.

Maddy stuffed the two remaining sticks into her fanny pack as Jace tucked the closed end neatly into the bundle, placing it directly over the spot where Hans had spilled the water.

"Are you ready?" he asked.

She nodded, and he struck the match on an exposed section of rock.

As the match head ignited, Jace turned. "Okay, go."

They ran up the two-hundred-foot soot-spotted ramp, past the artifact alcove, and up the thirty-foot incline toward a brilliant patch of daylight.

Scrambling out into the late afternoon sun, they found Torbald and Hans waiting outside.

"Where's Kit?" Maddy asked.

"He went that way." Torbald pointed toward the tent.

"Forget him." Jace ushered the others. "We've got to get out of range. Take cover beyond the ridge."

They had scrambled up the crevasse and positioned themselves on the downhill side of the rockfall when a rumble sounded deep inside the cliff. The ground shook and an amber-colored plume puffed from the cave entrance.

During the few minutes it took to let the dust clear, Kit reappeared. He carried a shovel.

"Where have you been?" Maddy asked.

"Back there." Kit pointed to the camp. "I just needed a few minutes alone. Maddy, I apologize for what I said in there. It was uncalled for."

Maddy patted him on the back. "Don't worry about it. We need you now."

Kit hoisted the tool. "I'm ready. Show me where to dig."

Even as Maddy ushered him over to the others, Jace was suspicious of Kit's feigned humility, but he let it go as everyone rechecked their gear. The sun was just beginning to set as Jace led them back into the tunnel.

The air was thick with dust as they worked their way back inside. Jace's flashlight cut through the gloom as he pushed on.

When they reached the alcove, Jace noticed the bone and pottery had been topped by a new layer of rusty sand. He panned the ceiling with his flashlight but found no sign of shearing rock. Yet the sight of the fresh sand bothered him, and a hundred feet into the "sooty" section of the tunnel, his uneasiness proved valid, as the crack of splitting rock shattered the air somewhere to the rear.

"Duck and cover," Jace yelled as a section of the ceiling collapsed behind Kit.

A fresh plume of dust blew forward, cloaking everyone.

Jace fought to see. He struggled to breathe, overcome by a horrific odor. Then he heard Maddy scream.

In the glare of the bobbing flashlight beams, the tunnel had come alive. The air itself seemed to churn with motion.

"Bats!" Maddy yelled.

"Hundreds of them!" Kit shouted from the rear.

Jace's natural impulse to escape to the outside was thwarted as Maddy and the others rushed in his direction with wave upon wave of flying rodents in their wake.

"Head for the entrance," Jace shouted.

"No way out," Kit yelled, covered by the swarm.

"We're trapped," Torbald exclaimed, his voice shrill with panic.

Claustrophobia momentarily gripped Jace, but the feeling passed quickly as he, too, was enveloped by flapping wings. Smothered by the disgusting creatures, Jace groped for Maddy's hand and, clutching her wrist, he took off at a run into the mountain's depths.

They scampered through the remainder of the sooty tunnel, reaching the cave, where Jace's flashlight beam revealed that the dynamite blast had blown a large hole in the floor.

An unnaturally shiny surface loomed ten feet below.

Hans, Torbald, and Kit stumbled into the cave behind Maddy. Trailing bats flew around their heads.

"Follow me," Jace shouted. "I'll let myself down."

"Hurry." Maddy took a swing at the fluttering rodents.

Adjusting his Beretta, Jace tucked his flashlight into his belt. By hanging on the rim of what had been the floor, he was able to step down onto the rubble below. As he jumped into a new subterranean tunnel, he realized it was completely different from the one above.

"Come on, Maddy," he called. "I'll catch you."

Maddy dropped into Jace's arms while Kit hopped down next to them. Then Hans helped Torbald, handing him off to Jace.

Torbald eased down onto the debris, panning his flashlight, creating a burst of color. "Dear God," he said, "what is this?"

The new tunnel's floor and walls were lined with opaque glass, radiating shimmering rainbows.

"Fused by intense heat," Maddy said as she stepped onto the shiny surface.

"But by whose hand?" Torbald gazed down the rounded tunnel that headed south into the darkness. It was seamlessly smooth, as if a molten fire ball had bored a shaft through solid rock.

More bats had entered the chamber above. "Let's lose those bastards." Jace took Maddy's arm and the party ventured farther into the mountain. After some seventy yards, the sound of flapping wings had been left behind and they stopped to catch their breath.

Jace noted that he could see everyone's features quite clearly, even without a flashlight. The rainbow colors had disappeared, replaced by an eerie green glow that flooded the passage.

"Explain this incandescence," Torbald said.

"I can't," Maddy answered. "No point of origination. It's as if the glass walls were phosphorescent."

"Natural energy, perhaps?" Torbald's eyes glowed.

Maddy responded with a smile. "One of your marvels, Torbald?"

Jace gazed ahead. He nudged Maddy. "Your party, lady. You want to take the lead?"

"No. I'm real comfortable right behind you."

Jace took the point once more, and they walked on, following the gently sloping curve of the shaft. The tube then took a sharp right turn. They were confronted with a triangular doorway.

Jace turned to Maddy. "Three-sided. Look familiar?"

"Same dimensions," Maddy added. "Identical proportions to the triangle in Nassau and the monolith outside."

"Look at these etchings, Maddy." Torbald pointed to the doorframe, which was lined with vibrantly illuminated hieroglyph engravings, carved in what appeared to be electric jade. The luminous art depicted a series of ancient humanoid shapes carved into a material that appeared technologically advanced—strong and smooth, like an alloy of glass and steel. "Why, they look positively Mayan. I've seen these before." Torbald unslung his bag and fussed inside, retrieving a sizable leather-bound volume. He leafed through the book, while the others trained their flashlights on the pages. "I found it." Torbald tilted the book so that everyone could see. "These figures stem from the Popol Vuh in the Mayan temples. It says, 'To him who watches over the happiness of the human race, who meditates on the goodness of all that exists in the sky and on the earth.'" Torbald turned to Maddy, his face ruddy with excitement. "Imagine that, three thousand miles and over two thousand years ago this artwork appeared in the Yucatán."

"Is this a reproduction? Or is it the other way around?" Maddy asked.

"In either case, the implications are earth-shattering," Torbald replied. "It suggests that the Anasazi, the Nazca, and the Mayans were culturally connected. It may even prove that the Nazcas were the ancestors of the Anasazi." Torbald pointed at the cranial shapes of humanoid figures. "Look at the long heads. Just as Wind Woman said."

Jace peered into the blackness on the other side of the portal. He took a step forward and aimed his flashlight through the opening. "I can't see a thing."

"Careful," Maddy whispered.

Jace wanted to step over the threshold, but he was unable to see the floor. "I'm going in. Follow me single file, in case the footing is hazardous." He stepped inside and panned his flashlight. The devastatingly black room seemed to soak up every bit of light. The ceiling and floor were coarsely textured, and the lack of refraction caused a blackout effect, making it difficult to estimate distance.

The sensation was unnatural and disturbing.

"I don't get this." Jace stopped in his tracks. "Kit, hand me the shovel." As the tool was passed forward, Jace used the handle to reach out and tap the floor. The sound indicated solid footing ahead, but it was impossible to tell the dimensions of the room. The walls appeared within reach, but when Jace tried to touch them, they inexplicably receded into darkness.

"It's the ultimate limbo," Maddy commented. "The sense of nothingness is overwhelming."

"Perhaps that's the desired result," Torbald called from his place in line. "This must be a transition point, meant to disorient the unwanted visitor."

"Well, it's working." Jace felt totally off balance. "If I didn't know better, I'd think were we were hundreds of feet in the air. I even feel some kind of draft."

"That's no draft," Kit said from the back. "My hair's vibrating on the back of my neck."

"I agree." Maddy shuddered. "There's a fuzzy sensation around my head."

"It's the singing," Torbald said. "Wind Woman spoke of vibrations. We're feeling an energy field."

Jace continued to tap with the shovel handle for footing like a blind man finding his way, but suddenly, a spiderweb of light shot through the floor toward a now visible far wall. The net of laserlike lines gathered at a point and climbed a vertical strip on the black surface directly ahead.

"God, what *is* that?" Maddy clutched Jace by the belt from behind.

The vertical strip split the wall with a turquoise slash that pulsed in the dark and disappeared.

Jace felt a gush of air hit him like a hot fever. "Hold on," he exclaimed. "Something's opening up."

52

The Memorial

LOOKING OVER JACE'S SHOULDER, MADDY watched as the narrow opening cleaved. Two huge walls were rolling apart without a sound.

Dull light appeared through the crevice, and Maddy suddenly experienced a sensation she could hardly describe: a constant buzzing that made her shiver, yet the air rushing past her face felt comfortably warm. The pleasant vibration touched her everywhere, as if a hundred fingertips caressed her skin.

The narrow opening was a portal into a new chamber.

Maddy surged forward, but Jace cautioned her, urging her to walk directly behind him as he stepped over the threshold.

Her feet touched the ground on the other side; the polished floor upon which she stood appeared to be composed of a seamless black onyx. The concave walls of the chamber were equally black and shiny, rippled and ribbed like melted rubber and rounded at both ceiling and floor, forming an oblong tube measuring some forty feet wide and stretching forward into a strangely shimmering darkness.

Maddy eased forward and bumped Jace by mistake. "What do you make of this vibration?"

Jace panned his flashlight from side to side. "Some kind of pulse," he replied, "like the hum of a dynamo."

"Undoubtedly electromagnetic," Torbald added as he joined Maddy, with Hans and Kit following. "Look. What's that?" Torbald aimed his flashlight ahead. His beam bounced off something highly reflective.

At first Maddy thought a thin sheet of water was pouring from the black ceiling to the floor, but the obstruction was much too delicate.

"It looks like cellophane." Jace referred to the eerie sheer that spread from rippled wall to rippled wall like clear plastic. Jace walked toward the shiny filament. He reached out, and his hand passed through.

"Holy shit," he exclaimed. "Feel that."

Maddy stepped up. She touched the membrane. As her fingers penetrated the gossamer veil, she felt a tingle run up her arm. "That's incredible, as if it were living matter."

"Might as well take the plunge." Jace took Maddy's hand and thrust himself through to the other side, pulling her along.

As her head passed through the filmy veneer, an image flashed though her mind. She momentarily visualized a desert. When she cleared the sheer to the other side, the image passed.

"Did you see that?" Jace asked.

"Some kind of mental impulse." Maddy looked across the thirty-foot enclosure toward yet another reflective sheer, which blocked the view beyond.

Torbald, Hans, and Kit stepped through the first sheer one at a time. Each exclaimed that they'd seen the image. They huddled together with Maddy and Jace, discussing the vision, and as they stood together energy suddenly seemed to flood the floor.

At Maddy's feet another silvery web shot across the onyx, and as the jagged spikes of radiance dissipated, the full expanse of the chamber began to glow.

Ether began to flow into the room; a protoplasmic mist drifted aimlessly at first, then quickly congealed into shapes, colors, and dimensions.

A holographic image formed, which Maddy recognized as one they'd all just visualized. Maddy and the others stood amid a three-dimensional replica of Cheops, Khafre, and Menkaure, the three great pyramids of Egypt. Under an azure sky and surrounded by endless desert, the great triangular monuments were cloaked in startling white granite.

"My God, what is this?" Kit asked.

"A display," Maddy answered.

"No. More than that," Torbald said. "It's a memorial. The alabaster stone that covers these pyramids was their original surface when they were built in the third millennium B.C. The white surface-granite was plundered by Egypt's conquerors until nothing was left but what we see today. Here, in this hologram, the original grandeur is preserved."

"What do you mean, a memorial?" Maddy asked. "To whom?"

"We may find that answer there." Torbald pointed to the next sheer, and before anyone could stop him, he walked forward and stepped through. "Oh yes," Maddy heard him say, "there is more."

The others hurried over, and as Maddy stepped through the filament, she experienced another desert vision. The same phenomenon took place: the floor of the new cell splintered into a web of light and the room filled with new ether that morphed into a completed hologram against an endless arid landscape.

Maddy now recognized the pristine shape of the Sphinx, its body untouched by the ravages of time.

"Look at the detail," Torbald exclaimed. "See how the Sphinx Temple stretches toward the sun, complete with its columns and limestone blocks. Look at the gardens that surround it." The sight of a pristine Sphinx with its facial features shining, its lion body totally intact, brought out the kid in the stoic Torbald. He relished the sight. "Do you realize what we're seeing? A time capsule with extraordinary implications. There's good reason to believe that the Sphinx was constructed over ten thousand years ago!" He turned and dashed for the next filmy veil, stepping through.

The others followed, and as they stumbled together into the next cell, a new hologram formed that Maddy recognized as Stonehenge—with one notable surprise. The circular formation of rectangular stone blocks was topped with a beautiful crystal dome that refracted sunlight and cast an incredible prism of light inside.

"You see," Torbald bubbled. "It's a tribute to the great architecture of the planet." Flushed with excitement, he moved on and the others followed.

The next cell filled with a green and blue aura.

"Easter Island!" Kit exclaimed. "Look at those black rocks, they are like the arrowhead boulder." Rows of great statues lined a cliff. The lush green mountain behind was dotted with over fifty carved monoliths standing watch over the Pacific Ocean. Like the others, this hologram was exquisite in detail—three-dimensional photographic clarity that defied description.

Maddy was awed by the display.

Each individual holographic chamber created an independent environment. The membranes that separated each image were as mysterious as the pictures themselves; each sheer curtain appeared transparent at first glance, yet became opaque when disturbed, concealing what had been viewed in the preceding cell.

Torbald could barely suppress his excitement as they moved on.

The next cell's panorama pictured a Mediterranean-style pantheon set near a craggy waterfall. Torbald looked frustrated. He couldn't name it, though he declared its origin to be Minoan, not Greek.

The following cell featured a pair of twin temples with narrow gold spires set in the depths of a vine-draped jungle.

"I don't recognize these," Maddy said.

"Somewhere in Malaysia," Torbald responded, "from the look of the architecture."

The next cell showed a long, winding esplanade that led to a mountainous Inca city crowned by a gold temple with a white dome. "Treasures," Torbald said, "lost to us forever if not for this exhibit." Torbald launched himself into the next cell, where the hologram showed a huge figure standing across a channel of water. Torbald gasped, "My God, it's the Colossus of Rhodes!"

Three more followed, all spectacular representations of presumably prehistoric architecture: the first, a tall, spindly observation tower domed like an observatory; the second, a turquoise temple with silver columns; and the third, a huge wall of rectangular stones that surrounded a crystal city on a cliff.

Torbald commented that the wall hauntingly resembled the symmetrical blocks he had seen in photographs of the undersea wall at the Bimini trench. "The crystal city," he said, "must have at one time been situated over what is now the eastern Atlantic Ocean."

They had arrived at what appeared to be the final filament.

Maddy and the others had stepped through, anticipating something to materialize, but nothing happened. They stood in a darkened space. Torbald shrugged and nodded to the holograms, now shielded from view by the opaque sheers. "I guess that's it."

"Quite a gallery," Jace glanced back at the veil. "As if an artist wanted them immortalized."

"Yes." Torbald rubbed his chin. "But the question remains . . . who is the artist?"

"Maybe *this* room will tell us." Maddy looked ahead. "Notice its familiar shape?"

Torbald turned. "Ah yes. Someone's assiduous creativity."

They had entered a large chamber shaped in the unmistakable triangular configuration they had seen before.

"Makes sense, doesn't it," Maddy said as she ventured ahead of the others. "Triangles as clues, triangular portals, and maybe . . . a triangular room as the conclusion?"

With Jace and the others on her heels, Maddy advanced from the narrowest end of the triangle toward the wide end, walking some eighty feet across a polished black onyx floor. As she reached the center of the room, she felt warm all over as a gradual glow emanated from the far wall. An indirect light revealed the silhouetted shape of a rectangular altar, eighteen feet wide, composed of the now-familiar jadelike glass.

Maddy recognized its ornately carved graphics as the earth drawings of the Nazca plain: a hummingbird, a monkey, a spider, and a variety of trapezoids and triangles framed the upper and lower cornices of the pedestal.

"Do you realize what this means, Torbald?" Maddy's excitement grew. "The artist that designed Nazca, fashioned this altar—"

"Shhh, Maddy," Jace said. "Something's happening."

Maddy listened and gasped as the vibration in the room intensified. It was as if someone had thrown a power switch, causing the air in the room to dance with specks of light.

"What the hell is that?" Kit covered his ears.

"A low decibel frequency," Jace shouted. "Deeper than the buzz in the tunnel."

"These airborne sparks are charged, decidedly electromagnetic," Torbald exclaimed.

Above the pedestal, an unearthly black light began to pulse. Like fireflies, the specks of light swarmed from the corners of the room toward the altar, gathering in what now revealed itself to be a translucent crystal sphere some two meters in diameter floating six feet above the altar surface. The moment Maddy saw it, she thought of the multiple concrete orbs Torbald had mentioned, buried in Central America. Were they tributes to this marvel?

Maddy and the others stood abreast, staring at the luminous sphere as the sparklets congealed inside, forming an energy field that began to throb with a liquid oscillation that flushed the globe's interior aura with tongues of fire.

They were witness to something that was theoretically impossible.

The sphere, suspended by its own power, exhibited a contained, yet terribly potent capacity for energy.

Maddy felt the resonance of the vibration in the hollows of her face, behind her eyes, and in the bones of her feet.

"Dear God, look at that," Torbald whispered as the globe flowed with new colors—metallic grays, charcoal blacks, the silver of mercury, and deep flaming crimson.

The sphere's sonic pulses continued and synchronized with the peaks of hypnotic rhythm, colors inside whipped into three-dimensional symmetrical figures, which momentarily froze into position. Each geometric form was outlined by a biting flame: cubes, octagons, pyramids, cones, an endless array of shapes formed and fluxed again into fluid elasticity.

The sphere's light danced in Jace's eyes. "It's as if the power of creation had been packaged into glass."

"Look at the exquisite precision of those geometric patterns," Torbald replied. "I've never seen some of them before. It's a living study of the properties of shape and space: a geometric encyclopedia." Maddy stepped up to the pedestal, easing under the globe, watching the luminous display.

She suddenly felt humbled in the face of such omnipotence. As the pulses radiated from the sphere, it was as if the dynamics within the orb had stirred something in her soul. The sensation caused an ethereal light-headedness. She was almost giddy as she smiled and turned to the others.

"It's Alca," she said, awed by the realization. "It must be."

53

Alca's Chamber

MADDY AND HER GROUP LEFT their backpacks and tools lying on the floor as they circled the altar, gathering like small children around a new-found marvel.

Jace felt the warmth from Alca's glow as it continued to pulse above their heads. He glanced at Maddy, who was beaming like a kid at Christmas.

Hans's eyes were wide with amazement. Kit looked intimidated, while Torbald seemed completely enraptured. With his face lit by Alca's glow and his mouth open in amazement, Torbald had moved around the altar and stood next to Hans between the chamber's rear wall and the pedestal.

Maddy nudged Jace, nodding at Torbald. She spoke up as if to break his trance. "Torbald, how do you feel?"

No response.

The older man's eyes were glazed with wonder, as if hypnotized.

"Torbald," Maddy called. "Talk to me."

Torbald's brow furrowed in concentration; he swallowed hard and gazed at Maddy. "Oh, I was . . . curious whether this globe is composed of the same transparent filament as those sheer partitions," he droned, nodding toward the other end of the darkened chamber.

Jace spoke over the hum of the sphere. "It has to be a hundred times as strong to contain that energy."

"Perhaps . . ." As if dazed, Torbald eased the shovel from Hans's hands.

Jace became suspicious. "What are you doing?"

"I just want to," Torbald guided the wood handle toward Alca's transparent enclosure, "tap it and see."

"Careful," Jace cautioned. "I wouldn't—"

The shaft came within inches of the Alca's surface.

Suddenly, Alca buzzed angrily and a white flash from the sphere's interior flooded the darkened room with light.

"Goddammit," Kit shouted in pain.

The strobe flash had turned everything gray and white, reversing color like a photographic negative.

Momentarily blinded, Jace heard rather than saw Torbald drop the shovel to the polished floor. Jace rubbed his eyes, trying to see. The all-encompassing whiteness had turned black, blue, and vacuous, slowly decaying like the fading burn from a huge camera flashbulb. Jace reached out for Maddy and apologized as he stumbled into her.

She stood numbed, blinking furiously.

"What the fuck was that?" Kit squinted at the others.

"A warning," Jace said.

Hans supported Torbald by the shoulders. The older man appeared stunned, shaking his head as he looked around. "I'm sorry, everyone. Apparently Alca wishes to remain undisturbed."

Jace glanced at the sphere.

Alca had resumed its routine; humming unobtrusively, its oscillating display continued as if nothing had happened.

"Alca's a bit cranky." Jace regarded the orb with renewed concern.

"You would be too," Maddy said, "if you'd just been bothered after a two-thousand-year nap."

"If we can't touch the damn thing, how are we supposed to carry it?" Kit asked.

"Perhaps we can't." Torbald had recovered his composure.

A thought suddenly occurred to Jace. "You don't think it's radioactive?"

"I doubt that," Torbald replied. "Alca seems to have given off some kind of photon emission. Radiant, but likely not poisonous. We'll have to import analytical equipment to measure what's happening inside."

Maddy smiled. "It has a mind of its own."

"As if it were alive." Torbald beamed. "Think of the marvelous intelligence that left this instrument behind."

Maddy stepped closer and stared at the sphere's underside. "But why leave it at all? Perhaps Alca's work isn't finished."

"Or, maybe it is," Jace said, "and it was left here as a memento." He gestured over his shoulder. "Like that holographic museum."

"That may be the case." Torbald ran a hand through his silvery-white hair. "But it's my guess that this spectacular artifact is a hyperdimensional tool kit. Contained within are new and advanced technological revelations, which we are now ready to claim."

"Ready? How do you mean?" Maddy asked.

"We must surmise that the designers of this device left Alca behind to be discovered *only* after we had gained the ability for flight . . . and with it, the wherewithal to read the Nazca map for what it was. Beyond that, we would have needed to become a global species, able to put together the clues left with widespread cultures around the world—an aptitude commensurate with space exploration. Alca is a time capsule of sorts left for when we would be ready to benefit from its secrets."

"And what do the holograms mean?" Jace asked.

"They're obviously edifices to the human race, and I would hazard that some interstellar Leonardo da Vinci contributed to at least the *principles* of their architecture. Perhaps, as Robert Marro believed, there's some inherent connection between the technologies used to erect the Martian monuments and what we see here." He fixed his gaze on Jace. "The mobility of your mysterious Martian moon may be indicative that there are forces in the solar system that touched not only the earth, but other planets as well."

Jace struggled with the premise. "But if that's true, Torbald, why isn't there some historical documentation?"

"There is." Torbald's eyes gleamed. "Quatel's myth, stories of Atlantis, accounts of angels, temples built to honor the gods through divine inspiration. We have accounts of unearthly intervention. Surely, Jace, you agree that even those holographic pictorials that we can *name*—the pyramids, the Easter Island statues, and the Sphinx—are still shrouded in mystery. There was never a *convincing* technological explanation as to how they were built." He pointed toward the holographs. "The pyramids alone were . . . were . . . oh Jesus." Torbald's face blanched as he stared toward the final sheer.

Jace followed his glance and startled as he saw the silhouetted figures in the gloom, some fifty feet across the chamber.

"No sudden moves," a voice boomed.

The strangers stepped forward into the light. Five were Chinese, dressed in dark mock T-shirts, holding semiautomatic handguns. The three remaining men were clearly Caucasian: one short, a bit overweight; another, a middle-aged man with almost reddish-blond hair and a mustache; and a third . . . Jace's stomach churned as he recognized the tall one with long blond hair. The man wore a safari vest and white silk scarf, and the face was that of the man Jace had seen bending over a dying Robert Marro.

Robert's killer spoke again. "You assholes in back—get out here."

Torbald and Hans edged out from behind the relative security of the altar's pedestal.

"That's him," Jace whispered as Hans and Torbald stepped forward.

"Who?" Maddy asked.

"In Vancouver," Jace said.

"Shut up and drop your guns," the blond man shouted.

Jace eased his hand toward the Beretta at his waist as the idea of using the weapon crossed his mind. But he decided against it—by the time he cleared the holster, he'd be dead.

"Go easy," Jace said to his friends as he unbuckled his gun belt and let go.

To Jace's right, Kit let the shotgun fall with a rattle, and Torbald, in turn, toppled his rifle forward.

"Now kick the guns over here," the husky blond man said. The weapons clattered across the floor, settling in the no-man's-land between Jace and the intruders.

Glancing casually at Hans, Jace noticed that Hans's crossbow sheath was nowhere to be seen.

As Jace caught Hans's eye, the Swede's mouth framed a pucker, making that hissing sound. Where had he left it? Was it across the room with the backpacks?

"Look at me," the blond man shouted, and Jace did, concentrating on the man's eyes, which were void of emotion.

The eerie stillness could be broken by gunfire any second.

A conversation might buy time.

"Who the hell are you people?" Jace shouted.

After a brief pause, a voice from the back said, "Don't you recognize me, Torbald?"

Torbald squinted in the dim light. "My God, it's Walsh." Torbald pointed at the man with the mustache. "Hector, you're alive! What is this, in God's name?"

"Priorities," Walsh said, casually.

"Priorities are something you should understand, Dr. Ürg," a new voice said. "You made great sacrifices for your work." The oldest Asian in the group had stepped forward. "I congratulate you." With exaggerated courtesy, the smooth-skinned man gestured to each of Maddy's party. "Ms. Marro. Mr. Kelton of course. Mr. Lassiter, and this . . ." he nodded toward Hans. "I don't believe I know—"

Jace bristled at the condescension. "Cut the bullshit. What's *your* name?"

"A fair question." The Chinese man moved forward into the light. Jace was struck by his widely set, oddly unfocused green eyes. "My name is Cho. These are my agents." Speaking in a smooth tone, he pointed to the Caucasian men one by one. "Mr. Walsh you've met, Vincent Scalbania is our guest here, and Shag is my trusted associate. I represent the future interests of the Chinese people. And that is why," he said as he pointed to Alca, "I am here to collect this most fascinating artifact."

Maddy edged forward. "Mr. Cho, Alca was meant to be shared by the world. Don't you see that?"

"What I see, Ms. Marro, is an uneven playing field. The United States controls most technology. Historically, Americans continue to make the same mistake; they view lesser countries as marketing zones. Your country traditionally sells technology—it doesn't give it away. So please don't patronize me. Why would Alca be different?"

"Because Alca could unite all people."

"Really?" Cho nodded his head cynically. "Like nuclear power did?"

While Maddy engaged Cho in conversation, Jace glanced around, assessing their situation. The only way out was blocked by Cho and his men, and the only measurable advantage was the lack of brightness in the room. There still might be a chance.

As Maddy continued to probe, Cho explained how the Chinese pursuit of alternate energy sources grew from his country's focus on UFO phenomena: his government's somewhat unorthodox view that the potential recovery of extraterrestrial artifacts would divulge new antigravitational technology. That policy had also bolstered Cho's position in Beijing and reinforced Cho's campaign to steal whatever he could from existing Western space programs. "Our intelligence network in the US was established decades ago," Cho continued. "We were fascinated with what we considered 'peculiarities' in NASA's Mars missions, particularly reports regarding the odd behavior of the Martian moons." Cho's unsteady glare roamed the room and settled on Jace. "As a telemetry analyst, your father was fully aware of those anomalies, Mr. Kelton. He was brilliant. Too bad he wasn't Chinese."

Jace was stunned. "You knew my father?"

"Oh, we never met." Cho nodded to his right. "Mr. Shag had that dubious distinction."

Jace felt heat rise up the back of his neck. So it was true. "So he is the one?"

"Yes. I was overwhelmed with the incredible irony that you were the one to discover Shag when he dispatched Robert Marro in Vancouver." Cho's face broke into a crooked smile. "Because two decades before, when Arthur Kelton was the courier of some rather sensitive photographs, Shag was the young Russian agent who commandeered those pictures."

During the pregnant pause that followed, Shag began to chuckle. "Father and son—a certain family resemblance, and a job not finished, until today."

Cho and Shag smiled at each another. Jace was the brunt of their tasteless joke.

"Goddamn you," he said through clenched teeth, barely able to control himself. He knew he'd probably be dead before he got his hands on Shag, but the fire in his gut told him it was worth a try. He started to lunge forward—a charge into vengeance at any cost—but immediately felt a restraining hand on his shoulder.

He glanced back and caught Maddy's pleading expression. Her eyes conveyed compassion, regret, and a desperation that hit him like a slap in the face. No, she was saying, don't lose it. Don't leave me. The appeal helped him harness his anger. He struggled to center himself.

"Your father fought well," Shag said, dismissively, "if it means anything to you." He gestured to the white scarf around his neck. "Damn near cut my throat with my own knife before I shot him."

Years of yearning had culminated in this absurd confrontation: Jace faced his father's murderer, unable to do a thing about it.

"Elimination is a deplorable necessity," Cho said coolly. "And elimination is unfortunately what we have in mind for all of you."

Cho stepped aside and nodded to his agents. The sound of guns being cocked echoed through the chamber.

Five men in black raised their weapons.
It was only a matter of seconds now.

54

Alca's Chamber

FORTY FEET ACROSS THE ROOM, five guns pointed in their direction.

"Mr. Cho. You're forgetting something." Jace instinctively stepped in front of Maddy, who clutched his waist. Jace gestured toward the sphere, humming and floating above the altar. "You'll never get out of here with Alca."

Cho raised a restraining hand before his men. "And why not?"

"Alca can't be moved." Realizing he'd bought a few precious seconds, Jace made eye contact with Kit and Torbald. "You must be blind not to see the problem," he continued casually, trying to telegraph his intent to Hans. Pretending to reach back and touch Maddy's arm protectively, Jace gripped the butt of the flashlight tucked in his back pocket. "Alca is protected by an impenetrable energy field."

Cho's eyes darted between the humming globe and Jace's face. "Then how had you intended to take—?"

"It's a question of timing," Jace cut in, and with an underhanded flip, he hurled the flashlight at Alca.

"No!" Cho screamed.

"Down!" Jace pulled Maddy to the ground, covering his eyes with his free hand as the room exploded with the anticipated flash.

Several Chinese were blinded and howled in pain.

On their hands and knees, Jace and Maddy blinked furiously, fighting to regain their eyesight as the photon strobe began to subside into a thousand retinal stars.

Jace could distinguish shadows in the room, the silhouettes of Cho's party brought to their knees by Alca's intensity. Cho and Scalbania still cowered from the shock. Shag had taken a couple of steps back and squatted with one hand raised to his face as if to fend off another flash. Cho shouted something in Chinese. From the rear, Shag barked an order and started firing at no one in particular.

"Be careful you don't hit the sphere!" Cho screamed in English.

With tears welling, Jace squinted across the floor at the rifle, shotgun, and Beretta. Kit was already slithering toward the guns.

At that moment, the Chinese agents opened fire.

Jace would have sacrificed himself gladly to reach the guns and kill Shag, but Maddy's safety loomed foremost in his mind. He grabbed her arm and dragged her toward the pedestal.

As he tucked Maddy closer to the floor, Jace glanced back, his vision now near normal, and saw Hans take a shot in the face as he moved to shield Torbald.

Maddy screamed as Hans toppled into Torbald's arms, and both men collapsed together.

Shag had dropped to a kneeling position, his pistol trained on Jace.

Jace flinched, expecting to be hit, but Kit rose with the Beretta and rushed toward the altar, firing three shots in Shag's direction. Two rounds brought Walsh down in a heap; a red splash burst on Shag's left wrist.

Jace used the distraction to shove Maddy further behind the pedestal and tumble in behind her. He turned to see Kit a few steps behind, still firing.

Shag recovered, steadied his gun, and fired twice.

Kit cried out, struck in the thigh and shoulder. The impact knocked him onto the onyx floor, just to the right of the pedestal, and just beyond Jace's reach.

Kit looked up, a splatter of blood on his cheek.

"Come on," Jace shouted. "Give me your hand!" As he reached for Kit, two more bullets splintered the stone wall behind Jace's head, forcing him to duck back behind the pedestal.

Kit groaned and tried to crawl the last few feet.

Jace leaned out as far as he dared and clutched Kit by the forearm. He had him by the biceps . . . the collar . . . but then Kit's back shuddered from the impact of two more rounds. With all his strength, Jace dragged Kit, whose wounds streaked blood across the floor.

Having Kit secured behind the altar, Jace rose with the Beretta and squeezed off a couple of shots at the Chinese, who lay prone, firing—the flames from their TEC-9s piercing the gloom.

Maddy knelt between the back wall and pedestal to cradle Kit's head.

Jace fired and ducked again. Kit blurted something to Jace that Jace couldn't understand over the gunfire.

Jace turned. "What?"

"The FBI. I called them." Kit's occasional absences when he'd "called his office" now suddenly made sense.

"Why do that, Kit?" Maddy frowned her disappointment.

"It was my mission too, Maddy. Robert wanted me. I cut a deal with the Energy Department. Big money. I would have given you—" Kit coughed blood.

Jace fired over the altar again. The Beretta's magazine held fifteen rounds. Eight had been spent.

Maddy tried to get more from Kit. "Is the FBI coming?"

"I couldn't tell." Kit's eyes were glazed. His head slumped into the crook of Maddy's arm.

Hope of rescue? Jace thought not. He reared again and squeezed off two more shots.

In reply, more bullets blew chips off the pedestal and splattered the back wall.

"He's dying," Maddy whimpered, holding Kit's head.

"And we will too, unless we get out."

"What about Torbald? Is he okay?"

Jace fired another shot as he peeked over the altar. No movement from Hans, who still lay sprawled atop Torbald's legs. Torbald's eyes were closed.

Shag lay on his side, binding his left wrist with his scarf as two of the Chinese agents fired, ricocheting more shots off the wall behind Jace's head.

Jace ducked, but suddenly, the firing ceased.

The room fell silent except for Cho and Shag, who were talking in hushed tones.

"Is Torbald dead?" Maddy whispered tearfully, still cradling Kit. "What'll we do? Do you think the FBI—?"

"Don't count on it," Jace said. Suspicious of the long silence, Jace leaned around the end of the altar and spied one of the Asians creeping forward toward Torbald.

Fearing harm to the professor, Jace took aim and shot the man, who fell to the ground only a few feet from Torbald. The commotion appeared to rouse Torbald, who suddenly stirred, as if awakened from sleep. To Jace's astonishment, the doctor stumbled to his feet.

"Help me," he shouted.

Jace wished Torbald had lain still; he had no choice but to spray the room with his three remaining shots to give Torbald cover. The doctor lurched for the altar, his face twisted in panic.

The other end of the room blossomed smoke as Cho's men returned fire.

"Don't hit Alca!" Cho screamed.

Torbald took a bullet high in the back. The exit wound below his collarbone sprayed red, and he went down in a heap.

"Oh God," Maddy shouted. "Did they shoot him?"

"Yes."

"Can you help him?"

"I can try."

Wanting to assess Torbald's chance of survival, Jace braced himself to see over the top of the altar, and a shot grazed his right shoulder, tearing his shirt into a bloody gash that sent a stinging sensation down his arm. Jace dropped to the floor to avoid being hit again and gripped at the searing pain. Under his bloody palm, Jace could tell it was a shallow laceration.

Letting Kit go, Maddy pressed to his side, whispering his name.

"I'm okay. It's a flesh wound." The room was quiet again. No doubt Cho was assessing his next move. Jace looked around. Jace's Beretta's magazine was empty and the spare ammunition was tucked uselessly in his backpack on the other side of the room. The shovel Torbald had used to probe Alca lay directly behind Maddy on the floor. Jace pointed. "Hand me that," he said, desperate for a weapon. She leaned back and grabbed the handle. Jace tucked his pistol in his belt as she handed him the shovel. Perhaps it could serve as a club. The man who killed his father was still out there. Could he get to Shag and still save Maddy?

Cho's voice boomed from the far side of the room. "Mr. Kelton, are you and Miss Marro still with us?"

"We're still here," Jace shouted. "Waiting for you." He counted on Cho not knowing Jace was out of bullets.

"Suppose we come to some kind of accommodation."

Jace didn't trust anything the man said. "Oh really? What do you have in mind?" As Cho began to rattle on about a proposal to cooperate and split any funds that might be garnered from Alca's potential energy, Jace tuned him out, looking around for any alternative to save their lives.

Then he saw it, tucked in a recessed shadow at the back wall at the other end of the pedestal. Hans had kicked his crossbow sheath as far behind the pedestal as he could when Cho's men surprised them. That's what he was trying to convey to Jace with his hissing before all hell broke loose.

"Don't move," Jace whispered to Maddy as he crab-legged past her to the sheath. He snatched it and returned to her side, pulling the stock and bow from inside.

"Let us think about that, Cho." Jace shouted, looking into Maddy's face. "How do we know we can trust you?"

"Neither of us wins, if we don't cooperate," Cho replied. "What do you say?"

"Give us a minute. This is Madison's mission," Jace yelled.

"What are you doing?" Maddy whispered, pointing at the crossbow. "Have you ever fired one of those?"

"Hell no." He snapped the weapon together. "But I better learn." Six arrows sat in the small quiver. Their tempered shafts felt cold and reassuring to the touch. "Grab the shovel," he said softly.

Laying one of the bolts in the firing groove, Jace drew back on the bowstring. He touched the button on the stock's barrel and lit the small laser target finder.

"On my signal, toss that shovel and poke Alca."

Maddy held the shovel in both hands. "The strobe?"

"You got it. Just cover your eyes. I'll be up firing this thing."

"Stop your stalling, Kelton," Cho bellowed. "What's the decision?"

Maddy bit her lip in concentration as she settled herself into a kneeling position. She glanced up at Alca, measuring the distance and, gripping the neck of the shovel, whispered, "Now?"

Jace laid the crossbow on the ground and covered his eyes with both hands. "Now!"

With eyes closed, Jace heard Maddy launch the tool and the following disconcerting buzz from Alca, saw the brilliance of the photon blast through closed eyelids, and heard the cries of the men on the other side of the altar as Alca dazzled the chamber with light.

Jace fumbled for the crossbow blindly—found it—and opened his eyes, blinking to clear the tears. He rose with the crossbow high on his right shoulder.

Shag was confused, rubbing his eyes. He had been trying to load a clip. The other Chinese men seemed similarly impaired, squinting in Jace's direction.

Jace sighted down the center of the bow. But because his eyes were still adjusting, he couldn't make out the laser pointer. He had to fire now. He squeezed the trigger. The dart fled the groove, its trajectory erratically high, and overflew everyone in the room.

Jace quickly reloaded. The gun smoke in the chamber made the fuchsia laser difficult to site accurately. But the beam now seemed to focus on Shag, who, in defense, had crouched near his men. Jace fired through the gloom, and the next dart found one of the agents to Shag's right, penetrating his neck.

The agent screamed as he fell, and Shag immediately took cover, using the writhing body as a shield.

Cursing under his breath, Jace reloaded again and panned right. He found another target. This time, the brass shaft flew straight and struck Cho in the arm. Cho cried out and, clutching a fist around the shaft, retreated toward the rear of the chamber. Jace caught a glimpse of him disappearing behind the far shiny filament.

The attack on Cho had allowed Shag to slap the clip into his gun, and Jace scarcely had time to duck behind the altar as Shag fired in Jace's direction. As shots splintered the wall near Jace's head, Jace loaded the fifth dart in the cross-bow. He glanced over at Maddy, who had recovered the shovel. "Are you ready? Smack Alca again."

Behind the protection of the pedestal, Maddy again threw the shovel, and with another racking drone, the blinding flash filled the room.

The moment Jace's vision cleared, he was up launching the fifth bolt. It found its mark; the bolt lodged in Shag's shoulder. With wide-eyed disbelief, Shag dropped his gun and clutched the shaft, falling to his knees. "Kill him, Xi! Kill him," he screamed.

A volley of fire followed, ricocheting off the back wall.

Maddy looked anxiously at Jace as he crouched, loading the crossbow. "Did you get him?"

"Not good enough. One more time with the shovel."

Maddy heaved once more, and with Alca's electrified whine, Jace rose and let fly. His accuracy had improved, and the laser showed him a clear target. The final dart struck Shag in the chest, and he was knocked to the ground with a thud.

Jace squatted next to Maddy, flushed with triumph.

Even in this moment of crisis, Maddy shared his taste for vengeance for her uncle's murder. She grabbed his wrist. "You got him?"

A gritty nod from Jace. "Yeah, I sure as hell did." After two decades, Jace had finally evened the score.

There were no more shots. The room had fallen silent.

"How many left out there?"

"With Walsh and Shag dead, I counted four," he said. "Cho's gone. And I don't see Scalbania either."

Then a voice. One of the Chinese agents. "Kelton, you may as well give up."

Why weren't they charging? Perhaps afraid of being caught by one of Alca's blinding flashes? The globe had taken on a new rhythm, sounding more ominous than before.

"You still want to deal?" Jace shouted. "Our safe passage if we show you how to disarm Alca?"

A feeble stall, but the only one he had. He peeked around the corner. The four men had gathered on the near side of Shag's prone body.

"We don't care what happens to you," one of the men yelled. "All we want is Alca. We'll let you go if you come out."

Maddy had leaned over to check on Kit, but now she turned from his body with an oddly peaceful expression and took Jace's hand. "We're going to die, aren't we?"

He marveled at her composure and had difficulty with the reply. "I'm afraid so."

"Well then, let's not go quietly." She reached around her back, tugging at her fanny pack, and pulled two sticks of dynamite and a six-inch length of fuse from the pouch.

Jace shrugged. "I hadn't forgotten that. I just wasn't ready to commit suicide."

"Let's do it and blow them to hell." Maddy's auburn eyes were cold with resignation. "Don't let them have the satisfaction." Of killing us, she meant.

Remarkably he felt no regret. The resolution in her eyes summed things up. No option. No hesitation. Shag's men would kill Jace and Maddy whether they retrieved Alca or not.

Jace took the length of fuse and stuck it into one of the sticks. He fished the matchbook from his pocket and lit the match. In the tiny glow of the flame, Maddy's face radiated peace. Jace looked hard at her, knowing this would likely be his last chance to tell her how much she meant to him. But there were no words and not enough time. "What the hell. I told you we'd finish this thing together." He lit the fuse and waited five eternal seconds. As the fuse burned to its quick, Jace stood and tossed the stick toward the huddled men.

He ducked to clutch Maddy, and holding her as close as he could, he wrapped her up with his arms and legs, trying to cover every inch of her body.

55

Alca's Chamber

THE BLAST HIT THEM LIKE a tidal wave.

Jace had witnessed countless dynamite explosions during the course of his professional career, but never one like this detonation.

The explosion was not only deafeningly loud, it was followed by a sudden howling . . . a high-pitched roar from a gush of air that originated from nowhere in particular, wailing like a hurricane through the chamber.

Dazed, Jace opened his eyes and helped Maddy scramble to her knees. "You all right?" he shouted.

Maddy's hair lifted in the wind. "I'm okay. What's happening?"

Jace glanced up at a ceiling, which looked miraculously intact. Above their heads, Alca appeared engorged and swollen, a deep-red color marbled with black ooze, as if it had absorbed the energy from the blast. Alca's geometric magic and strobe flashes were gone—replaced by an angry, darkened turbulence that swirled within.

Kit's body, which had been tossed a few feet, lay against the wall off to Jace's right. And as Jace stole a glance around the side of the altar, he saw the chamber strewn with bodies—Shag's among them.

Jace and Maddy's backpacks lay beyond, and where the opaque sheer at the chamber entrance should have been, there was . . . nothing.

Astounded, Jace looked down a cavernous thirty-foot-wide expanse that stretched some one hundred yards long—the area that had previously been divided into holographic compartments. But now, the dividing sheers had disappeared, and all that remained were rounded black sidewalls, pulsing with a feeble incandescence. Wind blew through the chamber from the dimly lit triangular portal at the distant far end.

Maddy scooted in behind Jace and peered over his shoulder. "Do you think all the Chinese are dead?"

"That's my guess," Jace said over the roar. "They took the full load of that blast."

"What about Cho?"

"Disappeared." He grabbed Maddy's hand and led her around the side of the altar. Hans and Torbald had been shifted by the force of the explosion, heaped together against the pedestal's far side. The shotgun and rifle had also been thrown next to the altar.

Jace picked up the twelve gauge and cradled it in his left arm.

Hans was clearly dead, having taken a shot in the right temple. The dynamite blast had blown him partially over Torbald.

Maddy knelt alongside as Jace rested his fingertips on Torbald's carotid. Miraculously, he felt a pulse. "Thank God, he's alive." Jace hoisted Hans's weight off the professor and, with Maddy's help, dragged Torbald a few feet away.

Jace touched the old man's forehead. "Torbald, can you hear me?"

The ragged exit wound under Torbald's right collarbone still oozed blood.

Maddy reached into her fanny pack and stanched the wound with a handkerchief under Torbald's shirt.

"Hans," Torbald whispered.

Maddy gave Jace a forlorn glance.

Jace shook his head, putting a forefinger to his lips. The less said about Hans's death, the better. Torbald opened his eyes, obviously dazed and somewhat incoherent.

"You're going to be all right, Doctor," Maddy said.

"Hans."

Jace skirted the subject. "We're going to take care of Hans too."

"But is he——?" Torbald's head tilted, his gaze drifting past Jace. He stared confused into the spacious vacuum created by the now nonexistent holographic cells. He rolled his head toward the other side, glancing at the bodies. He seemed to startle and gasped, "Good God, who's that?"

Maddy looked back and screamed.

From a kneeling position, Jace turned in time to see Shag stumble forward with a ten-inch knife in his hand. With the crossbow bolt stuck in his chest, he was covered in blood and lacerated by the explosion but had somehow survived.

Jace pivoted on his heels with the shotgun and tried to raise the weapon as Shag lunged, and they collided. The barrel deflected Shag's knife long enough for Jace to grab Shag's right wrist. At the same time, Shag clutched the stock of the shotgun as their momentum knocked both men, locked together, across Torbald and onto the polished floor.

As they tumbled over one another, each tried to gain the advantage.

Jace's mind worked as if in slow motion. How had Shag survived? His nose and his ears streamed blood from the shock of the dynamite blast. His shoulder was torn by the first crossbow dart. Another lodged in his chest—but no blood from that wound—yet several inches of the dart's brass shaft jutted from Shag's safari vest.

As they grappled with one another, Jace's gaze fell to the ragged scar that rippled the base of Shag's neck—the scar Jace's father left in his own death struggle.

"Maddy," Jace breathed. "The rifle!"

Out of the corner of his eye, Jace saw Maddy go for the weapon. "Shoot the son of a bitch!" Shag's blade neared Jace's throat.

Shag's pale eyes squinted with exertion as he jerked away from Maddy, rolling on his side to shield himself with Jace's body. Jace heaved Shag back on top.

The two men rocked back and forth.

"Shoot him."

"I can't, I'll hit you."

Jace suddenly didn't care. "Do it, goddamn it."

Maddy squeezed off a shot that ricocheted off the onyx floor. Jace winced as rock chips sprayed his face.

"Jace!" Maddy shouted. "Are you hit?"

He couldn't respond. Shag's knife was back at his throat.

Jace's left hand began to slip. He was stunned by Shag's stamina, particularly since he'd been severely wounded. Or had he? The bolt in Shag's chest hadn't penetrated too deep; it had lodged in something inside the vest. A familiar fragrance spilled from inside. Schnapps. A flask.

The searing pain in Jace's left shoulder affected the muscles in his arm. Shag's right-handed strength would overpower him.

Shag's knife touched Jace's neck. Jace pushed on the knife-hand and shot-gun stock to hold the knife back. But he was losing.

It occurred to him . . . if the bolt hadn't fully entered Shag's chest, would it perhaps come out?

"You want the gun, asshole?" Jace growled through clenched teeth. "Take it!"

Jace released his right-handed grip on the shotgun stock, and while Shag's face went blank with confusion, Jace grasped the dart in Shag's chest, yanked it loose, and jammed it up through the soft tissue under Shag's chin.

Shag's eyes widened in shock. His open mouth brimmed with blood. His bandaged left hand released the shotgun and clamped Jace's wrist.

Jace clutched the dart shaft and, using it as leverage, pushed Shag's head back. "Drop the knife."

Panting in pain, Shag gurgled unintelligibly, but he let the knife fall, clawing at Jace's wrist with both hands.

Jace struggled to a sitting position, once more yanking Shag into submis-sion. Jace kicked the knife away.

Shag lay on his side, reaching for Jace's face, but Jace jerked on the dart, and Shag yelped.

Jace reached over, retrieving the shotgun that lay nearby. Gathering the stock of the weapon in his left hand, Jace let go of the dart shaft and getting up, stepped away while cocking the twelve gauge.

Maddy stepped forward.

"Stay back. Don't get near this bastard," Jace said. He kept his eyes on Shag, who was writhing on the ground, struggling to remove the arrow from his throat. Shag cranked on the bolt and, with one fierce tug and an animallike scream, wrenched it loose.

Maddy retreated with the rifle and knelt with Torbald.

Blood poured from Shag's mouth as he sat on his haunches, the bloody bolt in his right hand.

Jace recovered his wind, watching Shag. "Don't move a goddamned inch." He glanced over. "Torbald, can you get to your feet?"

Torbald's feeble response, "I . . . can try."

Maddy attempted to help him. "He's too weak, Jace. He'll have to be car-ried. Besides, what are we going to do"—she pointed to Shag—"with *him*?"

Shag crouched, glaring at Jace like a caged cat.

"Bring him along. He'll have fun with the FBI."

Shag spit a stream of blood before asking, "What?"

"Didn't we tell you?" Jace backed toward Torbald. "By now, the FBI should be waiting outside. Before you killed Lassiter, he told us he'd called the Feds."

Shag flinched, eyeing the doorway at the far end of the chamber.

Jace turned to Maddy. "I'm going to carry Torbald." He handed her the shotgun. "Keep this pointed at Shag's chest."

Maddy laid the rifle on the ground and took the shotgun in both hands.

Apologizing to the doctor for any discomfort, Jace bent and put one of Torbald's arms around his neck. He was about to hoist the old man when the floor shuddered.

Jace glanced at the altar.

During the scuffle, Alca had changed. A spindly finger of light had dropped from the sphere to contact the top of the pedestal. A similar light band jutted to the ceiling, bisecting the sphere, which now revolved on a new illuminated axis that gained in width and energy.

As the room shook, Jace realized that the formerly suspended globe had reengaged itself with its surroundings. He now grasped the error they'd made: Alca wasn't just an energized sphere; "Alca" was an entity that could manifest itself as the entire hundred-yard-long tunnel structure as well.

"It's an earthquake," Maddy shouted as the chamber rumbled. She dropped to one knee.

Jace had to ease Torbald back to the ground.

Maddy screamed, "Oh God."

Shag had leapt toward Maddy, the dart clutched like a knife in his right hand. Maddy couldn't hoist the shotgun in time and, as Shag collided with her, the twelve gauge clattered to the floor as Maddy went down.

Jace hurled himself toward them and landed a kick to Shag's side. Placing both hands on Shag's armed hand, he twisted hard toward the thumb. The leverage brought Shag to his knees, and the dart fell harmlessly to the floor.

Blind with renewed fury, Jace landed two quick punches to Shag's face, and with a final kick to the head, he knocked Shag cold.

Maddy pointed a reviling finger. "We can't take this animal with us."

"You're right." Breathing hard, Jace stood over Shag's limp form. His desire to kill Shag was overshadowed by his will to help Maddy. "Let's just get the hell out." And that was advisable, since the floor of the chamber had begun to rock.

Jace stumbled over to Torbald and hoisted the older man into a fireman's carry.

Maddy picked up the shotgun and one of the flashlights from the backpack and, giving Shag one last look, the three survivors headed into a wind that now blew from the triangular portal at the distant end of the tunnel.

Hung over Jace's shoulder, Torbald asked, "What are we doing?"

"Escaping," Jace said.

"Hans is dead?" Torbald groaned.

"Yes. I'm sorry."

"Then go."

The floor shuddered more violently.

Jace looked back. Alca's angry red sphere had grown. The walls in the chamber glowed.

"What's with the wind?" Jace shouted.

"I don't know." Maddy's words were muffled by the rush. "A vortex forming maybe. I don't like it. Sounds like the place is coming apart."

With the sonic vibrations increasing and Jace burdened by Torbald's weight, they hustled across the void that had been the holographic chamber, stepping through the triangular portal only to find the jade-colored tube on the other side of the door becoming unstable. Its smooth, gleaming surface began to bubble.

"It's liquefying." Maddy gasped. "Hurry."

Hoisting Torbald higher on his shoulders, Jace tried to pick up the pace. They scrambled to the far end of the tube and climbed up into the cave, where a few bats still fluttered.

Maddy's flashlight cut through the gloom as they retraced their steps through the sooty section of the tunnel.

They came to the initial cave-in, and Jace gently set Torbald down as he checked the rubble. Cho's party had obviously removed parts of the cave-in to get through. That opening had been replaced by further dislodged material from above as tremors dumped loose dirt and rock. There were obvious soft spots in the new mound, as indicated by a stiff breeze that whistled through breaches in the debris, and Jace was able to find a place where he could clear enough rock to climb through.

As Jace scrambled out the other side, Maddy pushed Torbald from behind and Jace pulled him. Maddy followed. Jace hoisted Torbald once more, and they stumbled onward. As they passed the pottery alcove and scampered up the sloping shaft, the passageway began to reverberate with steady pulses.

Jace and Maddy were suddenly jostled from side to side.

"Keep moving!" Jace yelled, pushing her ahead.

"Jace," Maddy shouted in panic as they ascended the last 150 feet, "it sounds like something's going to explode."

A high-pitched whine within the butte filled the corridor. Jace would have plugged his ears, but carrying Torbald, he couldn't.

Maddy grimaced in pain, struggling to walk. "I wish it would stop." She dropped the shotgun and covered her ears.

"Run. Don't wait for me!" Jace yelled.

Maddy stumbled ahead as Jace tried to gather what was left of his strength. His back burned and his thighs ached as he followed her, negotiating the last thirty feet of passage—the final agonizing strides up the incline.

Suddenly, the cliff opening appeared. Maddy crawled through.

Jace shoved the doctor through the crevice, and they burst into the cool night air.

Maddy fell to her knees under the stars. "Thank God."

"Not yet." Jace pulled her to her feet. The tone within the mountain had risen several octaves. "We'd better get as far away as we can." Something huge was about to take place. "Let's try to reach the triangle rock."

Hoisting Torbald, Jace climbed down the rockfall, following Maddy past the base camp.

Out on the flat, staggering through the sage, they finally arrived at the black monolithic boulder.

Totally exhausted, Jace knelt on the sand and, with Maddy's help, gently rolled Torbald onto his back. He seemed to have passed out.

Jace collapsed to the ground, and Maddy slumped at his side. They stared back at the butte's silhouette.

The hum inside the cave had modulated to an ultrahigh frequency. It surged higher and higher in tone until it seemed to exceed the range of human hearing. As it lofted into nothingness, then silence, a strange hush fell over the land.

That stillness was followed by a subsonic drone—like the low rumble of a pipe organ's foot peddle. A rasping, racking bass note shook the ground. A series of three pulses from inside the mountain sent successive ground waves across the desert floor. Dirt danced as seismic tremors traveled outward from the butte.

"Oh no." Maddy got to her knees. "What is this?" She held on to Jace. A deep-seated concussion rolled through the countryside, causing the entire valley to shudder.

Torbald was rolled onto his side, and Jace and Maddy were bounced repeatedly.

A blossom of unearthly jade-colored light vaulted from the top of the butte as an explosion blew tons of sandstone off the mesa. With its lid removed, a resonance within the mountain echoed its discordance.

Torbald had stirred and come to. "Dear God," he groaned, his voice trembling as he tried unsuccessfully to sit up. "We have awakened the specter of a time gone by."

Maddy moved to steady him, but she was distracted by a massive pulse of red light several hundred feet wide that shot like a laser beam from the butte into the night.

As quickly as it had appeared, the light snuffed out, followed by more than a dozen photon bursts, each sending a golden ball of light into the sky. They trailed one another in succession, vaulting into the heavens.

Torbald had struggled onto one elbow, invigorated by the spectacle.

"What the hell is that?" Jace asked him, realizing it might be ridiculous to assume he would know.

"A sign," Torbald said.

"A sign?" Jace got to his feet. "Of what?"

"Alca's resurrection."

Jace watched in awe as eight gleaming gold orbs formed a hovering formation several miles above the earth.

"Look. It is the punctuation mark," Torbald said. "The formation emulates the configuration of the Orion constellation. It's the tie to Egypt, the reason the Nassau triangle touched Giza."

Alca followed with a fanning series of low-angle laser shots—multicolored fire-balls that sprayed the surrounding desert.

Like an erupting volcano, sparks mounded upon one another in a fountain of light that didn't stop; the mound of light punctuated by occasional laser bursts that pierced the night.

The display continued for some twenty minutes while Maddy maintained pressure on Torbald's wound and Jace kept watch.

Jace took a deep breath and looked back. Maddy knelt, supporting Torbald's head as they continued to gaze at the light show. "Someone's got to show up. This must be visible for thousands of miles," she said.

Jace stared off to the east. "And it's working. Someone's honing in." On the horizon, a series of airborne floodlights charged across the desert. "Helicopters."

"Could it be Cho's backup?" Maddy asked.

"God, I hope not."

The choppers rumbled in, arriving over their position, and Jace stepped over to face the lights as two of the choppers hovered overhead. A third landed some forty feet away. Several men in dark-blue uniforms jumped out. In the glow of the floods, Jace made out the letters F B I on their fatigues as they approached.

The first square-shouldered man waved a flashlight in Jace's face. "Mr. Lassiter?"

"No. I'm afraid he didn't make it."

"Then you must be Kelton. I'm Special Agent Gawdry." He glanced at Torbald and then at the butte, with obvious bewilderment. "What the hell happened here? That thing is visible from Ohio. We've gotten calls asking if a nuclear plant melted down. Holy Christ. Is that what I think it is? Laser fire? Mr. Lassiter's report claimed there was some kind of energy cache in the desert."

"That's exactly what it is," Jace said.

Torbald grunted and tried to sit up. "Special Agent . . . I assume you can contact Washington?"

"Through our field office, yes, sir. You must be Ürg."

"I suggest you call and tell the president."

"The president?" Gawdry asked as two other men edged in with a stretcher.

The doctor was able to raise a trembling hand. "The world must be told that Alca is a cursor, writing the future across the sky. A signal to whom, I can only guess. But we're at the brink of a new technological age. Alca may be merely the trigger to set things in motion." Torbald slumped, fatigued. "Explain it to him, Maddy."

In response to Agent Gawdry's inquisitive look, Maddy got to her feet and stepped over. She pointed to the light show as she put her arm around Jace's waist. "The world's been given a second chance."

Gawdry stared at Maddy, still confused. "For what?"

"We'll explain during our debriefing." Jace smiled. "Any sign of the Chinese?"

"Chinese? You're the first people we've seen, sir." Gawdry gestured to those assisting Torbald. "Medic, get that man aboard and see to his wounds." Gawdry noticed Jace's bloody shoulder, but Jace waved him off.

"I'll be fine."

"Any more in your party?"

Maddy shook her head sadly. "Just those left in there." She gazed at the butte.

Another agent rushed over, handing Maddy some coffee before turning to Gawdry. "Sir, there's an urgent call." He nodded to the chopper. "It's headquarters."

Gawdry excused himself and strode off with the other agent toward the slowly rotating blades.

Maddy took a sip from the thermos cup and handed it to Jace. Torbald's stretcher was being lifted into the far chopper. "Strange how we're standing here. I can't believe this miracle."

Jace turned. "Suddenly everything seems trivial compared to this fire burning in the desert."

"Nothing will ever be the same."

He glanced at her. "Frankly, I'd rather it wasn't."

She studied his face. "Well, it won't be. We're going to have to deal with that." She pointed to spewing sparks above the butte.

"So what do you think will happen?"

"If Torbald's right, there has to be an international meeting of the minds." Alca's glow was reflected in her amber eyes. "Think what we'll be able to accomplish with that energy."

"Your father's dream . . . and *your* dream."

"Yes." She nudged him. "Whatever it means, I want you to be involved."

Alca's glow threw a gentle light across Maddy's face. She looked bruised but beautiful. The fury of the adventure had taught Jace that the unexpected was the new normal, and in this moment of relative calm, he suddenly realized how much he'd fallen in love.

"I can't imagine not being involved," he said.

"With Alca?"

"With you."

"I hoped you'd say that." She smiled and quoted Jace's comment from days before. "Together," she said. "That's how we'll finish this thing."

He reached out to take her in his arms, but he hesitated as Agent Gawdry hurriedly returned. He was breathing hard, his face taut with tension. "Mr. Kelton. Does the name Dixon mean anything to you?"

Jace glanced at Maddy. "Yes, it does."

"Well, all hell's breaking loose. Dixon's apparently trying to reach you through our Washington office. He's just become world news." Gawdry shook his head. "Some damn thing about a Martian moon."

"What?"

"Reuters reports that Dixon slipped information to the press regarding several covert government projects concerning the Martian moon 'Phobos.' Dixon says the air force suspected the damn thing was partially hollow for years."

Jace remembered Dixon's wish for discretion. "Why would he do that?"

"Well, according to headquarters," Gawdry looked shell-shocked as he gazed up at Alca's pyrotechnics, "the minute this light show began, the Palomar Observatory in California reported that the moon, Phobos, disappeared from orbit."

"Jesus." Jace gripped Maddy's arm.

"And there seems to be some connection." Gawdry breathlessly pointed to Alca's glow. "My superiors have asked that you be flown to New York immediately."

Maddy suddenly looked overwhelmed. "New York?"

"Yes. There's to be a meeting tomorrow morning. Ms. Marro, you and Dr. Ürg will have the attention of the UN general assembly—to say nothing of the rest of the world."

"I don't understand."

"Tracking stations around the world confirm that Phobos reappeared—and is headed this way."

"Dear God." Maddy turned to Jace. "That's it. Torbald's theory. Maybe it's all timed to work like this." Maddy actually smiled. "If Alca is the ignition, perhaps the moon is the machine—a hyperdimensional database, filled with necessary tools to hurdle the human race beyond the solar system and into a new age. It's our cosmosis."

"Pardon me, ma'am?" Gawdry asked.

"Cosmosis, Agent Gawdry." She glanced his way. "Humankind's osmosis with our cosmic destiny." She looked up into the blackness of the night and, with awe, repeated the word. "Cosmosis."

Jace followed Maddy's gaze toward the skies above the butte.

He couldn't help thinking of Cory's fascination with the stars.

Conceivably, Cory's love for "something big out there" was more than intuition.

Maybe he simply knew.

Perhaps we all did.

EPILOGUE

Chinle Wash, Arizona

A GREAT DOME OF STARS hung over the dry darkness of the desert. The brilliant colors of the day had faded away into the pallid land.

Perched on the edge of the world on her hogan's porch, Wind Woman sat alone in her rocking chair, feeling the hot air rise up the cliffs as coolness sank into the crevices of the Chinle Wash.

Below, where the aspen trees shadowed the dankness of the creek bed, the moistened stones harbored the last rare frogs of summer; their September song echoed in the canyons.

Wind Woman heard them chirping. And though her ears had long ago lost their youthful hearing, she could imagine the whispers among the gray sage and slate-colored cacti, the slither of the sidewinder, the scurry of the field mouse.

Darla, her daughter, was away at the hospital at Akita's bedside. A hunter had found him crawling on a dirt road tonight. He was badly injured, but Wind Woman had sent the spirit of the hawk to heal the young man, and he would recover and gain wisdom from his suffering.

For now, Wind Woman would watch and feel the night.

Off toward the northwest, the glow from Monument Valley spoke of the prophecy fulfilled. She mused about the wise man with white hair who had come to visit, the tan-haired woman who walked like a fawn, and her strong friend.

Despite the fact that they had not returned to take her across the bridge to the sky, she knew she would go.

The red flame to the northwest had said so.

The things that were foretold would at last come to pass.

Wind Woman rocked in her chair and glanced into the inky heavens.

She had spoken of many things to the strangers—of the old ones, the Anasazi, and the cavern of infinity. There was much she had spoken, but also something she had not, because time had weakened her memory. It had not occurred to her until the buds of fire appeared over Monument Valley that she hadn't mentioned another ancient legend.

When the Anasazi could still count their generations, they told a myth about a flower of fire that would someday blossom in the desert: how on that day, the "Ku a tel"—the people of the moon—would return.

Her gaze swept the galaxies and came to rest on a luminous speck that appeared brighter than some of the others, creeping slowly to the west.

If the ancient legend was true, the hour of the union had arrived. The Anasazi, the Maya, and the Nazca would all be one again, and one with all peoples.

She fixed on the gleaming stardust that attracted both her eye and her imagination.

Seeing a vision, she sighed. Her toothless mouth parted in wonder.

"Ku a tel, Nì Ghxàà Nòh Kaah," she whispered in Navajo.

Quatel. Come for us.

A READER'S GUIDE

QUESTIONS AND TOPICS FOR DISCUSSION

1. Jace and Maddy are parallel protagonists who eventually collide as part of the plot. Considering the role their families play in the backdrop of the story, what factors in Jace's and Maddy's backgrounds are similar?

2. In the prologue of the novel, what similarities are portrayed in events surrounding Jace's and Maddy's parents?

3. Maddy's Uncle Robert is fascinated by unexplained prehistoric architecture. Using the Internet or other independent sources, list as many examples of architecture of unknown origins as you can. What does it mean to modern society if architecturally advanced societies existed before records were kept?

4. What aspect of Cory's character gives us a perspective on Jace's ambivalence about his career choice? How do Jace's father's death and Cory's death affect Jace's character development in regard to his career?

5. There are two sagelike characters who represent a global perspective in the book. How are those two perspectives delineated from one another and how do they also interrelate?

6. The artwork on the Nazca plain in Peru was discovered in the 1920s from the air. In *Cosmosis,* Torbald describes several theories about the earth drawings at Nazca and their origination. Among those theories

are: a) That they were drawn with the assistance of shamen who drugged themselves to levitate their consciousness in order to guide the artists; b) That the artists were assisted by lighter-than-air balloons that would allow them to view their art; c) That, as part of a religious ceremony, ancient natives walked the plain in processions, wearing the earth down with their feet to form the pictures; and d) That they were created as part of a large alien airfield that was used by interplanetary craft. How is each of these less plausible or more plausible than the legend of Quatel as described in the novel?

7. *Cosmosis* addresses our historic fascination with the planet Mars as one of its central themes. What hints are provided in the story as to why that Martian theme relates to Egypt?

8. The villains in *Cosmosis* are backed by the Chinese government. Why is China portrayed as the country involved in this type of mission?

9. There has been speculation for some time about the Martian moon Phobos being hollow. Why did that speculation originate?

10. As a man of faith, Torbald's views of an alien presence in the universe are particularly liberal. In an age in which interplanetary space travel is contemplated as a near-term reality, how do your views about creation compare with Torbald's?

11. Considering the themes involving the Nazca plain and its purpose, why is Wind Woman the character who makes the final observations in the story?

12. As the novel ends, it invites further revelations about what the moon Phobos might contain. Considering what the explorers in *Cosmosis* speculate when they discover Alca, what is your theory about the moon's contents? What is the impact, if any, those contents could have on human civilization? Could they affect the evolution of the human species, and if so, why?

AUTHOR'S NOTE

Why I Wrote *Cosmosis*

Even though the world appears far less mysterious as science allows us to learn more about our planet, ourselves, and our solar system, there are footprints of those who came before us that defy explanation. These footprints are evident in ancient walls, engineered so precisely that we are unable to match their exactness with our most advanced technology. The footprints are also evident in sophisticated sun-centric astronomy in structures that appeared thousands of years before Copernicus. And perhaps most startling is the evidence that human flight existed multiple millenia prior to the twentieth century.

Anachronistic cultures and architecture of technological societies that flourished before recorded history prompted me to speculate that our commonly accepted chronological development as a race is not the entire story at all, but merely an episode, perhaps in a series of cultural episodes that predate what we consider the beginning of our civilization.

Then came my awareness of a rogue science, namely extraterrestrial archeology, which claimed visual evidence of potential artifacts on Mars and other planets.

My fascination with these topics prompted me to write Cosmosis, which, while obviously a work of fiction, utilized story elements that are factual and can be traced by the curious reader, such as press about the Martian moon Phobos, which plays such an important role in this story, and ongoing speculation regarding the moon's origins as far back as the Eisenhower administration (http://www.rense.com/general20/eisenhowerwh.htm).

As for links regarding geoglyphs like those on the Nazca plain—the geographic hero of the Cosmosis tale—a Google search will yield multiple references to over fifty such art forms all around the planet (and to those that are still being discovered from the air as recently as this year).

No one knows why primitive diverse cultures on different continents would take the time to shape images that could only be seen from the skies, but in Cosmosis I enjoyed fashioning at least a partial answer as Jace and Maddy engaged in this adventure.

Are there more answers to the riddle for Jace and Maddy? Let's hope so.

In the meantime, if my story captured your imagination, you might enjoy looking further into the giant geoglyphs of the Nazca plain and others, because I believe this "sky art" will likely remain one of the greatest mysteries of our time.

Best always,
Rainer Rey